LOSING FAITH

LOSING FAITH

A THRILLER

ADAM MITZNER

GALLERY BOOKS
New York London Toronto Sydney New Delhi

Gallery Books
An Imprint of Simon & Schuster, Inc.
1230 Avenue of the Americas
New York, NY 10020

This book is a work of fiction. Any references to historical events, real people, or real places are used fictitiously. Other names, characters, places, and events are products of the author's imagination, and any resemblance to actual events or places or persons, living or dead, is entirely coincidental.

First Gallery Books hardcover edition April 2015

Manufactured in the United States of America

10 9 8 7 6 5 4 3 2 1

Library of Congress Cataloging-in-Publication Data

Mitzner, Adam.
Losing faith / Adam Mitzner. —First Gallery Books hardcover edition.
pages; cm.
I. Title.
PS3613.I88L67 2015
813'.6—dc23

2014031293

ISBN 978-1-4767-6424-5
ISBN 978-1-4767-6438-2 (ebook)

To my boys, Michael and Benjamin

One minute I held the key
Next the walls were closed on me
And I discovered that my castles stand
Upon pillars of salt and pillars of sand

—Coldplay, "Viva La Vida"

PART ONE

1

"You're wrong, Aaron."

Sam Rosenthal's tone suggests he's talking about much more than the topic at hand. It's as if he's addressing something innate about Aaron Littman himself.

Aaron smiles, and in that gesture, he belies Rosenthal's claim. In fact, if anyone seems completely right, it is Aaron Littman. A year past fifty, he's six foot two and not more than ten pounds heavier than when he was an All-American swimmer at Harvard. A strong jaw, piercing blue eyes, and thick, jet-black hair dusted with gray around the temples in exactly the spots you'd place gray hairs, if given the choice, complete the package.

Samuel Rosenthal is almost comically the opposite. He's more than a half foot shorter than Aaron, he doesn't have a single hair on his head, and his right side droops slightly, the last vestige of the accident that nearly killed him a decade ago. Yet Rosenthal is the personification of the expression that you shouldn't judge a book by its cover. At seventy-one, he's still a wartime consigliere of the first order. The type of lawyer who takes no prisoners and leaves no earth unscorched.

They met a quarter century before, the year Aaron clerked on the United States Supreme Court. Rosenthal had argued a case—it embarrasses Aaron that he can never remember which one, only that it wasn't a case that Justice Rellington had assigned to him to work on—and after the argument, Rosenthal came back to chambers.

"This is the young man I've been telling you about, Sam," Justice Rellington said. "Aaron Littman, meet Sam Rosenthal."

Aaron had heard of Rosenthal, of course. Back then, you couldn't be a law student without having heard of the great Samuel Rosenthal. Protector of the First Amendment. Confidant to power. Mr. Fix-it. A lot of other nicknames too. Before speed dial existed, those at the top of their field, any field, knew Rosenthal's phone number by heart.

"It's nice to meet you, Mr. Rosenthal," Aaron said, looking down at the top of Rosenthal's bald head. Little did Aaron know that he'd revisit that view a million times in the years to come.

"I suspect you two have a lot to talk about," Justice Rellington said. "I'll catch up with you later, Sam. And, Aaron, listen to what this man has to say—because the president does."

As soon as the door closed, Rosenthal said, "One of the things you learn when people pay you three hundred bucks an hour is that you need to get right to the point. So that's what I'm going to do. I'm here because I want you to come work with me at Cromwell Altman Rosenthal and White."

At the time, Aaron had more than three dozen job offers. Probably the only people more coveted professionally than Supreme Court clerks are Heisman Trophy winners. Virtually every major law firm, think tank, law school, and government agency had already contacted him.

"Thank you, Mr. Rosenthal—"

"Sam," he said, interrupting.

"I'm flattered . . . but I've already accepted a position at Yale. And please, Mr.— Sam, don't take this the wrong way, but I just don't see myself devoting my life to representing huge corporations and criminals."

Rosenthal laughed. "Is that what you think being a partner at Cromwell Altman Rosenthal and White is all about?"

Aaron didn't respond, making his answer quite clear. He most certainly did.

"Because I respect you, Aaron, I'm not going to tell you that we don't represent our fair share of giant corporations and criminals, but being a partner at Cromwell Altman is about much more than that. It's . . . let me put it this way. You wouldn't say that Justice Rellington's job is to interpret statutes, correct? His job is to shape the law in ways that will stand twenty, fifty, a hundred years or more from now. That's what being a partner at Cromwell Altman is about too. In a word: power." Rosenthal's expression turned even more serious. "The simple truth of the matter, Aaron, is that while I have little doubt that you would be great as a professor of law, the question you need to ask yourself is whether you want to make a difference in the law . . . or merely teach about others who make that difference."

The rest, as they say, is history.

In the years that followed, Aaron climbed the ranks at Cromwell Altman. At first that meant learning the trade at Rosenthal's side, then as a partner ready to assume the mantle of leadership. That transition happened earlier than either of them had expected, when Rosenthal was nearly killed in a car accident from which he emerged broken on his right side. It was in that crisis, however, that Aaron showed he was a worthy successor to the throne. When Rosenthal had returned to the firm after a six months' absence, Aaron offered to step aside, but Rosenthal wouldn't hear of it.

"The whole point, Aaron," Rosenthal told him at the time, "is that we're building something here that's bigger than any one person. Cromwell Altman is the monument to our time on earth."

Today, that monument comprises more than six hundred lawyers, who occupy seventeen contiguous floors at the top of a fifty-seven-story tower sheathed entirely in glass. On sixteen of those floors, there are seven offices on the northern exposure—two partner offices on the corners (each with six coveted windows), three associate offices on either side of them (two windows), and then a smaller partner office in the middle of the hall (three windows). On the northern exposure of the fifty-seventh floor, however, it's just Aaron and Rosenthal, their offices separated by a conference room, which is not accessible to anyone but them.

They meet in that conference room most mornings before eight. The space is dominated by a long, white marble table, around which sit twenty-two high-backed, black leather chairs, ten on each side and one at each head. The northern exposure is *all* windows, looking out onto Central Park, with a view stretching well past the park's northernmost point.

When it's just the two of them, they always sit catty-corner on one end, Aaron at the head and Rosenthal beside him. Usually they engage in the kind of breakfast chatter most men share with their wives before heading off to work—something of note that was in the morning news or the outcome of last night's game.

Today's topic is far more serious, however. It's about control of the firm that Sam Rosenthal and Aaron Littman have ruled since the Reagan administration.

"Sam, there's just no way Pierce gets four votes," Aaron says with confidence, even though Rosenthal has just told him that assessment is wrong.

Donald Pierce, the head of the firm's corporate department, fancies himself as the man who would be king. To achieve his coup, Pierce needs the support of four out of seven members of the firm's management committee—the Orwellian-named Committee on Committees.

Rosenthal shakes his head. "Say what you want about Pierce, but he's not stupid. He wouldn't be so open in the challenge if he didn't already have four votes."

"From who? Maybe Goldman is with him . . . but that's it. Abby, you, and me are solid. Jane thinks Pierce is a pompous ass, and Elliot Dalton is going to do whatever causes the least disruption. I mean, at his age, a civil war is the last thing Dalton wants."

Aaron's confidence does nothing to assuage Rosenthal's concern. His expression—a furrowed brow and tight jawline—doesn't relax in the least; if anything, Rosenthal appears even more alarmed that Aaron does not recognize the seriousness of the situation.

Rosenthal walks unsteadily to the window. He usually relies on a cane—a dark hickory stick with a mother-of-pearl handle—to provide balance, but when he meets with Aaron, which he does two or three times a day, for some reason he always prefers to limp.

Rosenthal takes a few moments to bask in the expanse of Central Park fifty-seven stories below him. At this height, it's easy to feel like a god, capable of controlling the world below as if it were actually composed of things as small as they appear. It's also easy to assume that being this high up makes you invulnerable to attack.

When Rosenthal turns around, his expression conveys greater worry than words ever could. It's apparent that he sees danger fast approaching.

Like most litigators of the first order, Rosenthal is predisposed toward pessimism. When your professional life is defined by trying to protect people from bad things, you realize how easily things can go bad. But Aaron knows better than to dismiss Rosenthal's concerns, because in those rare instances when Aaron and his mentor haven't seen eye to eye, Rosenthal has usually been right.

And so, despite Aaron's outward optimism that the COC still supports him, he is acutely aware that if Samuel Rosenthal believes Donald Pierce has four votes, he very well may have them.

2

The Honorable Faith Nichols knows what's happened solely from the Cheshire cat grin on Sara Meyers's face.

Sara is one of Faith's two law clerks this year. A judicial clerkship with Faith is a prized commodity among the law school graduates who can afford to spend a year by a judge's side at roughly the same pay as a public school teacher, rather than take one of the $175,000-a-year jobs offered by the large Wall Street firms. The very best students usually go to the appellate courts, but after that, as a young female judge sitting in Manhattan, Faith gets her pick of the litter.

Faith's other clerk this year is Kenneth Sadinoff. Sara and Kenneth have been working in Faith's chambers for nearly six months now, but it didn't take her six weeks to realize that Kenneth is smarter than Sara yet not as hardworking. He knows that a judicial clerkship is akin to taking a course pass-fail, and so he sees no reason to get an A. Sara, on the other hand, always wants to be top of her class.

Among Sara's other law clerk responsibilities, it's her job to alert Faith to new case assignments. Good news for clerks almost always heralds a hot new case. And today, that can mean only one thing.

Even though she already knows, Faith still has to ask.

"So, what do you have for me, Sara?"

"We got Garkov." Sara's voice is even more excited than her expression. "Can I have it? Please?"

Faith pauses a moment before replying: "We'll see."

It's an occupational hazard for a jurist to judge, and so here's Faith's assessment of how the next decade will unfold for Sara: After her clerkship, she'll join a top-tier law firm and put in the one-hundred-hour workweeks demanded, so that soon enough it'll seem normal to her never to see the sun, and she'll consider going to work at noon on Saturday as a mini-vacation. Maybe she'll go on dates, but more likely she'll think of a social life as something she'll have *after,* although that particular goalpost will be in constant motion—*after* she's established herself as a good associate, *after* she makes partner, *after* she gets a corner office. Then one day, she'll be sitting in that corner office wondering when exactly she made the decision for her life to turn out quite the way it has.

In short, she'll likely take the same path that Faith traveled. And while Faith knows that she's hardly a cautionary tale—forty-two years old and a federal district court judge—a part of her is still envious of Sara's ability to change course while she can, even as Faith strongly suspects Sara never will.

Faith's failure to immediately assign Sara to the Garkov case causes her clerk's smile to recede. But then, as if an invisible life coach has whispered in her ear to avoid pouting at work, Sara reclaims it and says, "It hit the docket last night at midnight. I came in early today and got the bench memo from one of Judge Mendelsohn's clerks. I also asked him to send us the complete file ASAP."

Brian Mendelsohn was the original judge assigned to preside over the trial of Nicolai Garkov. He's a dying breed of jurist, a card-carrying member of the ACLU who never met a criminal right he didn't go out of his way to enforce. Garkov certainly must have thanked his personal god when he saw Mendelsohn's name come out of the assignment wheel.

And then that deity had the last laugh. A week ago, in the middle of reading an opinion from the bench, Mendelsohn began speaking in Yiddish, and went on like that for more than two minutes before one of his clerks stopped him. Alzheimer's, which Mendelsohn had apparently believed he could hide for another year or so.

The Garkov case went back into the wheel for reassignment. The odds were forty-one-to-one that Faith's name wouldn't roll out.

That's why I never gamble, Faith tells herself.

"And it's a bench trial," Sara says, her excitement rising once more.

Garkov waived his right to trial by a jury of his peers, in favor of Judge Mendelsohn's rendering the verdict. It's a strategic decision that few defendants make, given that the likelihood of getting one out of twelve people to believe you is usually far better than convincing a judge of your innocence. Practically the only time that calculus shifted was when that judge was the Honorable Brian Mendelsohn. Going from Mendelsohn to Faith was the bait-and-switch of all time, however.

"Who's counsel of record?" Faith asks.

Sara looks down at the manila file folder in her hand. "Roy Sabato Jr."

Faith rolls her eyes, making her low regard for Garkov's counsel painfully obvious. "God knows that Roy Sabato certainly isn't the leading light of the criminal bar, but even he's smart enough to know that he should withdraw the jury waiver now that I'm presiding," Faith says.

"I've already done some quick research on that," Sara says brightly. "Garkov doesn't have an absolute right to a jury once he's waived it. It depends on how much going back to a jury trial would prejudice the prosecution."

That seems wrong to Faith. Simply as a matter of fairness, a defendant who waives a jury in favor of one judge should be allowed to withdraw that waiver when a different judge is appointed. But Faith learned long ago that the law is not always fair.

"Okay. So when's the trial scheduled to begin?" Faith asks.

"April fourteen."

That's less than a month away. Faith can already hear the prosecution screaming bloody murder if Garkov tries to withdraw the jury waiver. Whether true or not, they'll claim they've been preparing for a bench trial and don't have sufficient time to refocus their case so it's presentable to a jury.

"Also, there's a pretrial on for tomorrow," Sara says.

Of course there is, Faith thinks.

Everything could well come to a head then. It would have been nice if Faith had some time to think before being thrown into the lion's den. But, like the law, life isn't always fair, either.

"Is that the bench memo?" Faith asks, pointing at the manila folder.

Sara hesitates, as if she's reluctant to part with her prize for fear she'll never get it back. But when Faith opens her hand, palm up, Sara has little choice but to give up the folder.

For a moment, it looks as if Sara is going to ask for the case again, but she's smart enough to know that groveling will only hurt her cause. Nevertheless, as she leaves, Sara looks back at Faith with hopeful eyes.

"The case is yours, Sara," Faith says. "I appreciate the initiative. Please tell Kenny, and if you need to push a case or two on him to free up some of your time, that's fine. Just don't give him your worst ones, okay?"

"Thanks so much, Judge," Sara says through a beaming smile as she closes the door behind her.

Alone, Faith opens the folder. Inside is a one-page bench memo. The law clerks for all the judges rotate through the bench-memo assignment, and there's a special format that they follow: name of the case; the attorneys for the defendant; the bail disposition. Below that is a one-line description of the charges in the indictment, which liberally uses a preapproved set of abbreviations. For Garkov it reads: "Sec. Fr., ML, Obstr. Coll. SEC. SI possible."

Faith does the translation in her head. *The indictment charges counts of securities fraud, money laundering, and obstruction of justice. There is a collateral proceeding being brought by the Securities and Exchange Commission.* And the prosecutor must have mentioned something to

Judge Mendelsohn about a superseding indictment coming down, which means that additional criminal charges may be forthcoming.

The case-management synopsis is a bit like describing *Moby-Dick* as a book about a whale, however. Nicolai Garkov is the most reviled figure in America at the moment. The story everyone knows is that Garkov's hedge fund was laundering money for the Russian Mafia. As if that wasn't bad enough, the same hedge fund money had been traced to the accounts of the terrorists who claimed responsibility for the Red Square bombing that killed twenty-six people last New Year's Eve, including three American students.

Faith's been in the criminal justice arena for long enough to know how to read between the lines. The fact that Garkov hasn't been charged with anything having to do with the bombing means that there's likely no evidence of his involvement in that crime, and the threat of a superseding indictment for murder suggests that the prosecution's case on the charges they did file is shaky. In other words, the government is bluffing—trying to leverage Garkov into pleading guilty to the filed charges with the promise of giving him a pass on the Red Square murders, even though they seemingly don't have enough evidence to convict him of anything.

The fact that the trial is less than a month away tells her something else: Garkov's not falling for it. He's going to put the squeeze on the government to prove his guilt beyond a reasonable doubt.

Faith closes the folder and places it back on her desk. She can't help but smile at the irony. Perhaps this, too, is God having the last laugh.

Presiding over the Garkov trial is the kind of thing that can make a career. A year ago—hell, three weeks ago—Faith would have been no less excited than Sara to get it.

But now? It's the very last thing in the world she wants.

3

The Colburn Group is a multibillion-dollar conglomerate that pays Cromwell Altman upwards of one hundred million dollars annually. It operates in a dozen different industries, with a hand in everything from military defense to petrochemical manufacturing to operating fast-food restaurants.

And for the last ten minutes, Aaron has been getting an earful from Colburn's general counsel—a stern-looking man named Douglas Harrold—about how if Cromwell Altman wants to keep that plum business, it's going to have to offer a 20 percent discount.

"Aaron, it's not personal," Harrold says. "Your work on the tanker case was . . . what can I say, we reserved for a two-billion-dollar loss, and we thought that was too optimistic, and then you got us a resolution at less than half of that. But our board has given us a mandate to cut company-wide, and that's got to include outside legal, too."

Aaron's used to playing chicken over fees, but Colburn is Cromwell Altman's third-largest client, and their matters keep at least fifty lawyers fully subscribed. Losing that much business in one fell swoop would necessitate a round of layoffs, and profits per partner, the yardstick by which the firm's success is measured, would definitely take a hit.

Still, Cromwell Altman isn't JC Penney, and Aaron prides himself on never putting his services on sale. More to the point, he's not going to forgo $20 million in fees without a fight.

"Doug, belt tightening around legal fees is the very last thing Colburn should be doing," Aaron says. "The regulatory inquiry on the tanker ended well, but there's still the class action to worry about, and those plaintiffs' lawyers smell blood in the water. Besides, it's also a matter of principle for me. I don't reduce my rates for *any* client. That way, every client is assured that they're getting the rock-bottom best deal."

"Rock-bottom?" Harrold laughs. "C'mon, Aaron, you guys charge us a fortune."

"We charge you what the market will bear. Every one of our clients pays exactly the same rate that you do."

Harrold now looks like a man who's grown tired of this little dance. "All right. I don't want to play hardball here, but I guess I'm going to have to in order to make my point. You should know that I've already spoken to Steve Weitzen over at Martin Quinn. He's willing to offer us a twenty percent discount, and their rates are already lower than yours. So net-net, by switching our work to them, we'll save at least thirty million a year. That's real money."

"No, Doug, you have it wrong. We saved you a billion on the tanker case. Now *that*, my friend, is real money."

Harrold shakes his head. "Aaron, I'm sorry, but you gotta give me something here. Otherwise, I'm going to have to make the move."

Aaron looks squarely at Harrold. As the top legal officer of a Fortune 100 company, Doug Harrold normally gets his way, and he certainly gives every outward manifestation that he means what he just said.

"I hope you don't mind," Aaron says, "but while I'm still your lawyer, allow me to give you some advice. And because you're on an austerity program, I'm not even going to charge you for it." Aaron smiles but then quickly resumes a more serious demeanor. "I think you're looking at the relationship with Cromwell Altman in the wrong way. We're not just lawyers for your company. We're a personal insurance policy for you. Now, I know you'll take some heat from your board if you stay with us at our rates, rather than bargain-hunt with Martin Quinn, but you and I both know that you're not going to get fired over it. On the other hand, there's no way you're going to keep your job if the class action ends with a multi-billion-dollar verdict and you're left explaining to the board of directors that it was your call to switch lawyers."

The knock on the conference room door punctuates Aaron's point. It's Diane Pimentel, one of Aaron's two assistants. Aaron's other assistant serves as his legal secretary, but Diane is the gatekeeper. She controls his schedule and handles the emergencies that demand his time on an almost hourly basis.

"I'm so sorry to bother you, Mr. Littman," Diane says, "but Ms. London just called. She and Mr. Hahn are with a client and she asked that you come by as soon as possible."

"I have to deal with this other matter," Aaron says to Harrold as he comes to his feet. "So if your position is still the last word on this, I'll have your files sent over to Martin Quinn by the end of the week."

There's a momentary standoff. Having represented Doug Harrold for years now, Aaron knows he's the kind of man who's unwilling to go all-in when there's any chance of losing. Aaron's just waiting for Harrold to reach that conclusion, too.

Aaron extends his hand. "No hard feelings, Doug, and I wish you the best of luck with Weitzen."

That's enough to do the trick. Harrold takes Aaron's hand and Aaron can feel the yielding in Harrold's grip.

"You win, Aaron," Harrold says as they shake hands. "Let me talk to my board. I'll tell them that . . . I don't know what the hell I'm going to tell them, to be honest with you, but I guess I'll have to think of something. We really do need you on the class action . . . and whatever comes down the pike after that."

"Thanks, Doug," Aaron says. "You're making the right call. For you and the company both."

Rachel London hates it when supposedly grown men act like little boys, but that's exactly what Peter Hahn and Joe Malone are doing at the moment. She's voiced her disagreement with them, and in response they've actually retreated into opposite corners of the room. Malone has turned his back on her, while Hahn stands with his arms crossed.

She catches Hahn's glare, which is somewhere between icy and contemptuous. Hahn's the kind of senior partner who expects blind obedience from his subordinates, even if they're partners too, like Rachel.

Rachel was only recently assigned to the Malone matter. It was one of those unlucky convergences that define the big law firm life: on the day after Rachel's major trial concluded, Hahn demanded a junior partner to handle some of the witnesses for his own messed-up case.

Although she's not yet fully up to speed on the facts of Joe Malone's case, Rachel understands enough to know that, despite Malone's protestations of innocence, the odds of his conviction are, in her humble opinion, more than 70 percent. Conviction at trial means a long prison term, so the smart play would be to try to cut a favorable plea deal. But every time she's dared broach the subject of Malone pleading guilty in exchange for a shorter sentence, Hahn and Malone have shut her down.

Her latest effort is similarly falling on deaf ears.

"In any plea deal, the government is going to demand that Joe admit, under oath, that he stole those paintings," Hahn says, as if Rachel doesn't know this. "And Joe can't truthfully say that because he's *not* guilty. That pretty much rules out a plea, no matter what the government ends up offering us."

Rachel can't really believe that this is Hahn's actual basis for refusing a plea deal. There isn't a client who walks through Cromwell Altman's doors that doesn't profess their innocence, sometimes in the most extreme ways—on their children's souls, offering to take lie detector tests, you name it. *I didn't do it. You have to believe me* might just be the most commonly uttered phrase by Cromwell Altman clients. Probably in all of criminal defense. Yet nearly all of them ultimately plead guilty and admit everything . . . and the few who end up going to trial, in Rachel's mind at least, aren't any more innocent; they just have a greater risk tolerance, or are in denial.

Rachel is quite sure that the real reason behind Hahn's position has nothing to do with believing Joe Malone is innocent and everything to do with envisioning his picture on the cover of the *American Lawyer,* complete with some pun-heavy headline: WORK OF ART. Or maybe DEFENSE OF ARTISTRY. They don't write articles touting your legal genius when your client takes a plea. Even losing at trial will likely be a boon for Hahn's career—it'll add a few hundred thousand dollars to his billable-hours column and increase his stature just by keeping his name in the media. After all, Clarence Darrow lost the Scopes Monkey Trial and yet he's famous ninety years later.

"This is your call, Joe," Hahn continues. "No one can make it for you. If you're ready to stand up in open court and admit your guilt, then we'll call the prosecutor right now and see what kind of deal we can get. But if you want to prove your innocence, there's only one way to do that, and that's by winning at trial."

Joe Malone turns back to the conversation. Rachel thinks she sees uncertainty in his face about what to do, but then he says, "I told you guys from the very beginning, I'm innocent." And then, as if to convince himself, he adds, "I swear that I am."

I didn't do it. You have to believe me.

That's enough for Peter Hahn to declare victory. He nods at Malone and flashes Rachel a self-satisfied smirk before saying, "I guess that settles it, then."

Nothing is settled for Rachel, though. She's not going to let Hahn's ego be the reason that Joe Malone rots in jail for the next ten years. At least not while she has one more card to play.

"I'm going to get my witness folders," Rachel says, and scurries out of the room. Once in her office, she calls Aaron Littman.

Rachel knows that calling Aaron to come to her rescue will only add to the gossip about them, even if she is actually asking Aaron to rescue the client and not her. Still . . . every so often, someone, usually a guy who's been flirting with her, will lean in and whisper conspiratorially that people say she's sleeping with Aaron. The guy will make it seem as if he's imparting some top-secret information she needs to know in order to avoid embarrassment. Sort of like telling her that there's a stain on her blouse.

Years ago, she heard Kevin Bacon mention on a talk show that it never ceases to amaze him when people come up to him and say, "Do you know there's a game called Six Degrees of Kevin Bacon?" She feels just like that. Of course she knows. How could she not?

She tells herself that it's not her fault, and the gossip stems from the fact that she doesn't look the part of a big-firm law partner. Most people who ventured a guess at Rachel's profession would guess model, given that she's five foot ten with a slender figure and golden-blond hair that falls to the middle of her back. But she knows that's not the only reason. She brings some of it on herself. The way she looks at Aaron, as if he's the only man on earth.

Aaron's assistant, Diane, tells Rachel that he's behind closed doors with a client.

"Can you tell him that I need his help as soon as possible?" Rachel says. "I'm with Peter Hahn in conference room B on fifty-six, and we're meeting with Joe Malone. Peter's pressing to go to trial, but I think that will end badly, and there's a chance we can still get a sweetheart plea deal out of this."

Rachel returns to the conference room clutching the witness folders that were the pretext for her absence. Hahn and Malone barely acknowledge her return, and she sits quietly, waiting for the cavalry to arrive.

Within a few minutes, there's a knock on the door.

"Hi, I'm sorry to interrupt," Aaron says, entering the room. "I understand that you're on the verge of trial, and so I wanted to stop in and see if I can lend some support."

Rachel doesn't have to look at Hahn to know he's absolutely furious. She can't blame him; nobody likes being undermined. But her primary duty is to the client, and Hahn was clearly giving Malone some bad advice. Besides, Malone's smile tells her that he's more than happy to have an audience with the firm's chairman. Joe Malone originally came to Cromwell Altman for Aaron, but he was farmed out to Peter Hahn when the one-million-dollar retainer Aaron requires proved beyond reach.

Before Hahn can leap in, Rachel says: "Aaron, you'll recall the fifty-thousand-foot overview. Joe was until recently the studio assistant to Robert Attias, who I'm sure you know is, in many people's opinion, the greatest living American abstract expressionist master. The position of studio assistant is an extremely close one with the artist. Basically, Joe handled not only Attias's professional life but his entire life, for the last ten years. During the course of that relationship, Attias made eight gifts to Joe of his artwork. None were the serious types of paintings that sell at auction for tens of millions. These were more like sketches . . . but each still has considerable value because it's virtually impossible to buy an original Attias unless it's a fifty-million-dollar painting. There's a dispute about the value of these gifts, but we peg the sketches as worth somewhere between three million and five million. That's a lot of money for Joe, so he wanted to sell some of them, but Attias is the kind of guy who expects blind loyalty, and he would have fired Joe if he got wind that Joe had sold off the sketches."

"And just so you know, Bob once gave a painting to Brad Pitt and Angelina Jolie," Malone says. "And they donated it to some charity, and Bob was just livid. I swear. He couldn't see the big picture about how that canvas probably built a school somewhere in Africa. All he kept ranting about was what complete ingrates Brad and Angelina were."

"So to protect himself against Attias's finding out that Joe was selling the gifts," Rachel continues, "Joe sold them in private sales and required the buyers to execute confidentiality agreements and agree not to resell the works until after Attias's death. The buyers naturally demanded a cut in the price in exchange for agreeing to those restrictions, and so the works were sold at what we think was a thirty percent discount. The government is claiming it was more like fifty percent. And of course, somehow Attias found out about the sales. He got so pissed off that he called the FBI and claimed he never made any gifts to Joe and that Joe had stolen them. The prosecutor thinks that they have a winning hand here because Joe's selling the works at a discount, and in a private sale with confidentiality restrictions, and that could be deemed to indicate Joe was trying to avoid anyone knowing that these works were on the market, which is the typical MO for stolen art."

Hahn is now finally about to say something, but Aaron waves him off. Rachel wonders if Hahn's head is going to explode right here in the conference room. He's spent a thousand hours on the Malone defense, but Aaron's content to rely upon the two-minute recap he's just heard from the recently assigned junior partner on the case.

"What's the bid and the ask regarding plea negotiations?" Aaron asks.

"Um . . . we haven't really had any, but I figure that conviction on all counts likely means ten years, give or take," Hahn says. "The Assistant U.S. Attorney on the case is a woman named Stephanie Kessler and she's a . . ." He looks at Rachel and must decide not to use the term *bitch*, but says, ". . . tough one. I don't have a real feel for where she's going to land on this. Maybe three years is doable. I doubt we'd end up doing much better, though. The main issue is that there's no way Joe can allocute his guilt because . . . because it's not true."

Rachel's eyes meet Aaron's in a tacit *See what I'm dealing with* moment. Aaron's response is an almost imperceptible nod, reinforcing in Rachel's mind that she and Aaron share telepathy.

"I didn't do it, Mr. Littman," Malone says. "I know you must hear that all the time, but I swear, I'm innocent."

"Yes, I do hear that all the time," Aaron says. "And this may surprise you, but it's been my long-held view that when you're contemplating whether to take a plea, guilt and innocence are largely beside the point."

Malone looks as if he's just heard the Pope deny the existence of God, but Rachel knows exactly where Aaron is heading. She's seen him perform this particular bit of magic before: getting a man who has heretofore shouted his innocence from the mountaintop to do a one-eighty-degree turn and consider pleading guilty—for the right price, of course.

"Mr. Malone, are you married?" Aaron asks.

"Yeah."

"Kids?"

"Two kids. A nine-year-old girl and an eleven-year-old boy."

Aaron nods. "So, in three years, they'll be twelve and fourteen. I'm not saying that the next three years don't matter, because every day matters . . . but you need to think about not seeing your son again until he's twenty-one. And you need to think about the possibility that the worst case here *isn't* ten years, but say you get sentenced to fifteen. Or twenty. Now you're in territory of not seeing your grandchildren being born. What a plea does for you is, in many ways, more important than vindication. It assures you a future. Peter here thinks three years is doable . . . but what if he can get you two? So now you're looking at the certainty of being back at home before your daughter is interested in boys. On top of that, you've got to consider the financial cost of a trial. Conservatively, you're looking at two hundred and fifty thousand dollars, and more if you lose, what with post-trial briefing and appeals. That's college tuition for your kids, security for your wife. And while we win our fair share of cases, and Peter's as damn good a trial lawyer as there is, the sad truth is that the prosecution wins many more than they lose. I'm talking something like a ninety percent conviction rate. Those odds should give even the most innocent man something to think about."

Faced with the likelihood that he might well be convicted and sentenced to serious jail time—something that Peter Hahn has been soft-selling—Malone's barely keeping it together, which is exactly what Rachel had hoped this tête-à-tête with Aaron Littman would produce: abject fear. When Rachel previously tried to articulate the risk Malone faced by going to trial, Hahn belittled her concerns, at one point actually calling her a nervous Nelly. But when Aaron Littman tells you there's a very real possibility of conviction and a long prison term, that means in no uncertain terms that you have every right to be afraid. Very afraid.

"Now I'm going to tell you something else, which hits home for me," Aaron continues. "I'm sure you've heard, I just lost a very big trial for Eric Matthews, and he's now serving fourteen years. That was *twice* the sentence we thought he'd get. And I'm telling you that so you can see that no one has a crystal ball on these sorts of things. But to me, when it comes right down to it, this decision that you have to make—whether to plead guilty or go to trial—is likely the most important decision you'll ever make. For you and your family. And like any decision of that magnitude, you need to have all the available information. And part of that information is whether a guilty plea means five years or three years or, maybe, something less. That's just plain common sense, Joe."

Two knocks on the door and Diane steps inside. "Mr. Littman," she says, "I'm so sorry to interrupt, but there's someone here to see you."

"I'm very sorry that I have to go," Aaron says, "but let me make one last point. There's one thing I never say to my clients: that I'm with them all the way. The reason I don't is that I know it's just not true. The truth is that I'm with them until the verdict. If after that they go to prison . . . that's something they have to do on their own. Which is why only *you* can make this decision. But I'll tell you this—if someone offered me three years in jail to eliminate the risk of serving ten or fifteen, I'd think very hard about it. And whether or not I was innocent or guilty wouldn't be the only consideration, because the sad truth is that innocent men do get convicted." Aaron smiles at Malone and extends his hand. "It was very nice seeing you again, Joe. I know you'll make the right choice."

Malone shakes Aaron's hand and then puts his other hand on top, forming a handshake sandwich. "Thank you so much, Mr. Littman," he says.

Over Malone's shoulder, and out of Hahn's still-infuriated sight line, Rachel mouths: "Thank you."

4

When Aaron steps outside the conference room, he says, "Thanks for getting me, Diane. Right on time, too."

"You're welcome," she replies, "but there really is someone here to see you. Roy Sabato. He doesn't have an appointment, but he says it's a matter of some urgency."

At its highest echelon, the criminal defense bar in New York is fairly small and divided into factions. Roy Sabato and Aaron Littman are not members of the same clique, not by a long shot. Aaron and his ilk represent multinational corporations and CEOs involved in complex securities crimes, while Sabato's clients are by and large mobsters, drug dealers, and other allegedly misunderstood, albeit very wealthy, citizens from the lowest strata of society.

In the same way that owners sometimes end up looking like their dogs, from appearances alone you'd assume Roy Sabato was a client. Everything from his stocky build to his shiny suits to his pinky ring suggests he's a made man.

It's Aaron's usual practice to hold introductory meetings in the conference room. But something tells him maintaining a power advantage will be to his benefit, and so he directs Sabato into his office.

Sabato looks around the room. The chairman's office at Cromwell Altman Rosenthal and White isn't the Oval Office, but for lawyers it's a seat of power like no other. Floor-to-ceiling windows frame Central Park on two sides, while the main wall is blanketed with pictures of

Aaron with A-list movie stars, national political figures, and corporate chieftains.

Aaron takes his position behind a desk that costs as much as a Mercedes. It's more than three feet long, entirely made of stone, and held upright by a single pedestal positioned so far to one end that it creates something of an optical illusion that the structure is about to topple over.

After they're both seated, Aaron waits a beat, then two, assuming Sabato will come right out and state the reason for his visit. Sabato seems ill at ease, however; it's as if he's not looking forward to saying why he's here. It's the demeanor clients have when they fire you, but Aaron hasn't even been hired yet, and so he's at a loss as to the reason behind Sabato's hesitancy.

Finally, Aaron says, "So, Roy, what can I do for you?"

"I have a client who wants to retain your services."

"And who might that be?"

Sabato exhales and says: "Nicolai Garkov."

Now Sabato's hesitancy makes more sense. *He's* the one being fired.

Aaron was surprised when he first heard Garkov retained Sabato. He assumed Sabato got the nod because he was one of the few lawyers willing to take on Garkov at all.

Garkov's conduct had created a perfect storm of problems for most lawyers. Nearly every bank on Wall Street was a counterparty to his securities trading, which means that those firms are now at least six counselors deep in civil lawsuits. Although that type of conflict of interest didn't ethically prohibit the representation, it was disastrous for the bottom line. The big banks could be counted on to pull their corporate work from any law firm giving Garkov aid and comfort. Any lawyers of the first rank for whom that wasn't a problem—because they either were at smaller firms or, like Sabato, practiced alone—would have thought twice about taking on the case when the very-public terrorism angle surfaced.

“You looking for co-counsel?” Aaron asks.

“No. Garkov wants a straight substitution.”

“Pretty late in the game for that. Isn’t the trial coming up?”

“Next month. April fourteen. But I don’t know if that date will hold. You may not have heard, but Judge Mendelsohn lost his marbles. He’s out, and the lovely Judge Faith Nichols is in.”

Aaron tries to mask his panic. He heard about Mendelsohn’s meltdown, and so he knew that his days on the bench were numbered, but he hadn’t heard that Mendelsohn had officially withdrawn from the Garkov case.

Things are happening too fast for his liking. He needs to slow it all down, plan some kind of strategy here.

“Roy, my corporate group does a lot of work for . . . well, for everyone on the Street. That’s going to tie my hands.”

Sabato sighs. “Garkov’s got his heart set on you, Aaron. So much so that he’s willing to pay you a hundred grand just for the initial meeting.”

Aaron charges fifteen hundred dollars an hour. Clients have flown him around the world for an initial meeting, but no one has ever agreed to pay more than his hourly rate without any strings attached. Bonuses for good results, maybe. But never just for him to grant them an audience.

“Why the hell would he agree to do that?”

“Because he knows you won’t meet with him if he doesn’t.”

“Is that your way of saying that you don’t know why? Or are you just not willing to tell me?”

“Look, he didn’t tell me, and I didn’t ask. But, even if he had, I would have assumed it was a lie. I’ve been representing the guy for months now, and the only thing I know for sure is that it’s never clear if what he’s saying is actually the truth.”

"That's hardly a reason for me to take him on as a client, now, is it?"

"I imagine that's why he's offering you the other hundred thousand reasons to meet with him."

Aaron wonders if Sabato is being straight with him. Lawyers lying to other lawyers is hardly unprecedented, after all.

"Even though that's a lot of money, Roy, I'm still going to decline. Please tell Mr. Garkov that I'm sorry and I wish him the best of luck at trial."

Aaron rises, the universal signal that this meeting is now over. Rather than getting to his feet, however, Sabato instead lets out another sigh. A moment later he stands, but his posture leaves no doubt that he's not going anywhere just yet.

He presses a piece of paper into Aaron's hand.

"Aaron. You need to listen to me," Sabato quietly says. "My marching orders are to get you to Garkov's apartment right now."

Aaron takes a moment to study what Sabato has given him. As promised, it's a cashier's check in his name for one hundred thousand dollars.

"I'm not sure if you're bribing me or threatening me at this point, Roy."

"Aaron, believe me when I tell you that I don't know what the hell is going on here, but Garkov told me that . . . if the check wasn't enough to convince you . . . then I should tell you he has some very damaging information you do not want to find its way to the press . . ."

Sabato comes to a stop and shakes his head mournfully before continuing. "Please listen to me about this. I've represented some real animals in my time, but I've never met anybody who comes close to this guy. If I were you, I'd be at his place, pronto. Go tell him to fuck himself if he's bluffing, but, seriously, it would be a huge mistake to risk that he's not."

Roy Sabato's usual press conference–slash–courtroom tough-guy swagger is nowhere to be seen. To the contrary, he actually looks frightened.

Aaron has played this out long enough. He's known for the last five minutes that he is ultimately going to meet with Nicolai Garkov. Ever since Sabato uttered the name *Faith Nichols*.

5

Rachel London's office is one of the small partner ones, sandwiched between two associate offices on the building's south side. The office décor captures the conflicted nature of its occupant—the sleek furniture shows that she's serious about work, but her niece's crayoned artwork taped to the walls suggests there's more she wants out of life than her career.

Her office was one of the few things that changed when Rachel made partner. Well, that and her compensation. But the hours continued to be just as crushing and the work was largely the same, second-seating someone more senior, which more often than not amounted to taking notes in the important meetings and supervising the grunt work done by the associates.

Rachel joined Cromwell Altman seven years earlier, when she was an idealistic twenty-six-year-old, ready to save the world, which made her just like the fifty-nine other lawyers in the incoming Cromwell Altman class. Back then, the firm distributed a book with head shots of the new attorneys, with a short narrative indicating the department to which they were assigned, where they hailed from, and the schools they'd attended. Picture after picture of fresh-faced overachievers, all of whom graduated at the top of their class at a first-tier law school.

Fast-forward a decade and she's the only one left. The big-law equivalent of *The Hunger Games*.

To survive, Rachel has worked nonstop, missing more birthday dinners and holidays than she could count. And while the financial rewards are plentiful, she has little on which to spend her mid-six-figure income. Her two-bedroom apartment has one more bedroom than she actually needs, and she wouldn't know what to do with a home in the Hamptons or a Porsche. She'd like to travel, but putting aside the problem of not having anyone to go with, the partners never take vacations because God forbid a client needs to reach them when they're not in the office.

So for better or worse, for the past decade, Cromwell Altman has been her entire life. At least she's good at it. Her gambit of bringing Aaron in to talk some sense into Joe Malone is a case in point. Sure, Peter Hahn read her the riot act after Aaron left, telling her in no uncertain terms that he'd never work with her again, but to Rachel that was more of a prize than a punishment. Besides, so long as Aaron has her back, she isn't concerned that Peter Hahn can inflict any damage to her career.

True to form, Hahn was still being something of a passive-aggressive jerk about it, making her call the prosecutor to discuss the plea, so that he could, in his words, "wash his hands of the whole debacle." Once again, however, Hahn was actually doing Rachel a favor. At least this way, the negotiations might actually end up getting somewhere.

"Assistant United States Attorney Stephanie Kessler," comes the voice on the line.

"Stephanie, Rachel London here, over at Cromwell Altman. I'm working with Peter Hahn on the Joseph Malone case."

"Yes, hi. What can I do for you, Rachel?"

"Well, I'm a little out on a limb here," Rachel says, "because the client is adamant about going to trial, but between you and me, I really think that everybody is better off if this ends in a plea, and so I was wondering if we could talk a little about where the floor is on this one."

"I already told Peter that we're willing to be reasonable. Mr. Attias is in his mid-eighties, and we'd rather not put him through the trial if we can get a fair result. But that requires that your guy be reasonable, too."

This is the first Rachel's heard about any flexibility by the prosecutors. Of course, she's not all that surprised that Peter Hahn kept this nugget to himself.

"Here's my problem, Stephanie. Peter's all gung-ho to try the case, and the client won't budge on admitting he did anything wrong. So between them, there's very little interest in our side making an offer . . . but I think I have a way that you and I can break through that."

"Go on. I'm listening."

So far, so good, Rachel thinks. "I'm not going to argue the merits with you," Rachel says, "because this is a classic he-said-he-said situation, and so how can anyone know what went on between my guy and Mr. Attias, right?"

"I thought you just said you weren't going to argue the merits."

"Fair enough. I'm just looking for some middle ground here. What if . . . I can get him to make total restitution? Mr. Attias gets back the art, and the buyers are made whole. Everybody wins. Does that earn my guy a get-out-of-jail-free card?"

"Sorry, no way. Jail time is a deal-breaker for us. Probation sends the message that if you're a purse snatcher, you go to jail, but when it's a few million dollars in art, you get a pass."

No surprise there. Rachel knew jail time was going to be non-negotiable. The issue is how long.

"But in a purse-snatching case, you know there's a crime," Rachel counters. "Here, that's still a very open question. Like you said, Mr. Attias is in his eighties. Who's to say what he remembers about gifts of relatively insignificant works he made years ago? Not to mention that I hear his health isn't very good. If he dies before trial, which might still be six months or more away if we try to delay, your case dies with him."

"Come on, Rachel. I know you're repping your client, but jail time is a must for us. Period."

"Will six months do it?"

"Nope. We're not letting this go for less than a year."

Rachel smiles. That's exactly what she wanted to hear. "Does that mean a year might do it?"

"A year, plus a complete allocution of guilt, and he makes full restitution."

Rachel wants to jump through the phone and shout *Yes!* but she's got to play this out. "I don't want to mislead you, Stephanie, because that is still going to be something of a sell on my end. But, here's what I want to do. If you're willing to put that on the table, I'll go back to my client and tell him that it's my proposal—so then we'll make that offer to you, and do it on a take-it-or-leave-it basis. What I'm afraid of is that if *you* made the offer, he's going to want to see how much better than that he can do."

There's a pause on the other end. For a second, Rachel fears that she's overplayed her hand, and now that she's opened the door to a guilty plea, the prosecutor will demand more jail time. But then she hears, "I'm going to take you at your word on this, Rachel. It's a year. Not a day less. You understand?"

"How about if I want a day more?" Rachel says.

"Hah. Sure," Kessler says with a chuckle. It's a quirk of the federal sentencing system that inmates sentenced to more than a year get to serve the last six months in a halfway house. "A year and a day. Final offer."

"Thanks, Stephanie," Rachel says. "I'll get back to you later today, but I'm going to beat the hell out of Malone on this end so he takes the deal."

6

There was a time when the tourists lined up in front of Tiffany on Manhattan's Fifth Avenue, muffins in hand, to re-create Audrey Hepburn's famous pose from *Breakfast at Tiffany's*. Now they're much more likely to photograph themselves in front of its neighbor, Trump Tower, pretending to be fired contestants from *The Apprentice*.

Judge Mendelsohn had granted Nicolai Garkov's bail request that he be confined to his home as he awaited trial. There was quite a lot of outrage over that at the time, with every TV news report about the case shot in front of Trump Tower and making repeated references to Garkov's twenty-thousand-square-foot apartment's being the only five-star prison in the world. Now there's speculation in the press that Mendelsohn's Alzheimer's had something to do with the tone-deafness of his ruling.

Trump Tower's public spaces are clad in Breccia Pernice, a pink, white-veined marble, and mirrors are seemingly everywhere. The five-level atrium has a waterfall, various shops, at least three cafés, and a pedestrian bridge that crosses over the waterfall's pool. This morning it is also teeming with people, most of whom are speaking a language other than English.

Aaron walks past the kiosk hawking Donald J. Trump's signature clothing line to a booth marked CONCIERGE. He tells the white-gloved attendant that he's here to see Nicolai Garkov.

"The private elevator is down the end of the hall," the attendant says. He points to the back of the space. "Go through the doors, and you'll see it."

Through the door, the pink marble stops and is replaced by something much more industrial: a flat-weave, gray carpet. Two uniformed police officers and a man in a dark suit sit behind a metal detector.

"I'm here to see Nicolai Garkov," Aaron says. "I believe he's expecting me."

The man in the suit picks up a clipboard. "What's your name, please?" he asks.

"Aaron Littman."

"Yup. You're here. Mr. Garkov's ten o'clock."

Aaron grins at the thought. "Does he get many visitors?"

"You'd be surprised. The terms of his confinement are that he's only allowed to see immediate family, doctors, and lawyers, but somehow at least two of every type seem to show up each day. Which category do you fit in, Mr. Littman?"

"I'm a lawyer."

"Do you have any identification?" Aaron hands over his driver's license but immediately knows from Clipboard Man's frown that that's not going to suffice. "Anything to indicate you're a lawyer? A business card will do."

Aaron reaches back into his wallet, wondering why a business card is satisfactory proof that he's a lawyer, when anyone could have one printed up. Clipboard Man studies the card carefully, even though the only information on it is Aaron's name and the firm's name, address, and telephone number.

"Okay," Clipboard Man finally says, looking back at Aaron. "Please remove your coat, your suit jacket, your shoes, your belt, the contents of your pockets, and anything metal. Also, you're going to need to leave your phone, laptop, and anything with a camera in it."

Aaron doesn't have a laptop, but he dutifully hands over his phone for inspection. Then he places his belt, shoes, cuff links, and watch in the plastic bin and watches the accessories go through the X-ray machine.

After Aaron walks through the metal detector, the older of the two uniformed police officers says, "Please follow me, sir. I'll accompany you to Mr. Garkov's apartment."

Inside the elevator, the cop uses a key, rather than pressing a button. The lights above the doors don't go on until the fiftieth floor.

"I thought the Donald lives in the penthouse," Aaron says.

"He does. Mr. Garkov has the four floors below that."

Sure enough, the elevator doors open at the sixty-fifth floor. Aaron expects the cop to lead him out, but instead he gestures that Aaron should exit alone.

Two more police officers and another man in a dark suit await him. They sit at a desk with two computer monitors facing them. Even though Aaron doesn't get a clear look at the screens, he sees enough to know that they are transmitting video from inside the apartment.

Just like downstairs, the man in the suit has a clipboard. "Identification, please," he says.

Aaron mentally sighs and reaches back into his wallet. This time he pulls out his driver's license and a business card. This clipboard man spends much less time looking at them than his lobby counterpart.

From over Aaron's shoulder, one of the police officers says, "Please hold your arms out." He traces over Aaron's body with an electric wand, like they use at the airport. It rings at his belt, his cuff links, and his watch, but the cop doesn't seem to care.

"Visitor," he calls out while simultaneously knocking hard on the door with his fist. Without waiting for an answer, the cop opens the door and motions for Aaron to enter.

Nicolai Garkov is approaching seven feet in height, which makes him the tallest man Aaron's ever encountered. Garkov's hair is a straw-colored blond that can only be found on a Russian, and he has clear blue eyes that invoke Caribbean water.

If it weren't for the view of midtown Manhattan, Garkov's home could easily pass for a medieval castle. Tapestries cover the stone walls and all the fixtures are gilded.

Garkov is one of a growing breed in the financial world: Russian billionaires who made their fortunes in hazy ways and spend them ostentatiously. Latter-day Jay Gatsbys. The purported source of his billions is a hedge fund, although all that really means is that he has amassed a lot of money. Where the money came from, how he invested it, and where it went from there were likely known only to Garkov himself.

"Thank you for coming, Mr. Littman," Garkov says with only the subtlest accent.

"It didn't sound like I had much of a choice," Aaron replies coolly. "Here's my first bit of advice for you, Mr. Garkov: blackmail is not the best way to earn the trust of someone you want to retain as your lawyer."

"Ends and means, Mr. Littman. Ends and means. You've read *The Prince*, I assume?"

"Yes. And you're not the first person in your situation to recite that line to me. But I have to tell you, I've never found it to be a particularly persuasive defense. I'm more of a categorical imperative kind of guy."

Garkov smiles. "I'm going to enjoy working with you, Mr. Littman. I consider myself something of a student of political theory—it's not every day someone invokes Immanuel Kant. I'm impressed."

"Don't get too enamored with me. I doubt very much that I'm going to stay long."

"Then we should begin right away," Garkov says.

He leads Aaron into the apartment. An enormous fireplace in the shape of a roaring lion is the focal point of the room, with a four-foot-square opening for the lion's mouth, inside which a fire crackles. They sit on sofas positioned on opposite ends of the fireplace, staring at each other.

Aaron's first impression is that Nicolai Garkov is every bit as intimidating as his reputation suggests. Ironically, it's Garkov's calmness that's so disconcerting. It's as if he could snap your neck without his heart rate changing.

"Aaron. May I call you Aaron? And please, you need to call me Nicolai. I think we've gotten off to such a good start because we chose not to underestimate each other. Please don't deviate from that now. We both know why you're here and that you *are* going to stay."

Aaron looks to the ceiling. Garkov must understand what he's thinking, because he says, "Not to worry. The surveillance is video-only when it's a lawyer visit. Attorney-client privilege and all that. No one will know what we're going to discuss, if that's your concern."

Aaron's tempted to say that he has no concerns, but that would be exactly the type of underestimation Garkov warned him to avoid. Instead he says, "But you could be recording it yourself, for your own use later."

Garkov nods, indicating that he understands the point. "Yes. Yes, I could. I could tell you that I'm not, but I appreciate that you're not inclined to trust me. At least not just yet. So, allow me to prove it." Garkov waits a beat. "I, Nikolai Garkov, am guilty of the crimes for which I've been accused, and of many crimes for which I haven't. Specifically, I received one hundred million dollars from a Russian named . . . let's do first names only, because we're still getting to know each other . . . one hundred million dollars from a Russian named Yuri, and he is quite well-known in certain radical circles. In turn, I sent that money to a myriad of accounts that I control, and after considerable financial machinations, I arranged for those funds to wind up under the control of Arif Chedid."

Aaron is well aware that if Garkov is recording this as leverage for later, he could erase his confession and then digitally manipulate whatever remained as he saw fit. Nevertheless, Garkov's statement certainly evens the scales a bit, in that it ties him to the reputed mastermind of the Red Square bombing. Besides, Aaron isn't in any position to dictate terms, and so, like it or not, they are going to talk.

"Okay. Get to the point, Nicolai," Aaron says.

"Of course," Garkov says in an overly solicitous tone. "As I'm sure you're by now aware, Judge Brian Mendelsohn has withdrawn from my case, and he has been replaced with Judge Faith Nichols."

Garkov comes to a full stop. His only communication now is a sinister smile, which Aaron has the urge to smack off his face.

"And . . . what does that have to do with me?"

"You're doing it again," Garkov says. "One of the things I've read about you, Aaron, is that you're quite the poker player. I was particularly intrigued by an interview you did a while back—I apologize, but I can't remember the particular publication in which it appeared—but in it you said that being a first-class poker player requires similar skills as being a first-class lawyer. The ability to review facts dispassionately, adapt quickly to changing events, and find a path for success even when the odds are not in your favor." Garkov's smile vanishes, replaced with an icy stare. "Now, you'd be wise not to try to bluff me unless you think you can actually pull it off. And I think you and I both know that you can't, because I have the winning hand here."

Garkov's right, but Aaron's determined to play this all the way out. Poker is often as much about knowing your opponent as the cards, after all.

"You apparently believe that I hold some type of sway over Judge Nichols," Aaron says. "But I'm sure you know that the last time I appeared before her, it didn't exactly turn out well for my client."

That was something of an understatement. Aaron's last case before Faith Nichols was the one he had referenced to Joe Malone—the defense of Eric Matthews.

Matthews was the CEO of a small public company called Time Sensitive, which made low-cost watches. The company was acquired by a huge multinational, and Matthews's golden parachute on the deal netted him nearly four million dollars. Although that should have been more than enough of a payday, Matthews surreptitiously acquired another million shares of Time Sensitive stock and stashed it in offshore accounts, knowing that once the acquisition was announced, the value of those shares would double. That bit of trading on material, nonpublic information netted Matthews another three million bucks, and a seven-count criminal indictment as the cherry on top. A jury found him guilty and Judge Nichols sentenced him to fourteen years, the longest insider-trading sentence in history.

"Yes, I know all about your prior dealings with Judge Nichols on Mr. Matthews's behalf," Garkov says. "But there's a critical difference between my case and his."

Garkov waits a beat before delivering his payoff line: "He didn't know you were fucking the judge, and I do."

Aaron can't help but do a double take. It's not that he's surprised. He knew that this had to be Garkov's ace in the hole from the moment Sabato mentioned Faith's name, but the crude way Garkov's come out with it is startling nonetheless.

It takes Aaron's full effort to remain composed, trying to resist saying something imprudent. There's no good comeback for that type of charge other than denial, and that's not an option here.

"I hope we can now finally dispense with the posturing," Garkov says quietly. "I'm not an expert in legal or judicial ethics, but I'm relatively certain that sexual relations between a judge and defense counsel is not something condoned by the bar association or the committee on judicial conduct . . . Now, I'm not sure if they'd send a lawyer to jail for lying to his client, but disbarment seems inevitable, and I'm also quite certain that poor Mr. Matthews will sue you for millions. And that's to say nothing of the personal ramifications of such a disclosure. Your wife, Cynthia. Your two daughters, Lindsay and Samantha. They're seniors at Brunswick Academy, aren't they? It's a terrible thing when a father loses the respect of his children."

Aaron can feel a slow-burning rage taking hold, but he tells himself to keep it in check. It's advice he often gives to clients—no one is at their best when they're angry.

"How'd you find out?" he asks, largely because he thought he and Faith were very careful in that regard.

"How?" Garkov says with a smile. "It's always been my humble opinion that 'How?' is not a very interesting question. I find out so many things from so many different sources that it's difficult for me to keep track of the how. No, what you should be asking about, Aaron, is not *how* but *why*."

"I think I already know the why. It seems to me that you're less interested in securing my legal services than you are in finding someone to help you blackmail a federal judge," Aaron says in a measured tone. "Which brings me to this question: if you have evidence that Judge Nichols and I engaged in inappropriate conduct, why do you need me at all? You already have Roy Sabato willing to do your bidding. Just get him to blackmail Judge Nichols."

"I thought about that, and that's still a very real possibility," Garkov says, "but that would require bringing Roy into the loop. I don't see why you'd want that. Nor do I, because I believe you will be far more persuasive with Judge Nichols. So, in this regard, our interests are aligned."

"I'm sorry to have to burst your bubble, but my relationship with Judge Nichols is over. She doesn't do me any favors these days. Just ask Eric Matthews."

Garkov gives a small laugh. "I have confidence in you, Aaron. If you explain to her what's at stake, then I'm sure she'll see the light."

It's very rare that Aaron feels outmatched. Very rare, indeed. But Garkov has been a step ahead of him in every detail. If the poker analogy isn't a perfect one, it's apt enough—once the other side knows you're bluffing, you need to fold.

7

Sam Rosenthal storms into Aaron's office, looking nothing short of irate.

"No!" he shouts at Aaron. "What the hell is wrong with you?! You cannot do this. Not now!"

Rosenthal's rage is like clockwork. Two minutes earlier, an e-mail went out to the members of the Committee on Committees, explaining that Nicolai Garkov was the newest client of Cromwell Altman Rosenthal and White.

Rosenthal limps toward Aaron's desk. His expression is as grim as if someone has just died.

"Aaron, the man is a terrorist and a murderer. Worse than that, he's going to kill our corporate practice. Do you want to see Donald Pierce running this place? Because if you do, congratulations, this is precisely the way to do it!"

Aaron reflects for a moment, playing out the conversation where he tells Rosenthal everything. He's had this internal monologue a dozen times since his affair with Faith began and each time stopped short of letting the words come out.

He's not sure why he hasn't yet confided in Rosenthal. It's not fear of professional repercussions, as he trusts Rosenthal with his life. Rather, he surmises it's the same reason that his daughters don't tell him of their own failures—the fear of disappointing the person who thinks the most highly of you. And so he sits there mute, his eyes glued to his shoes, feeling like a scared child.

The silence between them lasts long enough to become a third participant in the discussion. "Did you ever read *The Old Man and the Sea*?" Rosenthal finally says.

Aaron knows Rosenthal's story is going to relate back to Garkov, but for the moment he's just happy to be discussing something else. "No. I read *The Sun Also Rises*, if that counts," Aaron says, managing a weak smile.

"Opposite lessons, I'm afraid. The point of *The Old Man and the Sea* was that sometimes having balls can be a problem, too. It's about an old fisherman who's down on his luck, and after months at sea, he captures this huge marlin. But he's too weak to pull it into the boat, and so he sails home with it hanging over the side. As he does, sharks attack the marlin. The old fisherman is fighting them to exhaustion, but by the time he finally makes it to shore, there's nothing left of the marlin but bones."

"What do you want me to take from this little lit class, Sam?"

"That sometimes it's not readily apparent whether you have the fish or the fish has you."

"So you think Garkov has me?"

"I can't think of any other reason you'd take him on as a client."

The lawyer in Aaron knows that speaking about certain things can only lead to trouble later, and the commission of a crime, like blackmailing a federal judge, is one of them. But lying to Rosenthal isn't something Aaron's ever done before, either.

"Sam . . . just give me a little time to work things out on this, okay? And believe me, I wouldn't be taking on Nicolai Garkov unless the alternative was far worse than anything you've imagined Donald Pierce will do."

"That hardly puts me at ease, Aaron."

"It's not supposed to, Sam. It's supposed to convey that I'm trying to protect you. You and the firm. Plausible deniability."

Rosenthal shakes his head in disagreement. "Aaron, I can't make you tell me, but I can tell you that you never have to shield me from anything. If you have a problem, it's my problem too. Whatever is going on, know that I'm with you. One hundred percent."

Aaron doubts many things—not the least of which is his own judgment of late—but the loyalty of Sam Rosenthal is not one of them. At the same time, he doesn't want to share what a colossal mistake he's made if there's any possibility he doesn't have to.

"I'm just asking for a few days, Sam. If I can't fix it by then, I'll come to you. I promise."

Rachel London looks much happier arriving at Aaron's office than Sam Rosenthal was when he left ten minutes earlier.

"Thanks for saving the day with Joe Malone," Rachel says. "Sometimes you make me feel a little like Lois Lane."

"My pleasure. How'd it work out?"

"Client gave the okay to start settlement talks."

"Good. I think that's the right call, especially if you can get him three years."

"Yeah, I didn't get that," Rachel says, deadpan. "I got a year and a day, though," she adds, breaking into a full-on grin. "And, needless to say, Malone jumped at it. All of a sudden, admitting guilt wasn't such a moral quandary for him anymore."

"Wow. Well done, Rachel."

"I try."

"That kind of good work calls for a reward. How would you like to work with me on the hottest case in the country right now?"

"I was hoping for a three-week paid vacation."

"C'mon, Rachel, what fun can you have on a Caribbean island that competes with working around the clock for Nicolai Garkov?"

Rachel's smile vanishes. "*He's* the client?"

"Since about an hour ago."

Rachel's professional enough not to show concern, but Aaron can see the tell, the small crinkle at the side of her mouth, which she attempts to hide by turning her head toward her notepad.

"I . . . thought Roy Sabato was repping him," she says.

"He was. Now we are."

"And it's before Judge Nichols now, right?"

Rachel was second-in-command during the Matthews trial, and so she saw firsthand how Aaron interacted with Faith, which gives her comment added weight. But Aaron dismisses the thought that Rachel has figured out his dirty secret and assumes she is referring solely to the harsh sentence Faith ended up handing down.

"You're not afraid of her, are you?" Aaron says, trying to return to their previous banter.

Rachel, however, appears to be in no joking mood. She looks very much afraid.

"The truth, Aaron?"

"I expect nothing less."

"This is going to give Donald Pierce a lot of ammunition."

"Maybe, but the decision's been made."

"And that's what worries me. You *know* you shouldn't be doing it, and yet you still are."

The statement equally applies to his affair with Faith. But unlike then, now he has little choice.

Through a soft smile he says, "So are you with me in this terrible mistake that I'm making?"

With Rachel, this is a rhetorical question. Her loyalty is a given.

"Of course," she says. "Always."

There was no more unwelcome a visitor Aaron could have imagined as he was getting ready to leave for the day than Donald Pierce.

Pierce hasn't called ahead, most likely because he knew he would have been told that Aaron was unavailable, which was Aaron's standing order to Diane whenever Pierce asked for a meeting.

It is undoubtedly for this same reason that Pierce does not stop at Diane's desk. Rather, he just walks straight into Aaron's office.

"I need to talk to you," he says. "It's important."

Everything about Donald Pierce is thin—his lips, his eyes, the few strands of hair still left on his head. He reminds Aaron of one of those little dogs that snarls and yips at everyone. The kind that seems crazy enough to strike at things twice its size.

Aaron debates saying that he's in the middle of something, but that will lead to Pierce's asking for time on Aaron's calendar. Scheduled meetings are presumed to go on for at least a half hour, whereas a pop-in could be cut short by the next phone call.

"I'm on my way out, Donald," Aaron says, laying the groundwork for his exit, "but we can talk for a second."

To prove the point that this is going to be a short meeting, Aaron doesn't offer Pierce a seat. Even worse, Aaron gets up and walks to his closet, retrieving his coat, which sends the unmistakable message that Aaron has allotted two minutes, if that, to whatever Pierce has to say.

Pierce gives the room a once-over—as if he's imagining how he'll redecorate when he becomes chairman of the firm—and then says, "I've already spoken with most of the other members of the COC. We're all in agreement on this, Aaron. We should not be taking Garkov on as a client."

"And why not? He's got a Sixth Amendment right to counsel, doesn't he?"

Pierce rolls his eyes. "I'm not a big believer in the whole everybody-deserves-to-be-represented thing, and even if everyone is entitled to a lawyer, that doesn't mean that they're entitled to Cromwell Altman. But let's not cite the Constitution to each other. This firm's mission isn't to defend the innocent. It's to make money for the partners. And taking on a goddamned terrorist like Garkov is going to cost our corporate group eight figures, easy. We'll be radioactive as far as the big banks are concerned. Not to mention that when the representation becomes public, it's going to send the associates flying to headhunters, and you can bet the press is going to be all over us."

"Come on, Don. This firm has taken on lots of unpopular causes. It's what lawyers are supposed to do."

"They're not supposed to piss away tens of millions of dollars in corporate business."

Just like with Rosenthal, Aaron knows Pierce is right. There is simply no logical argument for why Cromwell Altman would represent Garkov. Unlike with Rosenthal, however, Aaron doesn't give even a passing thought to telling Pierce the truth. Instead, he falls back on the old adage that the best defense is a good offense.

"If you're half the lawyer you're always telling me you are, Don, then I would think that the big banks would be rushing to retain your services no matter who *I* decide to represent. So if you can't hold on to your clients, don't go blaming me."

Before Pierce can respond, Aaron pushes past him and leaves for the day.

8

Faith Nichols lives in a Tribeca loft designed by her architect husband, Stuart Christensen. She bought the place when she was single and furnished it in a shabby-chic style. Stuart spent the first year of their married life replacing all of Faith's furniture and gutting the interior, right down to the studs. Now it's minimalist with a capital M, which means that the space is very beautiful but somewhat difficult to live in.

More than once Faith has mused that her home is a metaphor for her life.

"Something smells good," she says, catching a strong whiff of garlic.

"It's pasta night," Stuart calls out. "You know how I like my pasta, right?"

"Yes, I know," she says with a forced laugh.

One of Stuart's favorite jokes, which has been old for quite some time. She would say something like, *You like your pasta the way you like your women*, and Stuart would supply various punch lines—*spicy, hot, soaked in wine*, or in his bawdier moments, *filled with meat*. Tonight, she doesn't even bother with their little game.

"Well, today I've made it so hot, you can't keep your clothes on," Stuart says anyway.

Faith smiles politely and then excuses herself to change out of her work clothes. Stuart once told her that when Frank Lloyd Wright designed a house, he would also design the furniture (which Stuart did in their place too, for the most part), and he would even instruct the owners on what clothes to wear while inside it. Faith considers herself fortunate that she's still able to select her own wardrobe, even as she appreciates the irony that her work attire is a black robe.

Faith reaches for the baggiest sweatpants and T-shirt in her closet. She could wear something a bit more formfitting, but she'd just as soon not pique Stuart's interest tonight.

When she comes back to the dining table, Stuart is sampling his culinary creation. "Ahhh, 'atsa spicy-a pasta," he says in a cartoon Italian accent.

"Please tell me there's more wine," Faith says, noticing her husband has a nearly full glass beside him.

He pushes the bottle toward her but doesn't go so far as to get her a glass, even though he's standing in front of the cabinet where the stemware is stored. She nudges him aside and pulls one down herself.

"I got the Garkov case," she says in a flat tone as she pours.

Stuart's mouth forms a twisted smile. Faith knows that he's experiencing a bit of schadenfreude, which is about as unbecoming an emotional response as she can imagine.

It's moments like this, which occur far too frequently, that she can't believe she ever convinced herself that marrying Stuart was a good idea. She knew his faults—narcissistic, insecure, outsized sense of entitlement—but disregarded those alarm bells because she was thirty-nine and feared that he might be her last chance at not ending up alone.

"The nomination was always a long shot, Faith," he says. "Truth is, I never believed it was actually going to happen."

Faith isn't surprised that Stuart has jumped to the conclusion that the Garkov case is going to hurt her chances. She's tempted to put him in his place, which she could do simply by telling him that the assignment will likely help her cause. But the satisfaction she'd derive by knocking him down a peg is outweighed by her desire simply not to engage him at all.

The Garkov case doesn't come up again during dinner. Instead, Stuart discusses a project he's working on for a midtown law firm.

He looks annoyed when Faith can't recall the firm's name, which she knows he sees as some type of slight on his work, although that doesn't make any sense to her.

"So, every little thing is about the budget," he says. "You know, *Can we use cheaper materials on the secretarial stations? Can't we go with fabric rather than leather on the associate chairs?* But when we start talking about the two founders' offices, oh, now all of a sudden *no* expense is to be spared. One of them wants a state-of-the-art media center that he controls with a remote from his desk. You know, with a sliding panel that reveals three or four television screens and when it opens, the lighting simultaneously dims? And the other guy, he wants me to put in a safe that's as large as a walk-in closet. I half-jokingly asked if he was going to be hiding bodies in there."

Stuart's rant is interrupted by Faith's phone. She can tell that he's immediately annoyed and that he blames her. She wants to tell him that it's not her fault her phone is ringing, but she could let it go to voice mail and thereby demonstrate to Stuart his superior place in her life, and she's not about to do that. She knows who's calling, and for the record, that person *is* more important to her than Stuart.

"Hello?"

"Hi, Your Honor, it's Jeremy. The senator asked that I call you right away. He regrets that he couldn't do it personally but hoped that you'd understand. If it's not too much of an intrusion, can I come to your place to explain where things stand in light of today's case assignment? I'm in midtown now, so I could be there in half an hour."

Faith instinctively looks up at her husband. He's not going to be happy about this.

Who cares? she thinks.

The Littmans live on Fifth Avenue, between Seventy-Fifth and Seventy-Sixth Streets, in a prewar art deco building. A plaque outside identifies the building's architect as Rosario Candela, the gold standard of New York City residential architects.

The year that the twins were born, Aaron and Cynthia purchased a ninth-floor classic six—two bedrooms, living room, formal dining room, and small maid's room off the kitchen—facing Central Park. They had previously lived downtown, in a much hipper area, but the twins' arrival meant they had to think about schools and parks, and so the Upper East Side became their new home. As their neighbors moved or died, the Littmans annexed their apartments, like real estate conquistadors. Today their Manhattan castle stretches over three thousand rambling square feet, occupying most of the building's ninth floor, which connects by a staircase to a converted two-bedroom on the eighth that now comprises their master suite.

Tonight Aaron has arrived home with flowers in hand. Nothing that extravagant, just a bouquet of what the florist on the corner on Madison recommended. He knows that it's partly his guilty conscience that contributes to these romantic gestures, but they are about more than his making amends for transgressions of which Cynthia is unaware. He's trying to be more like the man he wishes he were, and that man brings his wife flowers just because he loves her.

He calls out, "Cynthia?" but she doesn't answer. His teenage daughters aren't likely to drop their time on social media to acknowledge his presence, so it's not until he has ascertained each of their rooms is empty that he's sure he's alone.

Aaron's being the first to come home at night is rarer than a blue moon. It places him in the uncomfortable position of being alone with his thoughts, a state of being that he seeks to avoid whenever he can. Especially because these days such introspection almost always leads him to reflect about Faith.

Aaron wishes that he could point to some cataclysmic event that resulted in his breaking his marriage vows—a brush with death that caused him to rethink his existence, or that Cynthia somehow betrayed him first, justifying revenge. But the simple truth is that he has no excuse and even less explanation. Opportunities had presented themselves before, and he'd never truly been tempted.

During the four months Faith and he were together, barely a day went by when Aaron didn't think about ending it. But he never did. Rather, he became even more immersed, buying prepaid phones like he was a drug dealer so his nightly calls to Faith would not show up on his phone bill, paying the Ritz-Carlton's nearly six-hundred-dollar nightly rate with cash fresh from the ATM to avoid the room charges showing up on his AmEx bill.

In its throes, Aaron felt like he was two people: his regular life proceeded as usual, and then once a week or so he met Faith, and during those two or three hours in her company, he felt as if he inhabited an alternative universe where his wife and children didn't exist.

They had met at a legal bar association dinner. It was the kind of event that honors whoever can strong-arm enough people to buy tables at five thousand dollars a pop. Members of the judiciary are part of the bribe and are allocated among the two hundred or so tables.

The honoree was George Vanderlyn, the chairman of Windsor Taft. Aaron later learned that the only reason Faith was even at the dinner was because she had worked at Windsor Taft before her appointment to the bench. She wasn't even originally seated next to Aaron, but when Jose Luiz claimed to have some fire to put out in a deal he was working on, Aaron felt compelled to slide over a seat so that a federal judge was entertained. He can scarcely remember how one moment they were talking, and before he knew it, they were in an upstairs room.

It might have been years before their sexual life intersected with their professional one. There were forty-one judges in Manhattan, and even though Faith had been on the bench for almost three years already, Aaron had never had a case before her. But a little more than a month after their affair began, Faith's name came rolling out of the wheel as the judge randomly assigned to preside over the trial of Eric Matthews.

Aaron had been representing Matthews for nearly a year by that point, and he expected Faith to recuse herself. But despite the fact that it violated every ethical canon in the book, Faith said that there was no reason they couldn't keep their professional and personal relationships separate. "Besides," she said, "you know cases like this always end in a plea bargain, and so where's the harm?"

Of course, the case didn't plead out.

During the trial Faith had been fair, or at least no more unfair to the defense than any other judge might have been. Certainly, Aaron didn't think it was due to any of her rulings that the jury found Matthews guilty. He had told his client that the odds of an acquittal were slim and had urged a plea deal even before Faith had been named as the presiding judge, but Matthews wouldn't hear of it.

Aaron expected Matthews to be sentenced to between four and five years, which was what similarly situated defendants had received from other judges. But then Faith dropped the hammer with fourteen years, explaining that the severity was necessary to send a message that financial fraud was every bit as destructive to society as street crime.

Aaron, however, received a very different message. He heard loud and clear that it was over between them.

9

Just one look at Jeremy Kagan makes it clear why he decided to be the man behind the man. His appearance not only inspires little confidence; it actually creates concern. It's something about his eyes. The way they seem to always dart around, as if he's on constant lookout for something to go wrong.

When Kagan extends his hand toward Faith, she can't help but suppress a laugh. Stuart believes Kagan's arms are too short for his torso and derisively refers to him as T-Rex.

As they make their way over to the living room, Faith is hoping that Stuart will let her speak with Kagan alone. But like a petulant child, Stuart takes his seat beside them.

"I'm sorry, Stuart," Kagan says. "Can your wife and I speak privately?"

Stuart looks insulted, although he would be morally outraged if Faith ever tried to sit in on a meeting he was having with a client. He skulks off, muttering something about being in the bedroom if anyone needs him.

Kagan isn't one for small talk, and so as soon as he hears the bedroom door close, he gets down to business.

"Your Honor, Senator Kheel wanted you to know that he's already spoken to the White House, and your assignment to the Garkov case is being viewed as a very positive development. So much so that they've asked Justice Velasquez to stay on until the end of the Supreme Court's term in May, in order to give you enough time to finish the case." He smiles, stretching out his scraggly beard. "In other words, you're a lock."

Faith isn't smiling, however. She knows the part that Kagan has left unsaid.

"I assume it's not a lock if Garkov's acquitted," she says.

Kagan's cheerfulness vanishes. "Hold on. Do you even see that as a possibility? The White House is banking on the fact that you're judge and jury on this one. The senator believes it's what put you over the top."

From the moment Faith saw Sara's face this morning, she's known that her nomination to the Supreme Court is going to rise and fall on the Garkov verdict. Nevertheless, now that it's actually been confirmed, she feels thrown.

"So the whole innocent-until-proven-guilty thing is . . . what? A technicality?"

Kagan's look hardens. He obviously didn't expect this reaction. Truth be told, Faith didn't anticipate it, either.

"Your Honor . . . I don't mean to suggest in any way how you should carry out your judicial responsibilities," he says with a deliberate tone, as if he suspects the conversation might be being recorded. "I'm here solely to apprise you that if Nicolai Garkov is convicted before July fifteenth, you're going to be nominated to the Supreme Court of the United States. Any other result, and you're not. And that's that."

"Jeremy, I'm relatively sure that Garkov is going to withdraw his request for a bench trial now that I'm the judge," Faith says. "That'll take it out of my hands and a jury will make the decision."

Kagan is shaking his head. "I don't know about the law, Your Honor. I'm just telling you the political reality here. It doesn't matter who renders the verdict—*you* now own the Garkov result. If he's convicted, you're America's judicial warrior against terrorism. But if he's acquitted . . . well, you become the judge who let a terrorist go free."

Faith knows that Kagan's right, but that doesn't make it any easier to digest. "And July is the drop-dead date?"

"Yeah. It wouldn't hurt if it was over a little earlier, just to give us some breathing room. The working assumption is that so long as the April fourteenth trial date holds, there should be more than enough time."

Faith has been thinking about a way out all afternoon. Kagan has shot down the jury option, but she has one other escape plan.

"What if I recuse myself? Let another judge own the Garkov case?"

Kagan seems confused. "Why would you do that?"

Of course that would be a politician's reaction, Faith says to herself. *All you need to do to get on the Supreme Court is make sure a terrorist gets the max, and you're thinking of stepping aside?*

"I'm just worried that the timetable won't work out," Faith lies. "You told me things were looking good before I got Garkov. If I recuse myself, there's no risk that the case drags on past July and the timing does me in. I can pass it off to another judge and it'll be just like I didn't get it in the first place. I don't have to give a reason for stepping aside. In fact, it's customary *not* to disclose why."

Kagan is shaking his head again, now even more vigorously. "I must not be making myself clear, Your Honor. This process is *highly* political. You don't get to keep things to yourself. Everything you do—everything you have *ever* done—is going to be scrutinized by the press the moment the president nominates you. Hell, you remember that guy who got bounced because he smoked a joint? Now, I know times have changed since President I Didn't Inhale, but my point is that the American people want nothing more than to see Garkov sentenced to death, and that's precisely what the president demands if you want him to nominate you to the Supreme Court."

"It's not a death-penalty case, Jeremy. The government never brought a murder charge."

Kagan waves off the mistake as if it's nothing. "Whatever the maximum penalty, Your Honor, Garkov's got to get that. Any other outcome and the president will pick someone else."

"The flowers are lovely," Cynthia says when she arrives home about an hour after Aaron. "Although I'm not sure what's a bigger surprise: the flowers or that you're actually home before me."

Cynthia smiles, and Aaron is struck by how infrequently he's seen that expression from her of late. And what a pity that is, because Cynthia's smile can light up much more than a room, a stadium at the very least, and her emerald eyes positively shine when she's happy.

"I was running away from the office," Aaron says. "Donald Pierce, to be specific."

Cynthia's expression drops slightly. "I'd prefer you think of it as running to us, rather than away from work . . . but I guess I'll take what I can get."

Aaron accepts the rebuke. "Will the girls be joining us for dinner?"

"No. Lindsay is at rehearsal and Sam is working on some project with Olivia."

"In that case, why don't we go out for dinner? Caffe Grazie?"

"Wow. I don't know what I did to deserve such attention from you—flowers and my favorite restaurant."

What she did, Aaron thinks, is not give up on him when he lost his mind and betrayed her. It hardly matters that she didn't know she was doing it; he still has a lot of making up to do.

At dinner, Cynthia appears to be in very good spirits. The two glasses of wine probably don't hurt her mood any, but Aaron can sense that she's missed him of late. She chats about her patients, the other doctors, general workplace gossip. Aaron's thankful that she's taken the lead, for the news at his office is not something he wishes to share, at least not tonight, when Cynthia is in such a good mood.

It's lightly flurrying when they leave the restaurant, and Cynthia leans up against Aaron, holding his hand as they make their way down Madison. The girls are both home when Aaron and Cynthia return. Lindsay tells them that rehearsal was boring and Samantha complains that she and her partner can't get their science project to turn out right.

At a little before ten, Aaron and Cynthia get into bed. Aaron puts the television on, but Cynthia suggests they do something else first, and slides down the sheets.

As he feels his wife's hot mouth around him, his body releases to the sensation of pleasure. But not completely. He knows how undeserving he is of her affection.

When Faith and Stuart get into bed, Stuart signals that he wants to have sex. She's glad it doesn't take long. *Small favors*, she thinks to herself.

He falls asleep immediately after, and she knows that's not going to happen on her end for several hours still. It's during this time, with her husband asleep beside her, that she feels most alone.

One thing that Faith learned early on as a lawyer was that there is no such thing as good and bad people. There are just *people*, who sometimes do good things and other times do bad things, and the idea that the guilty are punished is just something that people say; it isn't even remotely true.

In fact, quite the opposite. People doing bad things are sometimes even rewarded for their misdeeds.

She likes to think of herself as a person who mainly does good things . . . but for the past six months, no fly on the wall of her life would have described her that way. First there was the affair with Aaron, and although there are countless ways she could try to justify it—Stuart's own likely infidelity, his thoughtlessness toward her, his . . . general Stuartness—she knows that she was responsible for her own actions. And then there was the entire Eric Matthews debacle. Faith believed to her very core that every ruling she made in the case was right on the merits, but she also knew that her assessment was impossible to verify. No matter how you cut it, presiding over the case put her on the wrong side of the ethical divide.

In a just world, her conduct would have at least led to a divorce filing, if not impeachment proceedings. But Stuart didn't leave her (or even know about the affair with Aaron, as far as she knows), and she wasn't run off the bench in scandal.

Instead, Faith was rewarded, now on the verge of being nominated to the highest court in the land.

All she has to do to get there is engage in further misconduct: convict Nicolai Garkov and then sentence him to the max, regardless of the evidence.

She feels the pang of conscience, the angel on her shoulder telling her that even Nicolai Garkov is entitled to judgment by someone free from bias. And then she thinks about Roy Sabato telling his client about the pros and cons of Faith's assignment to the case, without the slightest notion that it was already over for Garkov the moment her name rolled out of the wheel.

10

Aaron can't recall ever being so nervous before a court appearance.

He's about to blindside Faith. She's expecting Roy Sabato, and instead she's going to be confronted by the one lawyer she doesn't want to have sitting at counsel table. But what choice does he have? Calling to give Faith a heads-up wasn't an option. For all he knew, she might have used such contact without the prosecution present—a big no-no called ex parte in legal jargon—as a reason to disqualify him, which would almost certainly have caused Garkov to go public about the affair.

The gallery is full of members of the press, the lucky ones who were granted access to report on the proceedings firsthand. A hundred or so of their colleagues have been shut out of the main event, relegated to shouting questions on the courthouse steps after the hearing.

From Aaron's presence at counsel table, the members of the media in the courtroom now know of the change in counsel. Faith won't become so aware, however, until she takes the bench and sees Nicolai Garkov sandwiched between Aaron and Rachel London.

Three hard knocks on the doorpost connecting the judge's chambers and the courtroom announce that the judge is about to enter. "All rise!" the court officer bellows. The massive wooden door leading to the judge's chambers swings open and all eyes turn toward the Honorable Faith Nichols.

Even cloaked in her loose-fitting black robe, Faith looks more like a 1940s Hollywood star than a United States district court judge.

Her dark hair is down and loose, and she flashes a glimpse of her calf when she walks.

Aaron feels almost light-headed. *Focus*, he tells himself.

"Please be seated," Faith says without looking up. Then her eyes meet Aaron's, and she swallows hard. After a momentary pause, she says, "Uh, counsel, please state your appearances for the record."

Aaron can only imagine that Faith is seething inside. He wishes he could convey somehow that this isn't his fault, convinced that she'd understand if she knew all that he did.

The prosecutor stands first. "Good morning, Your Honor. David Sanyour, assistant United States attorney, representing the United States of America. I am joined this morning by Assistant United States Attorney Michael Herrera."

Aaron knows Sanyour from past battles and respects him as an adversary. The person David Sanyour reminds Aaron of most is not a person at all, but Buzz Lightyear from the *Toy Story* movies. Erect, solid, sternly chipper, he looks the way you might imagine lawyers appeared in the 1950s, with short-cropped hair and black-plastic–framed glasses. There's something absurdly robotic about him, made all the more comical by the seriousness with which he believes in his own moral superiority.

"Good morning, Mr. Sanyour. And you, too, Mr. Herrera," Faith says. Then she turns and stares hard at Aaron. "And it appears we have two new lawyers present for the defense."

Aaron rises to address Faith. "Good morning, Judge Nichols. Aaron Littman of the law firm Cromwell Altman Rosenthal and White. With me is my partner Rachel London. If it pleases the court, we move to be substituted as counsel of record for Nicolai Garkov."

Aaron says this with a friendly smile, but Faith doesn't return the gesture. Her face is locked in a grimace, as if she's just swallowed something particularly foul tasting.

"This certainly does *not* please the court, Mr. Littman. Not even a little bit. In fact, I find it the height of arrogance for you to come to this proceeding and take your place next to Mr. Garkov as if my granting your application is a mere formality."

"My apologies, Your Honor. I didn't think—"

"I couldn't agree more, Mr. Littman. You clearly did not think. So now I'm thinking for you. I assume you're aware that my predecessor, Judge Mendelsohn, put this matter down for trial on April fourteenth?"

"I am, Your Honor. But given that the court and defense counsel both have to play a little catch-up, we were hoping for a short adjournment of that date."

"Well, you can keep hoping, Mr. Littman, because that's not going to happen. As far as I'm concerned, the fourteenth is etched in stone. I'm well aware of the game of musical lawyers that defendants with means attempt to play as a way of pushing out the trial date. But not in my court, I can assure you. So, Mr. Garkov, if that's why you hired Mr. Littman, then I'm afraid you're not getting your money's worth."

Aaron already knew it was a distinct possibility that Faith wouldn't postpone the trial. But it's Faith's phrasing that's the true concern. If Garkov didn't think he was getting his money's worth, what would he do to ensure a more adequate return on his investment?

"We'll be ready for trial on the fourteenth," Aaron says. "Will Your Honor please accept our substitution?"

"Hand it up," Faith says, followed by a sigh that reeks with displeasure.

Aaron passes the piece of paper to the court officer, who walks the document over to Faith. In her three years on the federal bench, Faith's seen hundreds of substitution forms, and all this one contains is a single sentence, stating that Nicolai Garkov consents to the substitution of Aaron Littman for Roy Sabato as counsel of record, followed by signatures from Aaron, Sabato, and Garkov. Nothing else. Nevertheless, Faith studies the single page intently. When she's finished, she lifts her head and addresses Sanyour.

"Does the government have any objection?"

Sanyour stands and buttons his suit jacket. "Your Honor, so long as there is no prejudice to the government by a delay of justice, we have no objection to Mr. Littman becoming counsel of record for the defendant." Then he unbuttons his suit jacket and sits down.

Aaron can almost see the wheels turning in Faith's head. With the prosecutor's consent, she's out of options for denying the change of counsel.

"Mr. Garkov," she says in a stern voice, "although you are entitled to counsel of your choosing, it is my responsibility to ensure that such counsel can be effective in his or her representation of you. I have severe misgivings in this case about allowing a substitution at this late date. As I just indicated, I'm unwilling to delay the trial, and you were previously represented by very capable counsel in Mr. Sabato."

Aaron touches Garkov's arm, the coaching signal that he's not to speak. Aaron too remains silent, as Faith has not posed a question so much as expressed displeasure at what's unfolding before her.

As if she realizes that the floor remains hers, Faith continues. "I can tell you firsthand, Mr. Garkov, having stood before the bench myself for quite a number of years, that litigation and wars are often won or lost in the preparation. For that reason, you have to be absolutely certain that your interests are better served by Mr. Littman trying this case with very little time to prepare than if Mr. Sabato remained as your lawyer." She looks firmly at Garkov. "So that there is no going back on this decision, Mr. Garkov, I need you to state in open court that you are aware of the time constraints that Mr. Littman would face if he were to become your counsel, and you nevertheless wish to proceed with him."

Aaron rises and pulls Garkov to his feet by yanking him at the elbow. When they're both upright, Aaron looks up at his client towering above him. He offers a subtle nod, telling Garkov to provide the confirmation Judge Nichols seeks.

"Yes," Garkov says.

Faith scans the courtroom, as if trying to come up with another way out. But if the prosecution and Garkov aren't going to give it to her, she has no choice but to sign the order.

"Given that Mr. Garkov is willing to proceed on the same schedule as previously established," she says, "and noting the prosecution's acquiescence, as well as Mr. Garkov's constitutional right to proceed with counsel of his choosing, with the reservations I've already stated on the record, I'm going to permit the substitution."

"Thank you, Your Honor," Aaron says, but his groveling doesn't seem to register with Faith in the least. She doesn't even make eye contact as she signs the document officially making him counsel of record.

When Faith does look up again, it's in the direction of the prosecution table.

"Mr. Sanyour," she says, "are there any matters that you would like to raise with the court at this time?"

Sanyour stands again and again buttons his jacket. "No, Your Honor," is all he says, and then he sits down.

Faith next turns her attention to Aaron. "Mr. Littman, I'm assuming that you are still too new to have an opinion about anything in this matter. But I'm going to raise an issue of my own. Although Judge Mendelsohn saw fit to permit Mr. Garkov to be in home confinement pending trial, it is my order that Mr. Garkov be held without bail, pending trial. Effective immediately."

There's a loud rumble in the gallery, reflecting the utter shock at Faith's ruling. Garkov has been out on bail for months, and there hasn't been any change in circumstances to justify incarcerating him now.

"Your Honor," Aaron says, quickly coming to his feet, "given that this is a departure from Judge Mendelsohn's ruling, and because the court has ruled without notice or the benefit of briefing, the defense requests that you hold your decision in abeyance until we can be heard on the matter."

"You can be heard now, Mr. Littman. In fact, I'm all ears. Please explain to me why your client should continue to be able to live in the lap of luxury. This is a man who has been indicted for crimes that, if he were to be convicted, would likely result in life imprisonment. He is probably one of the most egregious flight risks imaginable, given the seriousness of the crimes for which he stands accused, coupled with the fact that he is a man of considerable means who is not a citizen of this country."

Prior to making an argument before a court, Aaron is usually provided extensive legal memos outlining the state of the law and bullet points of the best arguments and sound bites to make. He takes that work and uses it as the basis for crafting his own presentation. As a general matter, every five minutes Aaron speaks in court are preceded by one hundred hours of other people's toiling. But that doesn't mean he hasn't had to wing it from time to time. Indeed, some of Aaron's best arguments have come in such circumstances.

"Thank you, Your Honor," he says, and then pauses for a moment as he mentally sorts through the points he intends to make. "First, as the court is aware, bail has nothing to do with punishment, but is a device to ensure the defendant's appearance at trial. Mr. Garkov has been out on bail for months without incident. Accordingly, there's no reason to believe that he is a flight risk now. If anything, the risk of flight was much greater back when Judge Mendelsohn initially ruled that Mr. Garkov should be placed in supervised home confinement. Second, Mr. Garkov is under extremely tight protection. I can attest firsthand that it would be virtually impossible for him to flee the jurisdiction. He is guarded by no fewer than six people at all times. Third, at the present time, Mr. Garkov's home incarceration is at no cost to the government. By contrast, time in the prison system imposes a cost, not only in terms of the dollars required to clothe and feed inmates, but also in the fact that the prison system is already overcrowded. And finally, Mr. Garkov has a constitutional right to aid in his defense. We understand that Your Honor has ruled that the substitution of counsel shall not delay the trial, and we respect that ruling, but it does mean that we have to get up to speed very quickly. That will be immeasurably more difficult if Mr. Garkov is held at the Metropolitan Correctional Center than if he were in home confinement."

"Thank you, counsel," Faith says in a perfunctory way.

For a moment she turns to Sanyour, as if she's going to ask the prosecution to weigh in. She must think twice about that, perhaps out of concern that Sanyour will cut her off at the knees the way he did on the substitution issue, because she quickly straightens up in her chair. Aaron knows from the Matthews case that it's the posture she assumes when she's about to rule.

Faith hesitates for a beat and then plunges forward. "It is the order of this court that the bail conditions previously entered are hereby revoked. Mr. Garkov is to be held in the Metropolitan Correctional Center until trial. The court officers should now take the defendant into custody."

The court officers move toward the defense counsel table. As Garkov's hands are being cuffed, he presses his face right against Aaron's ear.

In an icy-calm voice, Garkov says, "I want to see you tomorrow morning."

11

Faith is still trying to catch her breath when she closes the door to her office. She held her composure in the courtroom, but the moment she's out of sight, her head starts to spin.

What in the hell could Aaron have been thinking?

That's just it, she tells herself; like she said in court, he wasn't thinking. Or, equally likely, he was thinking only of himself. Typical Aaron. Goddamn it. He could never turn down a marquee case, even if it is for a terrorist.

Faith knows full well the furious activity that's about to kick into gear at Cromwell Altman. Half a dozen lawyers will work all night on a motion to reconsider. It will be one of the classic Cromwell Altman tomes, fifty pages long with two hundred case citations, despite being written in less than twenty-four hours, and will say little more than that she was wrong to revoke bail.

"Judge," her clerk Sara says, entering Faith's office. "I . . . Do you want me to do anything? Research bail revocations, maybe? Um . . . I don't know . . . Anything?"

Sara looks to be in as much shock as Faith over this turn of events, albeit for a very different reason. Sara knows that Faith normally doesn't make a judicial ruling, particularly one of such magnitude, without consulting her clerks and asking for research.

"No," Faith says, trying her best to sound like she's in total control. "Thanks, Sara. I . . . I would like some privacy, though. In fact, tell Kenny too. I don't want any interruptions this afternoon."

News of the drubbing Aaron took in court made it back to Cromwell Altman ahead of him. Even before he removes his coat, Diane is telling him that the phone has been ringing nonstop.

"There have been at least twenty press inquiries," she says. "And Paul Stillman called and said it was urgent. Mr. Rosenthal also asked that you see him right away."

Paul Stillman is the firm's public relations guru. Although Aaron doesn't fully understand what Stillman does to earn his twenty-five-thousand-dollar monthly retainer, handling the fallout from Cromwell Altman's representing a terrorist certainly falls within his bailiwick.

Aaron knows exactly how the conversation with Stillman will go. Stillman will complain that he can't do his job if he doesn't know what's going on, and then he'll want to meet to "brainstorm"—that's Stillman's favorite phrase—about how to best handle the press inquiries.

To Aaron's way of thinking, however, there are only two responses available: *"Aaron Littman, a lawyer for Nicolai Garkov, said that he was disappointed with the judge's ruling and was still considering his options, but noted that he was confident his client would be exonerated of all wrongdoing,"* or *"Lawyers for Nicolai Garkov could not be reached for comment."*

He concludes that it really doesn't make much of a difference, and so calling Stillman can wait. Besides, he'd much rather get Rosenthal's counsel at a time like this.

Just being in Sam Rosenthal's office makes Aaron nostalgic for a time when lawyers were truly counselors. The space has the feel of the sitting room of a mansion in the English countryside. The chairs and sofa are covered in rich, tan leather fastened by nail heads, the floor-to-ceiling bookshelves are crammed with old hardback volumes with cracked leather spines, and none of the paintings was created in the last two hundred years. Rosenthal sits behind a comically large desk, his head six inches from whatever he's reading, as if he needs to smell the words to understand them.

Aaron knocks on the door, even though it's open. "I hear you wanted to see me."

"Please, close the door, Aaron."

They usually meet behind closed doors, but Rosenthal rarely makes a point of it. The scowl on Rosenthal's face leaves little doubt that this will be the second unpleasant interaction Aaron's had in the last hour.

"I heard about what happened in court today," Rosenthal says. "She really put the hammer to you."

Aaron settles into Rosenthal's guest chair. "At least I get to spend the evening in my own bed," he says.

It's an oft-repeated lawyer joke. So much so that Rosenthal doesn't even smile.

Instead, he sighs before saying, "I always tell people that this firm is my only family . . . but the *only* part isn't right. *You're* my family too, Aaron. And just as I would do anything for this firm, you should know that I would do the same for you."

Aaron didn't have the kind of relationship with his father that permitted heart-to-heart talks. He was too young when his parents separated to even remember their ever being together. Thereafter, his father moved around a bit, remarried, and had a second family in a Chicago suburb. They apparently took up all of his time, because Aaron heard from his father only on his birthday via a telephone call, which didn't even come every year.

Aaron last saw his old man at his mother's funeral. She died of cancer a week after Aaron's high school graduation, which his father hadn't seen fit to attend. Nor did he visit his ex-wife during the last months of her life. In fact, it had been nearly ten years since he'd even seen the man. And yet, his father decided that showing up unannounced at his ex-wife's funeral was a good idea. It took all of Aaron's willpower to not deck the son of a bitch, but he decided then and there that his father would forever be as dead to him as his mother.

In many ways, Aaron had ended up replacing his father with Sam Rosenthal. He was really the one who taught Aaron how to be a man. In the early years, when the firm was smaller and billable hours were not the Holy Grail they are now, he and Rosenthal would share long lunches at top restaurants discussing everything—politics, literature, and, of course, the law. Aaron learned more during those lunches than he had in college and law school combined, and certainly more than he ever had from his real father.

After Aaron made partner, the lessons continued, as Rosenthal went out of his way to groom Aaron as his successor. When Rosenthal's accident caused that day to come much earlier than either of them had anticipated, their sessions morphed to address more philosophical concerns, with Rosenthal imparting what his brush with death had taught him and focusing Aaron on the things that comprise a well-lived life.

Right now, Aaron is sincerely moved by Rosenthal's sentiment. And truth be told, he loves Rosenthal too, and wants to say something equally moving . . . but like many a son, perhaps, he has difficulty saying it aloud.

"Thank you, Sam," is the best he can manage at first. Then, seeing that he should go on, he adds, "I hope you know I feel the same way about you too."

"You know that line from *The Godfather*?" Rosenthal says. "When Vito Corleone tells the Turk that he spoils his children by allowing them to speak when they should listen? Well, I think I'm guilty of the same thing, because I let you off the hook too easily before. But now I've given you some time to handle it on your own so you could preserve my—what did you call it? Plausible deniability? But that didn't seem to work out too well for you, and so it's time for you to tell me exactly what the hell went on between you and Judge Nichols, and how much of that Nicolai Garkov knows."

It doesn't surprise Aaron that Rosenthal has figured it all out. Rosenthal wouldn't be half the lawyer he is if he hadn't. Part of Aaron feels relief that his secret is finally revealed. The other part, however, feels shame.

"Okay," Aaron says with a heavy voice. As much as he wants to maintain eye contact, though, Aaron can't help himself and he turns away. His eyes fall to the floor, which at least will not offer any judgment about his sins.

"I had an affair with her, Sam. It started before the Eric Matthews case. Remember the George Vanderlyn dinner? When she was at our table? That night. When she got the Matthews case, we both figured it was going to plead out, and so she didn't recuse herself, and I stayed on as counsel. There really wasn't anything remarkable about the trial. She was fair, or at least no more unfair than anybody else might have been. But the sentence . . . That was certainly a shock. Maybe Faith really thought the crime merited that type of prison term. I don't know . . . I also don't know just how the hell Garkov found out about me and Faith, but he did. Somehow. Now he thinks I can blackmail Faith into acquitting him."

Rosenthal doesn't look horrified at the disclosure, which Aaron finds even more disconcerting in a way. Aaron's heard more than his fair share of confessions, and he knows the importance of not letting on that what you're hearing is incomprehensible to you. It's likely the reason that priests are shielded from their parishioners in the confessional.

"Is it over?" Rosenthal asks.

"Yeah. Right after the Matthews verdict, she cut off all communication. No explanation, she just stopped cold turkey. I guess it all just caught up with her. I mean, I kind of felt relieved, to be honest. Glad all that deception was finally over."

As Aaron's words hang in the air, he braces for the condemnation that he deserves. Instead, Rosenthal places his hand over Aaron's, patting it gently.

"You should have told me about this sooner," Rosenthal says. "I could have told you about some things you might not know about. For starters, why she likely ended it. She was told that she was on the short list for the Supreme Court."

Aaron's heard that Faith's name has appeared on such lists, but he never put any stock in such rumors. Those short lists are never so short anyway, and even his own name, and Rosenthal's too, in his day, were bandied about as potential high-court nominees.

"Right. And so are a few dozen others," Aaron says, "not to mention that there aren't any vacancies."

"No, it's for real. Justice Velasquez is going to step down at the end of the term. The president wants a law-and-order judge, and nothing says that like the longest insider-trading sentence in history. On top of which, I guess I don't have to tell you, but Judge Nichols won't exactly look bad on television for her confirmation hearings."

Aaron assumed all along that Faith ended their relationship and suddenly broke off all ties because she thought better of the double life of adultery. But now it seems that it wasn't her husband she was concerned about, as much as her career.

"Why didn't you tell me?" Aaron asks.

"Why would I tell you, Aaron? Senator Kheel told me in confidence. Besides, I didn't have any reason to believe there was anything going on between you and the judge before whom you were appearing. But if it's full-disclosure time, you should know that I had a few meetings with Judge Nichols and did some of the preliminary vetting of her background. Kheel's thank-you for the campaign contributions I bundle for him. At least one good thing in all of this is she didn't breathe a word about having a relationship with you. And I asked her point-blank whether there was any infidelity in her background."

"So tell the senator that there are such problems, and make the Supreme Court go away."

Rosenthal gives a bitter chuckle. "If it were only that simple,

Aaron. He'll want to know what I know, and how I came to know it. I don't think now is the time to be sharing your ethical issues with a U.S. senator, do you?"

The question answers itself, and so an uneasy quiet settles in between them. Finally, Rosenthal says, "Were you in love with her?"

"No," Aaron says reflexively. "At least, not enough that I ever considered leaving Cynthia," he adds, correcting himself.

Rosenthal nods, but Aaron knows his mentor has no frame of reference for what happens in the long middle of a marriage. In all the years they've known each other, Rosenthal has never mentioned a woman.

"Who else knows about the affair?" Rosenthal asks. "Besides Garkov, obviously."

"No one, Sam. Not even Cynthia." He shakes his head. "Although I didn't think you knew either, so perhaps I overestimate my ability to be clandestine in such matters."

"I take it, then, that you haven't told Judge Nichols about Garkov's threat?"

"No. I thought maybe she would figure it out by my appearance today and just decide to recuse herself."

Rosenthal rejects the suggestion with a shrug. "You're giving her too much credit. Clients retain you at the last minute all the time to take over the trial work. Why would she think this one is any different? And even though the Matthews case didn't end well, everyone gave you high marks for the defense. There's no reason for Judge Nichols to think that anyone who hires you in a case before her has blackmail on their mind."

"And yet *you* figured it out."

"That's because I know you have reasons not to take the case. You have no idea about the earful I've gotten from the other members of the COC, and none of them has suggested anything nefarious." Rosenthal smirks. "They just think you're a self-centered egomaniac, putting your interests above theirs. But they don't think for a minute you're being blackmailed by your client."

Aaron gives a small laugh at the gallows humor. "Good to know."

Rosenthal's expression returns to its previous grimness. "But you do have a serious problem here, Aaron."

"I know. Believe me, I know."

12

When she gets back from court, Rachel London calls her minions into the conference room nearest to her office. On the door, she's taped a paper sign: GARKOV WAR ROOM.

At least 50 percent of Cromwell Altman's interior conference rooms are designated as war rooms of one type or another. *War room* sounds much fiercer than *storage space*, but the latter description is actually more accurate.

Roy Sabato sent over his entire Garkov file—six banker's boxes and a thumb drive. A team of first-year lawyers is reviewing the thumb drive, tasked with printing out whatever they think Sabato didn't recognize as actually important. As first-years are inclined to do, they are being over-inclusive, and so now eight banker's boxes sit in the corner of the conference room.

As the junior partner on the case, Rachel serves as field general. She commands the rank-and-file (i.e., the associates) so that they can execute the battle plan drawn up by command (Aaron).

"Listen up," Rachel says to the six lawyers sitting around the table. They range in seniority from Harrison Geller, who is fresh out of law school, to Clare Ferguson, who's up for partner this year. "Aaron wants a comprehensive brief telling Judge Nichols why she was wrong to revoke Garkov's bail, and he wants to file it tomorrow morning."

They all know this means they're going to be here all night. Still, no one shows the slightest sign of displeasure. Pulling all-nighters is part of the job. Go big or go home.

"Here's how we're going to do it," Rachel continues. "I want

Chris, Harrison, and Amanda to begin the research right away. Figure it out among yourselves how to divide it up . . . but no matter how you do it, there shouldn't be a single decision concerning bail revocation in the last . . . let's say fifteen years, that you haven't reviewed. Rick, I want you to take the longer view. Your job is the historical analysis of the reasons to permit criminal defendants to be out on bail, and the factors that go into making that determination. Maybe we can do a statistical analysis of how many people accused of financial fraud ever jump bail—and let's remember, financial fraud is *all* Garkov's been charged with thus far. Clare, once you start to get a feel for what's out there, begin drafting. We're going to file a brief, a compendium of cases, and maybe an affidavit from Aaron himself, because he's seen what Garkov's home confinement looks like. You know what, on second thought, I'm sure the conditions for the home confinement are in either Mendelsohn's or the magistrate judge's order. Somebody fish that out, and if the terms are clear, we won't need an affidavit." She takes a deep breath, surveying her troops. "Okay. Any questions?"

Just smiles thrown back at her. As if there's nothing they'd rather do than work all night in the hope of returning an alleged terrorist to a life of luxury.

"I'd like to see the first draft by . . ." She looks at her watch. "It's noon now. How about by six, seven at the latest? Then we can order in dinner and spend the rest of the evening polishing. I'll be in my office if anybody needs me."

Aaron almost never walks around the hallways of the firm. Like a Mafia don, people come to see him. And so as he makes his way to Rachel's office, he encounters the kind of stares usually reserved for celebrities.

Rachel is furiously typing when Aaron knocks on her open door. The sound must startle her, because she jumps.

"I didn't mean to scare you," he says.

"No, it's fine. Come in."

"So, how was your day?" he says, taking a seat.

"You know, same old same old. Our big terrorist client had his bail revoked, so now he's in federal prison, undoubtedly planning the murder of his defense team. But otherwise, all's good."

Aaron laughs, which causes Rachel to break her deadpan expression and crack a smile.

"We're working on the motion to reconsider," she says. "We'll go in ex parte, by order to show cause, and ask Judge Nichols to put it down for the next day."

Filing ex parte, by order to show cause is legalese that means defense counsel will appear before the judge alone, without even notifying the prosecution, and request that the prosecution show cause as soon as possible why the order revoking bail should not be reconsidered.

"You know we have no chance, right?" Rachel says. "No way she reconsiders."

"I know," Aaron replies. "But the appellate court never reverses decisions that are within the trial judge's discretion, so our only hope is that Judge Nichols concludes that she acted in haste."

"Good luck with that," Rachel says with a smile.

"Actually, in the first instance, you're the one who's going to need the luck. I'm going to see Garkov at the MCC tomorrow morning, just in case he is, as you suggested, thinking about murdering his defense team. So, you're going to need to make the order-to-show-cause application to Judge Nichols."

"Sounds like we're both on suicide missions."

13

Just how much Faith wants out of her marriage is reinforced the moment she enters the apartment and sees her husband sitting in the living room. She actually feels as if the space has gotten smaller, the air harder to breathe.

Faith hasn't even removed her coat before Stuart says, "Do we get bodyguards now?"

"Don't start with me," she says. "It was a tough day."

"I'll bet," he says mockingly. "Not every day you get on a terrorist's hit list."

"Stuart, are you really worried for my safety? Or yours? Because they offered to put a security detail in front of the building, but I know how much you hate that."

"Just answer me this, Faith: is that what T-Rex told you to do last night? So long as you put the screws to Garkov, you'll be on the Supreme Court?"

"This your way of not starting with me, Stuart?"

"It's a fair question. I mean, you're doing everything you can, seemingly ethical or not, to get on the Supreme Court . . . even though you know what that's going to do to us."

"You're unbelievable. Jesus."

"*I'm* unbelievable? *Me?* Why is that? Because *we* decided to live in New York City? Because *I* have a life here? An architectural practice that I can't just up and move down to DC, which, by the way, has the worst architecture in the country."

"Yes, *you*!" Faith yells back. "This is unreal! I know you're not the most supportive of men, but is it too much to ask that you not do everything you can to make me feel like shit? Stuart, I could be on the Supreme Court of the United States. Do you understand what that means? The historical impact that I can have on this country? And yet boo hoo hoo, you're complaining that you'll have to live in Washington?" She gives a long, exasperated sigh. "You know what, Stuart? Don't come. Stay here if you want. It's not like we have kids to worry about—"

"That again? You knew I didn't want to have children when you married me."

Faith has lost the moral high ground, because Stuart is right. She knew he didn't want children, and yet she married him anyway. Besides, this fight isn't about that. It's about the fact that he's being a first-rate prick. She should just file for divorce and be done with it. It's not like being divorced would hurt her nomination, whereas she wouldn't put it past Stuart to sabotage her with a carefully planted off-the-cuff remark about her views on abortion. But for some reason she can't bring herself to end her marriage, and so the United States Supreme Court is now her exit strategy. She would move to Washington and Stuart would remain in New York, either because he claimed he couldn't leave his practice or because she asked him to stay behind. The lawyers could work out the rest with them three hundred miles apart.

"I'm tired, Stuart," she says, meaning more than that she's sleepy. She's weary of fighting the same battle over and over again. "I'm going to bed."

It's clear from her tone that her husband is most definitely not invited.

Cynthia is reading by the fireplace, although it's not lit—that being Aaron's job in the division of marital chores—when Aaron arrives home that evening.

"Are the girls here?" he asks.

"Not yet. But it's just as well, as I assume you have something to tell me."

There's an obvious edge to her words that leaves no doubt that Cynthia has learned of Aaron's newest client, and that has erased the goodwill from last night.

Aaron stammers, but words don't come out.

"I'll save you the trouble," she snaps. "I know that you're representing that terrorist."

"Alleged terrorist," Aaron says, trying to defuse her anger with a smile.

Cynthia doesn't see it as a joking matter. She has the look of someone ready for a fight.

"Same judge as the last case too. Right?"

He now realizes the source of Cynthia's discontent. Apparently he was right when he told Sam Rosenthal that he overestimated his ability to keep his affair with Faith a secret. But he knows Cynthia well enough to know that she's not going to confront him, at least not now. It's enough she's just given the signal that yes, she knows.

"Hopefully this one will end better," he says.

"I assume you're not basing that on how it's begun."

"Rachel is working tonight on motion papers for her to reconsider that."

"I see. So you're working with Rachel on this one too?"

"And what's wrong with that?"

"Nothing, Aaron. Nothing you do is ever wrong," Cynthia says, and returns to her book.

14

The first thing Rachel does when she wakes up each morning, even before brushing her teeth, is swallow four pills. She doesn't remember their names, as they change every so often, when she starts to experience side effects or she feels an episode coming on. She literally gobbles down this cocktail of antidepressants and antianxiety medications, as if they were the cure-all to a poison coursing through her body.

She's been on some type of pharmaceutical regimen since her first episode, which occurred shortly after spring break during her senior year at Stanford. At her midsemester evaluation, her adviser, Professor Gryzmala, told her that she was behind schedule on her thesis. Worse still, he said he was "disappointed," although when she conjures the memory now (with the benefit of the meds, perhaps), she's less certain that he actually said he was disappointed with *her*, which she always previously believed, rather than merely with the progress of the thesis.

She stayed on campus during spring break to do more research, and when she mentioned this to Professor Gryzmala, he suggested that they have dinner at the faculty club to discuss the direction she was taking.

Rachel recalls primping for that dinner more vividly than preparing for her high school prom. She must have tried on six or seven outfits, trying to achieve the perfect costume that said *grown-up woman*, with just the right amount of sexuality . . . all without being obvious, of course.

At dinner, Professor Gryzmala ordered a bottle of wine with the perfect Italian pronunciation, even though he spoke English with a trace of a Polish accent. It was the first really good bottle of wine Rachel ever had, rich and full-bodied. Her head began to spin midway through the second glass.

The conversation was just as intoxicating. He saw things—in art, books, the world around him—that she was convinced she'd never be able to see for herself.

After dinner, he walked her home, even after she put up a feigned protest that it was not necessary. She knew he was married but had nevertheless cleaned her room and changed the linens, so there was no way she could tell herself that she was surprised that the evening was going to lead back to her place.

When they reached her door, she didn't even ask if he wanted to come inside, so sure that they'd already tacitly made that agreement. She was more than startled when he said, "Thank you for a lovely evening. I think you're on the right track with your thesis and I look forward to reading it."

"Don't you want to come in?" she said.

"Oh no . . . thank you, but no," he said, as if the thought had never occurred to him. "I need to get back home. My wife and I always read to our kids before bed, and tonight's my night."

Rachel can't remember anything that happened after that. They must have said good night, but she has no recollection of those words passing between them. She knows that there was no physical contact, certainly not a kiss, or even a touch of the arm.

The next morning, she couldn't get out of bed.

It was as if every body part weighed more than she could lift. She somehow made it to the bathroom a few times, or for a glass of water that she didn't remember getting but that somehow appeared as if by magic on her night table, but otherwise stayed in bed. To this day she has no idea how long she persisted in that state. Her mother called campus security when she couldn't reach Rachel for the third day in a row. They brought Rachel first to the infirmary and then to Stanford House, a psychiatric hospital, where she spent the next month, some of it under a suicide watch, diagnosed with acute depression.

Rachel never returned to school. After her discharge from the psych ward, she spent the summer at her parents' home and arranged to submit papers for her spring-semester classes to get the necessary credits to graduate. Professor Gryzmala sent her an e-mail saying that she could submit her thesis in the same fashion and then defend it on campus whenever she wanted, but Rachel took the incomplete, deciding that it would be best if she never saw him again.

Her second episode occurred the year after she graduated from law school, while she was clerking for Judge Norman Davis of the DC Circuit Court of Appeals. Like before, her breakdown was triggered by an older man . . . although this time it had nothing to do with rejection.

Rachel met Lawrence Braithwaite, another judge on the circuit court, as part of her rotation to review habeas writs, the appeals that prisoners file by the thousands. One judge was assigned to hear such writs each quarter, and a different judge donated a clerk to assist in the review. The idea was to give the clerks an opportunity to work with different members of the court.

Even before being assigned to him, Rachel was well aware of Judge Braithwaite's reputation for sleeping with the clerks, and sure enough, he came after Rachel like a heat-seeking missile. Even though Rachel had never lacked for male attention, part of her found his advances flattering, as if she'd been specially selected out of the more than thirty female clerks on the court that year. Of course she knew full well the perils of a relationship with an older, married man in the workplace, but in this case Rachel saw it as a limited danger because Judge Braithwaite wasn't her boss, and her clerkship was going to end in a few months anyway.

Their affair lasted less than six weeks. Rachel ended it with him on a Friday and thought little of it until Monday morning, when Judge Braithwaite said that he'd asked his wife for a divorce so that they could be together. Rachel tried to let him down easy, explaining that was not what she wanted and that she was moving to New York when her clerkship ended.

Judge Braithwaite wouldn't take no for an answer, however.

He called her incessantly, sent her flowers at the office, and dropped in to Judge Davis's chambers unannounced, seemingly just to look at her. It all came to a head two weeks later when Judge Braithwaite's wife called Judge Davis to inquire why he employed home-wrecking sluts as law clerks.

Judge Davis assured Rachel that there would be no professional repercussions, and he saw no need to inform Cromwell Altman, with whom she had already accepted employment, to begin after the clerkship ended. But when Rachel asked if she could end her clerkship early, Judge Davis seemed only too happy to oblige her.

At least this time, Rachel avoided the hospital. She retreated to her parents' home for the summer, but once there, she could barely get out of bed again. She refused her mother's plea to get help, with the promise that she'd start at Cromwell Altman in September, as planned. Much to her parents' surprise, that's exactly what happened. On the day that she was to begin at Cromwell Altman, Rachel showered, put on a dark blue business suit, and went straight to work.

The next eight years went by without incident, so much so that Rachel believed the dark days were truly behind her. She thrived on the pressure of bet-the-farm litigation, and while the eighty-hour workweek of a big-law-firm associate didn't leave much room for a social life, she had her share of boyfriends, most of whom were age appropriate and none of whom were married.

Then she began working with Aaron Littman.

Six months before she was to come up for partner, Aaron asked her to second-seat him in the money-laundering trial of a Mexican banker named Alejandro Sanchez. In many ways, it was a standard

Aaron Littman representation—guilty client, lots of money involved, nonstop work for months, and then an acquittal.

After the case ended, they had a decadently expensive meal to celebrate. Over a four-hundred-dollar bottle of champagne, Aaron told her that he would enthusiastically support her for partner.

Everything Rachel had been working toward was coming to pass. And then she was completely blindsided when it all came crashing down around her.

Unlike the prior episodes, this one didn't all hit at once but built steadily over several weeks. The first sign was when she heard that Ellice Schwab, a senior associate who was very easy on the eyes, had been assigned to a new case that Aaron was handling. Rachel felt it like a stab to her heart. Each day that passed she missed Aaron that much more, as if she were withdrawing from an addiction. Rather than that feeling dissipating, the intensity of her emotions increased, to the point where she couldn't bear to wake up if there wasn't a reason to see Aaron that day.

When she started fantasizing about how much he would really miss her if she suddenly died, she checked herself into a private facility. The diagnosis was like before—acute depression—but her shrink, a little man with a white mustache, said that it was more than that. She was repeating the same pattern from Stanford: pursuing an idealized man who was unattainable and being unable to accept that her feelings were unrequited.

Rachel hadn't wanted to tell anyone at the firm that she was in a mental ward, but she couldn't go AWOL for a month, not right before she came up for partner, and so she told Aaron because . . . because she was in love with him. She didn't share that he'd played a role in putting her there, of course. Instead, she said that she had experienced a bad reaction to her meds, explaining that she suffered from depression and that every few years there needed to be an adjustment, although she had always previously seen it coming and was therefore able to avoid hospitalization.

"I'm so embarrassed," Rachel had said.

"There's no need," Aaron had answered. "This is a medical thing, Rachel. I get that."

"I'm not sure every partner is as enlightened."

"No one knows about this except me," Aaron said. "I told the partners that your father had taken ill and you were spending some time with your family. Don't worry about anything except getting better, and when you do, there'll be a partner's office waiting for you at Cromwell Altman."

She and Aaron never again discussed the episode. And at year's end, just as he'd promised, Rachel made partner.

15

The Metropolitan Correctional Center, or as it is more commonly called, the MCC, opened in 1975. Among its most famous residents have been Mafia don John Gotti, Ponzi schemer Bernard Madoff, and the Blind Sheikh, Omar Abdel Rahman, who was the mastermind behind the 1993 World Trade Center bombing. Given that Nicolai Garkov is something of a blend of all three, Aaron imagines that he'll fit right in.

The building itself is a particularly ugly brown, squat structure located in lower Manhattan. It is attached to the U.S. courthouse by an elevated bridge, which enables inmates to be shuttled back and forth without going outside. The facility houses approximately eight hundred inmates. Some, like Garkov, are awaiting trial. Others have already been convicted and are serving their sentences elsewhere, and are housed at the MCC during a court proceeding.

Attorney visits at the MCC can occur twenty-four hours a day and take place on the third floor. Aaron's been here enough times that he knows the schedule, which probably hasn't changed since the place opened. Inmates are awakened at six a.m., and breakfast is over by seven. At eight thirty, each inmate has to be back in his nine-by-seven cell (which he shares with another inmate) for the morning count, which occurs at nine.

It takes Aaron twenty minutes to go through security, and he arrives on the third floor a little after seven. He's directed into the visitors' room, a large space with ten tables, none of which are presently occupied.

Garkov arrives shortly before eight. He's wearing the orange prison jumpsuit, which is too short around the wrists and ankles. The MCC must not get many seven-foot-tall inmates. The guard who has accompanied him into the room unlocks Garkov's handcuffs but leaves the ankle shackles.

Aaron expected to see a seething-mad Nicolai Garkov. Instead, the man before him looks relaxed and confident.

"Well . . . you look good, Nicolai," Aaron says.

"American prisons are like fancy hotels compared to the places I've been in."

Aaron doesn't doubt that's true. That being said, they still aren't places where he'd spend an extra minute that he didn't have to.

"Do you remember what we discussed when we first met?" Garkov says.

Ever since law school, Aaron always hated the Socratic method. No useful information was ever imparted by asking questions you already knew the answer to.

"My recollection is that we discussed a great many things," he says.

"I asked that you not try to bluff me, because I always have the winning hand."

He comes to a full stop. As if that clarifies everything.

"We're asking Judge Nichols to reconsider her decision," Aaron says. "Rachel is making the application as we speak. Beyond that, I'm not certain what you expect me to do to get you out of here."

Garkov gives a theatrical sigh. "Aaron . . . you see, that's *exactly* what I'm talking about. I think you *do* know what I expect you to do. You are to tell Judge Nichols that if she doesn't put me back home tomorrow . . . well, I don't like to make threats, but as I'm sure you can appreciate, we're no longer talking about my going public with your indiscretions. She's increased the stakes by her little stunt, and so I'm not only calling that bet but raising. Public humiliation—the end of your careers—that's nothing compared to what I will do to the two of you. And don't kid yourself. I can get to you both just as easily from in here."

Aaron has never kidded himself about that fact. Nor is he anything but certain that he's quickly running out of time.

Wednesday is one of two motion days in Faith's court, Friday being the other. Faith likens it to the theater. Everyone dresses up and plays their parts: the lawyers in their fancy pinstripe suits and Hermès ties get to stand in front of a judge and try to persuade, and she wears the robes and makes judicial pronouncements.

And like a play, it's all scripted. The lawyers often read their arguments, and Faith has already decided how she'll rule on 99 percent of the cases before she hears a single word. As she often tells her clerks, it's the bad lawyer, not the good one, who says something persuasive in a five-minute oral argument, because it means that point didn't get through in a twenty-page written brief she's already reviewed.

This morning's smattering of cases is particularly mundane. Six motions to dismiss regarding pleading deficiencies, two discovery disputes, and a request for summary judgment on a trademark case that she already denied, but for some reason the plaintiff saw fit to make it again.

At half past noon, the last of the arguments is completed, and Faith hurries off the bench. She immediately goes into her office and shuts the door behind her.

Finally, some alone time, she thinks.

It's short-lived, however.

Two quick knocks on her door are followed by Sara's opening it and sticking her head in. "Judge, there's a lawyer from Cromwell Altman here on an order to show cause on Garkov."

Damn. Faith expected Aaron to make this filing, but she was hoping it would come at the end of the day—preferably after she'd left.

"Okay. Come in, Sara."

Sara enters clutching a stack of papers a foot high, which she drops on Faith's desk with a loud thud. On top is the legal brief, fifty pages,

VeloBound, with a clear cover. The title shows through: *Motion to Reconsider Bail Revocation.* Underneath that is another VeloBound volume, this one twice as thick. By the more than one hundred side tabs, Faith knows it's the compendium of the cases cited in the brief.

"My God, what a waste," Faith says. "A dozen lawyers must have worked all night on papers that I'm not even going to give a second thought."

Faith realizes a beat too late that she shouldn't have said this out loud. In front of her clerks, she likes to project that she's always open-minded.

"Okay, Sara, I guess you should send Mr. Littman back."

"It's not him," Sara says. "It's the woman lawyer from Cromwell Altman. Rachel London."

Faith can feel the heat rise in her. It was bad enough that Aaron showed up with Rachel in court yesterday, but now she can't help but feel that he's truly rubbing her face in the fact that she was quickly replaced by a younger model. She knows that her jealousy is misplaced—Faith was the one who ended the affair, not him.

"Have Ms. London come back then," Faith says, trying her best not to let on to Sara that anything is amiss.

When she enters chambers, Rachel London seems even younger to Faith than she did in court. Faith knows that, as a junior partner, Rachel must be older than thirty, but forty-two has never seemed as old to her as it does right now.

Close-up, Rachel appears more striking than she did at a distance in court. She's wearing a body-hugging black dress, no doubt from some high-end designer, like the clothes Faith wore back when she was buying them with her law firm partnership money. Smooth skin, not a wrinkle on her, and undyed hair, both of which Faith knows will undoubtedly change in the coming decade. She glances down at Rachel's left hand, trying not to be so obvious about it. No ring. Maybe Aaron finds having an affair with a single woman to be less trouble.

"Sara," Faith says, "can you give us a moment?" Sara looks crestfallen, but Faith doesn't care. "And shut the door on your way out, please."

Lawyers don't speak until judges ask them to, and so Rachel just stands there. Faith doesn't even offer her a seat. The power imbalance between them is further accentuated by Faith when she turns away, pretending to be reading something, solely to make Rachel wait.

Well past the time when Faith assumes that Rachel has become uncomfortable, Faith reestablishes eye contact. A half-dozen snide comments cross Faith's mind before she decides on: "So, I see that Mr. Littman has you doing his dirty work now, Ms. London?"

Rachel offers the awkward smile of someone who doesn't get the joke. "Mr. Littman apologizes for not making this application in person, Your Honor," she says. "Unfortunately, there was an emergency at the last moment that required his attention."

Bullshit, Faith wants to retort so very badly. *Aaron's just too much of a coward to face me.*

"What makes you—or Mr. Littman, for that matter—think that I'm going to reconsider my decision regarding Mr. Garkov's bail?"

"Your Honor, my purpose here is not to argue the merits, but to set the earliest possible date for oral argument. Our grounds are set forth in our papers. Stated succinctly . . ."

Faith has already tuned her out. She doesn't want to hear a legal argument. Interrupting Rachel, she says, "Stop right there. I don't care one bit about your application, Ms. London. You go back and tell Aaron that I said he's making a very serious mistake here. *Very* serious."

It surprises Faith that she's said this—the one-two punch of denying a motion without any consideration, followed by her not-so-thinly-veiled threat. Even her reference to Aaron by his first name was not something an impartial judge would ever do.

The shock on Rachel's face drives the point home.

"Excuse me, Your Honor . . . ?" Rachel says. "I-I don't think I understand."

"Oh, I think you probably understand very well, Ms. London."

Faith stares at Rachel, almost daring her to say something. It's an unfair fight. Faith is a federal judge, empowered to put Rachel in jail for contempt at her whim, and Rachel is still hoping to get Faith to consent to the application before her.

As if she just remembered the reason for this visit, Faith reaches for the briefs Sara delivered. Without saying a word, or even reading the papers, Faith reaches for a pen, and across the signature block writes: "DENIED."

"You go back and you tell Aaron what we discussed, Ms. London."

Then Faith hands Rachel the rejected order-to-show-cause application.

Sara must have started toward Faith's office the moment Rachel passed by her desk, because she's knocking on the open door before Faith has had a chance to get up to close it.

"What is it, Sara?" Faith barks.

"Uh . . . nothing . . . I wanted to know when I should calendar the motion."

Faith realizes that she has to get this part over with, and so as much as she wants to be alone, she says, "Never. I denied the application."

Sara doesn't say anything, which is the clearest indication of how unnerving she finds Faith's action. It's a rare judge who doesn't even give a litigant an opportunity to be heard.

"Judge . . . is everything okay?"

"I'm fine, Sara," Faith says coldly, a clear signal that Sara should back off.

Reading signals is not Sara's strong point, however, and so she continues: "You've seemed a little distracted lately."

Faith isn't listening. She just wants to leave.

"I'm going home," she says. "Please don't bother me with anything else, Sara. Whatever comes up can keep until tomorrow."

With that, Faith picks up her purse and then grabs her coat out of the closet. She walks by her law clerk without uttering another word.

16

"Let's just say that Nicolai Garkov is not happy about his present circumstances," Aaron says to Sam Rosenthal.

They're in Aaron's office, with the door shut. Diane has been told not to allow anyone entry and to hold all of Aaron's calls.

"I've reached out to Senator Kheel," Rosenthal says. "He tells me that if Garkov's convicted and she sentences him to life, she's got the nomination locked."

"I don't think Garkov is bluffing," Aaron says, "and he's not a patient man, either. He wants out of there right now. Rachel's at Faith's chambers now on an order to show cause, trying to get a hearing date tomorrow on a motion to reconsider the bail. But I have no reason to believe that's going to succeed, and every reason to believe that when it doesn't, Garkov will take matters into his own hands."

"Meaning what, exactly?"

Diane's knock prevents Aaron from answering. After Aaron says, "Come in," she pokes her head through the door.

"I know you said you didn't want to be disturbed," Diane says, "but Rachel London is here. She told me that you'll want to hear what she has to say right away."

Aaron looks over to Rosenthal. "Talk to her," Rosenthal says, getting up to head back to his office. "You know where to find me."

Aaron follows Diane out of his office, where he sees Rachel waiting. She looks like she's seen a ghost.

"I gather it didn't go well," he says.

Rachel turns to look over her shoulder, where Diane is hovering. Aaron understands that she means that this conversation is best had behind closed doors, and so he ushers Rachel inside his office and then closes the door behind them.

They're still standing, just inside his office, when Rachel says, "She denied the application."

"Damn it," Aaron says. "Did she give you a reason?"

Rachel sighs. "I . . . I don't know what happened, to be honest. She called me back to her chambers and said that I was supposed to tell you that you were making a very serious mistake. Emphasis on *very*. Then, after she denied the application, she told me to make sure that I told you that."

Aaron's response is a slow nod. He understands, he's saying, but he's not explaining it to her. That's apparently not good enough for Rachel, however.

"What the hell's going on here?" she asks.

"Were you alone when you met with her?"

"Yes, but that's not an answer to my question, Aaron. I thought she had it out for Garkov . . . but it now sounds like she has it out for *you*."

Aaron's confident demeanor doesn't crack, but his silence tells her that there are things he's not sharing.

"Aaron, after everything you've done for me, I want you to know that you can trust me. I know people say that all the time, but I mean it. You can trust me the way that I trust you . . . which is to say, completely."

The truth is that he does trust her. Almost as much as he does Sam Rosenthal. But unlike with his mentor, he sees no reason to embroil his protégée in his mess.

And so, rather than explain what was behind Judge Nichols's tirade, he says, "I know I can, Rachel. But don't worry about me. Worry about getting Garkov out of jail."

Faith spends the rest of the afternoon at home, drinking wine and channel surfing. Stuart comes home at seven and is still annoyed with her apparently, because he doesn't engage her at all, which is the first bright spot in her day.

Faith's normal routine is to be at the gym at eight, but when she pours herself the last of the wine, she realizes that she's not in any condition to work out. At the same time, she can't stomach the idea of spending any more time in Stuart's company. The horrifying specter of the fact that he might want to have sex tonight pushes her over the edge.

"I'm going to the gym," she announces.

"Okay," he says. He obviously hasn't been keeping track of how much wine she's consumed. "I'm kind of tired anyway. I may just call it a night early."

Good. There's nothing she wants more than for Stuart to be asleep when she comes back.

About five minutes later, while Stuart is in the bathroom, she calls out that she's leaving. She doubts he even noticed that she never changed into her gym clothes.

Along Fifty-Sixth Street, a row of black Lincoln Town Cars line up starting at 6:00 p.m. The Cromwell Altman version of mass transit. Every night Aaron gets into the first one and simply tells the driver where he wants to go. Somehow a client is always billed for the ride, but Aaron has no idea how that's determined.

Tonight, however, even though the air has a strong chill, a reminder that winter is hanging on, he walks past the cars without stopping and proceeds north to Madison Avenue. The various designer clothing boutiques in the Sixties give way to the art galleries that populate the Seventies.

If he were heading home, he would turn west on Seventy-Fifth, toward Fifth Avenue, but he keeps walking uptown. He enters Central Park at Ninety-Seventh, and when he reaches the West Side, he walks up to 102nd before going farther west to Amsterdam.

In the middle of the block on 102nd and Amsterdam is a convenience store that Aaron has never before entered. He steps inside and, after determining that it has no other customers, approaches the counter, where an older man of Indian descent greets him.

"Do you sell prepaid phones?" Aaron asks.

The man points to a few hanging on the wall behind him, beside the rows of cigarettes. "How much time do you want?" he asks.

"Twenty-five bucks' worth," Aaron says.

Aaron looks nervously over his shoulder. He wants the sale to be completed before any other patrons come in.

The man behind the counter fumbles around for a phone. "No twenty-five. I got a ten and a fifty."

"The ten is fine," Aaron says. He slaps a ten-dollar bill on the counter, then realizes that there's going to be tax and pulls out two singles, laying them on top. He doesn't want to wait for the change, but he knows he shouldn't do anything out of the ordinary, even if the entire transaction is nothing but unusual.

Once he's out of the store, Aaron moves as quickly as he can without breaking into a sprint back toward the park. Right before entering, he tears open the packaging and discards the cardboard and plastic in a garbage can on the corner.

When he's smack in the middle of the park, he activates the phone. Then he dials Faith's mobile number.

His heart rises and falls with each ring, until the fourth one, which he knows will lead directly to voice mail. He waits to hear her recorded voice. *"This is Faith Nichols and you've reached my personal voice mail. If this is related in any way to a court proceeding, please do not leave a message, and instead call my chambers at—"*

He hangs up and instantly calls again, hoping Faith might recognize the quick succession as some type of signal. When the second call also goes to voice mail, he realizes that his reasoning might be sound but his conclusion off—she might already know it's him, and that's precisely why she *isn't* answering.

Leaving a message is out of the question. A voice mail from him would be all Faith needed for his disqualification. Sending a text would be less risky, however. Particularly if it is vague enough that he could later deny he was the sender, if it came to that.

He types into the phone: *It's me. Urgent that I speak to you right away.* He knows at once that sounds too desperate, and so he deletes it. For his second effort, Aaron tries: *Faith, please call me at this number as soon as you can. Very important.*

After reading it over twice, he hits the send button.

Aaron comes out of the park on the East Side and considers waiting for Faith's response in the Dunkin' Donuts on the corner of Ninety-Seventh and Madison, or the pizza place across the street. He concludes that the fewer people who see him in this neighborhood, the better, however, so he starts to walk, very slowly, back toward his building.

If Faith is going to respond, she'll do it in the time it'll take him to get back to Seventy-Fifth and Fifth. If she doesn't call or text by then, she isn't going to.

Even though the phone is set to vibrate, Aaron checks it at least three times on every block: once when he crosses the street, again midblock, and a third time when he's about to cross again. But as he gets closer to his apartment, the realization begins to sink in that Faith is not going to answer.

Every year, as part of the orientation for the first-year associates, Aaron gives a speech titled "The *New York Times* Test." He tells the newly minted lawyers that everything they do professionally should be governed by one simple question: How would they feel if their actions ended up on the front page of the *New York Times*? Could they look their spouses, significant others, friends, or parents in the eye and defend their conduct? Because if the answer is no, then they shouldn't do it. Under any circumstances.

Aaron knows he's a complete hypocrite, having failed miserably at the *New York Times* test. Numerous times. When he began his affair with Faith. When he didn't disclose it to Eric Matthews or the prosecutors or the firm. When he entered his appearance on behalf of Nicolai Garkov.

Now he's going to pay the price. His transgressions will literally be splashed across the paper of record. He's going to bring shame to his wife and children, and Donald Pierce will have all the ammunition he needs to complete his coup.

In other words, life as he knows it is about to end.

17

During the week, Jorge and Julio work the front door of Aaron's building from 6:00 p.m. to 6:00 a.m. Someone once told Aaron that they're cousins, and there's a certain resemblance in that they're both Hispanic men with shaved heads, goatees, and somewhat sullen expressions. They're in full uniform, gray suits with red ties and dark double-breasted overcoats. And, of course, white gloves.

Julio opens the door for Aaron, but they both greet him in unison. "Good evening, Mr. Littman."

At exactly that moment, Aaron feels his pocket vibrate. He pushes the door back open himself and races against the traffic across Fifth Avenue, so as not to be overheard, without even turning back to see how the cousins have reacted.

"Hello?"

"Who is this?"

"Faith, it's Aaron."

"Oh . . . what the hell, Aaron?! You know—"

"I need to talk to you."

"Absolutely not. Even this discussion is extremely improper."

"Faith, be quiet for a minute and just let me say what I need to tell you." He doesn't wait for her assent. "Garkov knows about us. And he's going to use it to get what he wants. I need to see you. Right away."

"Aaron—no. I can't be seen with you. I shouldn't even be talking to you."

"Faith, I wouldn't ask if it weren't absolutely critical. And I just can't do it over the phone. Please. No one will see us, I promise. I'm begging you."

There's a long pause, during which all Aaron can hear is his own heart pounding.

"Where?" she finally says.

Thank God, he thinks to himself.

"The Alice in Wonderland statue."

"Of course," she mutters.

They met there once before, spending the evening necking like high schoolers. "No one will see us there," he says by way of explaining his choice of venue.

"If I can get away, I'll be there in a half hour. Maybe forty minutes. If I'm not there by then, I'm not coming, and if I get there and there are people around you, I'll leave."

He can't even thank her before the phone goes dead.

When Aaron's daughters were in grade school, the Alice in Wonderland statue in Central Park was just about their favorite place on earth. Even though there's a full-fledged playground closer to their apartment—complete with slide, swings, and a large sandbox—the girls never wanted to play there, always running toward the bronze statue and then jumping on top of the mushrooms in a race to be the first to climb to the top of Alice's head.

After nine on a cold school night in March, however, the area around the statue is empty, as are the nearby benches. Fifty or so yards to the south is the duck pond, where a couple sits tossing bread crumbs into the water, but they're far enough away not to be of any concern.

It isn't until nine thirty that Aaron first becomes concerned Faith might not show. But ten minutes later, she emerges from under one of the streetlamps as if she's an apparition. He expected her to be in gym clothes, but she looks like she's just left a party—high heels and what appears to be a tight dress under her open coat.

"Thank you so much for coming—"

"I'm not going to stay long," she interrupts, "so tell me what's going on."

He exhales deeply. "Like I said, Garkov knows about us. He hired me to get to you. He said that if you don't reverse yourself on the bail . . . I don't know what he's going to do exactly, but I'd just as soon not wait to find out."

Aaron thought Faith would share his concern, but he immediately knows by the angry way she's looking at him that she does not see them as common allies in this fight. She looks disgusted by the very sight of him.

"Garkov's *your* problem, Aaron. Get Sam Rosenthal to fix it. That's what he does, right? But whatever you do . . . just leave me out of it." She shakes her head in abject disgust. "I don't know what I was thinking by meeting you, Aaron. But I . . . I'm warning you to stay the hell away from me. If you contact me again, I'm going to remove you as counsel and file a formal complaint with the bar association."

She gets up, but he grabs her arm. "Please, Faith," he pleads.

"Let go of me," she snarls. "Coming here was a mistake."

She yanks her arm away from his grasp and then turns her back on him.

The last thing Aaron wants when he returns to his apartment is for Cynthia or the girls to see him in this state. His initial plan is to dart straight downstairs to their bedroom, but then he realizes that might be where Cynthia is, and so he calls out her name.

"Cynthia?"

No answer. Thank God.

One or both of the twins might be home, but they're likely holed up in their rooms. That gives him the opportunity to hurry downstairs to his bedroom without being seen.

Aaron takes off his suit and hangs it up, placing his shirt in the bin with the dry cleaning to go out the next day. Then he takes a shower, feeling the need to wash away the insanity of the last hour.

Before leaving the bedroom, he calls out for Cynthia again. Still no answer. He walks into Samantha's room, where he sees his daughter in her usual pose, staring into her laptop.

"Where's Mom?"

"IDK—wait, that's a total lie. She's at the hospital."

"Is your sister home?"

"Yuppers."

Aaron has a similarly abbreviated conversation with Lindsay and then heads to the kitchen, where he pulls a tumbler out of the cupboard and pours himself a generous amount of scotch. He takes his new best friend into the living room and tries to calm his nerves.

Shortly before 1:00 a.m., when Aaron is midway through his third drink, Cynthia finally appears. She looks a bit harried, which is not uncommon after she finishes a long night on call.

"Sorry I'm so late. There was this first-time mom," she says as she's taking off her coat, "and I'm told she's at eight centimeters, but when I got there, she was only at two, and so I was stuck at the hospital . . . you got my text, right?"

Cynthia has said this without even looking at Aaron. But when they make eye contact, her expression changes dramatically.

"Aaron, what's wrong? You look . . . like death."

"I'm not feeling particularly well," he says.

"And I see you're self-medicating."

She walks over and puts her hand to his head, checking if he has a fever the way she does with their daughters. She hesitates for a moment and then says, "You feel normal."

During his affair with Faith, Aaron always showered before returning home, and then worried whether the clean scent would be as incriminating as the sexual one he'd washed away. For a moment he has that same fear again, wondering if Cynthia can ascertain that he's lying by the sweet floral smell that clings to him.

"Why don't you just crawl into bed?" she continues. "I'll join you in a few minutes. You'll feel better tomorrow. I promise."

Aaron nods that he'll follow the doctor's orders, but he knows she couldn't be more wrong. Tomorrow will undoubtedly be the very worst day of his entire life.

18

Aaron feels like a man dressing for his own execution. Part of him wants to run. Run and never turn back. But he knows that the only thing he can do is go about his business as usual.

He puts on his favorite Brioni suit, a crisp white shirt, and a solid blue tie, and then heads out the door. Twenty minutes later, he steps into his office and sees Sam Rosenthal sitting there.

"What, are they painting the conference room?" Aaron asks.

Rosenthal doesn't smile.

"Judge Nichols . . . her body was found last night in Central Park. She was murdered. It's all over the news."

The lawyer in him knows that he should stay quiet, but Aaron can't help himself. "Sam . . . I *saw her* last night. In the park. I was trying to talk her out of staying on the case. Garkov must have someone following her . . . If he took pictures of Faith and me together . . ." Aaron shakes his head, as if he's in disbelief.

"Sam, I didn't kill her," he says.

I didn't do it. You have to believe me.

Aaron wouldn't believe a client who told him the same story, and so he fully expects Rosenthal's incredulity. But instead he sees in his mentor's eyes that Rosenthal will not abandon him. And that is oddly even more comforting than being believed.

Nicolai Garkov looks like a man who has just won the lottery. Even he must know how unseemly it is to gloat over another person's violent death, and yet here he is, grinning ear-to-ear before Aaron can even say hello.

Under other circumstances, Aaron would have brought Rachel to this meeting. But the last thing he wants is a witness to this discussion.

They are meeting in the same room on the third floor of the MCC where Garkov told Aaron not two days before that he would kill Faith Nichols—and maybe Aaron too—if she did not release him from this place. As he did then, Garkov is wearing the ill-fitting orange jumpsuit, and the guards who brought him in have left him constrained around the ankles but unlocked his handcuffs. Seemingly the only difference in today's scene is the look of pure joy on Garkov's face.

"I take it you've heard," Aaron says.

"Yes. Good news travels fast," Garkov says.

Aaron's only response is an icy glare. "You do realize that you're going to be the prime suspect in her murder?" he says.

"At first," Garkov says with an unconcerned air. "But"—he looks around the room—"I do have a fairly strong alibi, don't you think? Now, let's talk about something that matters, like when I can get out of here."

"It's not that simple—although I know you know that," Aaron says. "Everything is on hold until a new judge is appointed, and that's not going to happen until after the funeral. Then I'll make the bail application again. Be prepared for the fact that the new judge might well keep you here."

"Well, what's a few days in the grand scheme of things?" Garkov says. "And I suspect it *is* going to be that simple. I have every confidence that my next judge will see the wisdom behind house arrest, which apparently fell outside of Judge Nichols's understanding."

Aaron suspects that Garkov is correct. The next judge, being only human, will have severe concerns about ruling against Nicolai Garkov. Of course, Garkov could pull someone who is worthy of standing up to that challenge, but even if bail isn't reinstated, there is little doubt that whoever presides over Garkov's eventual trial will be more likely to acquit than Faith.

He also knows that another lawyer will be making that application. Now that he no longer has sway over the trial judge, Aaron Littman is superfluous to Nicolai Garkov's defense.

Most marriages have their demarcations. Like the equator, these are imaginary lines that take on navigational importance. Some you know going in—the wedding, the day your children are born—the things that forever change the way the world was before.

The night you tell your wife that you've been unfaithful and that your lover has been murdered—oh, and that you were the last person to see her alive—is certainly one of them.

Aaron wrestled all day with whether he should venture so far out on a limb with Cynthia. In addition to all the usual considerations that counsel against confessing infidelity to a spouse, he'd be creating evidence that could be used against him later by law enforcement. Spousal privilege would prevent Cynthia from testifying about the things he would share, but that didn't mean she couldn't still hurt him in other ways, like leading the police to admissible evidence that they might never have otherwise found.

But he pushed away such fears because he trusts Cynthia. He wants her to know that he might end up being a suspect in Faith's murder, so she'll know not to unwittingly say anything that might incriminate him.

At least, he thought it was a good strategy.

When he arrives at home, Cynthia is in the kitchen. Their housekeeper, Eunice, normally prepares dinner for the girls, and Aaron is usually wining and dining clients. But sometimes Cynthia likes to prepare dinner herself. She finds it relaxing, she says.

She's wearing the yoga pants she favors as her at-home attire, and the blue hoodie Aaron bought her as a gift from the Ugg store near his office.

Cynthia is one of those women who looks her best without makeup, with her hair tousled and . . . wearing yoga pants and a blue hoodie. Aaron can't help but consider the cruel irony that as he prepares to confess how unworthy he is of her love, she has never looked more beautiful to him.

"I didn't hear you come in," Cynthia says when she first sees Aaron in front of her in the kitchen. Cynthia's pique from yesterday over the Garkov case has apparently been put aside. She seems sincerely happy that he's here.

Aaron is trying to come up with some way to begin when Cynthia says, "I heard on the news about your judge. How terrible. Do they know who did it?"

"No. Not yet . . . Actually, I have no idea what they know. But . . . look, I have something to tell you and it's important."

Cynthia turns away from the stirring she's engaged in at the stove. "Okay . . . ," she says hesitantly.

He motions for her to sit down in their breakfast room. When she does, he takes a seat beside her. He wants to take her hand but knows that would be a mistake.

Despite Aaron's grave setup, Cynthia looks impassive. Aaron wants to turn back, but it's too late for that. All he can do now to limit the pain is come out with it quickly.

"I had an affair with the judge, Faith Nichols," he says. "It's been over since the Matthews trial ended, but that's why Nicolai Garkov hired me. He wanted me to blackmail her to get an acquittal. And I saw her last night, to try to tell her . . ."

Aaron can now see the fear in his wife's eyes, and although he had more he was going to say, he puts everything else aside and blurts out, "I didn't kill her, Cynthia. I would never do such a thing."

I didn't do it. You have to believe me.

Cynthia's face constricts, as if she's just been struck. He can tell that she's fighting back tears even as she processes how her life just went straight to hell.

Aaron's silent now, bracing himself for the barrage of questions he's sure is to follow: *How many times? Was it ever in our bed? Did you wear a condom? What do you mean you saw her right before she was murdered?*

But instead Cynthia asks something else. "Why . . . why are you telling me this now?"

"I . . . don't know if I should even be telling you at all, to be honest."

"You're being honest?!" Cynthia shouts at him. "An honest man doesn't fuck around!"

Aaron takes a deep breath. "You asked me why I was telling you now, and I was trying to answer."

Cynthia shakes her head violently. "Okay, sure. Go right ahead."

"I thought about telling you earlier, but I just thought that would hurt you for no reason. It was over, and the only rationale I could see for telling you was to make myself feel better . . . and that didn't seem to be good enough a reason. I-I'm so sorry, Cynthia."

"Stop it! Stop it! *Stop it!* I don't want to hear that you're sorry, Aaron. Sorry for what even? For having an affair or for telling me that you're going to be arrested for killing her?"

Neither of them says anything for a good ten seconds before Cynthia puts him out of his misery. "I can't even look at you anymore, Aaron. Just get the hell out of my sight. Go to a hotel or something, and give me some time alone."

PART TWO

19

Judge Nichols's murder is covered by the New York tabloids with the hyperbole for which they are famous. The *Post* plastered its front page with JUDGE MURDERED! while the *Daily News* went with JUSTICE DEAD. Under both headlines was Faith's photograph, the official shot from the court's website.

The *New York Times*'s coverage was more muted, but the story still merited two columns on the front page before jumping to the obituary section. Though long on biographical details (reared in Greenwich, Connecticut, attended Miss Porter's School before Smith College, then Yale Law School), the paper provided few details about the circumstances of Faith's murder besides the fact that she was bludgeoned to death in Central Park, with an anonymous source claiming the murder weapon was a tree branch. The article mentioned she was currently presiding over the Nicolai Garkov case and that she'd revoked his bail only the day before her murder, then left it to the reader to connect the dots.

In a sidebar story, the *Times* reported that Judge Nichols was only the fifth federal judge murdered since the Civil War. The deaths of two of the judges—John H. Wood of San Antonio and Richard J. Daronco of New York—were confirmed to have been in connection with their official capacity. Judge Wood was known as "Maximum John" for his tough sentences for drug traffickers and was shot in the back while leaving his home in May 1979. Charles Harrelson, the father of actor Woody Harrelson, was ultimately convicted and received two life sentences for the contract killing. A few years later, Judge Daronco was murdered by the father of a losing litigant. In 1989, Judge Robert Smith Vance of Atlanta was killed by a mail bomb, and while many speculated it was due to his refusal to overturn a conviction, that connection was never proven. The last federal judge murdered before Judge Nichols was John Roll of Arizona, who had the misfortune of being in the crowd on January 8, 2011, when a gunman opened fire, badly injuring U.S. congresswoman Gabrielle Giffords, as well as killing six others and wounding another twelve.

Faith's funeral is held the Monday morning after her death. It is a family-only event, the location itself a closely guarded secret.

The following day is the public display, a memorial service at Saint Patrick's Cathedral. As much as Aaron would rather not go, his absence would be conspicuous, and so he has no choice but to join close to one thousand of his fellow members of the bar to pay his final respects.

Despite the grim circumstances, the event has the feel of a bar association meeting. Nearly every member of the judiciary from the Southern District of New York and the Second Circuit Court of Appeals attends, and the city's most prominent lawyers jockey for their attention. There was some buzz that the governor, and maybe even the vice president, would be on hand, but according to the program that's given to Aaron when he enters the church, Edward Kheel, New York's senior senator, and Faith's benefactor for the Supreme Court, is the highest-ranking government official in attendance.

Even in the best of circumstances, Aaron's not a fan of any gathering of his fellow members of the bar, which is often little more than a mix of egotistical rantings and groveling for business, sometimes coming from the same person. Today's chitchat is even more labored than usual. In the ten minutes since he's arrived at Saint Pat's, Aaron has had two conversations in which the factoid about Woody Harrelson cited in the *Times* was referenced, and in both cases the lawyer who shared the information acted as if this were highly confidential information.

Aaron's now cornered by Steven Schwartzfarb, a short, pudgy bald man who works at a small white-collar boutique law firm. He chats Aaron up whenever he can in the hope that Cromwell Altman will throw some conflict work his way, which Aaron has never done and never will.

"I hear your man Garkov has a target on his back on this one," Schwartzfarb says.

Aaron offers a polite smile. He's not going to discuss with Schwartzfarb of all people the possibility that Nicolai Garkov killed Judge Nichols, that's for sure.

"I'll tell you one thing, this is definitely going to slow up the other prosecutions," Schwartzfarb continues. "All of the U.S. Attorney's Office resources are now going to be put toward finding who killed her. It'll be like 9/11 all over again. Remember? They stopped prosecuting securities fraud and focused entirely on antiterrorism. We had to let two associates go back then because there just wasn't enough work anymore." Schwartzfarb shakes his head mournfully, as if the two fired associates are casualties of the attack as much as the nearly three thousand souls who were in the two towers that day. "I guess the silver lining is that Garkov is going to end up being a full-employment act for lawyers, right? They're going to want to talk to everyone he ever spoke with. You got those guys lawyered up yet? Because, you know, I won't have any conflicts and so if I can help in any way . . ."

Aaron has tuned out even before Schwartzfarb's ham-fisted request for work. Someone is approaching the podium.

"It looks like the service is about to begin," Aaron says. "I'm going to grab my seat. Good to see you again."

Sam Rosenthal is sitting two-thirds of the way back from the stage on the aisle. He moves over a seat when Aaron joins him.

"How you holding up?" Rosenthal asks.

Rosenthal and Aaron haven't discussed Faith's murder since that first time in the office. Rosenthal hasn't even mentioned Nicolai Garkov, for that matter. Aaron is grateful for the respite, knowing it is likely the calm before the storm.

Aaron looks about for a moment. He wants to be absolutely sure no one is eavesdropping.

"I've been better," he says.

"I just finished chatting with your old buddy Fitz," Rosenthal says.

"And how is the good United States attorney?"

"Wanting to be mayor."

"Yeah, right. President is more like it."

"The good news is that he's focused on Garkov."

Aaron nods that this is indeed good news. There's no need for him to say what they're both undoubtedly thinking: that's subject to change if they ever find out that Aaron was sleeping with Faith, not to mention that he was with her right before she was murdered.

"Get this," Rosenthal continues, "Fitz actually suggested that he might try the case himself."

Aaron smiles at the thought of it. "I don't think he's even seen the inside of a courtroom in the last decade."

Rosenthal laughs with him, but this moment of levity is interrupted when New York's highest-ranking Catholic, Patrick Cardinal McKeowen, approaches the podium. He's dressed in the traditional ceremonial garb, pointy hat and all. McKeowen welcomes the crowd and then segues seamlessly into an invocation of God's awesome plan, which forever remains a mystery to those who are subject to it.

After the cardinal reads a few benedictions, George Vanderlyn, the head of Faith's old law firm, Windsor Taft, says that he knew Faith was destined for greatness from the first time he laid eyes on her, which makes Aaron recall that Faith referred to Vanderlyn as Vander*leer* because of the way he always stared at her breasts.

Judge Francis Petrocelli follows Vanderlyn to the podium. He tells the crowd that the entire judiciary has suffered a great loss, and then Senator Kheel tries to wax poetic, but it comes out sounding too much like a campaign speech.

The final speaker is Faith's husband, Stuart Christensen.

When you're sleeping with another man's wife, you learn quite a bit about the cuckold as well. And so even though they've never met, Aaron feels as if he knows Stuart intimately. According to Faith, Stuart is smart, but not nearly as much as he thinks he is; he never wanted children, which Faith knew going in but hadn't realized that it was actually a manifestation of his narcissism, which, to her mind, made it less acceptable than had it been a life choice; and he was not very good in bed, which Faith also knew going in, but she changed her mind about its importance somewhere around the two-year mark.

Nothing in the eulogy causes Aaron to doubt Faith's assessment. Stuart seems a touch too happy to be there, and he goes on ten minutes too long, which reminds Aaron of a comment Faith once made—that her husband took too long to do everything except the one thing where she wanted him to last.

When the service ends, as the others start a new round of glad-handing, Aaron tells Rosenthal that he's going to head back to the firm.

"Let's work the room a little bit," Rosenthal says. "We don't have to stay long, but you should say hello to some people."

Rosenthal is already thinking about a defense, in the event one is needed. He'd like the people in this room to tell the FBI that Aaron was no more upset about Faith's death than any other lawyer who attended the memorial service.

The truth interferes with that strategy, however. Aaron simply cannot stay another moment in this room. He feels claustrophobic and fraudulent, pretending to be a professional acquaintance of a woman he knew far greater than that.

"I just can't, Sam. I'm sorry, but I've got to go."

Rosenthal's nod releases him, and Aaron heads for the exit as fast as he can. He makes it only as far as the church steps, however. While his eyes are still adjusting to the bright sunlight, he hears his name.

He stops and turns to see Clint Broden jogging to catch up to him. "Just the man I wanted to see," Broden says when he finally catches up.

A few years back, the *American Lawyer* ran a profile of Aaron and Broden under the headline of THE TITANS, referring to them as the two best white-collar criminal defense lawyers in the country. It had the compare-and-contrast you'd see in a high school English term paper, with everything from their family upbringings (Aaron being Jewish, Broden a Roman Catholic) to their pedigrees (Harvard College/Yale Law for Aaron, Saint John's/Fordham Law for Broden) to their physical differences (Aaron at six foot two, Broden at five foot six) becoming a comment on how they approached their cases differently.

"Hey there. What can I do for you, Clint?"

"I met with Nicolai Garkov yesterday," Broden says. "He wants to make a switch."

Aaron's initial thought is that Garkov must have something on Broden. But Faith's successor as the trial judge hasn't been selected yet, so maybe Broden was picked on the merits.

"Did he offer you a hundred grand for the initial consult, Clint?"

Broden's grin reveals he understands the reference. "Look, Aaron, we're going to need to talk seriously about what's going on here, but this obviously isn't the time or place for that discussion."

That's fine by Aaron, who'd like nothing more than to extricate himself from this encounter. "Well, you know where to find me," Aaron says, and immediately starts his way down the stairs.

He's only taken a single step, however, when Broden says, "I almost forgot. Nicolai asked me to convey to you that he's very sorry."

Aaron turns a quarter so he's looking Broden in the eye, despite being a step below him. "I've been fired before, Clint. And, as Nicolai knows, I wasn't very enthusiastic about taking the case in the first place."

"I apologize," Broden says, not sounding at all contrite. "That was poorly phrased. I meant to say that he extends his sincere condolences for your loss."

20

Kevin Lacey knows that coming up to Stuart Christensen at his wife's memorial service isn't the classiest thing in the world, but as an FBI agent with over twenty years in, he also knows that etiquette takes a backseat to having the element of surprise on your side. Lacey was debriefed by the cops who spoke with Stuart the night of the murder, but hearing it secondhand isn't the same thing. Not by a long shot.

The rest of the FBI have their money on Garkov as the judge's killer, and Lacey has to admit that's the safe bet. But, at least statistically speaking, about a third of the time women are murdered, a sexual partner committed the crime, and that means that Stuart Christensen deserves a good hard look too, even if he isn't a terrorist.

When the crowd thins to just a handful of people, Lacey approaches.

"Mr. Nichols," he says, even though he knows that's not the man's surname. An interrogator's trick, to throw the suspect off balance.

"It's Christensen," Stuart says quickly, and with a sharp edge.

"My apologies, Mr. Christensen. My name is Kevin Lacey. I'm a special agent with the FBI." Lacey nonchalantly slides his suit jacket open, exposing the badge on his belt. "I know that this couldn't be a worse time for you, sir, but I was hoping that I could have a few minutes. I've secured a room so we can meet in private."

To Lacey, talking to a suspect is like going out on a first date: you know almost instantly how far they'll let you go. His initial impression of Stuart Christensen is that he is not going to be easy. His body language—crossed arms, turned shoulders, indirect eye contact—is the triple crown of noncooperative verbal cues.

Lacey knows that most people don't like talking to the FBI, but he never got that *Leave me alone* feeling from a parent whose child was kidnapped. They wanted him beside them 24/7. And usually spouses were all too happy to talk Lacey's ear off, throwing out the most mundane pieces of information in the hope that it would somehow crack the case wide open. But when loved ones weren't so inclined? That told Lacey they had something to hide.

"I've already spoken to the police," Stuart says. "I told them everything I knew."

"I understand completely, Mr. Christensen, and I wouldn't even ask if it wasn't important. The first twenty-four hours of any investigation are the most critical, and in this case the NYPD did a lot of that work on account of the fact that the whole jurisdictional thing wasn't ironed out until the morning after the murder. Unfortunately, that means the FBI's had to play some catch-up here. Leads can get cold in a hurry, and I just want to make sure that we're doing everything we can, which I know is what you want too. In this instance, doing everything we can means talking to you now, I'm afraid."

After the buildup Lacey just gave, if Stuart declines, he's practically begging the FBI to take a hard look at him as a suspect. Nevertheless, Lacey has the distinct impression that Stuart is weighing his options.

"Of course," Stuart finally says. "I want to help in any way I can."

Lacey directs Stuart out of the sanctuary, and they walk through the hallway until they reach the part of the church that is used for Sunday school classes. They enter room 19, and Lacey motions for Stuart to have a seat.

Lacey didn't check out the classroom beforehand, and so it isn't until he and Stuart are inside that he realizes the chairs are for very small children, kindergartners, maybe. When Stuart sits down in the tiny chair, he looks completely ridiculous.

"My apologies," Lacey says. "I asked to use one of the classrooms and they gave me this one." He looks around and sees a full-sized chair behind the teacher's desk in the other corner of the room. For a split second he considers wheeling it over for himself, but then thinks better of it for fear that the power imbalance will cause Stuart to shut down. The playbook is to put your suspect at ease in the hope that will make him open up, and if that doesn't do the trick, *then* you scare the crap out of him.

So Lacey pulls up another tiny chair and settles his six-foot body on top of it. It doesn't break under his weight and actually isn't as uncomfortable as he thought, and so whatever little sympathy he had for Stuart Christensen the moment before dissipates, which is good because now he can get down to business.

"I'm really not permitted to comment on the investigation," Lacey says, "but, off the record, we don't believe your wife was the victim of a random attack. I know the press is saying that the murder weapon was a tree branch grabbed in the heat of the moment, but one of the reasons that this is an FBI matter, and not being handled by the NYPD, is that the working theory is that your wife was killed in connection with her official duties. Here's a little bit of trivia for you: When JFK was assassinated, there wasn't a federal law making it a crime to kill the president. Had Lee Harvey Oswald been brought to trial, it would have been under Texas state law, and he would have been tried in a Texas state court. After the Kennedy assassination, the law changed so that the murder of a federal official—I mean everybody from the president down to a mailman—is a federal crime. But only if the murder occurs in connection with the victim's official duties."

Lacey sees the subtlest trace of relief in Stuart's face. One thing's for sure: if Stuart Christensen *did* murder his wife, it had nothing to do with her role as a United States district court judge.

"But like I said," Lacey continues, "we're early in the investigation, and we still have a lot of people to talk to. And I suppose that's a perfect segue for me to ask you about the night of the murder. Why was your wife in the park?"

Lacey knows the answer to this question, as well as most of the others he's going to ask, from the download he got via the NYPD. But that doesn't mean he's not acutely interested in the response.

"I already told the NYPD folks that I have no idea," Stuart says. "In fact, that's the question I keep asking myself. Faith told me she was going to the gym. It's in the basement of our building and she works out most nights at eight, and gets done anywhere from one to two hours later. That night, after she told me she was going to the gym, I went into the bedroom to read and must have fallen asleep, because the next thing I knew, I got a call from the police telling me that they'd found Faith's body in Central Park."

"And then what did you do?"

Stuart seems confused. "Uh, I cried, I think," he finally says.

"No, I'm sorry. I meant did you go down to the gym to see if your wife was there? You know, maybe thinking it must be a mistake and the body in the park was someone else?"

Lacey knew that Stuart didn't do this, or at least that he didn't tell the cops he did. He asked the question solely to get a reaction, and Stuart Christensen did not disappoint. For a guy who just lost his wife, he was clearly in self-preservation mode. Lacey could almost see Stuart doing the math: he wouldn't have checked the gym for his wife if he knew for a fact that she was dead in Central Park, and the only way he could know that was if he had left her there. At the same time, he likely also knew that the building's gym had cameras, and so had to assume the FBI had already verified that he didn't go there that night.

"I . . . I didn't go to the gym, no," Stuart says with pronounced deliberation, "but I did check the apartment. When I got the call, I remember seeing that it was already eleven thirty. She wouldn't still be working out that late. She obviously wasn't in bed, so I got up and checked the bathroom, the living room. You know, calling out her name."

Lacey nods and writes this down. Not because it matters, but solely so Stuart thinks that his lie about looking for his wife in the apartment has been believed.

"Okay. Are you aware of anyone who had threatened your wife recently? Anyone who might have wanted to hurt her?"

"Well . . . I mean, there were always angry defendants, but I'm not aware of a specific threat. There's the whole business with Nicolai Garkov, of course. She had just revoked his bail and she said something to me about being offered a security detail. She turned it down, though. Said it would make her feel like a prisoner and it wasn't fair to our neighbors."

Lacey already spoke to the people who offered Judge Nichols that protection. However, he was told that Judge Nichols said it was her husband who didn't want the security detail. Not a huge lie, but one that suggested that prevaricating to law enforcement was becoming something of a routine for Stuart Christensen.

That was where the NYPD cops had left off. But since the initial interview, the FBI had gone through Judge Nichols's finances, and that was the primary reason that Lacey was busting Stuart Christensen's balls at his wife's memorial service.

"Mr. Christensen, it's standard operating procedure in any murder of this kind for us to look at financial records," Lacey says, trying not to sound as if it's the gotcha moment it's about to become. "What we found was that most of your assets—the apartment you live in, the money you have in the bank, the securities account at Merrill Lynch—are comprised almost entirely of what your wife amassed prior to the two of you getting married. Is that right?"

"I don't know what you mean by *almost entirely*," Stuart says, sounding a little like Bill Clinton parsing the definition of *is*. "Faith was in private practice before we got married, and she became a judge right after. As I'm sure you know, federal judges make much less money than Windsor Taft equity partners, and so, yeah, Faith earned most of our savings and bought our co-op before we got together."

Lacey knew he was getting to Stuart. He could tell by the way Stuart looked around the room, as if scoping the exits in case he needed to get out of there fast. Lacey wouldn't be surprised if the *Maybe I should talk to a lawyer before we continue* card was played very soon. That means he needs to move quickly through the other questions he has or they might never be answered.

"And there's a large insurance policy on your wife that names you the beneficiary," Lacey says. "Two point five million. Are you aware of that?"

"Yes," Stuart says in a clipped voice, undoubtedly hearing how bad this sounds. "All the partners at her old law firm got large policies as part of their compensation. When you leave the firm, you can take it with you, which Faith did."

"I understand," Lacey says. "And how were things between you and your wife?"

"What do you mean?"

"Just what I said. Were you getting along well? Were you not getting along well? How were things?"

"Good. Very good, in fact. I mean . . . well, I imagine this is going to come out anyway, but Faith was being considered for the U.S. Supreme Court."

Lacey hadn't heard anything about the Supreme Court, but it was Stuart's smile when he made the disclosure, as phony as a bad toupee, that was the real discovery.

"You have your own architecture firm here, don't you?"

"Yes. Yes I do," Stuart says, smiling more naturally now, as if he's finally pleased to be talking about himself rather than his dead wife.

"Were you planning on moving your architecture practice to DC? Or were you two talking about a commuter-type relationship?"

Stuart looks like a guy who just stepped in shit. "We hadn't made definitive plans or anything," he says. "She had to, you know, get nominated first, and I wasn't sure she'd take it even if it was offered . . ." His voice trails off, seemingly in recognition that he was digging a deeper hole for himself with every word. "Look, I'm sorry, but I'm obviously not in a great frame of mind, which I'm sure you can imagine, given the circumstances."

There was one last topic. The reason husbands kill their wives other than money.

"There's just one more thing I need to know, and then we're done," Lacey says. "Was there . . . anyone in your wife's life that she didn't want you to know about?"

"Are you asking if my wife was having an affair?"

"I'm sorry to be indelicate, especially today, but the fact is that she was in Central Park when she told you she was at the gym . . . Sometimes—not always, but *sometimes*—when a wife lies to her husband about her whereabouts, it's because she's with another man. Or in some cases, another woman. So my question to you is whether you knew about anything like that."

"No," Stuart says flatly.

Lacey wonders if there's going to be more, expecting a flowery speech in which Stuart professes his undying love for his wife and hers for him. But that simple negative declaration is all he says.

"Okay," Lacey says. "I appreciate your time, Mr. Christensen. I may have some follow-up questions, and if I do, I'll reach out to you again."

As they shake hands good-bye, Lacey can see the unease in Stuart Christensen's face. Rather than give Lacey cause for empathy, it emboldens him to turn the screws a bit more.

"I promise you this, sir," Lacey says while still holding Faith's widower's hand tightly and staring at him good and hard, "we will catch your wife's killer. I guarantee you that."

21

After the memorial, Aaron returns to Cromwell Altman. He tells Diane not to disturb him and takes refuge behind his closed door.

Alone, he starts to organize the evidence against him. An order of proof, it's called. The traditional way is to divide a sheet of legal-pad paper in thirds the long way. In the left-most column the facts are set out, in the center is the evidence supporting those facts, and on the far right is the rebuttal, if there is any.

First, there's the affair. At least he and Faith were careful never to enter or leave the Ritz-Carlton together—or even be seen in public in each other's company, for that matter. And he always paid in cash, so there'd be no electronic record of his paying for the room. But the hotel always made a copy of his driver's license, and so if the FBI knew to go to the Ritz-Carlton, they'd have proof of his weekly visits.

Then there were the phone calls.

He always used prepaid phones so that Faith's phone number didn't show up on his cell bill. He didn't know if the FBI could tell that the calls were from burner phones, but he suspected they could, as the calls from one number stopped after a minutes threshold was met, usually a hundred, because Aaron bought prepaid phones in that denomination. Then the calls resumed from a different number. That would almost certainly be enough for the FBI to assume Faith was having an affair.

At least Aaron knew enough to always activate the phones outside of the place he bought them, and so he didn't think law enforcement could trace the phones to the place of purchase, which meant it was highly unlikely that they'd be able to link the calls back to him. Even if they flashed his picture at every place on the Upper East Side that sold burner phones, Aaron couldn't believe that anyone could remember who bought a phone a few months ago. They must sell tons of them every week.

The last set of phone calls was an entirely different matter, however. If the FBI traced the phone he used the night Faith was murdered back to the place where he bought it, the odds of identification were much greater, especially if they got to the store clerk soon, while his memory was fresh. *Calm down,* he tells himself. *Why would the FBI even think to go to 102nd and Amsterdam?*

Just as he was feeling a sense of peace, however, an even worse thought struck Aaron. If there was any physical evidence linking him to Faith and their meeting in the park—a single strand of his hair, his fingerprint on her coat, even some type of carpet fiber that existed only in his office—he'd be toast.

And he just couldn't rule that out.

Rachel didn't give any serious thought to attending Faith Nichols's memorial service. She never spoke to Judge Nichols outside of the unpleasant interaction they'd shared in the Garkov case, and she felt no need to use a murder to network. Besides, she knew that Aaron would be monopolized by the A-listers, and spending time with him was the only reason she would have wanted to be there.

So she waited patiently for his return, and when she heard the commotion of the others coming back, she made her way up to his office.

"He in?" she asks Diane.

"He said he wanted some quiet time," Diane answers, "but I'm sure he'd be happy to see you. Go on in."

When Rachel enters, she sees Aaron staring intently at a yellow legal pad, a pen in his hand. It's a startling sight, as Aaron never handles the first draft of anything.

"Hey, you," she says.

"Hey yourself," he says back.

Aaron looks pleased to see her, which, as always, instantly buoys her spirits. But she senses that something is off too, and that concerns her.

"How was the memorial?" she asks.

"About what you'd expect. Blowhards being blowhards. Senator Kheel was there. Judge Nichols's husband gave the main eulogy, so at least someone talked about parts of her life that weren't related to her job, although it sounded like he barely knew her too."

"Makes me glad I didn't go," Rachel says.

"I wish I'd opted out as well. Oh, and the cherry on the sundae of my day was that Garkov fired us. Clint Broden accosted me as I was leaving the church and told me that we're out and he's in. I can't say that I'm too upset about it, but I'm not looking forward to tomorrow's COC meeting. It's going to be a full-on assault. A lot of handwringing and over-the-top rhetoric about how I've put the firm's future in jeopardy."

There's a moment of silence, during which Rachel debates whether to say what's on her mind. Then she does.

"You know, I was thinking, it's a tradition that when a case ends to have a blowout dinner, and even though the Garkov case was short-lived . . . I think it merits some type of celebration, don't you?"

The moment the invitation is made, Rachel worries that she's been too aggressive. Aaron deliberates longer than she thinks he should, and so she tries to pull it back.

"You can say no if you have something else going on. But now that Garkov isn't in our future and we've got some downtime, I thought we should make the most of it."

"Sure," Aaron says. "Felidia? Eight o'clock?"

"Great. I'll meet you there," she says.

Rachel's too good a litigator not to know that when you get the answer you want, you say thank you and get out before anyone can change their mind. And so she leaves Aaron's office as giddy as a schoolgirl, visions of a romantic evening dancing in her head.

22

Clint Broden hates visiting clients in prison. He sometimes wonders why he hasn't come to terms with it by now, given how often he does it, but frequency has not made it any more bearable. He dislikes everything about it—from the way every article of his clothing seems to set off the metal detectors, to the impossible temperature of the facilities (freezing in the winter; stifling hot in summer), to the rancid stench of body odor that permeates the air. Worst of all, you can't bring in any food or drinks, and although there are soda machines for visitors, they stock only Coke products, and Clint Broden is a die-hard Pepsi man through and through.

Broden got the collect call from the MCC just as he was hearing about Faith Nichols's untimely demise. His first instinct was that Aaron Littman had thrown Garkov overboard, not wanting to sully his white shoes by representing a judge killer. But then Garkov gave him the full download of what was going on. Although years of experience had taught Broden not to believe half of what clients told him, he believed every single word of Garkov's story about his effort to get Aaron Littman to blackmail Faith Nichols into letting him go free. It was just too fantastic to be fiction.

Even before hearing that Garkov had been blackmailing his previous attorney, Broden knew that most of the city's elite lawyers wouldn't touch Garkov with a pole of any length. But even assuming Garkov was guilty of everything he had been charged with and the things he hadn't been—namely the Red Square bombing and, as of right now, the murder of Judge Nichols—he still wouldn't be anywhere near the worst client Clint Broden ever represented. That distinction went to Thomas Lee Curtis, who Broden should have known was twisted simply by the fact that he demanded to be called by his full name at all times. Thanks to Broden's good work, Curtis never spent a day in jail or even stood trial, despite the fact that he raped and murdered nine children and freely acknowledged to Broden that it might well be twice that number. He just couldn't remember.

Guilt, innocence, the severity of the crime—those issues were irrelevant to Clint Broden. He had only two criteria for taking on clients: money and challenge, and the former didn't matter if the latter was great enough.

Of course, Garkov had both in spades, which made him the perfect client as far as Broden was concerned. The fact that it also meant Broden got to personally fire the high and mighty Aaron Littman was just icing on the cake.

"Nicolai," Broden says, "sorry to be meeting under such circumstances, but my hope is that your stay here will be short."

Garkov didn't look any worse for wear. He had no bruises or other telltale signs that he wasn't making friends inside. Of course, Broden figured that even the toughest guy in lockup would think twice before tangling with a seven-foot-tall terrorist connected to the Russian mob.

"How was the funeral?" Garkov asks.

"Do you really care?" Broden says quickly.

"No, not really. So long as she's dead, I'm good."

Broden ignores the comment. "I ran into Aaron Littman at the memorial. Short conversation, just what we talked about."

"And what did he say?"

"Not much. He wasn't surprised you were making the switch. Told me that he never wanted to represent you in the first place."

"So, who'd we get?" Garkov asks.

"The honorable Milton Koletsky."

"Jew?"

"African-American."

"Same thing. Just as long as it's not some bitch again."

"Well, without endorsing your broad view of racial and gender generalizations, I will say that Koletsky is very good for us. I've already filed an application that house arrest be reinstated, and there's a hearing set for this afternoon. No guarantees, but my guess is that you'll be spending tomorrow night back on your twelve-hundred-thread-count sheets."

The news that he'll be home soon doesn't change Garkov's expression. It's as if he already assumed as much.

Believing that Aaron Littman was sleeping with Faith Nichols and Garkov's being a blackmailer was one thing, but Broden was far more skeptical about Garkov's protestation that he was innocent of Faith Nichols's murder. Not only was it readily apparent to Broden that Garkov was a man devoid of any conscience whatsoever, but Garkov was smart, and unlike some of the stupid actions clients have been known to undertake while awaiting trial—little things like trying to bribe FBI agents and lying about assets that are easily found—killing the judge was a very smart move.

A law-and-order devotee like Faith Nichols was almost certainly going to find Garkov guilty and then sentence him to the max. And if a superseding indictment were filed with a murder charge, it was a lethal-injection situation. But with Judge Koletsky, Garkov probably had an even-money shot at acquittal. Even if Garkov were convicted, a bleeding heart like Koletsky might sentence him to less than ten years. Garkov could probably do that standing on his head.

Broden takes a good long look at his client. Nicolai Garkov's smug expression suggests that it's entirely possible he's actually orchestrated everything from the get-go.

23

Felidia occupies the bottom two floors of a narrow town house just around the corner from Bloomingdale's. It's as close to a New York City institution as restaurants get, given that a five-year stint is considered noteworthy and Felidia has survived for a quarter-century.

Rachel knows that Felidia is one of Aaron's favorite dining spots, reminding him of a restaurant he loves in Rome, with its rich dark-paneled room juxtaposed with the lit garden in the rear. He took her here two years ago to celebrate her ascension to the partnership. The memory of that dinner—and the three drinks too many she consumed—rushes back to her as she enters the restaurant.

Rachel feels good being out of her work clothes. For tonight, she's opted for her favorite little black dress and three-inch Manolo Blahniks that a dominatrix might wear.

When she arrives, the hostess, a stick-skinny Asian woman with hair almost to her waist, tells Rachel that Aaron has already been seated. She follows the hostess upstairs, where she sees Aaron occupying a table against the window.

Aaron stands when she approaches, a gesture Rachel's always enjoyed. Very few of her dates do that.

The table is for four, and after a moment's hesitation, Rachel takes the seat next to Aaron, rather than across. Aaron signals for the waiter to come over and quickly orders a bottle of wine. When she takes the first sip, Rachel assumes the wine must be very expensive by virtue of the fact that it tastes so good.

Rachel mentions the news of the day, which is that Judge Koletsky reversed the bail decision, and Garkov is back under house arrest in Trump Tower. "Not quite a profile in courage," she says.

"Probably the right decision," Aaron says with a shrug. "Anyway, not our problem anymore, right?"

Rachel raises her wineglass. "To it not being our problem," she says, touching her glass against Aaron's.

The waiter is very attentive, refilling their glasses so often that the first bottle is finished before the entrées arrive. Aaron orders a second bottle, although Rachel is already beginning to feel a buzz taking hold.

"So, the COC tomorrow?" Rachel says. "What's on the agenda—world domination?"

"Besides me being handed my ass over Garkov? Something even more serious." He waits a beat. "The prom."

The derisive reference is to the annual Cromwell Altman black-tie gala, held every spring.

She laughs. "Will Cynthia be coming?" Aaron's smile drops, and Rachel realizes that she must have inadvertently touched a nerve. "I'm sorry, Aaron. Did I say something wrong?"

"No. No." Aaron's eyes circle the room, as if he's looking for the right words. "Cynthia and I . . . I'm staying at the Pierre for a few days while Cynthia and I give each other a little breathing room."

The news sends a jolt through Rachel. She's actually out on a romantic evening with a single Aaron Littman, or at least a separated Aaron Littman.

"I'm sorry, Aaron," she says, hoping it sounds sincere. "When did this happen?"

"Just a few days ago. This too shall pass," Aaron says with a taut smile.

As if the wine has taken over her judgment, Rachel places her hand on top of Aaron's and gently massages his thumb with her own. At the moment where things might escalate further, Aaron slides his hand away.

"What's going on in your life, Rachel?" Aaron asks. "Are you taking anyone to the prom?"

Rachel hesitates, wondering if she should say what she's thinking. But that rarely works in such settings, and so she plays along as if the last thirty seconds never transpired.

"God, no," she says. "Nobody in my life at the moment."

"I thought you were seeing that foreign banker guy. Paolo? Giovanni?"

"Alessandro," Rachel says.

"Right. So what happened there?"

"What always happens," she says. "One of us wanted more, and I didn't."

They don't finish the second bottle, but Rachel's still drunker than she's been in a while and in need of some air, and so when the waiter asks if they'd like any dessert, she suggests that it's time to go. Once outside, Aaron offers to hail Rachel a cab, but she doesn't want the evening to end, and she proposes to walk with Aaron the few blocks to the Pierre. As soon as she says it, she worries that she's being obvious, but Aaron doesn't protest, and they begin south down Lexington Avenue.

Three doormen stand in front of the Pierre, getting taxis for the guests. "Welcome back," one of them says to Aaron.

"This is me," Aaron says to Rachel. "Home sweet home." He motions to the first cab lined up in front of the hotel. "Your chariot, my lady."

The Manolos make it easier for Rachel to kiss Aaron on the lips. It lasts a second, maybe even two, before the seal is broken.

"Good night, Rachel," he says when they separate.

She hesitates for a moment, searching his face for a sign of whether he's playing hard to get or he means to end the evening like this. She so hoped that things would take a very different turn, but the look in Aaron's eyes leaves little room for doubt that, at least tonight, he's not ready for things between them to escalate beyond that one kiss.

Five hundred dollars a night at the Pierre gets you a king-size bed, an armoire that hides a forty-two-inch flat-screen, and a marble bathroom. The first few nights, Aaron was pleased to come back to this place. He knew all too well the contempt and disappointment that would have awaited him with Cynthia, and so he considered it something of a gift to be alone. A vacation from his life, from his mistakes.

Rachel's clumsy advance only crystallizes to him how much he loves his wife and how lonely he is without his family. He wants nothing more than to go back in time and not slide over that empty chair to chat with Faith. Then why did he in the first place? Because he could? Out of boredom? For the sheer thrill of it? How could any of those motivations have carried the day, especially when the danger was so great?

The answer, sadly, is the age-old one. He thought he could do both. That he could enjoy his time with Faith without risk to his family.

How wrong he was.

24

The Committee on Committees meeting begins promptly at 7:30 a.m., in the conference room between Aaron's and Rosenthal's offices. As is the case whenever the COC meets, there is no written agenda and no one is permitted to take notes.

The committee's seven members are charged with everything from approving firm expenditures to setting the compensation for the partners. The heads of the firm's five departments—litigation, corporate, tax, antitrust, and real estate—are members, as well as one partner at large, selected every two years by the chairman. Sam Rosenthal has an ex officio position as the former chairman of the firm.

Although the seating is not assigned, it never varies. Aaron is at the head of the table and Rosenthal across from him, which lends the meeting an air that they are the parents at a family dinner. Donald Pierce is stationed between Gregg Goldman and Jane Cleary on one side of the table, with Elliot Dalton and Abby Sloane across from them.

Abby Sloane is Aaron's own addition to the COC, and so he assumes her support for his continued leadership is a given. Not only because she owes Aaron her seat at the table, but because she owes him her partnership as well. A few years back, when she was an associate, she was involved in a somewhat messy sexual-harassment issue that ended with the ouster of the partner she worked with and her subsequent elevation at Cromwell Altman. Abby knows that it could have easily gone the other way, and might have but for Aaron's backing.

Goldman is head of the tax group and Cleary leads real estate, which puts both of them outside of Aaron's direct sphere of influence. Aaron had always assumed that they both saw through Pierce's act, but if Pierce's threat of having a fourth vote is true, and Aaron can count on Abby's support, that means both Goldman and Cleary have gone over to the dark side and are now in league with Pierce.

That leaves Dalton. Antitrust lawyers tend to be cerebral types, and Elliot Dalton certainly looks the part of the absentminded professor, with his half reading glasses perched atop his nose and the white tufts of hair that dust his scalp. What makes Dalton truly a wild card, however, is that unlike virtually every other Cromwell Altman partner, he doesn't outwardly appear to have any greater ambition than what he's already achieved. And that means Dalton can be counted on to vote for what he thinks is best for the firm.

Aaron calls the meeting to order and then asks Dalton to remind everyone about the prom. Dalton does not look amused by the reference to its colloquial name.

"Well, the annual Cromwell Altman *Spring Gala*," he says, "will take place at the Metropolitan Museum of Art. The cocktail reception is going to be in the same gallery as the Temple of Dendur, which is commonly called the Egyptian Room. Dinner will be in the main hall. Attendees will be able to roam the museum, at least on the first floor. Of course, that requires covering the costs of about twenty guards and a hell of a lot of insurance."

"Can I ask what this little soiree is going to run us?" Goldman asks.

"Ballpark, about a million, maybe a little bit more," Dalton says. "But, I remind you all, my marching orders were for this to be a true *event*, and it will most definitely be that. To that end, we expect a full turnout from the partners, and at least a fifty percent turnout from the associates. Please get the word out and do whatever you can to strong-arm your people to show up."

The prom issue now put to rest, the COC's next order of business is actual business. Aaron distributes the firm's monthly financials, which include several top-ten lists identifying clients in various categories: amount paid to date; hours billed; WIP, the abbreviation for *work in progress*; and firm investment, which identifies the clients with the highest unpaid bills. Although the order sometimes varies, the same ten clients appear on nearly every list.

The final page has the heading "Unapplied Retainers." Below it are nine of the names that appear on the other lists. The one exception occupies the top spot: Nicolai Garkov, who, according to this document, placed two million on retainer, of which $150,000 has been billed to date.

"How did the Garkov bill get to a hundred and fifty thousand dollars?" Cleary asks. "Didn't we just take that on a few days ago?"

"There was an up-front bonus of a hundred thousand dollars," Aaron says. "We only have fifty thousand dollars in the matter—"

Aaron is about to explain that they wouldn't be billing any time in the future, when Pierce interrupts. "I want to be on record that I expressed to Aaron my very vehement opposition to the firm taking on this client. Putting aside the moral aspect of representing a terrorist, this client will cost the corporate department dearly. I'm only sorry that I wasn't prescient enough to realize it was going to hurt the entire firm. I've already heard from headhunters that their phones are ringing off the hook from associates looking to jump ship, now that Cromwell Altman is the law firm of choice for judge killers."

Rosenthal is quick to answer. "Then I propose that going forward we only represent the most virtuous companies and individuals. Anyone who has legal problems of any kind is simply not welcome as a client of this morally superior law firm."

This elicits some laughter, although Aaron notices that Pierce does not seem amused. Goldman and Cleary aren't either, for that matter, but at least Abby and Dalton crack a smile.

Aaron decides it will be best to just get the bad news over with as quickly as possible. "There's no reason for this to take up any more of the committee's time. We're not going to continue in the Garkov representation. I spoke with Clint Broden yesterday, and he's coming in for us."

The bombshell disclosure only seems to embolden Pierce. "Wait. So, let me get this straight then," he says. "We lost ten million, maybe twenty million, in business and perhaps some of our best young lawyers over a less-than-two-hundred-thousand-dollar matter? Do I have that right, Aaron?"

"We haven't lost anything," Aaron says sharply. "The associates aren't going to leave, not with what we pay them, and we earned a hundred and fifty thousand dollars for a few hours' work. I fail to see what the problem is."

"I'll tell you the problem, Aaron. Craig Sinoway of Globe Tech told me point-blank that he's going to pull his corporate work—that's twenty million dollars annually—because of Garkov. That's the goddamn problem, Aaron."

"Isn't that convenient, Don," Aaron replies. "Blame me when you lose a client. You don't think the fact that you royally screwed up their secondary offering has anything to do with the loss of business?"

Aaron and Pierce are staring daggers at each other when Dalton chimes in. "That's uncalled-for, Aaron. Donald is making a valid point. No partner should take on a matter that's going to be a net loser for the firm. That's just common sense."

Across the table, Rosenthal and Aaron share a silent moment. They both now know that Elliot Dalton is Pierce's fourth vote.

25

Of all the time-wasting things that Agent Kevin Lacey could imagine, questioning Nicolai Garkov about the murder of Faith Nichols ranks near the top. There is no way a guy like Garkov, sitting next to a lawyer like Clint Broden, is going to give *anything* up.

When Aaron Littman was representing Garkov, he at least had the decency to tell Lacey no thanks over the phone, but the day after the memorial service, Lacey got a call from Clint Broden, who said he was in as Garkov's new counsel, and that he wanted a face-to-face. And when the prime suspect to a murder wants to talk, you drop everything to hear what he has to say, even when you know that it's likely going to be little more than a chain yanking.

The fact that the FBI has to go to Garkov—and at Trump Tower, no less—just makes it that much more distasteful. But the main reason Lacey is annoyed this morning has nothing to do with the venue or the task at hand, but with the fact that Tim Walker is coming along for the ride. Walker is the agent in charge of the original Garkov case, the money-laundering and obstruction indictments that landed Garkov on trial in front of Judge Nichols in the first place, and Walker is still trying mightily to transform those into a conspiracy to commit murder. If Garkov went down because of Judge Nichols rather than the American students in Red Square, the job would be considered just as well done.

The problem is that Lacey thinks Walker is a pompous ass, and not nearly as good an agent as everybody says. Worse still, Lacey has it on good authority that Walker thinks the exact same thing about him.

"I can't believe this asshole is back to living here," Walker says as they take the elevator to Garkov's apartment within Trump Tower.

"I guess Judge Koletsky didn't want to end up facedown in Central Park," Lacey responds.

Upon entering Garkov's apartment, they're greeted by Clint Broden, who looks as if he's about to give an opening argument, attired in a dark, finely tailored suit; bright tie; and gold cuff links in the actual shape of dollar signs. By contrast, Lacey and Walker are wearing jeans and sweatshirts. They dress for court only when they're going to court.

"Mr. Broden," Lacey says, "I'm Special Agent Kevin Lacey and this is my colleague Special Agent Timothy Walker."

"Welcome, gentlemen," Broden says. "Come in. Mr. Garkov is waiting."

Lacey has the feel of being at the circus, staring up at this giant approaching them. Garkov is also dressed to kill, although in his case that means a red velvet smoking jacket.

They all take seats in the living room. Lacey and Walker sit on the ends of a long sofa, while Broden and Garkov are side by side on the couch opposite them. The giant lion's-head fireplace breathes flame.

"Mr. Garkov, thank you for meeting with us," Lacey says. "As I'm sure your counsel has told you, we're investigating the murder of Judge Faith Nichols. We'd like to ask you some questions."

Garkov nods but doesn't give any other assent. Even so, it's enough for Lacey to continue.

"Look, there's no big state secret here, Mr. Garkov. You should be aware that we're looking hard at you on this one. Obviously, your reputation precedes you, but the timing of her murder—a day after Judge Nichols revokes your bail—also doesn't look too good for you.

So before we get our feet stuck in the cement that you're our guy, we figured we'd give you the opportunity to tell us otherwise."

Garkov doesn't look the slightest bit intimidated. "Well, I guess you have me, it seems," he says in a slow voice. "You've figured it all out. I confess. I was so upset at being put in prison that on my second night there, I simply walked out the front gate, hailed a cab, and luckily for me, the driver did not think anything of picking up a seven-foot-tall man wearing an orange prison jumpsuit, nor did he mind that I didn't have any money to pay him, and he took me straight from the correctional facility to Central Park. I knew that Judge Nichols would be there, because . . . well, it should be obvious, she confided in me her every movement. Then I killed her, of course, because she revoked my bail. Afterward, I left the park. Now, as luck would have it, the same cabdriver was nice enough to wait for me. He took me back to prison, where I reentered through the front door. So . . . *you got me!* Good work, Agent Lacey."

Garkov bellows laughter, and Broden joins in.

Walker rolls his eyes at Lacey, making it clear that he views this as Garkov's idea of a joke, jerking the FBI around.

"You're going to have to do better than that, Nicolai," Walker says, the anger evident in his voice. "All it would take is for you to have someone on the outside who's following her. He watches her leave her home, follows her to the park, and cracks her skull."

Lacey chimes in. "Yeah. It's not the most intricate murder scheme of all time. And let's not kid ourselves: there's only one person who avoids life in prison if she's dead. And I'm looking right at him." Lacey's stare says the time for fun and games is now over. "So let's start again, with some feeling this time, shall we?"

"Hold on. My client is not going to say anything further at this meeting," Broden says.

"Then why did you make us haul our asses up here?" Walker asks.

"Because I have something to say on his behalf. And I think that you're going to want to hear it."

Lacey and Walker share another look of mutual frustration. But Lacey figures that since they're already there, he might as well hear why.

"We're all ears," Lacey says.

Garkov nods at Broden, which apparently is the go-ahead for him to proceed, because Broden says, "I understand why the initial focus of the investigation might be on my client. But he didn't commit this crime, and you'd be better served focusing your attention elsewhere."

"Okay, then," Walker says. "Thanks for clearing that up. Let's go, Kevin. This is a fucking waste of our time."

Lacey doesn't move, however. "Where should our attention be focused, Mr. Broden?"

"Not so fast," Broden says. "In return for the mother of all cooperation that Mr. Garkov would be providing, you're going to need to give him complete immunity. That means on the indictment already filed, everything related to the Red Square bombing, and anything else that you might choose to tack on. We're talking a complete and total one hundred percent get-out-of-jail-free card. If you have him on jaywalking charges, it's going to be covered."

Walker explodes. "No fucking way! Do you honestly think for a second that we're supposed to recommend a free pass to *this* guy?! Who everyone in America wants to take a shot at right now?!"

Broden turns to Lacey, asking him to confirm that Walker's outburst expressed the FBI's official position. Lacey knows a more measured response will be more productive.

"You've got to offer us something much more concrete than that before we think about making *any* type of deal here," he says. "But I know that you already knew that. So, why don't we cut through all the bullshit and you just tell us what you brought us here to say."

Broden straightens up and whispers in his client's ear. When he's done, Garkov says, "Your murderer, gentlemen, is my former attorney, Aaron Littman. Is that concrete enough for you?"

Walker actually laughs through his rage. "You know, honestly, that's pretty funny. What, are you trying to get out of paying his bill?"

Broden looks at Walker with a mix of pity and disgust, like he's never been in the company of such an idiot. "I'm sure that you'll figure this out soon enough, but Aaron Littman and Judge Nichols were having an affair."

Broden's disclosure is met with the silence that such a bombshell deserves. How could a law-and-order judge like Faith Nichols and a lion of the bar such as Aaron Littman engage in such flagrantly unethical conduct?

Broden rises. "Thank you both so much for paying us this visit," he says. "You now know what we want, and you know how to reach us, and so I look forward to hearing from you."

Outside Trump Tower, Walker still hasn't calmed down. The vein in his neck is actually pulsating.

"You know we're not doing this, Kevin."

"I know," Lacey says. "We're not giving Nicolai Garkov immunity for two dozen murders. But that wasn't the purpose of what just went on back there."

"Sounded like it to me."

"No . . . that was cover. They wanted to put Aaron Littman on our radar. That's what that was about. The question is, why him? Garkov could have said anybody killed her, right? I mean, the judge's husband, a random mugger . . . anyone. But he specifically said *Aaron Littman*. There's got to be a reason for that."

"Maybe it's just like I said. He doesn't want to pay his legal bill."

Lacey smiles weakly, but he's already a step ahead. "No. Seriously, I'll bet you this: Garkov's telling us the truth about an affair between Littman and Nichols. Broden's smart enough to know we'd never offer Garkov immunity. This entire get-together was solely to make sure we were put on the right track. And if Garkov knew Littman was banging the judge . . . wow, that explains why he hired Littman in the first place." Lacey pauses, putting the pieces together in his mind first, and then says: "That motherfucker was blackmailing his own lawyer to turn around and blackmail the judge. He can't admit it to us without incriminating himself . . . and so he needed a way for us to figure it out on our own."

Walker looks hard at his colleague. Lacey may be a jack-off of the first order, but right now, damn, he's onto something.

26

The term is *shadow counsel.* At least that's what Stuart thinks it is. He heard Faith use it when she was in private practice. All he really knows about it is that the representation is to stay secret and that Faith hated it.

He didn't use the words *shadow counsel* when setting up this meeting with Jennifer Bennett. But after the security guard in the lobby knew immediately who he was, he wished he had. The last thing he wants is for people to know that Faith Nichols's widower visited a high-powered law firm.

"Stuart," Jennifer says when she enters the conference room where he's been for the last ten minutes. "I'm so sorry to make you wait. I was on a conference call and just couldn't get off." She says this with a smile but then catches herself, and with a much more somber tone, says, "So, how are you?"

"Somewhat in shock, actually."

"I wanted to say something to you yesterday at the memorial service, but there were just so many people around that I thought I'd give you some space. But I've been thinking about Faith . . . all the time, actually. I just can't believe that she's gone. I owe Faith so much. I mean, if it weren't for her, I know I wouldn't be here right now."

As she speaks, Stuart begins to catalog all the ways Faith undoubtedly saw herself in Jennifer. The most obvious, of course, is that they're both beautiful, in a way that defies the odds, unless you're on a movie set. Sometimes when he and Faith were watching some police procedural on television, *The Mentalist* or *Bones*, Stuart would say, *Is there any workplace on earth in which three-quarters of the people in any given room look like models? You'd think that someone as observant as Patrick Jane or as smart as Temperance Brennan might note that the odds of such an occurrence are statistically impossible.* Faith's comeback line was always, *What about when Jennifer and I worked together?*

Stuart called Jennifer the moment he left Agent Lacey after the memorial service. He knew he should have told her why he wanted to meet, and why it had to be as soon as possible, but for some reason, he just couldn't get the words out. Even now he wants to be cajoled into telling her, so he can continue to cling to the idea that retaining a lawyer isn't actually necessary, even though he's given up that idea by reaching out to Jennifer in the first place.

"So, what can I help you with, Stuart?" Jennifer finally says.

"I know this sounds crazy," he begins, saying the words as if they've just come to him even though he's run them through his mind a half dozen times, "but this FBI agent came up to me after the service yesterday and asked me some questions. He said it was all standard operating procedure, but I'd already told everything to the police, and this FBI guy . . . he seemed to have more of an agenda, if you know what I mean. Anyway, Faith always said that being involved in the justice system without a lawyer was as stupid as taking out your own appendix, and so . . ."

He was hoping that Jennifer would relieve his anxiety with a wave of her hand and say, *Why on earth are you concerned? No one in a million years would think that you killed Faith.* But what he gets is the opposite: a troubled look confirming his worst suspicions.

"You were absolutely right to come see me," she says. "Spouses are always the primary suspects. The sad truth is that some of them do end up in jail, and it would be naïve to think that sometimes they're not in there by mistake."

As if that weren't enough to suggest Stuart should be engaged in a full-fledged panic, Jennifer starts talking about things like conflict checks and opening a matter and retainer agreements and bringing on an associate.

"Hold on, Jennifer . . . I really thought that we'd just talk for fifteen minutes and then you'd be like . . . shadow counsel. Is that the term?"

Jennifer smiles, and for a moment Stuart thinks that perhaps the world is not ending. But then she says, "I'm so sorry, Stuart. I forgot for a second that you're not a lawyer. If Faith were here, she'd understand all of this without a second thought. I can't even begin to imagine what you're going through. First, there's the horror of Faith's murder and then the FBI—people you think you can trust to catch her killer—are suggesting that *you're* the one who might have done this. It's surreal, right?"

"I was going to say Kafkaesque," Stuart says.

"Okay, so let me try to put you at ease a little bit. This is a process. It's a scary one, I know. But it's still a process. I've always found that the more you're prepared for what's going to happen, the less frightening it is, so why don't I give you a step-by-step of what to expect. Okay?"

"That'd be great," Stuart says.

"First thing is that I know that Faith would want me to take extra-good care of you, which is what I'm going to do. But I can't do that until the representation is official. That means you sign a retainer agreement, and we have to charge you a retainer. Now, normally it's a hundred thousand dollars in a matter like this, but because . . . because Faith's family here, we'll only ask you for fifty. I charge seven fifty an hour, and I'll be working with an associate, who, depending how senior he or she is, will charge anywhere between three fifty and the high fours. If we don't use the retainer, we'll refund the difference, and if we exhaust the retainer, we'll ask you to replenish it. Sound fair?"

Fair is not the first word that pops into Stuart's mind. He wants to ask how many people ever receive a refund, but he's pretty sure he already knows the answer.

"Okay," Stuart says instead.

"Good. Now the next step is for us to do a very thorough debriefing so that I understand everything you told law enforcement and the types of questions that they were asking you. This will allow me to assess whether we can go in to see them again."

"Again?" Stuart says, hearing the panic in his voice.

"Yes. Our goal is to have a meeting with the prosecutor in charge of the case—not the FBI agent, but the person really calling the shots—and convince him or her that you're not the person who did this."

"Okay. When would we do that?"

"In the first instance it's not so much *when* as it is *if.* The only way that you can go in is if the story you tell them is going to be believed. And I won't know the answer to that until I hear the facts from you."

She doesn't let any time elapse for Stuart to proclaim his innocence before saying, "And there's no reason to put that debriefing off, and lots of reasons to get out ahead of this, so why don't we get right down to it? I trust you to wire the retainer tomorrow."

Jennifer reaches for a legal pad and for the next two hours she asks Stuart questions, most of which concern the thirty or so minutes between the time Stuart came home from work on the last night of Faith's life and when she told him that she was going to the gym. By and large, she approaches the facts from the vantage point of asking what the police and the FBI asked and how Stuart responded, rather than inquiring about the facts themselves.

When the Q-and-A ends, Jennifer rocks back in her chair, twirling her pen. Stuart knows better than to interrupt, as he has the feeling of a patient awaiting his test results.

"Stuart, I don't want to add to your worries," Jennifer says, "but you wouldn't be here if you didn't already know that you're at some risk. And what you need from me is not friendship or false assurances, but hard-nosed legal advice. So, here it is: you have every reason in the world to be concerned."

"I didn't kill my wife, Jennifer," Stuart says. "You have to believe me."

The moment the words come out, he feels the full weight of how serious this has become. He's actually denying being a murderer.

"I know you didn't," Jennifer says, but to Stuart it seems too pat, like something Jennifer is saying to be polite. The legal equivalent of *So nice to meet you.*

That would be bad enough, but Jennifer's not finished. "I do get the feeling you're not telling me the whole story, however. And if I'm getting that feeling, you'd better believe that the FBI has it too. Those guys never think anybody's being straight with them, and that might be the reason you got the impression that the agent . . . what was the term you used? Had an agenda? So, this is the part where I explain to you that whatever you say to me is subject to attorney-client privilege, and that means I'm duty-bound never to disclose it without your permission. Faith and I were close, and so I understand that there may be reluctance on your part to tell me certain things about your relationship with her, or even about her . . . but—and this is critically important—if that's the case, then you should get another lawyer. Someone who didn't know her. And you should do that right now, because you can't keep information from me and expect that I'm going to be able to do my best by you."

"Can I ask you a hypothetical question?" Stuart says.

He knows from Faith's war stories that hypotheticals are the loophole to the attorney ethical code. A client suggests that—*hypothetically*—he committed a crime, and the lawyer explains the *hypothetical* advice that would be given in such a case. The dubious theory on which the exercise rests is that because it's hypothetical, there's no perjury problem if the client later tells a completely different story on the witness stand.

"Sure," Jennifer says, not seeming put off by this transition.

"If I suspected, or let's say even *more* than suspected, that Faith was involved with someone else . . . would that be good or bad for me?"

Stuart wonders if Jennifer already knew about Faith's affair. Would she tell him if she did? Probably not, he concludes. Best friend privilege being right up there with that of attorney-client. Perhaps that's even the reason that Jennifer so quickly saw through the story of marital bliss that Stuart recounted to law enforcement. Maybe Faith previously told Jennifer all about their problems.

"So the *hypothetical* you're positing is one where a husband knows his wife has been unfaithful, and then the wife is murdered?" Jennifer asks. "Do I have the *hypothetical* facts right?"

Stuart nods. He's already forgotten this is supposed to be speculative.

Jennifer considers the fact pattern for a moment and then says, "Okay. So my view, under this hypothetical set of facts, is that the husband should stay quiet about the affair. One reason is that you already denied it, and I'd just as soon not hand the FBI proof that you've lied to them. But more importantly, the issue only comes up if the FBI concludes the murder is some type of crime of passion. Faith's personal life doesn't matter if the attack is a random mugging or the killer is someone out for revenge for a judicial ruling. If the focus of the investigation turns to people with whom she had a romantic attachment, however, then the fact she was having an affair is highly relevant. But in that case her lover also becomes a suspect. The reason I say that you should keep quiet about it is because I'm assuming the FBI will discover the affair without your help. I take it that the FBI agent didn't share any of that with you during your meeting, did he?"

"No," Stuart says, fully recognizing that Jennifer has now abandoned the pretext of this being a hypothetical. "But he asked me if she was having an affair, and I said she wasn't."

"Okay . . . Well, maybe they haven't discovered proof of the affair, or maybe the agent just didn't want to tip his hand. But at some point, they'll come back to you with that evidence." Jennifer rubs her face, deep in concentration. "The danger for you now is that if you know about Faith's infidelity, then you have even more of a motive: on top of the financial angle that they're already onto, there's also jealousy to consider. Are you with me here?"

Stuart nods. He understands all too well. Things do not look good for him.

As if she senses that he's desperate for good news, Jennifer smiles. "*But* . . . if she *was* having an affair and you didn't know about it, then the affair is irrelevant to you. You're not a jealous husband. You're not fearful of a divorce and its financial implications. For all you know, you're the happiest married couple on earth."

For the first time since he's arrived, Stuart can feel himself relax. "Oh, got it. Thanks, that's what I thought too," he says.

"That's not the end of it, though." Stuart thinks that Jennifer is going to call him on this being a hypothetical, but that's not the way she plays it at all. "I'd have a different response if I thought the FBI was going to find evidence that you knew about the affair and then lied to them about it. People don't lie to the FBI to protect their wives' reputations. They lie to protect themselves. So—hypothetically speaking, of course—if the husband is going to keep the affair to himself, he'd better be damn sure the FBI doesn't find evidence that says he knew about it before the murder."

27

Rachel cleared out most of her work over the coming weeks so she could devote her full attention to the Garkov case. As a result, she now finds herself in the very rare situation of having downtime. She knows her type-A personality, as well as the partner billing committee, won't permit this state of affairs to persist very long, but that doesn't mean she can't bask in it for a few hours.

As is so often the case, her thoughts immediately turn to Aaron. Although she knows her glee over the possibility that Aaron may be on the road to a divorce is unseemly, she can't deny that's precisely how she feels. And while their "date" didn't lead back to his hotel room, she's now convinced it's only a matter of time.

And there is no better time to take that next step than after the prom.

Her mind flashes on the image of Aaron in formal wear, looking like James Bond, right down to holding a martini, shaken, not stirred. When she conjures herself standing beside him, she realizes that something new is called for, a dress that is going to blow Aaron Littman's mind.

She types into her search engine *Dolce & Gabbana.* She could walk up Madison and actually shop in the company's showroom, or better yet, travel the even shorter distance to Bergdorf's or Barneys, but she's still not ready to make that extra commitment to decadence—shopping in public during a workday.

A few screens in, she comes upon a silk chiffon in platinum, with two jeweled straps. It makes the model in the picture look like she has a chest, and Rachel figures she's a cup size bigger, if not two, so the effect on her will be that much greater.

She has just completed inputting her credit card information when the phone rings. The caller ID says "Restricted Number."

Rachel figures it's most likely a snotty judicial clerk about to tell her that some filing she made last week has been bounced. She considers whether to let the call go to voice mail, but law clerks are often difficult to get on the phone, and so she answers.

"Rachel London."

"Ms. London?"

She knows from the way he's said her name that it's not a clerk. The caller is a man, not a boy.

"Yes?"

"This is Special Agent Kevin Lacey of the Federal Bureau of Investigation."

Rachel has at least ten clients who are currently subjects of ongoing FBI investigations, and she hasn't a single clue as to which one this call is about. The FBI is notorious for putting people through the wringer and then not following up again for months, sometimes even years. She's had clients who gave the FBI interviews and were contacted three, and once four, years later, always on the eve of the statute of limitations' running out, and been told that the U.S. Attorney's Office was about to indict.

"And which one of my very lucky clients are you calling about, Agent Lacey?"

"I'm afraid *you're* the client on this one, Ms. London," he says in a voice that's too confident for Rachel's liking. "I'm investigating the murder of Judge Faith Nichols, and I wanted to talk to you a little about that."

There's a standard operating procedure at Cromwell Altman for calls with the FBI: act friendly, get as much information as you can without giving up any, and when that effort has been exhausted, say that you need to discuss the issues with your client.

She's never had a case without a client, however.

"I'm . . . not sure I understand," she says to stall him. "If I didn't know better, I'd think that the FBI is trying to encourage me to divulge attorney-client privileged information concerning Nicolai Garkov."

"The FBI would never think of such a thing," Lacey says in a tone that makes it difficult for Rachel to discern whether he's being sarcastic. "I'm just making a very straightforward courtesy request for you to come down and speak with us, informally. If we ask you about something that you believe is privileged, you don't have to answer. And I hate to have to resort to clichés about this, but, as I'm sure you understand, this is the easy way. The alternative is that we'll issue a grand jury subpoena, in which case you'll still have to speak with us, but it'll be under oath and on the record."

Just as Cromwell Altman has an SOP, so does law enforcement, and Lacey just followed it: first *ask* a witness to talk, but if the witness says no, *compel* the discussion with a subpoena.

Rachel expects Lacey to fill in a little more about what's going on here. But instead he says, "We're willing to offer you the full queen-for-a-day protection, Ms. London."

This is the government's carrot for cooperation. Whatever Rachel tells them during the meeting will not be used against her if the government later indicts her. It's not the best protection in the world, but at least it's something.

The fact that Lacey would even offer it is cause for concern, however. It tells Rachel that there might be some universe in which she's at risk of prosecution.

That's enough for her to decide it's time to end the conversation.

"Well, Agent Lacey, I'm really going to need to discuss this issue with my partners, as well as with Mr. Garkov," she says.

"Ms. London, while I appreciate you have client concerns, we're on a very tight time frame. I can't even say it's on a fast track. It's more like a rocket ship to the moon. So I don't have much flexibility with regard to time. If I don't hear back from you within the next twenty-four hours, you can expect a subpoena."

"Can we make it forty-eight?"

"Wish I could, but I can't."

Christ. They were really taking a hard line on this.

Aaron knows it's Rachel from the sound of her knock. She has a particular rhythm, although he'd be hard-pressed to repeat it exactly.

His first thought is that she wants to do a postmortem on last night, something that he'd just as soon avoid, if possible. It's as close to an inviolate rule as there is: nothing good is ever accomplished by discussing a kiss.

When she walks in, however, Aaron can tell that she's got something more important than that on her mind. She looks as if there's been a death in her family.

Even before sitting down, Rachel says, "I think I need a lawyer."

Damn. It's even worse than he thought a moment ago.

"Let me guess," he says, trying mightily to maintain a lighthearted tone. "An FBI special agent named Kevin Lacey just called you."

She looks like she could be knocked over with a feather. "Yeah, how'd you know?"

"You're not the only one on his call list. I just spoke with him too."

Aaron held out some flicker of hope that Lacey was asking him to meet to have Aaron formally assert the attorney-client privilege on Garkov's behalf. But there's no reason for the FBI to have two lawyers do it. That they've reached out to Rachel can only mean one thing: the FBI has Aaron in its sights.

And therefore he needs to be extremely careful. The FBI will question Rachel at length about this conversation, so his next words should be as self-serving as possible.

"No reason to look so glum, Rachel. Garkov must have shut them down, and so they're trying to get something on him by going through us."

Even to himself, this sounds like whistling past the graveyard. Aaron is reasonably sure that Rachel has already reached the same conclusion he has, that this isn't about Garkov at all.

"Well, I'm glad that if I'm going to jail, you'll be there to keep me company," she says with a nervous laugh.

Although Aaron's thankful for the levity, he'd just as soon not be making jokes that could be misconstrued. "So . . . what did you tell the very special agent?" he asks.

"That I was concerned about the attorney-client privilege and needed to speak with you. He told me that if he didn't hear from me in twenty-four hours, I'd be getting a subpoena. I tried to push back, but he wasn't having it."

"That doesn't give us much time, now, does it? Let me talk to Sam about how to handle this. Until then, don't talk to anyone about this."

As soon as Rachel leaves, Aaron walks into Sam Rosenthal's office. He assumes he looks every bit as nervous as Rachel did a few moments ago.

"Sam, I just got a call from the FBI. They want me to come in on Judge Nichols's murder. They called Rachel too."

Rosenthal is stoic. Lawyer 101—never let your client think that you're worried.

"Does Rachel know anything that can hurt you?" he asks.

"No."

"Are you sure? She saw a lot of you and Judge Nichols together."

"In court, Sam. She saw us together in court. But, to answer your question, how can I be sure? I didn't think *you* knew."

Rosenthal sighs, as if mentally stepping back, and then says, "It's probably a safe bet that the U.S. Attorney's Office already knows about the affair anyway. That must be why you're getting this attention. Unfortunately, that also means we need to go outside the firm for Rachel's representation. You know that they're going to scream conflict of interest if I show up representing you and her, and I don't think that's something we want to litigate."

Aaron feels like a weight has come off his shoulders. As long as Rosenthal's in his corner, he feels safe.

"Thank you, Sam."

"For what?"

"For agreeing to represent me?"

Rosenthal laughs, as if the mere thought of his not doing so would be absurd. "Of course, Aaron. I'm with you. Always. Never forget that."

Aaron nods. "Richard Leeds," he says. "For Rachel."

Leeds was the firm's usual go-to conflict counsel. He didn't work at Cromwell Altman in the technical sense that his paycheck didn't come from the firm, but he relied on Aaron, and lawyers beholden to Aaron, for most of his clients. Which meant that Leeds would do everything within his power to make sure that nothing Rachel told the U.S. Attorney's Office would hurt Aaron or Cromwell Altman.

"Okay," Rosenthal says, "I'll reach out to Fitz and see what I can get out of him about the way this is breaking. Then I'll tell Leeds that he's our guy for Rachel."

One last issue remained: the FBI's request to speak to Aaron.

"You know you can't go in, right?" Rosenthal finally says.

"I realize the problems that would arise as a result, yes."

They're both experienced enough that those difficulties do not need to be articulated. In any interview, Aaron would be asked about his relationship with Judge Nichols, and if he answered truthfully, he'd be serving up his motive on a silver platter.

Worse still, if he told them that he met Faith in the park on the night she was killed, they'd likely arrest him on the spot.

28

That night, Aaron goes home. It's been less than a week since Cynthia told him to get out, when he confessed his affair with Faith. He's been away from home for much longer periods of time, of course. His record is four months—this was about seven or eight years ago, when he tried a case in Albuquerque.

It feels different this time, however. He's unwelcome.

He called earlier to ask Cynthia if he could come by, explaining that he had something he needed to discuss with her face-to-face. She was cool on the phone, but she didn't make him beg, at least. Nevertheless, he knows his wife well enough that he has no doubt she's still furious, and he has every reason to believe that she's only going to be even angrier when she hears why he's there.

He enters the apartment and calls out her name. "I'm in the living room," she says.

Cynthia is sitting in one of the matching leather chairs, which Aaron knows is her favorite spot in the apartment. Diana Krall is playing on the stereo, a Cynthia favorite, and there's a glass of red wine on the table beside her.

She's still in her work clothes, a pair of gray slacks and a black silk blouse. She looks good, he thinks. Almost disconcertingly so, as if his absence has been a boon to her.

Cynthia must see Aaron spying the wine, or else she realizes that she's the host in this situation. "Do you want something to drink?" she asks. "There's a bottle of Chianti already open."

"No, thank you." He looks past the living room, down the hallway that leads to the bedrooms. "Are the girls home?"

Cynthia shakes her head. "Lindsay's at rehearsal and Sam had a yearbook meeting. Lindsay called and asked if they could go to Starbucks with some friends afterward."

"Have the girls said anything? About my absence, I mean."

"I told them that you were traveling."

Aaron nods. "How have you been, Cyn?"

"Me? Oh, I'm just peachy." She looks even angrier than her words, which is a tough feat. "You're still wearing your wedding band, so I'm assuming that you're not here to ask me for a divorce."

Aaron instinctively looks down at his ring finger. It hasn't even occurred to him to remove the platinum band. He quickly eyes Cynthia's hand. She, too, is wearing the symbol of their union.

He decides it will be best if he just gets to the point. "I got a call from someone at the FBI. I think they might know that I was with her that night."

Cynthia's previous posture as furious wife has vanished. The blood drains from her face and she slumps back in her chair.

"On second thought, maybe I am going to have a drink," Aaron says.

He walks over to the kitchen, and like he did the night Faith was killed, he pulls out a bottle of scotch and a tumbler. After pouring himself a generous amount, he takes it over to the chair opposite Cynthia.

Aaron takes a long, slow swallow. "I've asked Sam Rosenthal to represent me in all this, but I think it's important that I move back home. I don't want there to be a record of my staying at the hotel because—"

"Yes, of course. Because you want us to look happy. Have to keep up appearances," Cynthia says with a tight-lipped smile.

"Yeah . . . So is it okay if I come back home?"

"Do I have a choice?"

"Please, Cynthia. We don't have to share a bed or anything like that. I know how angry you are, and believe me, I know it's totally justified, but there are things going on besides you and me here. Do you really want to see me in jail over this?"

"So I take it that the answer to my question is no. If I don't want my children's father in jail for murder, I don't have much of a choice, do I?"

"I guess not."

"Then welcome home, Aaron."

"Thank you," he says with some relief.

Cynthia isn't going to be so easily placated, however. "Oh no, thank *you*, Aaron."

There's no reason to prolong this, and so Aaron quickly says, "I'm going to go back to the hotel and get my things. I'll be back in about an hour."

Cynthia isn't finished with him yet. "Just one more thing, Aaron. I don't want to see you moping around here about her. Not for a second. If you're going to live in this house, you're going to understand that her murder wasn't a tragedy. If anything, it *averted* a tragedy. Just remember that."

Aaron returns a little more than an hour later. His daughters are now home.

He visits them in the order they are usually dealt with—Lindsay and Samantha. Hardly ever Samantha and Lindsay. Perhaps that's because Lindsay is the eldest, albeit by twenty-two minutes. But it's also because she demands the attention, being the much more aggressive of the two. The one more like him, Aaron thinks.

Although she matches her father more in temperament, Lindsay is the spitting image of her mother. The same sparkling emerald eyes and radiant smile. He catches himself almost every time he sees her, remembering Cynthia the first time he looked in her direction.

"So, what's going on?" he says.

"Oh, hey, Dad. NM."

" 'NM'?"

"Not much."

"Has speech become so labored for you that you need to abbreviate *not much*?"

"Mhm," Lindsay says, but this time with a smile.

"I haven't chatted with you in a while. Catch me up."

Lindsay doesn't look up at him, but instead focuses intently on her iPhone, tapping away at the keys.

"Nothing to say," she says, still tapping.

"How's the play going? All good there?"

"Mhm."

Aaron laughs to himself, as he's sure that Lindsay finds nothing odd about this exchange. "Okay, then. I'm going to see if your sister is as scintillating a conversationalist as you."

He finds Samantha in a similar pose as her sister—lying on her stomach in bed, except instead of staring at her phone, Samantha is looking at her laptop screen. Unlike Lindsay, who possesses more of a classic beauty, there's something exotic about Samantha's looks. Aaron imagines that even now, the boys think Sam's the sexy one of the Littman girls, which might account for why she's had no fewer than six "serious" boyfriends over the past two years.

"Hold on," Samantha says the moment Aaron steps toward her. "Hey, Dad. How was your trip?"

Aaron falters, momentarily forgetting that Cynthia had told the girls he was traveling, but then he says, "Good. Glad to be back home."

"I'm talking to Jason," she says.

"Jason, huh. How about taking a minute away from Jason to talk to me? I won't be too long. I promise."

She doesn't agree, but instead turns back to the computer screen, which must be where Jason exists. "I gotta go. Later." Then she closes the laptop. "What?" she says.

"Nothing," Aaron says. "I just haven't seen you in a few days. Tell me . . . I don't know, tell me anything."

Samantha is more of a caregiver than Lindsay, and so it doesn't surprise Aaron that she's going to give him what he wants—some attention. He doesn't know if that quality is going to make Samantha happier later in life, but he's confident it will at least make Samantha's life partner happier than Lindsay's.

"Let's see . . . ," Samantha says. "So, Jason got mad at me today because I told him that I didn't think his presentation in English was very good because . . . it really wasn't. And he was telling me that I need to support everything he does and tell him it's great, even if I think it's crap, and so I told him that I thought *that* was crap, and just because we're, you know, boyfriend-girlfriend doesn't mean that I've had a lobotomy and can't tell the difference between an insightful presentation about *The Stranger* and one that makes it seem as if he didn't even read the book."

"Camus," Aaron says, because that's all he can think to say.

"Yeah. *The Stranger.* Anyway, it turned into this whole big thing. You know, he apologized and all to me after, but I'd already had enough and I said, you know, whatever."

"But you guys are okay now?"

"Yeah . . . but he's such a jerk sometimes."

Aaron smiles. He can only imagine his daughter will be saying that about the men in her life for a long time to come.

"I'm glad you're home, Dad," Samantha says. "Can I call Jason back now?"

"Yeah, sure," Aaron says, and kisses his daughter on the head.

Aaron spends that evening in the guest room. He's done this before a handful of times in his marriage, but usually out of some sense of pique, and always under circumstances where he knew he could grant himself dispensation to return to his bedroom.

Tonight he takes a moment to reflect on how lucky he is to be living this life. He wonders why he's so rarely stopped to consider his good fortune, although he assumes that few people ever do, and it's probably even rarer for those on top of the world to consider how fleeting their success might be.

And now, with all of it coming apart around him, he spends these sleepless moments trying to figure out a way to salvage what's important. It doesn't take him very long at all to realize that the professional repercussions are meaningless to him. All that matters is that he make things right with Cynthia and his daughters.

29

The Viand is not the most upscale meeting place that Thomas J. Fitzpatrick—Fitz, as he's known to friends and those who like to pretend they're closer to the U.S. attorney than they actually are—could have chosen. The restaurant's official name is the Viand Café, but other than the fact that a chef's salad costs twenty-two dollars, it's like any diner anywhere—right down to the vinyl booths, linoleum floors, and breakfast that can be ordered anytime.

Sam Rosenthal arrives early and takes a seat in the last booth in the back. It's a habit he's adopted since the accident, so as not to look frail by entering a room with the use of a cane. Rosenthal's always viewed litigation as combat, and so even though he's twice as fit as Fitz, he doesn't want to show his adversary the slightest trace of weakness.

The meeting was set for eight o'clock, but at eight fifteen, Fitz still hasn't arrived. Three years as U.S. attorney have made Fitz accustomed to people running on his schedule.

Rosenthal sits there, nursing a pretty bad cup of coffee, until Fitz finally enters the diner at eight twenty. He offers Rosenthal a wave to signify his arrival and then takes a good five minutes to make it the twenty-five feet from the door to the back of the restaurant, stopping at each booth to shake some hands.

Since getting the U.S. attorney gig, Fitz has dropped twenty pounds, shaved off his beard, and stepped up his wardrobe. But even with the makeover, he's still far from a handsome man—his jowls hang like saddlebags on his face and his chin is almost nonexistent.

When Fitz finally makes it to Rosenthal's table, he slides into the booth and smiles at the waitress, a young woman in her twenties who's wearing too much makeup. The smile is all it takes for her to bring a cup of coffee to the table.

"Thanks, Sylvie," Fitz says to her. "This here is my good friend Sam Rosenthal. Sam, meet Sylvie, the finest waitress in the city."

Rosenthal smiles. "Do you want a warm-up, hon?" Sylvie asks.

"No, I'm still good," Rosenthal says.

Fitz pours a splash of milk and mixes in two teaspoons of sugar in the time it takes Sylvie to pull her order pad from her apron pocket. "What can I get you, gentlemen?" she says with a smile.

"You should have the waffles, Sam. Second to none."

"I'm game if you are."

"I truly wish I could, but I can't. I got a fire raging back at the office, so I'm afraid this is going to be an in-and-out thing for me."

Rosenthal's first impulse is to tell Fitz off. First he's almost half an hour late, and now he's only allotted a few minutes? Rosenthal stifles the impulse, however. Even five minutes with Fitz is better than nothing.

"In that case, I think I'll stick with the coffee," Rosenthal says.

Sylvie closes her pad and briskly moves back to the counter to wait on a newly arrived patron. When she's far enough away from the booth that Rosenthal assumes they won't be overheard, he says, "I appreciate you making time to see me, Fitz."

"My pleasure, Sam. What can I do for you?"

"Well, I'm sure you know the FBI agent on the Judge Nichols investigation has reached out to Aaron Littman and also to one of my junior partners, a woman named Rachel London. She was second-seating Aaron on the Garkov case. We're going to give your office our fullest cooperation, of course, but we also have to be concerned about our client confidences. And, to be frank . . . it seems like overkill to make two lawyers tell you the same thing. I think one should suffice, and based just on billable rate, we'd rather it be Rachel. If you need Aaron at trial later, that's fine, but for information-gathering purposes, Rachel can give all you need on Garkov, consistent with our professional obligations, of course."

Fitz takes a long sip of coffee. "How long have we known each other, Sam?"

"Twenty-five years, I'd guess."

"I thought about it on my way over here. I met you when I was the number two guy prosecuting state senator what's his name, the guy in the Bronx. I remembered because it was 1984 and that guy wouldn't shut up about how everything that was happening was like from the George Orwell book."

"Okay. I stand corrected. We've known each other since 1984."

"So . . . that type of longevity requires that we dispense with the bullshit, don't you think?"

"If you've got some non-bullshit to share, Fitz, please, by all means, let's hear it."

"All right, I will. For starters, don't sit there with a straight face and tell me that you don't understand why we'd want to talk to Aaron. You wouldn't be here if you didn't already know that he's in a shitload of trouble."

"C'mon, Fitz," Rosenthal says, leaning closer. "This is Aaron we're talking about. *Aaron Littman.* Do you really think he murdered a federal judge, for chrissakes?"

"Look, I know how you feel about the man. Surrogate son and all that, but . . . facts are facts, Sam. I'm sure I'm not telling you anything you don't know, but we have evidence of the affair, and that it was going on during the Eric Matthews case. I mean . . . what the hell was Aaron thinking?"

Damn. They know about the affair. At least that means Rosenthal can stop maintaining the façade with Fitz that he has no idea what's going on.

"That's for the bar association to deal with," he says. "Not the fucking United States Attorney's Office."

"Ordinarily I'd agree with you, Sam. But, you see, I got a dead federal judge on my hands. Somebody killed her. You want to tell me whodunit?"

"Yes. Not Aaron. You know as well as I do that you have a terrorist with a pretty goddamned good motive sitting under house arrest this very moment over at Trump Tower. And from what I hear, everything wasn't paradise in Judge Nichols's marriage, either. That's two good places where you should be looking instead."

"We're running down every direction, Sam. But one of those paths leads to Aaron. You'd do him a lot of good if you bring him in to talk to us."

"Like I said, we're going to cooperate with you as best as we can, but not if you're engaging in some kind of witch hunt."

The battle lines have now been drawn, and they can both read into what the other is saying. Fitz is telling his old buddy Rosenthal that his protégé Aaron Littman is a prime suspect in a federal judge's murder, and Rosenthal is telling his good friend Fitz to go straight to hell.

Fitz reaches into his breast pocket for his phone and quickly scrolls through a few messages. "I'm really sorry, Sam . . . but like I said, I got an emergency back at the ranch. Look, it's your call whether you bring Aaron in, and I don't need to tell you that his silence says a lot. But you need to represent him as you see fit. I just don't see why either you or he would want to play it that way. If he's not the guy, okay, come on in and tell us that. Otherwise, how can you blame us if we reach the opposite conclusion?"

Rosenthal rises with Fitz. He's tempted to show his annoyance by refusing to shake Fitz's hand but thinks better of acting out in such a juvenile fashion.

"Thanks for meeting with me, Fitz. You'll be making a big mistake if you focus on Aaron. Believe me on that."

"Good seeing you too, Sam. You think about bringing him in, so I don't make that mistake."

The moment Fitz leaves the booth, Rosenthal sees that whatever emergency requires his immediate attention is not so great as to delay him from shaking some more hands and slapping a few backs on his way out of the diner.

Rosenthal decides to salvage something positive from this meeting.

"Excuse me, Sylvie . . . I've changed my mind. Can I get an order of those waffles?"

30

The thing about being an architect is that there are very few pressure-packed moments. Every day is more or less the same. There might be a rush when pitching a new client or when a project is finally unveiled, but it's not like there's a point when you need to rise to the occasion or else all is lost.

Stuart remembers Faith telling him that being a lawyer is quite different. Although she always made clear it was far from the thrill-a-minute ride portrayed on television, with a different high-stakes trial every week, she said that there were occasions that rivaled the unfettered excitement of the most important athletic contest. Faith believed that was the most apt analogy: as in sports, in trial work you prepared for months and then entered the arena, where decisions you made on the fly would lead to victory or defeat.

Stuart has never played sports, but while waiting to be interviewed by Assistant U.S. Attorney Victoria Donnelly, he finally understands what Faith meant. His every sense is heightened, and nothing but adrenaline pulsates through his veins.

Jennifer Bennett sits on one end of the table with Ryan Oberlander, an associate at her firm, on Stuart's other side. Stuart will end up paying twenty-five hundred dollars for the pleasure of Ryan's company, but Jennifer explained it was necessary to have a designated note-taker present.

"Best case, it's a waste of a few thousand dollars," she said. "Worst case, he's an insurance policy against a one thousand one."

When Jennifer started to explain, Stuart told her that he understood the lingo. Faith had talked enough about cases involving the charge of lying to a government official for him to know that it was simply referred to by its section number in the criminal code: 1001.

The other side enters the room en masse. Jennifer warned him that prosecutors often travel in packs, but Stuart doesn't like the feeling of being so outnumbered.

Victoria Donnelly introduces her entourage. "This is FBI special agent Kevin Lacey, whom I believe you've already met, Mr. Christensen." Stuart thinks she says this with snark, as if in that one meeting he already hurt his cause. "And also from the FBI is Special Agent Timothy Walker. Next to him is my colleague here at the U.S. Attorney's Office, Leonard Stanton, and Christopher Covello, the head of the Criminal Division." As if that weren't enough people to sit in on a single interview, Donnelly adds, "We may be joined by the U.S. attorney at some point as well."

There are things about Victoria Donnelly that might be considered attractive—her eyes are a deep blue, almost turquoise, and her hair is a long and luxurious chestnut, like out of a shampoo commercial—but her overall thickness overrules everything else, so that she's one of those people of whom you say, *She has a pretty face*, and it's understood to mean she might be attractive if she weren't thirty to forty pounds overweight.

"So, Fitz is now sitting in on witness interviews?" Jennifer says.

"He does when they involve the murder of a federal judge," Donnelly replies curtly. "I would think Mr. Christensen would appreciate the U.S. attorney's personal involvement in bringing his wife's murderer to justice."

In preparing for this interview, Jennifer told Stuart not to say anything unless it was in response to a direct question, but he assumes the instruction doesn't apply now. "Of course," Stuart says, "anything and everything you can do is greatly appreciated."

Jennifer softly pats Stuart's hand, her way of telling him that he's now said enough. When he turns a quarter to catch her expression, he sees a faint smile, which he interprets to mean that he's done well.

Donnelly begins exactly the way Jennifer said she would. Nonetheless, it sounds significantly more frightening coming from her than it did when Jennifer said the same thing during prep.

"Mr. Christensen, I am going to ask you some questions this morning. As I'm sure your counsel has explained to you, even though you are not formally under oath, that makes no difference regarding your legal obligation to tell the truth. It is a felony pursuant to title eighteen, section one thousand one, of the U.S. criminal code to lie to a federal officer in the course of an investigation, and we are all federal officers for the purposes of that provision. So, if you lie to us today, you will be committing a crime for which you may be imprisoned. You are here voluntarily, and therefore you may end this interview at any time you choose. However, be advised that we will draw certain conclusions from your refusal to cooperate with our investigation, and we have the power to subpoena you to testify before a grand jury. If that were to occur, you can only refuse to answer if you elect to assert your Fifth Amendment privilege against self-incrimination."

She pauses and then smiles at Stuart. "Do you understand what I've just explained to you?"

He wants to say, *Yeah, that I'm so screwed.* Instead he says, "I do."

"And are you nevertheless willing to continue with this interview?"

Stuart turns to Jennifer, and after she offers a subtle nod, he says, "Yes."

The preliminaries complete, Donnelly looks like a switch has flipped in her head. Her game face is now on.

"Mr. Christensen," she says, "since you met with FBI special agent Lacey, have you had time to consider whether anything you said to him during that meeting was incorrect?"

"No," Stuart says, following Jennifer's instruction to answer as succinctly as possible.

"No what?" Donnelly says, as if she's cross-examining a hostile witness. "No, you haven't had time to consider the issue, or no, you believe everything you said to Special Agent Lacey was completely accurate?"

"C'mon, Victoria," Jennifer says. "Try to remember that Mr. Christensen lost his wife only a few days ago. A little more respect would be appropriate."

"I'm sorry if you don't find my tone sufficiently cuddly, Jennifer, but I tend to get that way when witnesses lie to the FBI. That's true even if they're the victim's spouse. In fact, that pisses me off even more."

Stuart's heart sinks. They know about Faith's affair. Worse, they know *he* knows.

"You've made your point, Victoria," Jennifer says calmly. "Allow me to make the following proposal: let's adjourn for the moment. I'll talk to my client and go over his recollection of the interview with Agent Lacey, and see if there's anything he thinks might have been misstated or which could have been misconstrued. After I've spoken with him, we can reconvene."

Victoria looks to Covello, who nods. They must have assumed that it would play out exactly like this.

"We're on a very tight time frame here, Jennifer," Donnelly says. "Why doesn't Mr. Christensen step outside for a little bit instead, and we'll explain our concerns to you. After that, you can tell us what protections you'd like for your client in order to proceed with the interview."

"Just give me a moment alone with my client first," Jennifer replies. "To translate all this legalese for him. We'll be right back."

With that, Jennifer gets up and heads to the door, and Stuart follows her. Jennifer doesn't stop walking until she's standing in front of the elevators. Stuart wonders if that's because the offices are bugged.

"Shit," Stuart remarks.

Jennifer shakes her head in disagreement. "No, no. This is good. It's a gift, actually. If they were *really* going after you, they'd be more than happy to have you lie to them right there. That gives them far more leverage. *They want your help*, Stuart. Did you see that no one on their side took notes during the exchange I had with Victoria?" Stuart actually didn't notice that, which he conveys with a stiff head-shake of his own. "Well, that's because they don't want any record that they had to pressure you to get the testimony they want."

"What testimony do they want?"

"That's what they're about to tell me, but I'll bet you anything it's the name of whoever Faith was seeing."

"But I already told Agent Lacey I didn't know Faith was even having an affair."

"They are apparently willing to give you a pass on that. That's what Victoria meant regarding the protection I'd be seeking. They must know about the affair . . . or they suspect it, but they can't prove it. That's where you come in. It's Economics 101—supply and demand. You have something they need, and so they're willing to pay for it. When I go back in there, Donnelly's going to tell me that you lied to Agent Lacey when you said you didn't know that Faith was having an affair. I'll then tell them that Agent Lacey must have misunderstood you, but that's beside the point . . . because the real issue isn't what Agent Lacey might think you said *then*, but that *right now* you're more than willing to tell them that Faith was having an affair. Are you following me?"

"I think so, yeah."

"I'm also going to say that, before I let you talk, I have to make sure that they're not contemplating any type of obstruction or false-statement charge against you. After they give me assurances that you get a full pass, you'll come back in and you'll tell them what they want to hear." She smiles confidently. "Sound like a plan?"

"You're telling me the promise of no charges will include the murder too, right?"

"Definitely. Stuart, they're not offering you this deal unless they already have their sights set on somebody else as Faith's killer. My guess is that whoever Faith was seeing is number one on their list."

"But I don't know who that is," Stuart says. "I knew . . . well, was pretty sure she was screwing around, but I didn't know with who."

Jennifer's smile trails off. "Back to the economics metaphor. You can't buy something with nothing. They want the name, and I don't see you getting a free pass without giving them that."

"I swear, I don't know," Stuart says again. "Believe me, if I did, I'd be more than happy to have that motherfucker fry for killing Faith."

Jennifer takes this in. "Maybe they know. Or at least think they know. How about this: if I can get them to give up the name, will you confirm it for them?"

Stuart pauses, his head spinning, having some difficulty breathing due to the pressure he feels. But he thinks he understands what she's suggesting—that he lie to save himself.

"Sure," he says hesitantly. "If you think that's the way to go."

She looks at him. "Stuart, I'm not telling you to lie, because that would be a crime," Jennifer says with all the conviction of a POW denouncing his country on videotape. "But if they give us a name and that somehow jogs your memory that . . . you saw Faith with this man somewhere, I think the case against you goes away, and the full focus is on the other guy."

She doesn't wink at him when she says this, but it's obviously implied.

Jennifer reappears in the U.S. Attorney's Office's lobby an hour later. Stuart sweated every second of this period, figuring that the longer Jennifer was with the enemy, the worse it was for him.

"Follow me," she says without breaking stride, and heads out of the building. They walk past the security guards stationed in the makeshift structure on the bridge leading to One Saint Andrews Plaza and don't stop until they've reached the center of the plaza, where there is no one within twenty feet of them.

"Aaron Littman," Jennifer says.

"What? The lawyer?" Stuart says in disbelief.

"Yes. They have a theory that Nicolai Garkov hired him to exert pressure on Faith."

Stuart still doesn't understand. "Why would Garkov's lawyer want to kill Faith?"

"It's more complicated than that," Jennifer says, "and I'm not sure that they have evidence that he killed Faith. They played that kind of close to the vest. What they told me was that they did have evidence that he was having an affair with Faith, and they think that's relevant to the investigation."

"What evidence?"

"Apparently Faith and Aaron would meet at the Ritz-Carlton in midtown. The hotel has some evidence. I'm not sure what exactly, but it must not be conclusive because they need you to corroborate it. And I'm really sorry you have to hear this from me."

Stuart rubs his face, as if trying to wake himself up. Even though he was almost sure that Faith had been unfaithful, he still clung to the hope that he was being paranoid. Proof confirming his suspicions, and worse, a name and a face being attached, are more than Stuart bargained for. In his mind's eye he can imagine Aaron Littman, conjuring the photo of him that ran in the *Times* on the day of the Eric Matthews sentence, and he can't help but transpose that image on top of his naked wife.

Jennifer has waited for the shock to sink in, but now she's talking again, going over the next steps. "What they want you to say, Stuart, is that you saw Aaron Littman with Faith at the Ritz-Carlton."

Stuart isn't making eye contact, although he's heard what she said. A rage is running through him now.

"Can you do that, Stuart? Can you tell them that you saw Faith with him at the Ritz-Carlton? You don't have to know the date, although it would be at night, so you'll have to supply some detail about why you were there, where you were standing, that kind of thing. I think the easiest thing to say is that you were suspicious and so you followed Faith. Then you can say that you saw her enter or leave with him, and you've given them what they want. And in return, you get what you want."

"Fuck him," Stuart says quietly. "I'll say whatever they want me to."

31

Rachel London learns that the firm has decided to go outside for her lawyer when she receives a call from Richard Leeds, who tells her that he's spoken to Sam Rosenthal about representing her. The immediate thought that comes to Rachel's mind is disappointment that Aaron didn't break this news himself. Just as quickly, she forgives him, realizing that it makes perfect sense that Aaron and she shouldn't discuss the investigation.

As soon as she starts to feel that Aaron hasn't betrayed her, however, Rachel begins to wonder why she needs conflict-of-interest counsel at all. She knows that the technical reason is that the firm believes that her interests conflict with those of another Cromwell Altman client. But that client certainly isn't Nicolai Garkov, because Aaron is being represented by Sam Rosenthal, and the conflict rules prohibit the same law firm from representing clients with divergent interests.

Which means it's *her* interests and Aaron's that aren't aligned. And that concerns her greatly.

Richard Leeds's law firm is called Leeds, Jonns, and Williams. Stepping off the elevator, Rachel is surprised how much it looks like Cromwell Altman.

Sometimes smaller firms have a home-office feel to them—no receptionist, cramped space, boxes in the hallways, and little, if any, natural light. But Leeds's firm has the trappings of a mega-firm—leather furniture, large conference room, and a view of the Statue of Liberty.

If she didn't know otherwise, Rachel would assume two hundred lawyers work there, rather than the fewer than ten who actually do.

A few minutes after Rachel arrives in reception, a woman with a disproportionately large chest and shoulder-length blond hair, who can't be more than twenty-five years old, introduces herself as "Mr. Leeds's assistant" and escorts Rachel to Leeds's office. That's enough to set Rachel's preconceived notions about Leeds in stone. What senior partner at any law firm has a twentysomething secretary, let alone one who resembles a porn star?

"There she is, the guest of honor," Leeds says when Rachel enters his office. Then he extends a hand. "Rich Leeds," he says as if it's a privilege to meet him.

Leeds is one of those men where the parts are much greater than the whole. If Rachel were to describe him—medium build, good head of sandy hair, nice enough features—it would leave the impression of someone much handsomer than Richard Leeds. She finds something extremely smarmy looking about him, however, reminding her of a carnival barker.

Also in the room is a young woman whom Leeds has not even bothered to introduce. She's pretty too, although in that *for a lawyer* way. Blond hair, thin, and young must be Leeds's type.

"Hi," Rachel says, extending her hand to the woman. "I'm Rachel London." Then she adds, "But I guess you knew that since I'm the client."

"Alyssa Sanders," the blonde says. "It's nice to meet you."

Rachel surveys Leeds's office. It's the corner, naturally, and the views go straight out to the New York harbor, capturing Lady Liberty without obstruction.

"So, Rachel, does it feel strange to be on the other side of the proverbial table?" Leeds asks.

"A little," Rachel concedes.

"First rule. Your job here is to be the witness. Let me be the lawyer. Okay?"

"Sure."

"Okay, then. The AUSA wants to see you tomorrow. I would have preferred to have a few more days to prepare, but they wouldn't budge. My guess is that they're going to move soon with an arrest on this thing. She wouldn't tell me who, of course, but you don't have to have a crystal ball to see that your buddy Nicolai Garkov has a bright red bull's-eye on his back. I reached out to Clint Broden, just to give him a heads-up, and to get whatever I could out of him. He wasn't giving me ice in winter, but he did make it very clear that Garkov wasn't waiving his attorney-client privilege with Cromwell Altman."

"Did Sam Rosenthal say why I needed conflict counsel?"

Leeds looks at Rachel with a perplexed expression, as if he's never questioned why he's retained on any matter.

"It's just standard operating procedure," he says dismissively.

Rachel nods as if she accepts the explanation. She knows, however, that there is nothing standard about what's going on here.

"Who's the assistant?" Rachel asks next.

"Oh, I thought you knew. A woman named Victoria Donnelly."

Rachel shakes her head. She was hoping it was someone she knows, someone who likes her. But there are lots of assistant U.S. attorneys in Manhattan, the office being the size of a large law firm. On top of that, attrition is high; a faster revolving door would be hard to find. The most common path is two years at a big law firm, three to five at the U.S. Attorney's Office, then back to the big law firm.

"Victoria's . . . how do I put this diplomatically," Leeds says with a self-satisfied smile. "Well, she's not going to win any popularity contests, that's for sure. But even though she can be very abrasive at times, she's smart and a hard worker. She's also pretty experienced. I think she's probably been in that office for at least a decade by now."

"Funny that I've never had a case with her," Rachel says.

"She's out of the OC unit," Leeds says. "That may be why."

Organized crime. Most of Rachel's cases are brought by the securities fraud unit. The fact that an assistant out of OC is handling the case means that Nicolai Garkov *is* the main suspect, or at least was at the time when they had to decide what prosecutor to assign.

Leeds lays out the instructions for tomorrow's session, which are nearly word for word what Rachel tells the witnesses she preps: *Listen to the question, wait until it's finished, make sure you understand it, think about your answer before saying anything, answer the question and* only *the question, and then stop. And above all else, don't volunteer anything.* He omits the most important one—to tell the truth—but perhaps that's because he thinks it's implied.

They spend the next four hours going through a mock interview. Leeds plays Donnelly's part, asking the questions in a surly manner, and Alyssa acts as defender, the role Leeds will play when they do it for real. Rachel has done this playacting as inquisitor a hundred times herself and finds it easier being a witness than a questioner. She doesn't have to strategize or plot, but simply respond to the questions as succinctly as she can.

"I think you're ready," Leeds declares after the question-and-answer game. "Just follow my rules, and you'll do fine."

Rachel smiles at him, suggesting agreement, but something tells her that it's not going to be that easy.

32

As soon as he returns to Cromwell Altman, Sam Rosenthal enters Aaron's office to run down the particulars of his almost-breakfast with Fitz.

"They know about the affair, and so we need to assume you're at least a target, if not the main target, in all of this," he says, even before taking a seat in Aaron's guest chair.

Aaron greets the news with a heavy sigh. "If they already know about the affair, why can't I go in and tell them my story about Garkov's blackmail? Maybe that will get them to refocus their energies on him."

"Among other things, because you can't tell your story," Rosenthal says. "The attorney-client privilege is going to block you from revealing anything Garkov said to you."

"The threat Garkov made isn't privileged. Crime-fraud exception."

Rosenthal's response is the slightest raise of his brow. It might be indiscernible to most people, but Aaron reads it as a strong rebuke. If it were translated into words, it would say, *Do you* really *need me to explain this to you?*

"Even if that's true," Rosenthal says slowly, "and you know as well as I do that it's a debatable issue, admitting that Garkov was blackmailing you, or that you were in a conspiracy with him to blackmail Judge Nichols, would be suicide. They may know about the affair, but God willing, they'll never learn about the blackmail. And it's the blackmail that gives you a motive. Besides, are you actually thinking you're going to admit you saw her on the night of the murder? And you know as well as anyone else, you can't go in there half-pregnant. You tell the truth or you shut the hell up. I know it's frustrating not to defend yourself, Aaron, but this is not the time or the place to put on your defense. If they want to indict, nothing you say is going to change that. All talking to them does is lock you into a story, which very likely will not be the best defense when all the evidence is known."

Aaron feels appropriately chastened. He's thinking like a client, not a lawyer.

Just like when a hurricane approaches, the safest course in a criminal investigation is to hunker down and pray that it passes you by. And if it doesn't, then you pray that the damage can be contained. The one thing you *never* do is anything that makes you an easier target.

"Okay, you're right. We stay away."

Even though he knows inaction is the proper course, Aaron still can't help but wonder just how complete the destruction is going to be once this particular storm passes.

Rachel has the distinct impression that Aaron is avoiding her. She can't really blame him if he is. She's said it to clients a thousand times herself: when the prosecutors ask, *Who did you speak to about the facts of the case?* you want the answer to be *My lawyer and no one else*, so as to not permit the claim that they were conspiring with anyone to get their stories straight.

But she can't let the opportunity of Aaron alone at the Pierre go untapped. She needs him to know that she's his for the asking.

"Hey, you," she says after knocking on Aaron's open office door.

When Aaron smiles at her, she realizes she was worrying about nothing. He's just as happy to see her.

"Hey yourself," he says.

"I was wondering if you wanted to get a drink after work today."

Aaron's smile recedes. She can actually see his face tighten.

"Is something wrong?" he asks.

"Oh, I'm sorry. No. I didn't mean to worry you. I met with Rich Leeds this morning, and I'm meeting with the AUSA tomorrow, but all is good. I just hate the idea of you being all alone in a hotel room, ordering room service, that's all."

For the second time, Aaron looks concerned. "I'm sorry, Rachel. I should have told you sooner . . . but I've moved back home. It turned out to be just a minor kerfuffle after all."

"Oh," she says.

Just then, Sam Rosenthal enters Aaron's office. Rachel wonders if it's her imagination, but she senses that Rosenthal is looking at her like a protective parent who thinks that she's not a good influence on his son.

"I need to . . . I'm late for something," Rachel says, trying to come up with an excuse to leave before Rosenthal asks her to go.

As if he senses her nervousness, Aaron smiles to put her at ease. "If we don't talk tomorrow because . . . of your other engagement down at the U.S. Attorney's Office, I'll find you at the prom for sure. Just so you'll recognize me, I'll be the guy wearing a tuxedo."

When Rachel's out the door and not within earshot, Rosenthal says, "You know she's a witness now, right?"

"I trust her, Sam. I daresay almost as much as I trust you."

Aaron knows that he has not assuaged Rosenthal's concerns. Part of that is because Rosenthal worries about everything. But on this score, Aaron knows there's some cause for concern when a woman who knows him as well as Rachel is providing evidence to the U.S. Attorney's Office.

33

Jesus Christ Superstar.

That is the Brunswick Academy high school musical this year. There was some grumbling about whether it was appropriate because of its religious theme, which became louder when the school cast Lindsay as Judas and another girl as Jesus, with the explanation for the unusual casting being that none of the boys who auditioned could sing.

The Brunswick auditorium is the size of a small Broadway theater, with a capacity of more than a thousand. The Littmans have seats toward the middle, on the aisle. Samantha, who's never been one for public performing, sits between her parents.

After the overture, Lindsay has the first song. Her singing voice has always been something of a marvel to Aaron. It's a skill he does not possess, but one that is so present in his daughter that at times it seems like magic to him. Cynthia credits her side of the family for Lindsay's soprano range, but to Aaron's way of thinking, it is something unique to Lindsay, setting her apart from him and Cynthia both.

After the show, the four of them go to a Mexican restaurant a few blocks south of the school. It's one of the girls' favorite after-school haunts, the kind of place that only has tacos and burritos on the menu.

It is the first time since Aaron's return that Cynthia seems happy. The girls, too, appear to be in excellent spirits. Lindsay is pleased with her performance, and Samantha, as always, is her number one fan.

"I thought Cameron was great too," Lindsay says, referring to the girl who played Jesus. "She was so freaked out that we had to kiss, though. You know, when Judas signals to the Roman guards to arrest Jesus with a kiss? I kept saying, it's no big deal. It's a kiss on the cheek. So, once, during rehearsal, she turns to allow me to do the kiss, and then I just planted one on her lips."

"You didn't!" Samantha squeals.

"Swear to God," Lindsay says. "And, for whatever reason, after that, Cameron didn't mind at all when I kissed her."

Aaron is brought back to years of this dynamic. The way the girls talk to each other as if no one else is around. In the past, he and Cynthia would sit quietly by, the only communication between them expressions of parental pride.

Tonight, however, when he catches Cynthia's eye, she looks away. It's as if she is sharing the same memory but wraps it with an entirely different meaning. For her, perhaps, those times are forever behind them, whereas Aaron still clings to the hope that their past has been a prelude to an even happier future.

The moment they arrive back at the apartment, the girls rush to their respective bedrooms, leaving Aaron alone with his wife. "That was really nice," Aaron says, trying his best to make it sound like a peace offering.

"I think the girls enjoyed all of us being together," Cynthia says.

"I'd like to . . . I was going to say make amends, but what I really want is to be better, and for us to be happy. We have so little time before the girls go off to college, and I don't want to waste it."

Cynthia is not a cruel person, and so Aaron knows that her first instinct will not be to hurt him. But she's also not a hopeless romantic. It's the scientist in her, he thinks, that causes her to think about love and life through a more pragmatic lens.

"I know you do, Aaron. I just don't know if it's possible. We've been . . . *drifting* for so long . . . and all during that time I was hoping that we'd find some way to come back together. To what we once had. I mean, if you'd come to this epiphany then . . . But what can I say—you didn't."

"All I can do is try to be a better person now, Cynthia. I wish I could undo the past, but I can't."

"I hope there's a happy ending in store for us too, Aaron. But sometimes, I don't know . . . things happen and they're just too heavy for a relationship to support. I'm not saying that's what's happened between us, but I guess I am saying that I'm not sure it hasn't. But the good news is that I'm trying too. And tonight was nice. So, I guess let's keep trying and see where that takes us."

Where it takes Aaron that evening is back to the guest room.

In the darkness, he contemplates the extent to which his love wreaks such havoc on its recipients. Faith. Cynthia. The twins. Maybe Rosenthal and the firm too.

The lawyer in him sets up the argument. He's made mistakes, yes. And those mistakes caused suffering for others, it's true. But he now repudiates that conduct and is willing to live a better life. What more can he do than that?

Aaron knows, however, that any judge hearing that plea would dismiss it out of hand. The entire criminal justice system is predicated on the principle that it's the conduct—not the contrition after being caught—that determines the appropriate punishment.

Which means that in a fair world, he would not be entitled to another chance. Not after all he's done. And that leads him to pray that the world is truly not fair.

34

Rachel sits beside Richard Leeds at a badly nicked wooden table as they wait for the prosecution team to arrive. On Rachel's other flank is Alyssa Sanders.

Sanders's role is one that Rachel knows all too well. She's the record. She'll attempt to transcribe every word that's said, like a human Dictaphone. It would be far more efficient if someone actually recorded the proceeding, but if they did, the prosecutors would have to turn that recording over to the defendant in discovery, which they're loath to do. So instead, Sanders takes notes for the defense, and a junior prosecutor does the same for the other side. Because these notes are not verbatim transcripts, they magically become shielded from discovery by the attorney work-product doctrine, on the theory that they have become infused with attorney thought process.

Victoria Donnelly is not at all the way Rachel imagined her. Rachel doesn't know why, but she pictured something of a seductress. The first word that comes to mind upon seeing Victoria Donnelly, however, is *intense*.

After a hearty, "Good morning, everybody," Donnelly introduces her entourage. "This is FBI special agent Kevin Lacey, whom I believe you've spoken to, Ms. London. And my colleague here at the U.S. Attorney's Office, Leonard Stanton, and Christopher Covello, the head of the Criminal Division."

While everyone is still trading business cards, the U.S. attorney enters. "I hope I'm not late," Fitz says.

Rachel's immediate instinct is that Fitz's presence is a harbinger of very bad things to come. The U.S. attorney doesn't sit in on meetings to hear the attorney-client privilege invoked. If Fitz is taking the time to be here, this meeting is most certainly about something other than Garkov.

After Donnelly gives the standard U.S. Attorneys' spiel about the perils of lying, she begins the interview by asking Rachel to recite her educational background. Rachel tells the group that she received her undergraduate degree from Stanford (leaving out the part about how things ended there, of course) and thereafter graduated from Columbia Law School. She anticipates that the next question will be to go through her employment, and so she volunteers that she clerked for Judge Davis (again omitting the way her clerkship ended) and then joined Cromwell Altman.

Richard Leeds takes the opportunity to whisper in her ear. "Don't volunteer. Not even on something like that."

She nods, bracing herself for the fact that now that the preliminaries are over, Donnelly is going to get to the stuff that matters.

Donnelly says, "Ms. London, did Mr. Garkov ever say anything to you that suggested he might harm Judge Nichols?"

"Don't answer that," Leeds immediately says, looking at Rachel as if he's a knight in shining armor. "Come on, it's privileged, Victoria. You know that."

"No, it isn't, Rich. The violent-crime exception trumps the privilege."

"Not *after* the crime," Leeds counters.

Rachel slumps back in her chair as Leeds and Donnelly start arguing. She knows this exchange will end with both sides agreeing to disagree, but without Rachel providing an answer. That's the way disputes always end between lawyers. But it's also why judges exist—to later break such stalemates.

"You worked with Aaron Littman on the trial of Eric Matthews, didn't you?" Donnelly asks Rachel after the argument ends.

So much for a focus on Garkov, Rachel thinks. Second question in and they're already asking about Aaron.

"I did," she says.

"How would you characterize Mr. Littman's relationship with Judge Nichols during that trial?"

"Like a defense lawyer with a judge."

Donnelly whispers something to Fitz, and then he whispers something back. When their private exchange ends, Donnelly says, "So, how'd the Matthews case turn out for your client?"

"Not so well. He was sentenced to fourteen years."

"Did it strike you as odd that right after Judge Nichols was assigned to the Garkov case, Mr. Garkov retained Aaron Littman to represent him . . . even though Mr. Littman's previous experience before Judge Nichols had turned out, as you just said, not so well?"

Rachel forces herself to chuckle. "No. Aaron Littman is probably the best lawyer in the city, maybe the country. It makes total sense that a guy in serious trouble like Nicolai Garkov would want to hire him."

As Donnelly shuffles her notes, Leeds leans in again. "What's this all about?" he whispers.

"I don't know," Rachel whispers back.

"Did you know that Mr. Littman was having an affair with Judge Nichols?" Donnelly says as if she were asking about the weather.

"What?!" Leeds exclaims.

"Please don't interrupt, Counselor," Donnelly snaps. "I will represent to you that Mr. Littman and Judge Nichols were engaged in a sexual relationship. My question is very simple: did you have any knowledge of that relationship, Ms. London?"

Rachel feels her body clench, but without missing a beat, she says, "No, I didn't know that."

Donnelly doesn't seem thrown by Rachel's denial. She simply plows ahead with a new question.

"Did Mr. Littman ever say anything to you to indicate that he needed to get Judge Nichols off the Garkov case?"

Rachel is trying to gather her bearings and thinks that there might be a basis to invoke privilege—if, say, as part of the Garkov defense, they considered a disqualification motion, perhaps—but decides that it's better to just offer a denial, which also has the benefit of being true. "No."

"What is the nature of *your* relationship with Aaron Littman, Ms. London?" Donnelly says with a full-on sneer.

"What the hell is this, Victoria?" Leeds says.

"It's a valid question," Donnelly shoots back.

"Uh, for a reality show, maybe. But not for a criminal investigation where Ms. London is a fact witness only."

"Who said that?"

"Wait a second . . . are you saying that you have any evidence, or even a suspicion, that my client is involved in this crime? Because that's news to me."

"This is an ongoing investigation, Counselor, and we have recently learned new facts which have caused us to view certain people in a different light. For example, perhaps Ms. London saw Judge Nichols as a rival for Aaron Littman's affections, which is a conclusion I'm inclined to give much more serious thought if the witness continues in her refusal to answer this question."

Rachel is about to say something when Leeds holds out his arm as if she's the passenger in a car that Leeds has just stopped short. He turns his focus to the U.S. attorney and says, "Fitz, we're here voluntarily, and you're seriously making me regret that decision. I'm about a second away from pulling the plug on this little circus."

"Your call, Rich," Fitz says, "but that's just going to escalate things. It would seem to me that it's far preferable if your client gives us the information we're seeking in a less formal way, with you present, rather than through the grand jury process."

Leeds wears his displeasure on his sleeve. On her other side, Rachel is acutely aware of Alyssa Sanders scribbling down the exchange.

"Ms. London, are you going to continue to answer my questions?" Donnelly asks.

Rachel looks at Leeds, who nods. "Yes. Until my counsel tells me otherwise."

"Okay, then. I asked about your relationship with Mr. Littman."

"We're . . . we're law partners. Nothing more."

"So you and Mr. Littman were never romantically involved, is that right?"

"That's right."

She can feel herself flush, but no one else seems to notice. Donnelly hasn't even made eye contact and instead stares at the paper before her, no doubt reformulating the questions now that the romantic angle has been denied.

"Ms. London, did you ever hear Mr. Littman threaten to harm Judge Nichols in any way?"

"No," Rachel says quickly, as if the very thought is absurd.

Donnelly smiles, as if the next question just occurred to her. "Do you know if Mr. Littman killed Judge Nichols?"

"No," Rachel says with a laugh.

"No, you don't know?"

"No. I mean that I have no reason to think that he did."

"Does that mean you have reason to think that he *didn't*?"

"Yeah, about a million reasons," Rachel says.

"Would you care to share them?"

"Absolutely not," Leeds says loudly. "This is getting ridiculous, Victoria. How could she possibly know such a thing unless Aaron Littman confessed to her, and you don't think she might have mentioned that little tidbit to you by now if that had happened?"

"Not if she's trying to protect him, she wouldn't," Donnelly snaps back. "Or if she was his accomplice."

Donnelly glowers at Leeds, but Rachel can see that her champion is going to back down. Donnelly sees it too, because she turns away from Leeds and resumes her questioning.

"Okay, then, as I was saying, Ms. London, was Mr. Garkov blackmailing Mr. Littman?"

"Privileged! Next question!" Leeds shouts back at her.

"It's not, Rich. Crime fraud."

"*Next* question!" Leeds says.

Rachel stifles a laugh. At long last, Richard Leeds has found his spine.

Retreat isn't Donnelly's style, and so she forges ahead. "Where were you, Ms. London, on the night of the murder?"

"Nope," Leeds says, steam coming out of his ears. "If you're asking for an alibi, then you should have designated her as a target. She is not answering that. Period."

"Really?" Donnelly says as if she's never heard anything so ridiculous. "A member of Cromwell Altman Rosenthal and White is not going to provide an alibi if she has one regarding the murder of a federal judge?"

"You know what," Leeds says, "we're done here."

He gets up and bolts toward the door. It takes Rachel a second to react, but she's more than happy that this is over.

35

The first thing you learn as a criminal defense attorney is not to utter a word until you're well clear of the U.S. Attorney's Office building. That makes the twenty-five-foot-tall orange sculpture in the center of Saint Andrews Plaza the unofficial post-meeting debrief spot.

When Richard Leeds and Rachel arrive at the designated area, however, instead of talking to Rachel, Leeds pulls out his phone.

"Sam, Rich Leeds here. Yeah, we just got done . . . Not good. Much different than the way I thought it was going to go. Rachel's still here, and I haven't gotten her take on it yet, but I wanted to reach out to you right away . . . You know, maybe the best thing is for me to come up there, and we can sit down and talk this whole thing through."

Sam Rosenthal can't say that he's very surprised by the turn of events, but it's certainly unwelcome news. Even after his meeting with Fitz, he still held out some hope that Rachel's interview would primarily focus on Garkov, and even without Leeds's giving an explanation, he knows that isn't even close to what transpired.

Leeds arrives at Rosenthal's office forty minutes later with Alyssa Sanders in tow.

"Traffic was murder on the FDR," Leeds says. "I told Rachel that she shouldn't be here for this meeting. I think she's back in her office. I hope that was okay."

"That's fine," Rosenthal says. "It's safer to hear it from you anyway. We're subject to an oral joint defense, right?"

"Yeah," Leeds says.

That means this conversation, in which neither lawyer's client is present, is protected by the attorney-client privilege as inviolately as any discussion that Rosenthal has with Aaron alone or Leeds engages in with Rachel. There was a time when lawyers scrupulously committed joint defense agreements to writing, but the U.S. Attorney's Office began demanding the production of those agreements, arguing that the terms of the joint defense weren't privileged, even if the substance was protected. Some judge somewhere agreed with the government, and as a result now such agreements are almost always oral.

"So, what happened?" Rosenthal asks.

Leeds shakes his head, as if he's being asked to recount a gruesome car accident. "I still don't have my head around it . . . but man, it sure as hell sounded to me like they're thinking either Aaron, or maybe even Rachel, killed Judge Nichols."

"I need a little more specificity, Rich. What kinds of questions were they asking?"

"Alyssa here took notes, and we'll make them available to you as soon as they're typed up . . . but my recollection, and correct me if I'm wrong, Alyssa, is that they started out asking some things about Garkov, but pretty soon after that, they were asking solely about Aaron. Did he have an affair with Judge Nichols? Were Rachel and Aaron having an affair? Was Garkov blackmailing him? Did Aaron ever express to Rachel that he needed to get her off the case? That kind of stuff. I finally just shut it down. You know . . . maybe I should have pulled the plug sooner, but I had no idea that this was an angle they'd pursue."

Rosenthal doesn't care much about Leeds's performance. His focus is whether the prosecution has any evidence to support their suspicions that Aaron killed Judge Nichols. Otherwise it's all conjecture. "Did they show you any proof of the affair?" Rosenthal asks.

Leeds laughs. "Which one? Aaron and Judge Nichols, or Aaron and Rachel?"

"Either," Rosenthal says without any hint of amusement.

For Rosenthal, this isn't two lawyers gabbing about a stupid client. This is personal.

Leeds apparently gets the message. "No," he says, this time with a much more somber expression. "Rachel denied any sexual relationship with Aaron and said she didn't know about him and Judge Nichols. But the assistant U.S. attorney represented to us that it was true. So is it, Sam?"

Joint-defense privilege or not, Rosenthal's objective is to get information, not give it, and so he doesn't even consider Leeds's question. Besides, right now, Rosenthal's got much bigger concerns than satisfying Richard Leeds's curiosity.

"Did they tell you anything about their evidence?"

"No," Leeds says. "There were only about ten minutes of questions before I shut it down."

Rosenthal takes this in. He doesn't want to read too much into it, because it could mean that the prosecution was saving their evidence for the end, but he's hungry for any good news and takes some solace in the fact that it may also mean that Fitz doesn't have anything.

"I really appreciate you coming down and sharing this with me," Rosenthal says as he gets up to escort them out. "What I'd like to do is get your notes by this afternoon. Is that possible?"

Leeds answers for Alyssa Sanders, even though she's going to be the one tasked with preparing the document. "Yeah, sure, no problem."

Rosenthal knows that keeping Leeds in the fold is going to be important. And that means he's got to keep him happy.

"It sounds like you did everything you could in there, which I'll certainly pass along to Aaron. And it wouldn't surprise me if we need to bring more of our people in. You should be Cromwell Altman's outside counsel on this, conflicts permitting, of course." He pauses a beat, allowing Leeds mentally to tabulate how much that will mean in fees, and then says, "As soon as you can run off a bill, send that to my attention, and we'll pay it within twenty-four hours."

"Great. I appreciate that, Sam. I'll send you the actual notes as soon as I get back to the office. We're also going to do a memo that memorializes the meeting, and so that will take a few days to complete. When it's done, we'll send that your way, too."

That's Leeds's way of paying himself a bonus for this work. The assignment is over, but he's going to churn another twenty thousand in legal fees by preparing a redundant memo.

Rosenthal doesn't care, though. It's a small price to pay for loyalty.

After Leeds leaves, Rosenthal heads straight to Aaron's office. Aaron must be wearing a look of concern, because Rosenthal's first utterance upon entering his office is: "I take it you've already spoken to Rachel?"

Aaron knows that Rosenthal will not be pleased that he's speaking directly to Rachel because such communications aren't privileged, whereas the circuitous route from Rachel to Richard Leeds to Rosenthal to Aaron *is* protected. But things are often lost in translation in that game of telephone. Besides which, Aaron has no fear that Rachel is going to turn against him.

"Yeah, but she was very general," Aaron says, in an effort to placate Rosenthal. "Just that they were asking more about me than Garkov. She didn't think she gave them anything. Why, what did Leeds say?"

"The same thing, except in his version, he was the hero."

"Have you gotten back to the assistant yet?" Aaron asks. He means whether Rosenthal has officially told Victoria Donnelly that Aaron's not going to submit to an interview. "That may be the reason she took such a hard line with Rachel."

Rosenthal gives Aaron a sad smile. "I haven't, but I will now. I'll tell her that in light of her unprofessional treatment of our partner, we regrettably have no other option but to decline her request."

Aaron nods that he's on board for the strategy, but he also knows exactly how Rosenthal's message will be translated by the prosecutors.

Aaron Littman has something to hide.

36

The prom is always held at some over-the-top locale, and an early topic of conversation for the attendees is how the current space compares to that of previous years. The conventional wisdom is that the best one so far was the whale room at the Museum of Natural History, but that was six months before the economic collapse. Since then, the prom has been held in more understated spaces, although that was entirely for show. Like organized crime and Hollywood, Cromwell Altman Rosenthal and White is recession-proof. Clients need even more legal advice in bad times, and the more serious the trouble they're in, the more they're willing to pay for it through the nose.

With the economy finally back on track, the COC (Rosenthal, primarily) decided that it was time for a blowout party again. And it doesn't get any more over-the-top than the Metropolitan Museum of Art.

More than four hundred people are in attendance tonight. Nearly all the first- and second-year associates are present—the lure of an open bar and the opportunity to don formal wear too much of a siren song for them to resist—but the midyear associates largely send regrets, either because they have to work (even though the prom is held on a Saturday night) or they so thoroughly hate their colleagues that they can't bear to spend another minute with them. Those who are still on partnership track by their eighth year make their inevitable return, working the room like candidates at a nominating convention. Of course, the partners never miss any opportunity to strut around like cocks of the walk, and so they're out in full force.

The Egyptian Room, where the cocktail hour takes place, is as large as a football field. A narrow reflecting pool runs nearly its full length, and for tonight's party, the water is framed by candles flickering in paper bags, each approximately a foot from the next.

A sixteen-piece band plays from a stage running along the long side of the room, while each of the shorter sides has a fully stocked bar manned by four bartenders. The food is designed to appeal to every conceivable taste—Kobe beef tacos, yellowtail sashimi, vegetable dumplings for the vegetarians, and roasted-pepper skewers for the vegans—all served by a cadre of white-gloved waiters carrying silver trays.

In the corner farthest away from the band is a discussion circle led by Donald Pierce. He has a drink in one hand and his other clutches his date's waist. She's a twentysomething wannabe actress/model type. For the past ten years, Pierce has taken a different woman to each prom, each of whom bore a striking resemblance to the last and looked nothing like the ex–Mrs. Pierce. Like a twisted version of *The Picture of Dorian Gray*, Donald Pierce gets older each year, but his dates do not.

Two junior partners, Roland Singleton and Ira Greenberg, are laughing at Pierce's jokes as if they've never heard anything so funny in their lives. They're each wearing a twenty-five-hundred-dollar tux, which does nothing to camouflage that they were given wedgies on a daily basis back in middle school. They're both pasty complexioned, vampirish almost, the fluorescent tan that many of the Cromwell Altman lawyers sport.

As is the case with nearly every Cromwell Altman partner, their dates are several notches above them in looks, but unlike Donald Pierce, who is almost salivating at the prospect of what's going to happen after he pours enough alcohol down the throat of this year's chippie, Singleton and Greenberg seem completely uninterested in their female companions.

They're talking about work, which is pretty much all they ever discuss. For more than a month, they've been going 24/7 on a merger involving two giant telecommunications conglomerates. They speak in pronouns and coded phrases, ostensibly so as not to disclose non-public information, but a casual observer would likely conclude it's because they enjoy pretending to be spies, just like an eleven-year-old might.

"I put up a fight for close to a week," Greenberg says with obvious relish, "and then I said, 'Okay, okay, you win. Your guy can be the chairman of the board, but only if our guy is CEO.'" Greenberg begins laughing at his own triumph but still feels the need to dot that *i*, just in case someone missed it. "I think he actually thought *he* pulled a fast one on *me*."

"Who's the GC?" Pierce asks.

"Who do you think?" Singleton replies.

They laugh as one, while the women look on with bored expressions. Pierce takes it upon himself to explain the joke.

"After a merger is consummated," he says slowly, like a second-grade teacher, "there's a battle between the law firms that represented the two parties in the merger as to which one of them is going to get the legal work of the company *post*-merger. To ensure that it's going to be us, we insist that our client's head guy become the CEO of the new company, and that our client's general counsel, or *GC*, becomes head of legal. They're the two guys who are responsible for hiring law firms. In exchange for that, we'll let the other side's guy be the chairman of the board or president for life, or whatever title he wants to pump up his ego. All we care about is making sure that we keep the client's business after the merger."

Greenberg and Singleton laugh again, even though it's the same joke as before. The women smile politely.

"Enjoying the party?" Sam Rosenthal's disembodied voice asks the group.

He's approached them so quietly that Greenberg and Singleton both are startled by the interruption. Pierce, however, remains composed, staring right at Rosenthal, whom he clearly sees as his enemy.

"Very much so," Pierce answers for the group.

"I remember the very first gala I ever attended," Rosenthal says wistfully. "Nineteen seventy-four. Only the partners were invited." He chuckles. "All sixteen of us. We went to dinner at La Côte Basque. We didn't even have a private room, just a table in the back." He looks out over the crowd like a proud parent. "My God. And now look at us."

Rachel couldn't have been more pleased with her Dolce & Gabbana gown. As she anticipated, the plunging neckline has captured the attention of every man she's spoken with this evening. Even Aaron had difficulty making eye contact.

Aaron's avoided asking her more about her session with the government, but that doesn't surprise Rachel. She knows that Rosenthal's gotten the full download via Richard Leeds, and that he, in turn, passed on the information to Aaron, keeping it all within the attorney-client privilege.

Aaron has come alone tonight, claiming his wife had a headache. Rachel knows that's code for all is not good in the Littman marriage, and she's taken full advantage of Aaron's being without a plus-one, not leaving Aaron's side unless he's getting them both a drink. She is in the midst of telling him a story about a recent dating disaster when it's obvious she's lost Aaron's attention.

"Everything okay?" she asks.

"Yeah. I'm sorry. Over there, Sam's talking to Pierce and his cronies," Aaron says. "Did I ever tell you what Sam told me when I became chairman of the firm?"

"No," Rachel says.

"After his accident, I ran the firm, but I fully expected him to return as chairman. When he came back to work, I offered to step aside, but he said no. I assumed it was because he was thinking about retiring, devoting his time to other things, but when I said as much he gave me this look because I'd so completely missed the point. He said that he'd never been married, never had any children, and that he'd devoted his entire life to the firm. 'I'm not stepping aside because I want to end my involvement here,' he said. 'I'm doing it because I'm trying to ensure that day never comes.' "

"And he was right," Rachel says.

"Sometimes I wonder."

Before Rachel can ask what Aaron means, Simon Fairbanks approaches. Fairbanks holds the title of Cromwell Altman's director of operations, which basically means he's the guy who handles everything that's required to make a large New York City law firm run.

"Is it time?" Aaron asks.

Fairbanks nods back.

"Excuse me, Rachel," Aaron says. "I've got to sing for my supper."

Aaron strides toward the stage. As he approaches, the bandleader announces, "Ladies and gentlemen, may I please have your attention. It is now my honor to introduce the chairman of Cromwell Altman Rosenthal and White, Aaron Littman, to say a few words."

There is a smattering of polite applause as Aaron takes the microphone.

"Thank you," Aaron says as the applause dies down. "Today is a day for us to celebrate, and not for me to speechify . . . but I would be remiss if I didn't thank you all for coming and for your dedication to our firm. The great philosopher Jerry Seinfeld once said that in the game of life, the lawyers are just the people who have read the rules on the inside of the top of the box." He pauses to allow a few chuckles and then continues. "But not here at Cromwell Altman Rosenthal and White. No, my friends, here we are the masters of the game. And so, I ask that you all raise your glasses for a toast. To our continued success."

"Hear, hear!" Rosenthal shouts.

Rachel favors Aaron with a broad smile, which she's sure is received, because he smiles back at her. Everything about tonight has been perfect, like a dream. Looking up at him on the stage, dressed in his formal wear and basking in the warmth of the applause of those he leads, she lets herself imagine that tonight will end up with their finally consummating their relationship.

The fantasy shatters the moment Rachel sees out of her peripheral vision three men wearing identical clothing—long black overcoats, dark gray suits, white shirts, nondescript dark ties—enter the room. Men dressed like that, walking with such purpose, can only have one of two occupations—FBI agent or assassin.

37

Sam Rosenthal raises his glass and lets out a loud, "Hear, hear!" when he sees the dark-suited men enter the room. With the champagne flute still in one hand and his cane in the other, he limps over to the podium, a step behind the newcomers.

The light's reflection focuses Rosenthal's attention. He knows they're feds, but somehow it doesn't connect that they're here to arrest Aaron until he sees the handcuffs.

The first thing Rosenthal does is call out: "Mr. Littman invokes his right to counsel and will not answer any questions put to him unless I'm present."

No one answers him. Instead, one of the agents, not the oldest of the three, but the one clearly in charge, is in the process of clicking a cuff around Aaron's wrist.

"Agent . . ."

"Lacey," the man says, turning around after the cuffing is complete.

"Agent Lacey, I'd like you to acknowledge that you've heard my request."

"I heard you. He won't be questioned without you present. Now, if you'd please step aside, sir."

"Are the handcuffs really necessary?" Rosenthal asks.

"Yes, they are. This man is under arrest for murdering a federal judge."

"This man is one of the most respected lawyers in the country."

"As I said, sir, please step aside."

With that, Agent Lacey moves in front of Aaron. Another agent, the oldest of the trio, gives Aaron a shove in the back, pushing him forward.

Aaron's face, which was previously hanging low, comes into Rosenthal's view. There's a glaze in Aaron's eyes, suggesting that all of this has not truly computed for him yet.

"Aaron," Rosenthal says, "do not talk to *anyone*. Do you understand me?"

Aaron nods weakly, as if he has limited control of his body.

The FBI agents have by now grabbed Aaron by the elbows and are leading him out of the museum. Rosenthal is moving as fast as he can to follow them, but never before has he been so acutely aware of how damaged he's become. With each clank of his cane, his distance from Aaron increases.

When Rosenthal finally makes it out the museum's front door, he sees firsthand what he's imagined: an out-and-out media circus. Fitz's handiwork, no doubt. There are at least twenty vans parked along Fifth Avenue, most of which have antennas on top. Hordes of reporters are on the sidewalk, seemingly shouting questions at Aaron as he approaches, although Rosenthal is too far away to hear them, or to know if Aaron has offered a response.

Aaron and his FBI escorts approach the black SUV parked at the bottom of the museum's steps, and Aaron is unceremoniously pushed into the back. One agent follows him, and the two others take their seats in the front.

Rosenthal watches the SUV recede from view. When it's finally gone, he turns back and begins to ascend the steps to return to the museum, at which time he's nearly knocked over by Rachel London racing the other way.

Rachel's eyes are filled with tears. To Rosenthal, she looks like a lost child, almost begging him to tell her that everything's going to be fine, which is the one thing he can't do.

Rosenthal grabs her hand. "Go to Aaron's apartment," he says. "Right now. Hurry. Tell his wife what's happened. Explain to her that if the FBI has not already obtained a search warrant, it's very possible they will do so in the next few hours."

Rachel's dazed expression suggests she doesn't grasp that he's asking her to destroy evidence. He looks around, making sure there's no one to overhear, and then, looking Rachel squarely in the eye, says, "Rachel. You need to focus. Now *listen*. Aaron told me that he trusts you with his life. Do you understand what I'm asking?"

It takes her a few moments, but then everything clicks. "Yes. There won't be anything there," she says.

The Egyptian Room is quiet when Rosenthal returns. The band is still on the stage, but they're not playing. People are talking, intermittently checking their phones, undoubtedly for the latest news of what they just witnessed. Far from the normal buzz you hear when entering a party, it feels like a wake.

Rosenthal makes a beeline to Donald Pierce. Stepping between Greenberg and Singleton, Rosenthal says, "I need a moment with you, Don."

Pierce doesn't even make his apologies to the others. He follows Rosenthal to a corner of the room, away from everyone.

When they're alone enough not to be overheard, Pierce says, "What the hell just happened?!"

"Aaron was arrested for murdering Judge Nichols."

"Oh my God. Did you know anything about this?"

"Now's not the time to play who knew what and when, Don."

"So what *is* this the time to do, Sam?"

"Protect our firm, of course. To do that, you need to go up to that microphone and make an announcement that the party is over. Under the circumstances, I'm sure no one will disagree. Get the car service to send every goddamned car they have. I don't care if they have to hire pedicabs, just make sure everyone goes straight home. And that goes double for anyone working in the office tonight instead of being here—I'm going down there right now and throwing everybody out. I don't want anyone except the cleaning people there this weekend. Tell everybody that on Monday, the firm will issue a statement. And make it clear that no one is to talk to the press. I mean *no one*. Not one person is to say a word about this until we've thought this through."

"The partners are going to want to know what just happened, Sam."

"For Christ's sake, look around you, Don. They already know."

Sure enough, there are a dozen or so reporters in front of Cromwell Altman's building, and each one shouts at Sam Rosenthal as he enters.

"Did Aaron Littman kill Judge Nichols?"

"Was he having an affair with her?"

"Was it going on while he was representing Eric Matthews?"

"Did Nicolai Garkov hire him to influence Judge Nichols?"

Rosenthal doesn't even say *no comment* as he pushes past them. When he enters the lobby, there's an odd silence, broken only by the rhythmic clacking of his cane against the marble floor. The lone security guard seems oblivious to the commotion outside, saying hello to Rosenthal as he passes, without even a reference to the fact that Rosenthal's entering the building at 10:00 p.m. on a Saturday night wearing a tuxedo.

When Rosenthal steps off the elevator on the fifty-seventh floor, Margaret, the firm's weekend receptionist, is not so in the dark. She looks positively panicked.

"Mr. Rosenthal, thank God you're here! The phones have been ringing nonstop. Not just the general number, either—I can hear the office phones ringing too. It's like someone is calling every lawyer in the firm. I've seen online that Mr. Littman . . ." She doesn't finish the thought, as if saying it out loud would be some type of offense.

"Did you say anything to anyone?" Rosenthal asks.

"No, of course not."

"Good. I need you to go office by office and tell anyone who's here to go home immediately. No exceptions. I don't care what they're working on. Tell them those are my orders, on penalty of immediate termination. Also tell them that I said they are not to talk to the press, but to go straight home and come back on Monday morning. The same goes for you, Margaret. As soon as you've finished your rounds, go straight home. There are some reporters outside, but I want you to just walk right past them without saying a word. If they follow you, just ignore them and keep going. Thank you . . . good night."

Rosenthal leaves the stunned receptionist in his wake, knowing she will do his bidding without question. A minute later, he's behind the closed door to his office, ready to spring into action, battle to the death as he's done so many times behind this desk, when he realizes that there really isn't anything for him to do.

Aaron will be booked, and then he'll be sent to a holding facility for the night, all of which means the earliest Rosenthal can see him is tomorrow morning. Rosenthal could work the phones right now, harass a judge to hear Aaron's application for bail tomorrow, but he already knows that's not going to yield success. None of his buddies on the bench are going to go out of their way to spare Faith Nichols's accused murderer at least a night in jail.

Rosenthal dials Fitz's cell number. He's not surprised when it goes directly to voice mail. Fitz is probably working on his remarks for tomorrow's press conference and doesn't want to be disturbed.

"Goddamn you, Fitz!" Rosenthal shouts after the beep. "It's Sam! If you have any decency at all, you'll call me back tonight! Do you hear me?! So help me God, if I don't get a call back from you, I'll do everything I can to make sure that this is the last fucking job you ever have in this city!"

After slamming down the phone, Rosenthal sits in silence. His heart goes out to Aaron. He can only imagine what must be going through his mind.

And then he realizes there is something he can do. He dials Elliot Dalton.

38

It takes Rachel less than ten minutes to walk from the Met to the Littmans' building, but when she arrives, there's already a large police presence erecting a barricade to hold back the press. The reporters must think that Rachel's a resident because they shout: "Did you ever see Judge Nichols in the building?" and "What's your reaction to the news that one of your neighbors might be a murderer?"

She rushes past them but is stopped by the doorman at the threshold. "No press!" he screams at her. "I'll get a cop in here right now!"

"I'm a friend of the Littmans," Rachel says. "I'm here to visit Cynthia. I'm also their attorney. Call upstairs, and tell Mrs. Littman that Rachel London from her husband's office is here."

The doorman makes the call, although he mangles the message. "Let me talk to her," Rachel says, and reaches for the phone.

"Mrs. Littman, this is Rachel London. I'm a partner at Cromwell Altman. Sam Rosenthal asked that I come over. It's very important that we talk."

Rachel hands the phone back to the doorman. He nods a few times before saying, "Of course," into the receiver, and then telling the second doorman, "Take her up."

The elevator has no buttons, only a lever that the second doorman operates. When they reach the ninth floor, the doors open into the apartment, and Rachel is face-to-face with Cynthia Littman. She's wearing sweatpants and a man's white T-shirt, is without makeup, and looks as if she's been crying. *At least that means she already knows what happened*, Rachel thinks.

Rachel has met Cynthia a handful of times. She came away from each interaction with the distinct impression that Aaron's wife was not at all pleased to be in her company. Rachel didn't begrudge Cynthia her suspicions. She understood all too well the threat she posed.

"Mrs. Littman, thank you for seeing me. I don't know if you remember me. I worked with Aaron on the Eric Matthews trial."

"I know who you are, Rachel."

Rachel decides not to read too much into Cynthia's harsh tone. Her husband has just been arrested for murdering his mistress, after all. That is more than enough to make any woman angry.

"Sam Rosenthal asked me to come over right away. He wanted someone from the firm to tell you what happened, which I gather you already know."

"The phone started ringing about twenty minutes ago," Cynthia says in a slow voice. "The first reporter, somebody from CNN, I think, said that Aaron had been arrested and would I care to comment. I just hung up on him and turned on the TV. There was nothing about Aaron, and so I went online . . . and it was everywhere."

"Did you talk to anyone?"

"No. And I unplugged the phone. It started ringing nonstop pretty quickly. The girls are out tonight at a friend's house. I called over there and explained it to them . . ." She shakes her head, fighting back tears. "I thought it was better if they stayed there for the night. There were already reporters downstairs."

Rachel nods, having passed that gauntlet herself. "Can I sit down?" she asks.

"I'm sorry," Cynthia says, actually sounding contrite. "Of course."

The Littmans' living room is enormous, maybe fifty feet long, with at least ten windows looking west onto Central Park. There are two separate seating areas, and Cynthia shows Rachel to the one closest to the fireplace.

Once seated, Rachel is about to continue, but Cynthia's eyes are shut tight, as if she's trying to block out everything around her. When she opens them, she stares hard at Rachel, almost as if she's trying to bore into her thoughts.

"So. Were you also fucking my husband?"

Cynthia has said this without emotion. Not an accusation as much as a simple question. Like, *Can I get you something to drink?*

"Excuse me, Mrs. Littman?"

"I believe you heard me. The least you can do is give me an answer."

For as long as she could remember, Rachel wished it to be so, and yet she's suddenly glad that she can answer Aaron's wife honestly. "No, ma'am," Rachel says.

"Please don't call me *ma'am*. It's not flattering to either of us. You're not married, are you?"

"No, I'm not."

"And you're what . . . thirty?"

"Thirty-three."

Cynthia shakes her head with a look of disgust. "My my, you must have really turned some heads tonight in that dress. I bet the partners' wives thought you were this year's arm candy with that asshole Donald Pierce, and then they find out, oh no, she's a partner. She's with our husbands every day."

Cynthia laughs, and right then, Rachel realizes what she didn't before. Cynthia Littman is very drunk.

"Are you okay, Mrs. Littman?"

"*Mrs. Littman* is hardly better than *ma'am*. If you *are* fucking my husband, the least you can do is not to refer to me like I'm some goddamn old lady."

"Cynthia," Rachel says with a soft voice, looking into her eyes in an effort to ascertain just how inebriated she is, "there's nothing going on with me and Aaron. I don't know what happened between him and Judge Nichols, but Aaron needs you now." She pauses, and even though there's nothing she wants to say less, Rachel adds, "Cynthia, I think you've had a little too much to drink."

"Of course I've had too much to drink. Wouldn't you?"

Rachel laughs. "Yeah, I guess I would."

This coaxes a smile from Cynthia, and Rachel decides not to let the shared moment between them go to waste. "Sam Rosenthal thinks that the FBI might try to execute a search warrant, and he wanted me to—" Rachel catches herself. Not knowing where Cynthia is going to come out in all of this, she doesn't want to say what she's there to do. The irony isn't lost on Rachel that while she's certain of her own loyalty to Aaron, she's looking at his wife with suspicion.

"You can tell Sam not to worry. There's nothing incriminating here."

Rachel wonders if Cynthia meant to include herself among the things in the apartment that wouldn't potentially hurt Aaron.

"Are you sure?" Rachel asks. "Have you searched his clothes for blood? His e-mails? His phone for texts? Anything linking him in any way to Judge Nichols?"

"Yes. There's nothing. Believe me. Aaron thought he was so clever that I would never know about them, but a wife always knows . . ."

Rachel wants to ask Cynthia what that means but decides that now is not the time to cross-examine her. Cynthia Littman needs to be contained. God forbid she wanders downstairs drunk and starts talking to the press about Aaron's cheating ways.

"Cynthia, here's what I'd like to do. If it's okay with you, I'd like to stay here tonight. In the morning, we can talk more about what the next steps are going to look like, but right now, I suggest that you go lie down and try to get some sleep."

Cynthia squints at Rachel, seemingly uncertain of what to make of the offer to babysit. "I'm glad she's dead . . . you know that? I don't deny it. How could I? That bitch deserved to die."

After making this sweeping pronouncement, Cynthia Littman stands up and walks to the bedroom.

39

Booking is one of those things that defendants do alone. Not completely, of course, as the FBI agents conduct the process and stand guard during it, but the suspect is denied the presence of counsel.

Aaron wonders if Sam Rosenthal made the request that he himself made a thousand times: to stay with his client through the booking process. Not that it matters. If Rosenthal did, Agent Lacey would have given him the same answer Aaron had heard each time: no.

Aaron's escorted down a long corridor, turning into a room with the acronym *JABS* on the door. A sign in the room spells it out—JOINT AUTOMATED BOOKING SYSTEM.

The JABS room is ten by ten with battleship-gray walls. A machine occupies the center of the room with chairs on either side of it. For a moment Aaron thinks it might be a polygraph, but then he realizes it's a high-tech fingerprint machine. The only other things in the room are a sink and a three-foot bench with a metal bar behind it on the wall, the kind you might see in a handicapped shower stall.

The youngest of the three agents, the one who read Aaron his rights in the SUV, unlocks Aaron's right handcuff and reattaches it to the metal bar. He's identified himself as George Kostopolous, and Aaron figures he's no more than thirty. Everything about him screams meathead—his thick neck, shaved head, and suit that pulls across his pumped-up physique.

"I'll do the pedigree," Kostopolous calls out. He reaches into the single drawer under the table upon which the computer sits, and then turns to Agent Lacey and asks, "Is he a safekeeper?"

Aaron doesn't know what the term means. He's tempted to ask but resists, reasoning that his questions should be reserved for moments when the answers really matter.

"Yeah. I'll work the phones," Lacey says, and then leaves the room.

Kostopolous pulls up a metal chair so that he's beside the bench where Aaron sits cuffed to the bar. "Okay," he says, "I'm going to ask you some questions, and even though you've been Mirandized, you need to answer truthfully." He doesn't wait for an acknowledgment before he begins. The first question Kostopolous answers himself: "Name . . . Littman, Aaron." He looks back at Aaron. "You got a middle name?"

Aaron's initial reaction is to refuse to respond. He could say something like, *I invoke my rights against self-incrimination. When my counsel is present, he may choose to instruct me to provide fuller responses.* There's no doubt that's the answer he'd advise a client to give.

Aaron doesn't take his own advice. "Lewis," he mutters.

"Lewis," Kostopolous repeats. "Date of birth?"

"July eleven, nineteen sixty-four."

Kostopolous scribbles it down. "Seven-eleven," he says, as if it's meaningful.

In response to Kostopolous's questions, Aaron next provides his address, social security number, and home phone number.

"You're married, right?" Kostopolous asks.

Aaron hesitates for a moment, as if the answer to this question might somehow incriminate Cynthia. Then, realizing that couldn't possibly be the case, he says, "Yes."

"You got any drug dependencies? On any prescription meds? Anything like that?"

"No."

Kostopolous fills in some information that apparently doesn't need Aaron's input before asking, "Do you have any scars or tattoos, or any other distinguishing features or peculiarities?"

Aaron can't hide a slight smile as he contemplates what constitutes a peculiarity. "No," he says again.

"Any prior arrests?"

Another question that probably shouldn't be asked without counsel present. "No."

"Employer?"

"Cromwell Altman Rosenthal and White."

If Kostopolous is impressed, he doesn't show it. Then he proves the name means nothing to him by asking, "Can you spell that?"

Aaron slowly spells out all four names, including *White*, even though he suspects Kostopolous will think it's a smart-ass response.

If Kostopolous is insulted, he doesn't show it. Instead he does a little more scribbling on the intake form and then reaches for the phone.

"He's ready," Kostopolous says into the receiver.

A minute or so later, a skinny man wearing jeans and a flannel shirt enters. He introduces himself as "the tech" but doesn't give his name.

Kostopolous unlocks the handcuffs, but not before he makes a point of telling Aaron that the door will be locked from the outside. Aaron rubs his wrist, thankful for this brief moment of freedom.

The tech says, "The good news is that we don't fingerprint with ink anymore. We did up until about two years ago. Now it's all computers."

He grabs Aaron's wrist. One by one he places each of Aaron's fingers on the machine, then each palm. Finally, he tells Aaron that they're going to do "the roll" and demonstrates by rolling his own hand over the machine. After Aaron does likewise, the tech walks over to the door and knocks twice.

Kostopolous comes back into the room, reapplies the handcuff to Aaron's left wrist, and fastens the right cuff back to the bar. Both the tech and Kostopolous then leave the room without saying a word to Aaron.

Aaron sits there for more than an hour with a single thought going through his head: *How are Cynthia and the twins coping?* He can imagine the girls in tears and Cynthia trying to remain calm in order to comfort them.

The last thing the girls said to him was that he looked hot in his tuxedo. Sure, they said it in the sarcastic way of teenagers, but he still thought that they meant it as a compliment. Their way of telling him that they were proud of him. And now, he would never be the same man to them again. There would always be a before and an after. Perhaps with Cynthia, he had already breached that divide when he told her about Faith—or when he started his affair—but for the girls, tonight will be the night when they lost their innocence about their father.

When Kostopolous finally returns, he says, "There's no judge on call now. The Saturday judge went home at three and no one sits on Sunday. That means you're going to be a guest of the federal marshals for the next two nights. We're looking for an open bed somewhere. Usually Nassau County helps us out, so it's possible you're going to be heading out there. As soon as we know who's going to take you, we'll move you, but it may be a while. So sit tight, and don't go anywhere."

Kostopolous says this with a smile, and Aaron wonders how many times he must have made that joke.

After another hour alone, Aaron assumes that they've forgotten about him. He lies down on the bench, figuring that it could well end up being his bed for the night.

Forty minutes later, while Aaron is still staring up at the pockmarked tiles on the ceiling, Agent Lacey reenters the room.

"You're a lucky man, Littman," he says. "There's an empty bed at MCC, so you're not going to travel very far tonight."

Aaron offers a pained smile. Right now, he doesn't feel very lucky.

40

It's pitch-black when Rachel is startled awake. Her first thought is that it's still the middle of the night, but then the phone alarm goes off again, and that's enough for her to remember she has to meet Sam Rosenthal at six o'clock that morning.

Everything else rushes back in an avalanche of bad news: Aaron has been arrested, and she spent the night in his apartment babysitting his drunk wife, who believes that Rachel has been sleeping with her husband.

Rachel recalls the light being dim last night, but when she flips the switch, the illumination is harsh enough to take her a few blinks to adjust. When the room comes into focus, she spies the gown she wore to the prom folded over a slipper chair. More bad news: she has no clothing here aside from that dress.

With little choice, she puts the dress back on, like prepping for a walk of shame. Even without the benefit of a mirror, she knows she can't step into a prison dressed like this, or even past the reporters camped outside the building.

It takes Rachel a few minutes of wandering about the duplex, but she finally manages to find the master bedroom downstairs. She pushes open the door and hears Cynthia snoring lightly. In a whisper, she says, "Cynthia," and when that does not elicit a response, she returns to her normal voice. "Cynthia, you need to wake up."

Cynthia groans, a deep guttural sound that makes Rachel think that she was even more inebriated last night than she previously believed. That perception is further reinforced when Rachel flips the light on and Cynthia violently places her forearm over her eyes and groans again, as if she's a vampire.

"Cynthia, wake up. I need to talk to you."

Cynthia opens a single eye. "Oh my God," she says, and then tries the other one.

Rachel holds in a laugh. No one with a hangover enjoys being made fun of.

"How are you feeling?"

"I've certainly been better." Cynthia glances over at the clock on the night table, then straightens herself and rubs her eyes.

Cynthia lets out another groan as she gets to her feet. "I haven't drunk like that in a long time. . . . Thank you, Rachel. Very much. I don't remember everything from last night, but I remember enough to know that I owe you an apology. So . . . I'm sorry."

"No apology necessary. This is a very difficult time for all of us," Rachel says. "I'm going to go downtown to the U.S. Attorney's Office to find out where they're holding Aaron. As soon as I know where, I'll text you the address."

Cynthia looks Rachel up and down before saying, "You're going like that?"

"Yeah, that occurred to me, too. I was actually hoping that maybe I could borrow something of yours."

Cynthia slowly makes her way to her closet. "I think this might fit," she says, handing Rachel a simple blue dress with a J.Crew label.

"Thank you," Rachel says. "My suggestion is that you not bring the twins. Aaron will be arraigned on Monday, and they can see him there. Sometimes seeing someone in prison . . . it's hard."

Cynthia's eyes begin to tear up, and she rubs her face with her hands. "Okay," she says quietly. "I'll see you soon."

And then Cynthia reaches forward and hugs Rachel.

The U.S. Attorney's Office visitors' entrance is a makeshift structure that sits in the middle of the plaza outside the actual building. Two guards man the space, both of them twenty pounds overweight. One has a mustache and the other sports a beard.

"The building doesn't open until eight o'clock," the bearded guard says.

"I'm not here to see an AUSA," Rachel explains, using the acronym for an Assistant U.S. Attorney so the guards know she speaks the lingo. "I want to visit someone who was arrested last night. I'm trying to find out where he's being held. Aaron Littman."

After she spells out the last name the mustached guard clicks some keys on the keyboard. "Littman. Aaron?" he says.

"Yes."

"Looks like he's over at MCC. That's just across the way here."

Sam Rosenthal is sitting in the lobby area of the MCC when Rachel arrives. He's wearing a three-piece suit and tie, and with his bald head and cane, Rachel thinks that he looks a little like Mr. Peanut, sans top hat and monocle.

Rachel proceeds to fill Rosenthal in on last night.

"Cynthia knew about the affair," she says.

Rosenthal nods. "Yeah, Aaron told her. After the murder."

"No. She knew before. She'd figured it out somehow."

Rosenthal doesn't react, although she's certain he understands what she's saying: if Cynthia knew that Aaron was having an affair with Judge Nichols, then she had a motive.

They sit for the next few minutes in an uncomfortable silence. Rachel has a million questions, but she can tell that Rosenthal is in no mood to answer any of them.

After what seems like an eternity in awkward purgatory, the guard behind the desk shouts out, "Counsel can enter now."

Rosenthal and Rachel go up to the third floor. Once there, they're led by another guard, this one a woman, to the visitors' room—the same place where Aaron met with Nicolai Garkov.

"We'll be bringing the defendant in shortly," the guard says.

"He's not a defendant," Rosenthal answers.

"What?"

"There hasn't been a formal charge yet, and so Mr. Littman is not a criminal defendant. He's merely been arrested."

"Oh," the guard says, the distinction obviously irrelevant to her. "Either way, he'll be here in a few minutes."

Aaron enters the room wearing a light blue smock. It looks a bit like a hospital gown, although it fully closes in the back. *Small favors*, Aaron thinks.

He has no idea where his Brioni tux, the antique platinum cuff links and shirt studs, and the A. Lange & Söhne chronograph watch he had on eight hours ago are at this moment. He hasn't showered, and he has a day's growth of stubble. Worst of all, he knows his breath and body stink.

He resists the urge to hug Rosenthal and Rachel on sight.

"How are you holding up?" Rosenthal asks.

"Not the best night of my life," Aaron says with a pained smile. His mind flashes on Garkov and how stoic he was in the face of adversity. "But, truth be told, not the worst, either."

Aaron shows Rachel a slightly sturdier smile, but she looks away. Although he would have thought it impossible, he must look even worse than he thinks.

"How are Cynthia and the girls?" he asks.

Rosenthal turns to Rachel for her answer. "Cynthia's doing okay. I spent the night at your place. I think she's hanging in there. She talked to your daughters and said that they were at a friend's house last night, and she thought it was best if they stayed there for the night. When I left your house this morning, she was getting ready to go and get them. She's going to come down here as soon as she brings the girls home. I told her that she shouldn't bring your daughters. I hope that was okay."

"Yes, of course," Aaron says. "Thank you, Rachel."

He can feel the tears welling up in his eyes. How much more is he going to put Cynthia and the girls through?

Rosenthal is seemingly oblivious to the emotion overcoming Aaron. He uses the silence to get down to business.

"They're reporting on your affair with Judge Nichols," he says, "and it does seem as if they have some evidence you spoke with her that night. On the bright side, I don't think they have proof that you saw her in the park. If they did, I'm sure Fitz would have leaked that too."

Aaron can tell that until that moment Rachel didn't know that he saw Faith right before she was murdered. He looks at her earnestly, hoping it conveys his apologies for keeping her in the dark, but all he sees back is overwhelming sadness.

Rosenthal continues to make the point that the case against Aaron is extremely weak. "I truly think that all they have is a circumstantial case. That's why they're doing what they can to pressure you—arrest you at the prom to poison the jury pool, two days in jail to soften you up, and then offer you a deal and hope you take it."

Aaron laughs, a reaction as inconsistent with his circumstances as any could be. "I almost forgot. How was the rest of the prom?"

Rosenthal smiles back. "Pretty good, actually. I think everyone had a nice time."

When Rachel and Rosenthal return to the waiting area, Cynthia is there, sitting impassively, staring down at her hands. Although Rachel can't hazard a guess as to what's actually running through Cynthia's mind at a moment like this, the visual is that she's contemplating her wedding band.

As they approach, it becomes obvious to Rachel that Cynthia's in need of any news, good or bad. Rosenthal, however, doesn't pick up the cue. It's almost as if he doesn't want to be reminded that other people are suffering as much as him as a result of Aaron's plight.

Rachel takes it upon herself to fill Cynthia in. "He's good," she says. "Very good, in fact. His spirits seem high. He was smiling and joking with us. He asked about you and the girls. He's obviously concerned about all of you. How did it go with them?"

"Not something I ever saw myself doing," Cynthia says. "But they're strong kids. I think they'll be okay. At least I hope so."

Rachel looks at Rosenthal, trying to will him to say something to comfort Cynthia. Instead he says, "I'm afraid I need to get back to the office."

After Rosenthal leaves, Cynthia says, "Aaron absolutely adores Sam, but I swear, the man is something of a stranger to human emotion. It's as if the empathy bone just isn't in him."

Even though Rachel feels the same way, for some reason she feels the need to defend Rosenthal. "I think this is hitting him pretty hard. It always seemed to me that Aaron was like a son to him."

Before Cynthia can respond the guard says, "Mrs. Littman. You can go in now."

Aaron can't say that he's pleased to see his wife enter the visitors' room. The pain in her face is so blinding that Aaron has to turn away. It's as if she's become disfigured by her suffering.

"I'm so sorry, Cynthia," he says.

Cynthia places her hand on top of his. Aaron wonders if such physical contact between inmates and visitors is permitted, but none of the guards at the corners of the room tell him otherwise, and so he takes refuge in the warmth of Cynthia's touch.

"How are the girls doing?"

Cynthia's expression falls even lower. "Honestly, I'm not sure. They must be terrified. But they're trying to hold it together. They told me to tell you that they love you."

Aaron can't recall the last times the girls told him that they loved him. As he's wondering if they actually said that or Cynthia is being kind, she removes her hand from Aaron's and her posture stiffens.

"Can you answer one question for me, Aaron? And do it honestly?"

"Okay," he says tentatively. He's already declared his innocence to Cynthia, but he knows that she's not going to ask him anything about Faith.

"Do you still love me?"

"Of course I do. I love you, Cynthia."

As much as Aaron knows anything anymore, he knows that's true. He loves his wife, and believes he always will.

He only fears that this realization has come too late. That his love will also be a prisoner in this cell forever.

41

In the nearly fifty years that Sam Rosenthal has been associated with Cromwell Altman, he does not recall there ever being an emergency meeting of the COC. But on the Sunday morning after the prom, the entire COC is assembled around the conference room table, with the exception of Aaron Littman, of course.

Rosenthal feels his age, which is unusual for him. Most of the time, his limp notwithstanding, he feels stronger than he did twenty years before, but this morning every movement seems labored. He barely slept last night and then awoke before dawn to go see Aaron. Worse still, he knows that there will be many sleepless nights to follow.

Sitting across from Aaron's empty chair, Rosenthal calls the meeting to order. There is usually considerable cross talk among the members of the COC before the meeting gets under way, but today you can hear a pin drop. To a person, they're waiting to hear what Rosenthal has to say.

"Thank you for coming this morning," he begins. "There are two things I want to do today. First, I want to tell you about what's going on, as best as I know, and as best I can share consistent with the attorney-client privilege."

"Wait a second," Pierce says, interrupting. "What privilege do you have that we don't?"

"I'm acting as Aaron's counsel. As such, there are communications between us that I cannot share with the rest of you."

"When was this decided?" Pierce says. "I don't remember a conflict check going around the firm. And there was no new matter opened to indicate that Aaron was seeking representation by the firm."

Abby Sloane comes to Sam's defense. "Donald, let Sam say what he brought us here to say," she snaps. "Then you can make whatever points you want, but I'm telling you right now that it would be a huge mistake if the firm did *not* represent Aaron. He's our partner, for God's sake. The one thing we most certainly don't want to do is send the message to our clients that our own partner—the head of the firm—chose another law firm to represent him."

That's enough to quiet Pierce down, at least for the moment.

"How is Aaron doing?" Jane Cleary asks.

"He's fine, under the circumstances," Rosenthal says. "Obviously, he's looking forward to clearing his name. There is no doubt in my mind that Aaron is innocent and will be vindicated. Tomorrow we will appear before a magistrate judge and ask for bail."

"What's the likelihood of his making bail?" Gregg Goldman asks.

"Realistically . . . it's even money," Rosenthal says. "A lot depends on which magistrate judge gets assigned, but this type of situation—the murder of a fellow judge—makes it difficult to handicap how even the most lenient judge will rule."

Rosenthal makes direct eye contact with each of his fellow COC members before going on to the next point. Other than Pierce, he has their attention.

"But I understand that we need to do more than just protect our partner. We also need to protect the firm. And that leads me to the second matter for which I called this meeting. Given Aaron's incarceration, we need to elect a new chairman."

Like clockwork, Pierce says, "And let me guess. You propose that you will—with a heavy heart, of course—take on the mantle of leadership. Do I have that right?"

Rosenthal and Pierce stare hard at each other, like two gunslingers in the Old West.

Elliot Dalton breaks the silence. "I know that you've been patiently waiting, Donald, but this is not the time for a new direction."

"I couldn't disagree more, Elliot. Now is *precisely* the time for new leadership. We need to do everything we can to distance ourselves from Aaron. To tell our clients that his transgressions have nothing to do with the way we conduct business at Cromwell Altman. We should cut him loose and make it crystal clear it wasn't that *he* went outside the firm for counsel but that *we* didn't want to represent him."

Rosenthal is ready to spit fire. "That is never going to happen!" he shouts. "I am going to do everything in my power to protect Aaron. End of discussion. And, Don, I'll either do it here or I'll do it somewhere else—and make no mistake about it, I'll take my fucking name off the door on my way out!"

"There's no reason to prolong this," Sloane says. "Let's just vote. I'm with Sam."

"Me too," Dalton says.

"My vote and Aaron's proxy makes four," Rosenthal says.

Donald Pierce looks angry enough to split in half, but there's nothing he can do. Samuel Rosenthal has the votes to become the chairman of Cromwell Altman Rosenthal and White for the second time.

Aaron's second incarcerated night is far worse than the first.

No longer does it feel like a curiosity that will someday make a good story, to be told in the comfort he's always known. Now it seems he might well have to live out his days in an eight-by-ten windowless room with three other men.

It is a common narcissism that people view their lives like novels in which they are the protagonist. It's a comforting thought, because it means that even when the story twists and all looks lost, there remains the unshakeable belief that a happy ending awaits.

Part of Aaron clings to that belief like it's a life raft. It's simply unfathomable for him to imagine being taken from his family. And yet he knows all too well that the unthinkable sometimes occurs. Faith, of course, being the prime example. She undoubtedly thought that her story's next chapters took place at the Supreme Court. How wrong she was.

Of all the insincere gestures known to man, prayer by an agnostic has to rank right up there. And yet, that's what Aaron does. Silently, he asks for forgiveness and pledges to be a better man, a better father, a better husband, if only he's given the chance.

42

Unlike their more prestigious district court counterparts, who are nominated by the president, confirmed by the Senate, and serve for life, magistrate judges are appointed by a judicial panel and serve eight-year terms. They're tasked largely with doing the busywork that district court judges would rather not be bothered with, which includes bail hearings.

Also befitting their lesser status, a magistrate judge's courtroom is half the size of the palatial space where a district court judge presides. There are seats for twenty-five spectators, but twice that many cram the courtroom, many crowded together in the back or along the sides.

There's something of an assembly-line feel to the proceedings. The bailiff calls out a case name and number, and then the side door to the courtroom opens, so that the court guards can escort in a man, usually of color, who's wearing an orange prison-issued jumpsuit and in some state of dishevelment, handcuffed behind the back and about the ankles.

None of the prior cases are bail hearings. Two are pleas, and the other three are status conferences of one type or another.

When the clerk calls out, "United States v. Aaron L. Littman, criminal case number eight five five seven two," the previously established rhythm breaks. The guards still enter, with Aaron in their wake, but unlike the men who preceded him, Aaron looks positively regal, dressed in a tuxedo.

The first faces Aaron sees are in the back. Cynthia, flanked on either side by Lindsay and Samantha. For a moment he feels comforted by their presence, but that emotion quickly gives way to shame.

He always tells clients to wear to court what they'd wear to church, and apparently Cynthia has taken that advice literally because she's wearing the navy blue suit she wore for the Jewish holidays earlier in the year. Lindsay is in a bright peach dress, and he appreciates the burst of color she brings to the room. Samantha, always the more serious of his daughters, is in all black, as if she's in mourning.

Rachel sits beside them and offers a pained smile when she catches Aaron's eye. Aaron wonders why she's not at counsel table, but this must have been Rosenthal's decision, another indication that Rosenthal doesn't trust her.

When Aaron reaches counsel table, Rosenthal puts his hand on Aaron's shoulder. Aaron appreciates the gesture for its reminder he's not completely alone.

"Appearances," Judge Gruen calls out.

Jonathan Gruen has been a U.S. magistrate since before Aaron passed the bar. In that time, he's developed a reputation for inconsistency, which makes it difficult to handicap how he'll rule on any given issue. Most lawyers believed that whether he's for you or against you could ride on something as irrelevant as whether his sciatica was acting up.

Victoria Donnelly stands and says, "Assistant United States Attorney Victoria Donnelly. Good morning, Your Honor."

"And good morning to you, Ms. Donnelly," Judge Gruen says. "Been a long time since I've seen you in for an arraignment, but you're always welcome in my court. And for the defense?"

Rosenthal rises. "Samuel Rosenthal of the law firm Cromwell Altman Rosenthal and White. I represent my partner Aaron Littman."

"Welcome to you too, Mr. Rosenthal. Now, before we begin, a disclosure is required. Judge Nichols and I were colleagues. Of course, any magistrate in this courthouse would be in the same position, but,

Mr. Rosenthal, if you see that as a basis for my stepping aside, please make that request on the record at this time."

"Your Honor," Rosenthal says, "the defense seeks to have Mr. Littman arraigned as soon as possible, especially given the fact that the government sought to arrest him on a Saturday evening, which means he's already been incarcerated for thirty-six hours."

Translated into non–lawyer speak, this means that the defense will not object to Judge Gruen's presiding over the bail issue, despite his connection to Judge Nichols, but reserves the right to challenge a trial judge on the same grounds, if he or she isn't to the defense's liking.

"Very well," Judge Gruen says. "Waive reading of the indictment, Mr. Rosenthal?"

Criminal defendants have the right to have the charges against them read aloud in open court. Exercising that right, however, is the fastest way to piss off a judge.

"We waive reading, Your Honor, but would nevertheless like a copy of the indictment."

As Rosenthal is saying this, Donnelly's second chair, Leonard Stanton, is already handing the indictment to him. Rosenthal immediately passes it to Aaron, who doesn't even look at it before setting it down beside him.

"That solves that problem," Judge Gruen says. "Mr. Rosenthal, would you like a few moments to review the charges against your client and discuss them with him, or is the defense now ready to enter a plea?"

It's the usual practice at Cromwell Altman to have the lawyer enter the plea because clients can find any number of ways to screw up saying just two words. But with a nod, Rosenthal tells Aaron to do it. Even though there's no camera in the courtroom, the press will still report that Aaron, and not his counsel, made the declaration.

"Not guilty," Aaron says in a strong, clear voice. For a moment he sounds like a lawyer again. After which he and Rosenthal return to their seats.

"Very well," Judge Gruen says. "Which leads us to the issue of bail. Mr. Rosenthal, would you like to be heard on that issue?"

"Yes, thank you, Your Honor," Rosenthal says, again coming to his feet. "As the court knows, Mr. Littman is a man who has devoted his life to a belief in the judicial system. There is nothing—*nothing*—that would keep him from appearing at trial because that is the only way he can ever be completely vindicated. In addition, Mr. Littman has extremely strong ties to the community, including a wife of twenty-four years, and his two teenage daughters attend school here. The Littman family is all present in the courtroom."

Rosenthal turns to the gallery and gestures that Cynthia and the twins should stand. They do as requested, and sit down almost immediately after coming to their feet.

"Finally, Mr. Littman has the constitutional right to participate in his own defense," Rosenthal continues, "and if he is incarcerated, that participation will be greatly restricted. For those reasons, Your Honor, we ask that the court release Mr. Littman on his own recognizance."

"Thank you, Mr. Rosenthal," Judge Gruen says. "Any response by the government?"

Donnelly now stands. She's wearing what must be her best suit for her star turn, a serious black number with a cream-colored blouse poking through. Like Judge Gruen said, seasoned prosecutors normally don't make bail arguments. Then again, bail arguments normally don't warrant a courtroom packed with reporters, either.

"Just as the prosecution does not dispute that Mr. Littman has been a lawyer in this city for many years," Donnelly begins, "the defense cannot dispute that he is not in this courtroom today for that particular reason, but because he has been accused of brutally murdering a member of this court. The proof against him is overwhelming. In addition, the defendant is a man of considerable means, who can easily live out his life abroad and in luxury, and thereby escape being brought to justice for his crimes. As for the supposed family ties that Mr. Rosenthal mentioned, the evidence in this case will show that Mr. Littman was having an affair with Judge Nichols, and therefore there's absolutely no reason to believe that his wife is sufficient reason for him to stay within the jurisdiction. And his children can just as easily visit him in Paraguay or Venezuela during school breaks as they could in prison. For these reasons, the government strongly urges this court to remand Mr. Littman to custody without bail, pending trial. He deserves no special treatment and should be treated like any other accused murderer."

"What a surprise," Judge Gruen says. "The defense says that Mr. Littman wants nothing more than to have his day in court, and the prosecution says that the moment he walks out this door, he's on the first flight to any country without an extradition treaty." Gruen looks at Donnelly and asks, "Is this a capital case?"

Aaron swallows hard. He hasn't even considered that the prosecution might seek the death penalty.

"We are still considering that issue," Donnelly says as matter-of-factly as if the issue at hand were what color to wear and not whether to seek to put a man to death.

"Here's what I'm going to do," Gruen says. "I think that a cash bail, in any amount, frankly, is too lenient under these very unique circumstances. As the prosecution stated, this is a very serious crime, and therefore the impulse to flee is proportionately strong."

Aaron sucks the air around him hard. It sounds very much like Judge Gruen is about to deny him bail.

"But I also think that the government is overreaching a bit," he continues. "So, in my best impression of King Solomon, I'm going to issue a ruling that I'm quite sure will make neither side happy." He smiles, although he must realize that it's inappropriate to think anyone is amused, and then says, "It is the order of the court that Mr. Littman shall post ten million dollars' bail, but thereafter he will be confined to his residence pending trial. During that time, he shall only be permitted to leave for a medical emergency. Visitors shall be restricted to immediate family members, medical personnel, and counsel who are on a preapproved list. When the trial begins, and subject to the trial judge's rulings, the terms of the confinement shall be modified to include visits to the defendant's counsel's office."

The air comes back into Aaron's lungs. He's being allowed to go home.

Aaron doesn't care that he won't be permitted to go anywhere else. There's no other place he wants to be.

PART **THREE**

43

Seventy days.

That's how much time stands between Aaron and the trial.

Most federal criminal cases take a year, and sometimes longer, to get to trial. The defense is to blame more often than not for the delays, especially when the defendant is out on bail. It's pretty straightforward logic: every day before trial is a day out of jail, and the passage of time can only help memories to fade or, if you're lucky, witnesses to die.

Rosenthal, however, decided to buck the conventional wisdom by invoking Aaron's constitutional right to a speedy trial, which requires that it begin no later than seventy days after the indictment. Rosenthal was convinced that because the prosecution rushed to get an indictment, it wouldn't have all its ducks in a row. It was more than a little bit of guts ball. The shortened time frame also means that the defense has to get ready in record time too, but as Rosenthal said when Aaron made this point, the defense doesn't have to prove anything.

The trial judge is the Honorable Jodi Siskind. At thirty-six, she is the youngest member of the bench in the Southern District of New York, and looks like a mom in a children's aspirin commercial, with her short brown hair cut in a bob and excited-just-to-be-here expression. She's only been on the bench for four months, and before that, she was a partner at Taylor Beckett, where she specialized in intellectual property matters. As a result, she has no criminal law experience and probably never tried a case in her life.

With the Constitution telling her she had little choice, Judge Siskind set down the trial for June 4—seventy days after the indictment was filed.

Seventy days.

Not very much time in the big scheme of things, but when it's all the time there is before you stand trial for murder, the entire concept of time takes on a very different significance.

As they wait for Aaron's day of reckoning, the other Littmans try to hew to their normal routines. Cynthia sees her patients and makes her rounds, and the twins continue to go to school and out with their friends.

But try as they might to feign normalcy, Aaron knows that a sea change has occurred in his family. The girls can barely make eye contact with him, and when they do, their disappointment in him is so glaring that it makes Aaron wish they hadn't.

The change in Cynthia runs in the opposite direction. She has seemingly decided that seventy days is too little time to spend even a moment of it angry, and so she has turned her emotions on a dime. Aaron has been permitted back into the bedroom, and there is barely mention of Faith Nichols at all—not an easy feat when the trial hangs over them like the sword of Damocles.

While his wife and daughters have their daily grind to shroud their upheaval, Aaron's day-to-day existence is completely foreign from the life he once led. He wakes up and has absolutely nothing to do. No client calls. No court deadlines. No firm administration matters. Nothing. He spends the day reading, watching old movies, and trying not to think too much about the future.

Of course, time has not stood still. Eric Matthews has sought a new trial, citing Aaron's misconduct, and filed a one-hundred-million-dollar malpractice suit against Cromwell Altman. Rosenthal told Aaron not to worry about it. With a shrug, he said, "Matthews will get convicted again when his lawyer isn't sleeping with the judge, and so where's the harm? Besides, this is why the firm carries a billion dollars in malpractice insurance. So we can all sleep easy when something like this comes along."

Aaron appreciates the words of comfort, but he cannot sleep easy. In fact, it's worst of all at night. When the lights go out, Aaron's mind reels with the horrors that await him in prison.

Nearly all of Aaron's clients who had the misfortune to become involuntary guests of the federal government were sent to minimum-security facilities. Even the few who weren't so lucky served their time in medium-security.

But that's not where Aaron would do his life sentence. A judge killer spends the rest of his years in a place worse than hell.

Which is why the impulse to run is so overwhelming.

Everything Victoria Donnelly said during the bail hearing is true: Aaron Littman is a man of means, and so living his life abroad wouldn't be too much of a hardship. Although Cynthia tells him at every opportunity that they're in this together, Aaron can't help but think she would be secretly relieved to be released from that obligation. And if by some stroke of the imagination Cynthia really wants only death to part them, she could always leave the country with him.

Lindsay and Samantha are a far different matter, however. He can't expect them to live their lives in hiding. And while visiting him as a fugitive might not make them criminals, he couldn't guarantee that the prosecutors wouldn't present them with the Hobson's choice of giving up their father's location or committing perjury. On the other hand, how often will he see them if he's spending the rest of his life in maximum security in another part of the country?

Even though the smart move is to flee, Aaron is determined to stand trial. It's not because he believes he will be acquitted, however. Having spent most of his adult life navigating the criminal justice system, Aaron knows that beating the prosecution in a criminal trial is like winning in Vegas—possible, but not very likely. He's going to place his fate in the hands of the jury for the least noble reason there is: he doubts he could get away with jumping bail. He doesn't know the first thing about false identification, or accessing funds without leaving a trace, or blending into a country where he doesn't speak the language, and he doesn't know anyone he trusts enough to teach him. And when he thinks about it, life on the run, cut off from his family, is just a different kind of prison.

At times, he likens his predicament to a cancer diagnosis. Thinking about percentages of survival, trying to enjoy the little time he has left.

44

Sam Rosenthal served a comprehensive discovery demand on the prosecution the day after Aaron's arraignment. The request sought all documents, video footage, audiotapes, and electronic data in any way relevant to the murder of Faith Nichols, the investigation of the crime, and the evidence against Aaron Littman, as well as any exculpatory evidence.

The prosecution has still not handed over a scrap of paper or a single e-mail, however. Weekly requests demanding compliance are met with the standard U.S. Attorney's Office reply that the government understands its discovery obligations and will fully comply in a timely manner.

When or how they will do that is always unstated, but Rosenthal can read between the lines. Those sons of bitches would comply at the last possible moment, and the extent of that compliance would be the least amount they could get away with.

The day before the last pretrial conference, which is a week before trial is scheduled to begin, Rosenthal's executive assistant of more than forty years, a frail woman named Dotty—an unfortunate diminution of *Dorothy* because nowadays she does seem more than a little bit out of it at times—knocks on his door.

"This just arrived for you, Mr. Rosenthal," she says.

Dotty hands Rosenthal a light gray, legal-sized envelope. The return address indicates it's from the U.S. Attorney's Office. The lack of heft confirms Rosenthal's suspicion that the government's discovery response would be paltry at best.

After thanking Dotty and giving her time to leave and shut the door behind her, Rosenthal opens the envelope and removes its contents. The top two pages are Victoria Donnelly's cover letter, in which she objects to the discovery request as overly broad, unduly burdensome, vague and ambiguous (as if they were two different things), and not reasonably calculated to lead to the discovery of admissible evidence. Then she reserves her rights with regard to admissibility, relevance, and privilege, and whatever other rights she possesses but hasn't listed.

Behind the letter are Faith Nichols's cell phone bills. The first one contains the calls during August, a month before Aaron's affair with Judge Nichols began, and they continue month after month until the day she died.

Rosenthal skims the first few pages. A week into September, the calls began. Every day. From the same number. Usually at the same times, 8:15 p.m. and 7:45 a.m. Every so often, one number vanishes from the bill, replaced by another that makes and receives calls with equal frequency, at the same two times. That pattern continues the next four months, until the calls abruptly stop two days after Faith handed down the Eric Matthews sentence.

The last calls were all incoming, and each a minute in duration. After the sentence, Aaron was undoubtedly trying to reach her and she was ignoring his calls. The final page of the phone records contains the two calls Aaron told him about on the day Faith died: a one-minute call at 8:03 p.m., and after that, the return call from Judge Nichols, which was made at 8:36 p.m. There's also a call at 8:04 p.m. from Aaron to Judge Nichols's phone, again one minute in duration. Aaron didn't mention this one, but Rosenthal assumes it was an oversight; the 8:03 call must have been dropped and so Aaron simply tried again. Easy enough to have forgotten.

The phone bill shows one more call on that last day. The last call to or from Faith Nichols. Three minutes and three seconds in duration, to Aaron's office number. It was placed at 9:48 p.m.

Damn.

The prosecution might not be able to link the burner calls to Aaron, but the final entry is indisputable evidence of contact between Judge Nichols and Aaron, smack in the middle of the window in which she was murdered.

Rosenthal stares at the page the way you might focus your attention on a child who's disappointed you. And like that child, the page offers nothing back.

The next document is a text message that Aaron sent Judge Nichols at 8:05: *Faith, please call me at this number as soon as you can. Very important.*

Alone on the white page, the text looks more threatening than it likely did on Judge Nichols's phone screen. Still, like the calls from the burner phone, it's far from a smoking gun. It could have been sent by anyone and could be referencing anything.

Behind the text message are multiple copies of Aaron's driver's license on Ritz-Carlton letterhead, each bearing a different date. They follow roughly the same pattern as the phone calls—beginning on September 6 and ending January 12. Behind the driver's license papers are the invoices for the room, indicating that Aaron always paid in cash.

This will be more than enough to prove the affair. Aaron Littman, a married man, checking into a hotel once a week that is less than a mile from his home, and paying cash so there's no record of the event. There's no other explanation to sell to the jury.

The one glimmer of hope is that the prosecution's discovery doesn't include any direct proof linking Faith to these visits. That means the Ritz-Carlton must not have surveillance cameras in their common areas. But Rosenthal assumes that the prosecution can plug that hole. A witness will appear who saw them kissing in the lobby, or a desk clerk will testify that Judge Nichols asked what room Mr. Littman was in.

The bulk of the production is composed of various forensic reports.

The cause of death is blunt-force trauma, and diagrams indicate that Judge Nichols suffered wounds to the back of the head. The prosecution can be expected to play this to mean that she was attacked from behind, likely taken by surprise, perhaps trying to flee from a raging Aaron Littman.

There are six crime-scene photos. In them, Judge Nichols lies on her side, her eyes closed, with her head resting on her arm. The blood is visible but not readily apparent, blending in with the leaves and dirt around her, muting the brutality of the scene.

The defense's experts would have to translate the medical jargon, but Rosenthal has seen enough of these types of documents to be able to separate the wheat from the chaff. Very good news here: nothing appears to place Aaron in Central Park with Judge Nichols.

As he places the pages back in the envelope, Rosenthal thinks again about that last phone call—the one from Judge Nichols's cell phone to Aaron's office. If it weren't for that one call, he'd really be celebrating.

The Littman dining room table seats twelve, but two hours after he received the prosecution's discovery, Sam Rosenthal, Rachel London, and Aaron are huddled on one end, with Rosenthal sitting at the head. The lawyers fit the part—Rosenthal in his standard three-piece suit and Rachel wearing a black pantsuit and jacket—but the client is in jeans and unshaven.

Rosenthal warned Aaron that Rachel might still end up being a witness, which meant that she shouldn't be privy to defense strategy. The prosecution might call her to testify about her nasty interactions with Judge Nichols during the failed request for the order to show cause on Garkov's bail revocation. And if called by them, Rosenthal wanted to leave open the possibility of using Rachel as a character witness.

Rachel's involvement was one of the few points about the defense on which Aaron would not acquiesce to Rosenthal's judgment, however. He made it crystal clear that he only wanted people he trusted implicitly handling the case, and that meant it could only be Sam and Rachel.

A compromise was reached. Rachel would second-seat for the pretrial work, which included reviewing the discovery, participating in witness interviews, and crafting an overall defense strategy, but she wouldn't be present at counsel table when the trial began.

"We finally got some discovery," Rosenthal says, and then nods to Rachel. She reaches into her briefcase and pulls out the gray envelope.

"This is it?" Aaron asks, taking the packet from Rachel.

"Donnelly claims that what you have in your hand is the full extent of the government's discovery obligations," Rosenthal confirms. "And you know the only reason she produced it now is so that Judge Siskind doesn't take her head off at the pretrial tomorrow."

Aaron takes the pages out and turns his attention immediately to the phone bills. He flips the pages until he comes to the end, and there he lingers.

The 8:03 entry gives rise to the despair he felt when he got Faith's voice mail, as if it's happening all over again. A second call at 8:04. Aaron forgot that he called her twice, hanging up both times in frustration before sending the text.

He next focuses on the 8:36 call from Faith's cell to the burner phone. That he remembers all too well. The coolness of her voice, clearly not pleased to be hearing from him.

But the last entry is a complete bombshell. A call from Faith's cell to his office number at 9:48. For three minutes and three seconds.

Aaron repeats the timeline in his head, as if maybe he doesn't remember parts of the night that are inextricably etched into his brain. He called Faith, got her voice mail, and hung up. Twice, apparently. Then he sent the text a minute later. She called him back—the 8:36 call—and that's when they agreed to meet at the Alice in Wonderland statue. She showed up around 9:30. They talked for five or so minutes, and then she left. That was at 9:40, maybe 9:45, but no later than that.

He didn't speak to her from the office at 9:48. He was still in Central Park when the call came in.

"The receptionist on fifty-seven can testify that I wasn't in the office that night," Aaron says hopefully. "Or maybe the building's security guard."

"Yeah, we should definitely consider that," Rosenthal says, which to Aaron's ear sounds a lot like the opposite.

He quickly realizes what Rosenthal has already grasped. There's no way that the firm's receptionist or the security guards in the lobby will remember what time Aaron left the building two months ago. Usually a car voucher would indicate his departure time, but he knows he walked home that evening, and so there is no such record.

"I left that day around seven," Aaron says. "Maybe it'll show up on the building's security cameras."

"Even before we got the discovery we checked that out," Rachel says. "It's tough to make anyone out definitively. There's just too much traffic in the lobby at that time. We can point to a figure and claim it's you, but . . . to be honest, I really can't be sure that it *is* you."

"And even if it is," Rosenthal adds, "all it proves is that you left the building at that time. The prosecution can easily argue that you returned, careful to avoid the security cameras. Or they'll point to some shadowy figure about your size coming back into the building and claim it's you."

Aaron continues to stare at the phone records. "How is this possible? I didn't get a call from her," he says. "I wasn't even in the fucking office!"

Aaron's declaration is met with silence. Worse still, Rosenthal and Rachel both look away. They might have just as well said that they've heard such denials before from guilty clients.

I didn't do it. You have to believe me.

"Um . . . I'll check the firm's hard drive for voice mail," Rachel finally says. "Best case, there will be three minutes of static on your voice mail that you might have deleted without giving it a second thought. I get those sometimes . . . you know, butt dials."

"We can deal with the call," Rosenthal says. "Garkov knew you were having an affair with her, and I suspect that her husband might have too. Either one of them could have dialed your number after they killed her, as a way of pointing the police in your direction. And no time-of-death analysis is that precise. There's no way anyone knows if the call was made before or after she died."

Aaron doesn't see it that way. A phone call to him coming around the time of death may not be a smoking gun, but it sure as hell doesn't look good, either.

45

Among Judge Siskind's standing rules is that before the last pretrial conference, the parties have to meet in person and confer about the possibility of a plea. It is one of the many things judges do that sound good in practice but in reality are a complete waste of time.

Rachel and Rosenthal arrive at the U.S. Attorney's Office right on time for their 2:00 p.m. meeting, only to have the guard in the building's lobby tell them to wait. They sit in uncomfortable metal chairs aside a mural of children of various nationalities—someone's idea of a political statement, no doubt. The nicer part of the lobby is where press conferences are held. For the press, the chairs are covered in fabric.

"Petty power-play shit," Rosenthal says, ostensibly to Rachel, but as much to himself. "Meeting with an AUSA is like going to the doctor," he continues to mutter. "Show up on time, then wait out here. Fifteen minutes after the scheduled time, they finally call your name, but then you wait in a conference room upstairs for another ten minutes."

That's exactly what happens. Fifteen minutes after they've arrived, a heavyset African-American woman enters the lobby and calls out: "Sam Rosenthal. Rachel London." She introduces herself as Victoria Donnelly's assistant, but doesn't provide her own name, and then asks Rachel and Rosenthal to follow her to the seventh floor.

Once there, the anonymous assistant directs them to the same small, windowless room with the badly nicked wooden table that Rachel recalls from her interview.

"You're on that end," she says, pointing to the side with two chairs. On the other side are six seats.

They aren't offered coffee or water. The U.S. Attorney's Office doesn't provide such niceties. Instead, their guide says, "Ms. Donnelly and others will be here shortly," and then she shuts the door behind her.

"Six people for a meet-and-confer," Rosenthal says when they're alone. "Imagine if we tried that with a client. The bill would be ten grand."

Rachel smiles. "No, it's more like we have two people attend the meeting, and then twenty read the memo about that meeting. Probably comes out to more our way."

Rosenthal likes Rachel, but that doesn't mean he trusts her. He knows part of his bias is unfair, but he's had more than his share of encounters with beautiful women, and not one of them ever caused him to reconsider his prejudice against them.

Fifteen minutes later, Victoria Donnelly strolls into the room with the usual pack behind her: Assistant United States Attorney Leonard Stanton, FBI special agents Kevin Lacey and Tim Walker, and Christopher Covello, the head of the Criminal Division.

Donnelly doesn't take a seat, but instead makes her way to the corner of the room and reaches for the phone. "We're all here," she says. "Conference room two. On seven."

After she hangs up, she turns to Rosenthal and says, "The U.S. attorney will be here in a minute. I trust that you received the discovery we sent over this morning?"

"Yeah, thanks. You decided not to put anyone in the grand jury?"

Rosenthal knows that there has to be at least one witness in the grand jury, or else they couldn't have gotten the indictment. If he had to guess, he'd point to one of the FBI agents, most likely Lacey, who seems to be the guy in charge. It's common for the prosecution to put their case in through their investigator.

Under the Jencks Act, the transcript of a witness's grand jury testimony must be produced to the other side before that person is called as a witness at trial. Even more important, the prosecution is also required to turn over whatever documents were relied upon by that witness. That means that if Special Agent Lacey did testify before the grand jury, the defense would get not only the transcript of his testimony but also his notes, which would include the witness interviews he conducted. That's exactly what Rosenthal wants, and the sooner, the better.

The rub, however, is that Jencks requires the prosecution to provide such materials only if Lacey *testifies* at trial. That might be reason enough for Donnelly to make her case without calling him to stand.

Donnelly smiles. "We understand our obligations. If we call a witness at trial who gave grand jury testimony, we'll provide the transcript at that time, just like the rules require."

Rosenthal looks past Donnelly to Covello. "Chris, help me out here," Rosenthal says, "because this is utter bullshit. I've never had a case where you didn't provide Jencks materials with the other discovery. Bad enough that you withheld it until now, but we're flying blind here."

"Sorry. Rules are rules, Sam," Covello answers.

Covello is a large man, probably more than two hundred and fifty pounds. Unlike Fitz, who sees the U.S. Attorney's Office as a springboard to elective office, when Covello ends his stint as head of the Criminal Division, he'll go back to earning two million dollars a year to represent the same types of people he's prosecuting now.

Rosenthal makes a mental note to add Covello to his ever-growing enemies list. When Covello's back in private practice, Rosenthal will thoroughly enjoy making Covello pay dearly for being such a hard-ass today. Count on it.

"While we're waiting for Fitz," Donnelly says, "I can also tell you that it's a no on the witness list."

The prosecution's witness list is something of a Holy Grail for the defense. It not only limits the universe of people the defense has to prepare to cross-examine, but it gives insight into the prosecution's trial strategy. Rosenthal can't say he's surprised he's getting stiff-armed on that, however. It's pretty clear that the prosecution is pulling out all the stops.

Rosenthal offers a sad laugh. "Okay, have it your way. It's just going to make it that much sweeter when Aaron walks on this."

Before Donnelly can respond, Fitz enters the room. He's decked out in a politician's navy-blue suit, white shirt, red tie, and American-flag pin on his lapel. His side of the table stands, as if royalty has entered.

"Sorry I'm late," Fitz says with a smile. "Did I miss anything?"

Rosenthal feels nothing but contempt at the sight of the U.S. attorney. Whatever camaraderie they once shared is now a thing of the past. Sam Rosenthal now truly and unequivocally despises this man.

"I was just about to make the plea offer, but I was waiting for you," Donnelly says.

"I'm here now," Fitz says.

This is Donnelly's cue. "In light of the fact that we suspect this was a crime of passion," she says as if reading from a prepared text, "we have authority from the attorney general to offer a plea to murder in the second, with a sentencing recommendation of twenty."

That is exactly what Rosenthal predicted. It isn't a terrible offer, given that the prosecution hasn't formally taken the death penalty off the table. But Rosenthal and Aaron both know the Department of Justice guidelines don't permit seeking a lethal injection in cases of a single murder—even that of a federal judge—and so the maximum sentence Aaron could face is life without the possibility of parole. If the actuarial tables are correct, Aaron only has another 27.6 years to live, which means that the prosecution's offer isn't much of a bargain.

"Thanks, but no thanks," Rosenthal says.

"We'll also support your application that Aaron serve in a

medium-, maybe even a minimum-, security facility," Covello adds. "Nobody on our side of the table wants to see Aaron in supermax with those animals. You may not think that's a big concession on our part, but I tell you, for an inmate . . . well, it makes all the difference in the world. Believe me."

For a split second, Rosenthal thinks about negotiating. He could ask for manslaughter or confirm that minimum security is truly on the table. But no deal would be acceptable, and so there's no point in discussing it further.

"Okay. Sounds like we're done here?" Rosenthal says, and rises to show that he means it. Rachel does likewise. The other side of the table stays put, however.

"Sam . . . look, could you please sit down?" Fitz says. "I really wish you'd consider this offer. We had to go to the mat with the attorney general to make it."

Rosenthal waits until enough time has passed that Fitz probably thinks he's actually reconsidering his prior rejection. Then he says: "What part of *go to hell* do you not understand, Fitz?"

Fitz shows no reaction, as if Rosenthal's venom has no impact on him. "All right, we'll let the jury decide. But I'm still asking you to please sit down. We have something else to discuss with you. Something important."

There's a moment's hesitation by Rosenthal, but he eventually does as directed. Rachel, once again, follows suit.

When they're both seated, Fitz says, "As you know, my office believes that every defendant has the right to counsel of his choosing . . . but not when it compromises the trial."

Fitz comes to a complete stop, daring Rosenthal to say something. Sam isn't going to fall for that trick, however. He stares back, waiting for Fitz to finish.

After a moment's standoff, Fitz resumes. "As I'm sure you've read in the press, there is speculation that Judge Nichols was on the short list to take Justice Velasquez's seat on the Supreme Court. At the time she was killed, very few people knew that. Hell, no one even knew Justice Velasquez was going to be stepping down. But *you* did, Sam. You knew that there was about to be a vacancy on the Supreme Court, and you knew that it was going to go to Faith Nichols, but only if she convicted Nicolai Garkov."

Out of his peripheral vision, Rosenthal can see a look of shock on Rachel's face. Rosenthal isn't surprised, however. He knew it was only a matter of time before Senator Kheel opened his big fucking mouth.

"Fitz, is this your way of telling me that you arrested the wrong guy? Because it sounds to me like you just admitted in a room full of lawyers that Nicolai Garkov had a pretty strong motive not to have Judge Nichols decide his fate."

Rosenthal has said this with a smile, as if he doesn't have a care in the world. That smile vanishes, however, when Fitz shoots back: "Sam, we're going to call you as a witness at trial on this issue."

Fitz has him by the balls, no two ways about it. Under the rules of professional ethics, an attorney can't simultaneously serve as trial counsel *and* appear as a witness in that trial. When it's the prosecution that wants to call the lawyer at trial, the judge weighs the relative prejudice to each side . . . but if the testimony is indispensable, the defense lawyer is disqualified.

"Fuck you, Fitz, and the horse you rode in on," Rosenthal says, pure hatred in every syllable.

Fitz's response is a patronizing chuckle. "Sam, we're just extending you a courtesy," he says. "Tomorrow, bright and early, we're going to ask Judge Siskind to disqualify you as Aaron's counsel."

An hour later, Rosenthal arrives at Aaron's apartment.

Aaron expected this visit, as they discussed a debriefing after the meet-and-confer. But to Aaron's surprise, Rosenthal is alone.

"Where's Rachel?" Aaron asks when Rosenthal enters the apartment.

"Good to see you, too," Rosenthal responds. "She went back to the firm. I thought it made sense to talk . . . just the two of us."

Aaron leads Rosenthal to the living room, where they each take a seat in the leather club chairs. Rosenthal looks around, clearly wondering if anyone else is home.

"It's just us, Sam," Aaron says.

"Good. Well, the meet-and-confer went just like we thought," Rosenthal says. "They told me to go and pound sand on the witness list and then offered a plea to murder two, sentencing recommendation of twenty."

Aaron smiles. "And medium security?"

"Of course. Covello said that minimum might be doable."

"Well, they're nothing if not predictable, at least."

Rosenthal sighs heavily, indicating a more serious matter is about to be raised. "They also know about my involvement in vetting Judge Nichols for the high court. Fitz said that tomorrow they're going to move to disqualify me as counsel."

All of the blood drains from Aaron's face. The prospect of losing Sam is unimaginable. In fact, one of the few reasons Aaron has maintained any hope is because he has Rosenthal in his corner.

"Sam . . . I can't do this without you."

"My theory is that they're just trying to yank our chains a little bit. Which I'm going to make them regret. Believe me on that. So tomorrow, after they tell Judge Siskind they want me to testify that Judge Nichols was led to understand that her nomination to the Supreme Court only happened after Garkov got convicted, I'll tell her that half a dozen people could testify to the same thing. And God willing, she'll make Donnelly call one of them."

Aaron nods that he understands, but his expression must betray his concern because Rosenthal places his hand atop Aaron's on the table. "Don't worry, Aaron. I'm with you all the way. That, I promise."

46

The last pretrial conference is a proverbial forever-hold-your-peace moment, constituting the last opportunity before trial for each side to raise any issues. Such motion practice normally doesn't interest anyone but the litigants, but Aaron Littman's case is far from usual.

The gallery is standing room only, and the snippets Aaron's overheard from the reporters sitting behind him indicate Fitz must have leaked that the main event today will be the prosecution's motion to disqualify Sam Rosenthal.

"Good morning," Judge Siskind says brightly. "I take it that counsel followed my rules and met and conferred?"

"Yes, Your Honor," Donnelly and Rosenthal say in unison.

"And are we still going to trial?"

"Yes, Your Honor," they say together again.

"Okay, then. Are there any issues regarding discovery that either side would like to raise at this time?"

Donnelly, as the prosecutor, goes first. "We've fully complied with our obligations to the defense," she says.

"Mr. Rosenthal, any complaints?"

"We only received the government's discovery yesterday, Your Honor, so we're still reviewing it. This much we already know, however: they've refused to give us a witness list."

"Ms. Donnelly, may I ask why not?"

"Your Honor, as Mr. Rosenthal well knows, we're under no

obligation to provide a witness list. In this case, we have serious concerns about witness intimidation."

This is the kind of thing you say to an inexperienced judge. Someone with a few years under her belt would know it's a crock. Witness intimidation might be the battle cry in organized crime cases, but Aaron's certainly not going to have anyone whacked. But there's no percentage in it for Judge Siskind to risk having a witness killed during her first trial, and so she denies the request without a second thought.

Rosenthal displays no emotion at the ruling, even though it's a significant setback. Instead he says, "We also didn't receive any grand jury testimony."

Donnelly is already speaking over him. "I explained to Mr. Rosenthal at the meet-and-confer that, to the extent that we call a witness at trial who previously testified in the grand jury, we will produce the transcript at the close of the prosecution's direct examination. Although our office sometimes produces grand jury transcripts earlier, we are under no legal obligation to do so."

Judge Siskind shrugs. "That's your prerogative, Ms. Donnelly. But if you're going to be so literal about it, I'm going to give Mr. Rosenthal ample time between direct and cross to review. Now, is there anything else?"

"Not from the defense, Your Honor," Rosenthal says.

"The government does have something of importance to raise," Donnelly says. "Your Honor, as part of our case in chief, we will prove that Judge Nichols was being considered for the United States Supreme Court. Mr. Rosenthal was one of a handful of people who knew about this. The prosecution plans to call Mr. Rosenthal as a witness on this issue, and that necessitates his disqualification as defense counsel."

Judge Siskind looks hard in Donnelly's direction. Judges, like everyone else, don't appreciate having their world turned upside down without any notice.

"Hold on there," Judge Siskind says. "That's not going to cut it, Ms. Donnelly, and you know it. Before I'm going to deny a defendant counsel of his choosing, I'm going to need a detailed proffer from you regarding the expected testimony that Mr. Rosenthal will provide, and a representation that the government cannot introduce that evidence through another witness. And, if you can do those things, then I will balance the government's need for this testimony against Mr. Littman's Sixth Amendment right to counsel of his choosing."

Donnelly does not seem fazed by Judge Siskind's demand. "We will call Mr. Rosenthal to testify that Mr. Littman was well aware of Judge Nichols's potential elevation to the Supreme Court," Donnelly says. "And, to answer the court's second point, while there may be other witnesses who can testify that Judge Nichols was being considered for the Supreme Court, we believe that Mr. Rosenthal is the only witness who can say that Mr. Littman was aware of that fact other than Mr. Littman himself, and he, of course, has the right not to testify. As for the government's need for this testimony . . . it speaks to motive, proving that Mr. Littman knew Judge Nichols was not going to acquit Nicolai Garkov because her nomination was only going to happen if he was convicted."

Aaron didn't anticipate that this would be their play—to argue that it was *his* knowledge of Faith's possible Supreme Court nomination that is relevant, rather than the nomination itself. It's a smart move. Donnelly's right that only Rosenthal could testify about such communications, and therefore he becomes an indispensable witness.

Aaron's stomach tightens. Rosenthal is going to be disqualified.

Judge Siskind looks to the defense table. "What about it, Mr. Rosenthal?"

Rosenthal doesn't answer at first, and Aaron assumes he's running through different responses before committing to a position. Finally he says, "Your Honor . . . I never told Mr. Littman about Judge

Nichols's possible nomination to the Supreme Court, and I have no reason to believe that Mr. Littman knew about it until after it appeared in the press, which, of course, was after her death."

Needless to say, this isn't true, but that hardly matters. Rosenthal's testimony is only relevant *if* he told Aaron.

If they weren't in court, Donnelly might have shouted *bullshit*, but she says the legalese equivalent. "If Mr. Rosenthal is going to testify, he should be sworn and cross-examined on this point."

Judge Siskind considers the request for a few moments. "No. No, I'm not going there, Ms. Donnelly. Mr. Rosenthal is an officer of the court and therefore I'm going to accept his representation."

"Your Honor, we're entitled to sworn testimony," Donnelly says.

Judge Siskind straightens up a bit. Even though she's new to the bench, she knows enough to make it clear that she's not going to be pushed around.

"Ms. Donnelly, you'd be wise to watch your tone. If you have a problem with my ruling, the appellate court is in the next building. Until then, we're adjourned."

Aaron savors the moment. The defense will certainly get its fair share of judicial contempt during the trial, but it's always nice when the other side pisses off the judge. Better than that, he'll have Sam Rosenthal at his side at trial, and not testifying against him.

47

Rosenthal wants to put on a reasonable-doubt defense, where they poke holes in the prosecution's evidence and hope that gives rise to sufficient uncertainty about Aaron's guilt to obtain an acquittal. It's a tried-and-true strategy to be sure, and one that Aaron has used more often than not. And yet for his own defense, Aaron thinks it's lacking. He's convinced a jury will not let him go free without being firm in the belief that someone else must ultimately be punished for Faith's murder. In his mind, that means the defense must present an alternative theory of the crime clearly identifying Faith's murderer.

There's very good reason why Rosenthal disagrees. Without the vast resources of the prosecution—the ability to compel testimony, conduct forensic analysis, review computer databases for matches to DNA and fingerprints—the defense can easily get it wrong. They could end up pointing the finger at someone who turns out to have an airtight alibi.

Still, Aaron has pressed for a defense that's uncompromising in the claim that Nicolai Garkov murdered Faith. After all, it's not every defendant in a murder trial who can point to a terrorist with equal motive. But, as Rosenthal has countered, putting their eggs in the Garkov basket is not without problems. Among other things, the defense has no evidence linking Garkov to the murder, not to mention that he was in jail at the time of the attack.

Plan B is Stuart Christensen, Faith's husband. Aaron knows from his pillow talk with Faith that Stuart became accustomed to a certain type of lifestyle, and that she completely financed it. More than once she told

Aaron that her husband would be up shit creek without a paddle if they divorced. The apartment was in her name alone, purchased back when she was a partner at Windsor Taft, and she brought all of their net worth into the marriage, which meant that it wasn't marital property, and she could take it with her when they split. Aaron also knew that big law firms offered their partners outsized life insurance policies, and so he suspects that Faith's husband profited considerably from his wife's death.

Rosenthal is against this approach too, pointing out that going after Stuart has even greater risks than accusing Garkov. For one thing, he might have an airtight alibi too, and unlike Garkov, he wouldn't know the kind of people who would commit murder for hire. For another, there is a great risk of jury backlash when you accuse a member of the victim's family of murder.

Mainly to placate Aaron, Rosenthal agrees to reach out to both men in the hope that they'll say something that the defense could use. Everyone understands, however, that it's a very long shot.

Stuart Christensen meets Rosenthal's expectation. His lawyer, Jennifer Bennett, is nice enough about it—high-priced white-collar practitioners never piss off potential business referrers—but the message is clear: her client will do everything he can to make sure Aaron is convicted.

They expect Clint Broden to also decline, but to their very pleasant surprise, Broden says that Garkov will meet with them. Aaron knows not to get his hopes up, as Broden is way too smart a lawyer to allow his client to say anything that would incriminate him. But the fact that they're granting the defense an audience means Garkov isn't cooperating with the prosecution.

And that's grounds for cautious optimism.

After going through the double set of security procedures, Sam Rosenthal and Rachel London are greeted in Garkov's entry foyer by the tall Russian, decked out in a purple velvet bathrobe, as if he's channeling Hugh Hefner. Clint Broden is more appropriately dressed, but at a foot shorter than his client, he looks something like a child playing dress-up.

Aaron wanted to be present—to stare Garkov down if for no other reason, but home arrest prohibited that kind of showdown. The defense could have made a request to Judge Siskind for special dispensation, but that would have given the prosecution notice, which likely would have caused Broden to refuse to meet. So Rosenthal and Rachel are without their client.

Ever the host, Garkov brings his guests into the living room, with its wall of windows overlooking Central Park. Sam and Rachel arrange themselves on one sofa, while Garkov and Broden take the sofa opposite them.

"Quite the fireplace," Rosenthal says, remarking on the open lion's mouth.

"Thank you," Garkov says. "I saw it in a palazzo near Lake Como, and I just had to have it. Bought the entire goddamn palazzo, actually, just so I could bring the fireplace over here."

Rosenthal politely smiles, but he's eager to get down to business. "I suppose the first and only thing on our agenda is to ask if you'll be testifying for the prosecution."

Broden answers for his client. "No. Needless to say, they asked, they threatened, they offered inducement, but Nicolai is not going to help them."

"What about helping us?" Rachel says, her smile focused like a laser on Garkov.

"No. I'm afraid not," Broden says, grabbing Garkov's arm to ensure that he doesn't speak out of turn simply because he's being asked a question by a beautiful woman. "If either side calls Mr. Garkov to the stand, he will assert his Fifth Amendment privilege against self-incrimination."

That settles it then. Garkov is a dead end.

"That seems like the kind of thing you might have told us over the phone and saved us the trip here," Rosenthal says.

Broden smiles. "There's something else. Something that Nicolai wanted to tell you face-to-face."

All eyes turn to the Russian, who clearly has no qualms about being the center of attention. He holds everyone's stare until the silence is palpable.

"I was hoping you could convey a message to Aaron Littman for me," Garkov finally says.

Rosenthal says, "Okay. What is it?"

"Thank you."

Rosenthal knows it's a setup, but he's got to play it through nonetheless. "And for what are you thanking him?"

"For killing Judge Nichols, of course," Garkov says with a full-on smile. "I know I didn't do it, and so I can only assume that he did. So, please tell him: thank you."

It's less than a five-minute walk from Trump Tower to Cromwell Altman's offices, but the silence makes it seem longer. It isn't until they're in the elevator that Rosenthal finally opens his mouth.

"Don't let what Garkov said upset you," he quietly remarks. "All we care about is that he's not going to help the prosecution. Without Garkov's testimony, they can't prove any kind of blackmail. And without that, there's no motive."

Rachel is not assuaged. "I really thought it was him," she says.

"And it still might be him, Rachel. Garkov's a sociopath and a murderer. What makes you think he's telling us the truth?"

"I don't know. Maybe it's because I don't see any advantage he gains from lying to us."

"It doesn't matter," Rosenthal says in a stern voice. "Trials aren't about the truth. They're about winning. And if Garkov is sitting this one out, then our best shot is to put the blame directly on him, just like Aaron wanted. So that's exactly what we're going to do."

48

On Sunday evening, the night before the trial is scheduled to begin, Aaron feels the full weight of what is about to unfold. He has done yeoman's work to keep it all together in the days since his indictment, but this night, lying in bed beside his wife, all that emotion is ready to burst free.

Aaron's not so naïve as to think that the last two months, in which nothing has been normal, are a good indicator of future happiness, but he's also not so far gone that he doesn't recognize the possibility that he's being given the rarest of all gifts: a second chance.

"I love you so very much, Cynthia," he says, choking on the words.

Cynthia looks at him and is also near tears as she kisses him on the lips very softly. "I love you too," she says. "And we're going to get through this. Together."

The irony is powerful enough to bring a broad smile to his face. For the first time in . . . he doesn't know how long, Aaron is optimistic about the future.

Even as tomorrow, the trial of his life begins.

A Lincoln Town Car picks Aaron up in front of his home to take him to court. As he gets in the backseat amid the popping flashes, Aaron suspects the spectacle in front of the courthouse will be twice as bad.

And holy God, it is.

There are actually two federal court buildings in lower Manhattan. The original structure was built in the 1930s and has the majestic columns denoting a courthouse of that era. The newer building was erected twenty years ago and is positioned diagonally behind its predecessor. It has two entrances that are open to the public, which means that at least the press factor is cut in half at each one.

Aaron opts for the back entrance, which is still blocked by at least a hundred reporters. He smiles for the cameras and then quickly ducks inside. Cynthia will come separately, the thought being that if she doesn't arrive with Aaron, she might not attract the attention of the paparazzi. Aaron knows now, however, that is very unlikely.

Inside the courtroom, the gallery is at capacity. Even so, when Cynthia finally arrives, she's allowed to sit in the front row behind the defense table. All have agreed it's best if the girls are not present for any of the trial, the thinking being that if the jury believes Aaron is subjecting his children to the prurient details of his life, they'll be more likely to be angry with him than feel sympathy for his daughters.

Faith's husband, Stuart, sits on the opposite side from Cynthia, directly behind the prosecution team. He will almost certainly be a witness against Aaron but is permitted to watch jury selection—or voir dire, as Judge Siskind prefers to use the French term—and opening statements, after which the judge has ordered that all potential witnesses will be barred from the courtroom, so as not to taint their testimony. Erring on the side of caution, Cynthia will also be absent during the testimony, just in case she's needed as a character witness. It is for that reason, too, that Rachel is back at the firm and not here.

Jury selection goes quickly. Most federal judges don't stand for the weeks of vetting that can occur in the state courts. The questions designed to ferret out bias are submitted by the lawyers, and then Judge Siskind asks the prospective jurors only the ones she deems relevant. Proceeding in that fashion results in all twelve being seated in less than a day.

Although some lawyers swear that picking a jury is the most important part of any trial, Aaron likens it more to the scoring system of Olympic judges—you throw out the high and the low, and the rest are going to be fine. *The low*—those predisposed to convict—means anyone with a background in, or penchant for, law enforcement. The only juror who fits that bill is a retired air force colonel who now teaches sociology at John Jay College. Had he been in the first chair, Aaron might have struck him, but Rosenthal waved off Aaron's concern, reasoning that the professor is an academic more than a military man, and that makes him more inclined to acquit on grounds of reasonable doubt.

In the end, the jury's composed of six men and six women. Five of them appear to be minorities. They range in age from twenty-two to seventy-two.

Aaron considers it a fair enough jury, at least insofar as he can make any assessment based on physical appearance and the answers to rudimentary questions intended to root out only the most severe prejudices. If he's ultimately convicted, he won't blame it on the jury composition, which honestly is all you can ask out of voir dire.

The next day, June 5, begins with opening statements. Victoria Donnelly is no more pleasant in front of a jury than she is in real life. She still carries herself with that particularly noxious combination of superiority and contempt for others. Perhaps the jury will find her to be a no-nonsense prosecutor, but Aaron can't help but think that it's good for him that Donnelly has taken the lead and not Covello or, as he once threatened to do, Fitz himself.

It's immediately apparent that Rosenthal's decision to rush to trial hasn't impacted Donnelly's preparation. She speaks without notes, and the exhibits she plans to introduce appear on cue on the forty-eight-inch television screens on either end of the jury box.

"Think of my opening statement like the printout you get from Google Maps," Donnelly tells the jury, a rare instance when she smiles.

It was once part of the U.S. Attorney's Office's standard opening-statement monologue to tell the jury that they were presenting a road map. Apparently, this is their effort to get with the times.

Aaron's given instruction to enough clients to know not to react to anything Donnelly says. Nevertheless, when Donnelly tells the jury about his affair with Judge Nichols, it takes all of his willpower not to turn to the gallery to ascertain Cynthia's reaction.

"Ladies and gentlemen," Donnelly says, "the defendant was in love with Faith Nichols. They had a torrid affair during which nothing else mattered to him. Not his wife of more than twenty years, not his children, not even his professional standing. You will hear evidence that, subsumed by this obsessive love, Mr. Littman did something unthinkable for a defense lawyer. He appeared as counsel for a client named Eric Matthews in a case in which Judge Nichols—his lover at the time—was the judge. This type of conflict of interest could, and indeed should, result in a lawyer never practicing law again."

Donnelly pauses and shakes her head in disgust. Aaron notices that some of the jurors seem to squirm in their seats.

"If that was the only infraction Mr. Littman committed," Donnelly continues, "it would be a matter for the disciplinary committee that governs attorney conduct, and not you, ladies and gentlemen. But after Eric Matthews, the defendant represented Nicolai Garkov. Mr. Garkov was on trial for very serious crimes. So serious, in fact, that he likely would have received life in prison if convicted. And so when Faith Nichols became his judge, Mr. Garkov immediately hired Aaron Littman, even though he already had a very competent trial attorney representing him. Why did Mr. Garkov do this? For one simple reason: he knew about the defendant's affair with Judge Nichols, and he was blackmailing Mr. Littman to blackmail her. You see, ladies and gentlemen, unlike this trial, where you, the jury, will ultimately decide guilt or innocence, Mr. Garkov waived his right to a jury, which meant that Judge Nichols, and she alone, would render the verdict. It was a very simple plan. Mr. Garkov told his new lawyer, Aaron Littman, that he was to convince his lover, Judge Nichols, to find him not guilty, or else he'd go public about their affair, which would end both of their careers.

"And that's precisely what Mr. Littman set out to do. The evidence will show that the defendant met with Judge Nichols right before she was murdered," Donnelly says, without explaining what that evidence would be. "They met in Central Park at night, a place where no one would see them. And when they did, the defendant told Judge Nichols about Mr. Garkov's threats."

Aaron scribbles on the legal pad in front of him, *OBJECT!* but Rosenthal dismisses it with a shake of the head. Jurors often view objecting during an opening statement as discourteous, and truth be told, Aaron can't recall ever having done it himself. That being said, Donnelly has gone far beyond what is permissible under the rules, making arguments based on inferences rather than merely recounting what the evidence will be.

"But Judge Nichols told the defendant that she would not compromise her office," Donnelly continues, as if there is no doubt that this is what occurred, even though there is no possible way she could know what Judge Nichols said. "And that meant that Mr. Littman would be disbarred for sure, not to mention that his wife might divorce him when news of his extramarital affair became public. And so in the heat of the moment, Aaron Littman beat Judge Nichols to death."

It's a truism of criminal practice that only two people know what actually happened—the victim and the perpetrator. In a murder case, that means no one who knows the truth is going to reveal it. And yet Donnelly has gotten a lot of it right.

Sam Rosenthal could easily make it to the podium without his cane. Yet he leans on it heavily to make the five-foot trek, an unspoken communication with the jury that he is a man who has known struggle.

"Ladies and gentlemen of the jury . . . I disagree with much of what Ms. Donnelly told you," Rosenthal says in a slow voice, almost like he's sharing a sad story. "About the evidence indicating Mr. Littman's guilt, of course. But about so much more, as well. Even about the purpose of our opening statements. Ms. Donnelly told you that her opening statement was a map. I don't see it that way at all. I believe that what Ms. Donnelly and I tell you to begin this case is a promise. No, it's even more than that. It's a sacred vow about what each side will demonstrate during this trial. And like all vows, be wary of those who make them cavalierly and then do not follow through."

Aaron wishes Rosenthal chose a different phrase. Having never been married, Rosenthal might not have made the connection to Aaron's own broken marriage vows.

"Ms. Donnelly promised you a great many things in her opening statement," Rosenthal continues, his voice growing stronger. "She promised you proof of an affair between Mr. Littman and Judge Nichols. She promised you a motive: blackmail. She promised you that at the end of this case, you would not have a single reasonable doubt that Aaron Littman committed this brutal murder."

Rosenthal stops and tries to make eye contact with each of the twelve in the jury box. It appears to Aaron that most of them have accepted his lawyer's gaze.

"I make you one promise, and one promise only," Rosenthal says with a closing crescendo. "And that is this: Ms. Donnelly will *break* her promises. The government, with all its vast powers and resources at hand, will *not* prove Mr. Littman's guilt beyond a reasonable doubt. Of that you can be certain."

With that, Rosenthal limps back to counsel table and sits down. Aaron had wanted Rosenthal's opening to go on longer, hitting back at the evidence and setting up Garkov, but Rosenthal overruled him.

Aaron is questioning Rosenthal's judgment right up until the moment he spies Donnelly's scowl. It is the surest measure of the effectiveness of Rosenthal's presentation. Perhaps the old man was right to quit when he did.

49

The afternoon begins with Victoria Donnelly calling her first witness to the stand. Stuart Christensen is wearing a black suit, undoubtedly to remind the jury that he's still in mourning.

In something of a monotone, Stuart answers Donnelly's open-ended questions to explain that he suspected his wife was having an affair, and one night he followed her to the Ritz-Carlton, and then waited three hours for her to leave.

"Did you see who she was meeting?" Donnelly asks.

"Yes. She came out of the hotel holding Aaron Littman's hand." Even without Donnelly's prompting, Stuart knows to make the in-court identification. "The man I saw with my wife is that man, there," Stuart says, pointing at Aaron.

As revenge fantasies go, this must rank pretty close to the top. *You may have fucked my wife, but now I'm going to send your sorry ass to jail for the rest of your life.*

"Let the record reflect," Donnelly says quickly, "that the witness has identified the defendant, Aaron Littman."

Aaron wants to scream *Liar!* Instead, he leans over and whispers to Rosenthal: "He never saw us. Faith and I never left together."

Victoria Donnelly has already asked her next question, and rather than answer Aaron, Rosenthal instead gets to his feet and shouts, "Objection! Hearsay."

Judge Siskind seems surprised, as it's the first time Rosenthal's objected. "Counsel, please approach," she says.

Although Aaron is technically not included in the request that counsel approach, he joins Rosenthal at the bench anyway. When everyone is assembled, Judge Siskind places her hand over the microphone in front of her and leans forward to address the lawyers below her.

"It's your objection, Mr. Rosenthal, so it's your turn."

"Your Honor, Ms. Donnelly's question suggests that she's trying to elicit from this witness the testimony about Judge Nichols's consideration for a nomination to the Supreme Court," Rosenthal says. "My objection is that such testimony should be precluded on hearsay grounds because Judge Nichols was his sole source for that information. As a result, he's really just testifying to what *she* told him, and that's classic hearsay."

Thank God Rosenthal was listening to Donnelly and not his complaint that Stuart Christensen was lying, Aaron thinks. This is a critical issue for the defense. If Donnelly can get into evidence that Faith knew her Supreme Court nomination was linked to Garkov's conviction, the prosecution has gone a long way to show motive.

Judge Siskind's eyebrows rise, suggesting she thinks Rosenthal's made a good point. She turns to Donnelly. "Any rebuttal, Counselor?"

"This witness will establish Judge Nichols's mental state," Donnelly counters. "Therefore his testimony meets an exception to the hearsay rule. As the victim's husband, he was well aware that Judge Nichols *believed* she was under consideration for the Supreme Court. That belief caused Judge Nichols to reject the defendant's attempt at blackmail, and that's what we're putting before the jury."

Like a spectator at Wimbledon, Judge Siskind turns back to Rosenthal, as it's now his turn to volley. "What do you say to that, Mr. Rosenthal? Can't a husband testify to his wife's mental state?"

"Not if that conclusion is based solely on hearsay," Rosenthal replies. "Mr. Christensen is free to testify about what he observed, but a conclusion that is based on nothing more than a statement made by his wife is no different than testifying to the truth of the statement itself. Either way, it's hearsay."

When Donnelly tries to offer a rebuttal, Judge Siskind stops her in her tracks. "No, I think Mr. Rosenthal's got you on this one," she says. "The objection is sustained. Ms. Donnelly, move on to something else with this witness. If you want to get into evidence that Judge Nichols was being considered for the Supreme Court, I suggest you get the White House on the phone."

As they walk back to counsel table, Rosenthal whispers to Aaron, "That was huge for us."

Now unable to establish motive through Stuart Christensen, Donnelly decides to pull at the jury's collective heartstrings. Stuart recounts how much he misses his wife and how grief-stricken he was upon hearing the news of her murder. Aaron can only imagine that somewhere up there Faith is rolling her eyes.

When Judge Siskind says that Rosenthal may begin his cross-examination, he rises slowly and says, "No questions for this witness, Your Honor."

"In that case," Judge Siskind says, "the witness is excused, and we're adjourned for a twenty-minute recess."

Aaron holds his tongue until the last of the jurors leaves the courtroom, and then a few moments longer to allow Judge Siskind to depart the bench. The moment the coast is clear, however, he turns on Rosenthal.

"What the hell, Sam?! Why didn't you question him?!"

Rosenthal looks away from the papers he's shuffling. "It was too risky," he says. "Did you look at the jury while he was testifying? They wanted to hug the little shit."

"But he's lying about seeing Faith and me together at the hotel! That wasn't true at all, and you didn't call him out on it."

Rosenthal grasps Aaron by the elbow and says, "I know the lawyer in you knows this, Aaron, but without proof, what's calling him a liar going to do for us? And it's not going to help us win any sympathy points with the jury, that's for damn sure."

Aaron feels himself deflate. He knew the Ritz-Carlton records would establish he'd been at the hotel, but he had held out hope that the prosecution couldn't prove he'd been there with Faith. And now they have.

"Keep your eye on the ball, Aaron. Garkov's the real play here. If we can get his assertion of the Fifth before the jury, we're home free."

Aaron wants to ask, *What if we can't?* but he already knows the answer. Having passed on the opportunity to go after Stuart Christensen, without Garkov the defense has nothing.

50

Victoria Donnelly's next witness is a desk clerk at the Ritz-Carlton. Donnelly's strategy is now clear. She's going to go all-in on the one thing she can prove without any shadow of a doubt—the affair—in the hope that when she's done, the jury will be poisoned against Aaron to such an extent that they won't much care that the evidence that he committed murder is wholly circumstantial.

The clerk's name is Dana Luria. She's in her early twenties, at most, and has the attractive but unthreatening quality that a luxury hotel would look for in someone to meet their guests. She speaks so softly that Judge Siskind has to ask her more than once to speak up so the jury, which is sitting less than fifteen feet from her, can hear.

Donnelly's direct is straightforward. She establishes that hotel procedure is to copy identification for every guest checking in and then submits into evidence the hotel's records indicating each and every time that Aaron was there.

"Ms. Luria, let me call your attention to the line that indicates the form of payment," Donnelly says, a copy of the Ritz-Carlton bill for September 6—the day of the Vanderlyn dinner, the first day Aaron slept with Faith—shown on all six television monitors. "Please tell the jury the amount of the charge for the room on that night."

"Six hundred and sixty-five dollars, which includes taxes."

"And how did Mr. Littman make that payment?"

"In cash."

One by one, Donnelly systematically goes through the rest of the Ritz-Carlton bills. As each invoice flashes on the monitors, the clerk takes a few moments to carefully study the paper copy in her hand—as if she hasn't already reviewed it numerous times in preparation—and then announces the nightly charge and that Aaron paid in cash.

Donnelly walks back to counsel table and whispers something in the ear of her second chair, Stanton. A moment later, Faith's picture comes on the computer screens, the same photo that the newspapers ran for her obituary.

Donnelly asks, "Did you ever see this woman at your hotel?"

"Yes. Many times."

"Tell the jury about that."

"She was something of a regular. Once a week or so, she would come in and head straight to the elevators. She never checked in, and I never saw her with any luggage. She just always went straight to the elevators."

"Thank you, Ms. Luria. No further questions, Your Honor."

Rosenthal's cross is brief, but he drives home the only point there is to make.

"You must see thousands of people in your job?" he asks.

"Yes."

"And you don't recall ever seeing Mr. Littman, do you?"

The answer must be no. Otherwise, Donnelly surely would have had Luria make the identification during direct questioning.

"Not that I remember," she says.

"And that must necessarily mean that even though you *claim* that you saw Judge Nichols at the hotel on various occasions, you have no reason to believe that Mr. Littman was meeting with her at any of those times. Is that correct?"

"I know that he checked into the hotel because of the records."

"Ms. Luria, is that something that Ms. Donnelly told you to say?"

"Objection!" Donnelly calls out.

"Sustained." Judge Siskind gives Rosenthal a sharp look. "Counselor, please. You know better than that."

Indeed, Rosenthal does. Still, Aaron is thankful that the effort was made.

"Let me phrase it a different way," Rosenthal says. "Ms. Luria, I grant you that you know from the hotel records that Mr. Littman was a guest at the Ritz-Carlton on certain dates. And your testimony is that you recall seeing Judge Nichols in the lobby from time to time. Is that correct?"

"Yes."

"And so, all that I'm asking is if you can say, under oath, that you know, for a fact, that Mr. Littman and Judge Nichols were ever in the hotel on the same day."

Luria hesitates, but again Rosenthal knows that if she could have put them together, Donnelly would have made this the center point of her direct examination.

"No," Luria says softly.

"And isn't it a bit odd, Ms. Luria, that you recall seeing Judge Nichols in your hotel—a woman who *never* actually checked in—but you *don't* remember seeing Mr. Littman, who stood at the front desk for probably five minutes at a time, week after week, and handed over his driver's license each time?"

Luria looks confused. "I'm not lying," she says defensively. "I just don't remember seeing him."

"I don't think you're lying about *that*," Rosenthal says. "Who could remember seeing someone months ago? It's the part about you remembering that you saw Judge Nichols in your hotel that I'm suggesting is highly doubtful."

"Objection!" Donnelly shouts.

"I agree," Rosenthal says quickly, "it is highly objectionable, which is why I have no further questions for this witness."

When Rosenthal sits down, Aaron whispers in his ear, "Nicely done, Sam."

51

The last witness of this busy trial day is Sara Meyers. Upon hearing her name, Rosenthal leans over to Aaron and asks, "Who the hell is that?"

"One of Faith's law clerks," Aaron whispers back. "I never spoke to her."

Aaron assumes Meyers will provide further evidence to support the affair. After all, no one knows more about the comings and goings of a judge than her law clerks. But when Donnelly asks if Sara was assigned the Garkov case, Aaron realizes that's not the reason she's testifying. She's been called as a witness to provide evidence of motive.

"Ms. Meyers, what was your perception of Judge Nichols's reaction to being assigned to the Garkov case?" Donnelly asks.

"I was super excited. It was a very high-profile case."

"I understand that, Ms. Meyers. But my question was whether you noticed *Judge Nichols's* reaction?"

"Oh, sorry. Yeah, I was kinda surprised because the judge didn't seem happy about it at all."

"Why did that surprise you?"

"Like I said before, it was a very high-profile case, with lots of interesting legal issues. As soon as we got it, I asked Judge Nichols to put me on it."

"Did you do any legal research concerning Judge Nichols's decision to revoke Mr. Garkov's bail?"

"No. That's why it was so surprising when she did it," Sara says.

"Explain to the jury why you were so surprised."

"Well, before Judge Nichols made a ruling, she'd always ask me to review the briefs and do extensive legal research. Then I'd present her with a bench memo, which had my findings, and a suggestion of how I thought she should rule. She almost always agreed with my analysis. Sometimes, she'd even have me write the decision. Then she'd edit it, but a lot of the time what I wrote stayed in."

To hear Sara Meyers tell it, she was really the federal judge and Faith Nichols her assistant. Donnelly doesn't seem to mind much, so long as she's getting into evidence for what she needs to prove—that Faith's conduct with regard to the Garkov case was aberrational.

"After Judge Nichols revoked Mr. Garkov's bail," Donnelly asks, "did the defense ask her to reconsider her bail decision?"

"Yes. The next day. An attorney from Cromwell Altman came to chambers. Not Mr. Littman, but his partner, Rachel London. I wasn't with Judge Nichols when they met."

"Was that unusual, Ms. Meyers? For Judge Nichols to meet with counsel without one of her clerks present?"

"Yes. Honestly, it had never happened before. The only way you really can learn is to be there. So, it's important for the clerks to be in every argument or conference on one of the cases that you're assigned. And since I was assigned the Garkov case, I was very surprised when Judge Nichols said she didn't want me to sit in."

"Why was Ms. London there?"

"She was making an order to show cause application."

"Please explain to the jury what an order to show cause application is, Ms. Meyers."

"It's really just a request for a hearing date. In this case, the defense wanted Judge Nichols to schedule a hearing for the next day, at which time they were going to ask that she reverse her decision to revoke Mr. Garkov's bail and reinstate his house arrest."

"And what happened after Ms. London left Judge Nichols's chambers?"

"I assumed that she'd granted the order, and so I asked her when the hearing was going to be and if she wanted me to prepare a memo.

You know, like I always did. But she told me that she'd already denied the motion. I was . . . honestly, *shocked* isn't even the right word. I would say, flabbergasted. She'd never before denied an order to show cause. She might deny the underlying request, but not the request to just set up a hearing date. She always granted them."

"What did Judge Nichols say to you after she told you she was refusing to even set up a date for the hearing?"

"She said she wasn't feeling well and was going to go home."

Donnelly's face is screwed up tight, as if this is the oddest thing she's ever heard in her whole life.

Judge Siskind gives the defense a ten-minute break after Donnelly finishes with Sara Meyers. During that time, Aaron and Rosenthal huddle about the cross-examination. The strategy they agree upon is to tread lightly, reasoning that Meyers can only hurt them.

And so when court resumes, Rosenthal focuses on Sara Meyers's lack of experience. The goal is to convince the jury that even though Sara believes that Judge Nichols's behavior in denying the order to show cause was odd, *they* shouldn't.

"How long were you Judge Nichols's law clerk, Ms. Meyers?"

"Six months."

"And you never practiced law, did you?"

"No. I was a student before my clerkship."

"I take it then that all you know about how often judges deny requests for orders to show cause is from that six months' worth of experience."

"Yes, but we had a lot of them."

"Fair enough," Rosenthal says with a smile. "Let me just get to the bottom of it, then. I'm assuming, Ms. Meyers, that if you believed that Judge Nichols was doing anything in her official capacity that was unethical, you would have been troubled by that. Am I correct in that assumption?"

"Um . . . if I thought so."

"That's my point exactly. You *never* thought that Judge Nichols was ever doing anything improper, did you?"

"No."

"And I take it that means you didn't think Judge Nichols had already made up her mind to convict Nicolai Garkov, did you? Because it would have been highly improper for her to have done that, correct?"

"I guess."

"No, no, Ms. Meyers. This is very, very important. A man's freedom is at stake. Please, just like this jury, you must be sure. You were with Judge Nichols every working day for six months, and I take it that, in that time, you knew her well. And my question is simple: did you think, even for a second, that Judge Nichols was acting unethically toward Nicolai Garkov? In other words, did you think she had already made up her mind to convict him even if the evidence at trial were to indicate that he was not guilty?"

Sara hesitates. Obviously, Victoria Donnelly has gone over the government's theory of the case with her ad nauseam, and she doesn't want to contradict it now.

Rosenthal decides to put his thumb more firmly on the scale. "Please, Ms. Meyers. Did you think that your mentor was engaging in the most horrific abdication of her judicial responsibilities imaginable and was really going to sentence a man to life in prison who didn't deserve it?"

"No. I didn't think she'd do that," Meyer says. You can almost see in her eyes that she hopes Donnelly isn't too upset with her.

It's as good as they're going to do with this witness. But Aaron knows it likely wasn't enough. Even if Sara Meyers's loyalty to her employer caused her not to be able to see it, the jury most likely has concluded that Judge Nichols's bail revocation and then denial of the order to show cause—both coming without any consultation with her loyal law clerk—meant that she was going to convict Nicolai Garkov.

The only saving grace is that so far, at least, the prosecution hasn't been able to prove that Aaron had anything to fear from such a result.

Aaron returns to Cromwell Altman after court to help Rosenthal prepare for the next day. It's the first time he's been back in his office since his arrest. He expects it to look different, but he's the only thing that's different.

"I expected that Pierce would have moved the furniture around by now," Aaron says, only half joking.

"He couldn't get the decorator in yet," Rosenthal says back.

Rachel enters Aaron's office a second after she knocks on the open door. "I asked Diane to call me when you got back," she says by way of explaining her stalking them. "How'd it go today?"

"Just great," Aaron says with obvious sarcasm. "They put on Faith's husband, her law clerk, and a woman who worked at the hotel. The husband said he saw Faith and me at the hotel together. Then the hotel employee corroborated it, and Faith's law clerk drove home that Faith had decided to convict Garkov even before the trial started."

"It wasn't that bad, Aaron," Rosenthal says. "We kept out any evidence that she was up for the Supreme Court, and that teenager from the Ritz-Carlton couldn't put you and Faith together."

Rachel's sad smile makes clear that she understands it was a better day for the prosecution than the defense. "I wish I could be there with you, Aaron," she says. "I just feel so useless sitting at the firm. And I'm getting nowhere on the phone call to your office. I must have spoken to everyone at AT&T, and to a person they claim that the call happened. And our IT people say that there's no record of any three-minute call on your voice mail that night."

Aaron knows that this call will be his undoing, linking him and Faith right before Faith's murder. The fact that they never spoke doesn't matter. Truth and evidence are sometimes very distant cousins in a criminal trial.

"I know it's frustrating to be away from the action," Aaron says, "but you definitely are helping."

Rosenthal seemingly doesn't appreciate being a third wheel and says, "Rachel, can you give us time alone?"

"Of course," Rachel says, trying to mask her embarrassment. "I'll be in my office if you need me. Good luck tomorrow, Aaron."

As soon as Rachel has made her exit, Aaron says, "Sam, you don't have to be so hard on her. She just wants to help."

"I'm sorry, Aaron, but I don't trust her the way you do. Call it one of the benefits of being seventy-one. You become immune to beautiful women."

Aaron shakes his head in disagreement, but there's no reason to fight this particular battle now. "Do you think they'll do the phone call tomorrow?" Aaron asks instead.

"I do."

"And we've got nothing to rebut it."

"I'm not going to let you go to jail, Aaron. I swear, that will never happen."

Aaron says thank you, because there's nothing else he can say to a promise that he knows Sam Rosenthal is powerless to keep.

52

Wednesday is composed of the scientific evidence. One by one, forensic experts take the stand to offer brief testimony describing the tasks they did and the conclusions they reached. It's mind-numbingly boring, and the jury, at most, grasps only the headlines, which amount to: cause of death was blunt-force trauma to the head; time of death was between 9:00 p.m. and midnight; the murder weapon was some kind of stick, which may well have been a tree branch; and there was no physical evidence left at the scene by the attacker.

Rosenthal's cross gets the defense's main arguments into evidence. No, they did not find Mr. Littman's DNA or fingerprints at the crime scene. No, there wasn't any evidence directly linking Mr. Littman to the murder. That's correct, they did not locate the murder weapon.

The expert parade concludes with the representative from AT&T, an Asian woman in her forties with a sharply angled haircut. She testifies that Judge Nichols received numerous calls from different prepaid phones in the months before her death, and at 9:48 p.m. on the night she was murdered, she called Aaron Littman's office number, and that call lasted three minutes and three seconds.

Donnelly milks this piece of evidence for all it's worth. She has the phone bill passed around the jurors, waiting patiently while each one sees what they've just heard Ms. AT&T say.

"Is there any way—any way at all," Donnelly says when the last of the jurors has looked at that bill, "that this call did not happen?"

"None," Ms. AT&T says. "The simple fact is that phone bills don't lie."

On cross Rosenthal gets the defense's response to the phone call before the jury. Hearing it, Aaron thinks it doesn't sound half-bad.

"You testified that this call definitely occurred, correct?" Rosenthal says.

"Like I said, phone bills don't lie."

"But you don't know who actually dialed the phone, do you?"

"How could I know that?"

"That's right, you couldn't. In fact, no one could, simply from looking at the phone bill. And you're not a medical coroner, are you?"

"No. I work for a phone company."

"And so, it is possible, is it not, that after Judge Nichols's murderer killed her, he took the phone out of her pocket and made that nine forty-eight call, and that is the person who stayed on the line for three minutes and three seconds, just so the police would later think that Judge Nichols called Mr. Littman?"

Ms. AT&T seems at sea. "I guess," she says meekly. "I really have no idea who made the call. I just know that it was made."

Aaron decides that there's little point in going back to the office after court to do a postmortem. Even with Rosenthal's sleight of hand regarding the 9:48 phone call, the trial is not going well, and he'd rather spend the evening at home because he knows that his days with his family might well be numbered.

Later that evening, just before he and Cynthia turn off the lights for the night, Aaron says aloud what he hasn't been able to fathom before.

"I think I'm going to be convicted."

Having not been privy to the actual testimony, Cynthia's only frame of reference is what Aaron's told her each night, and from what she's heard, it doesn't sound good. Still, she views it as part of her job to keep Aaron's spirits up, and so she replies, "Even if some of the testimony has been less than great, you said that they still don't have motive yet. Right?"

"They don't need motive to convict," Aaron says. "Sometimes they can never prove why. And even if they can't prove the blackmail, they'll just say it was jealousy or something else."

"I've heard you say it a million times, though. Trials are like roller coasters. There are always low points."

Aaron *has* said that before, and there's some truth to it. But for his own trial, it seems much less of a roller-coaster ride than a full-on free fall.

The next morning, when Victoria Donnelly announces her first witness, it's a name that means absolutely nothing to Aaron. The man who answers the call is young, under thirty, and dressed in a preppy suit, right down to the button-down collar and school rep tie. Aaron assumes that he must be another law clerk.

He states his name for the record as Jeremy Kagan and answers Donnelly's question regarding his current employer: "I work in the office of Senator Edward Kheel."

Rosenthal leans over to whisper in Aaron's ear. "Goddamn Kheel. He'll never see another penny from me."

Aaron appreciates the sentiment, but it only reinforces what he's already surmised: Kagan's testimony will prove that Faith Nichols knew the Supreme Court was hers if Garkov was convicted.

In a way, Aaron's got to hand it to Donnelly. She wasn't going to get anyone with real clout to testify about the quid pro quo offered to Judge Nichols—a Supreme Court seat in exchange for Garkov's conviction—and Kagan must have been offered up as a sacrificial lamb. For Donnelly's purposes, the man who speaks for Kheel is just as good as if she'd called the senator or even the president himself to the stand, because Kagan can testify to what Stuart Christensen could not: that Judge Nichols *believed* she needed to find Garkov guilty in order to get the nomination. Kheel and the White House could then take refuge behind the oldest Washington defense—the overly enthusiastic staffer.

Donnelly says, "Mr. Kagan, did you ever have a discussion with Judge Faith Nichols about the fact that she was being considered for nomination to the Supreme Court?"

"Yes," Kagan answers.

"Did any of those occur *after* she had been selected to preside over the trial of Nicolai Garkov?"

"Yes. One time."

"Please tell us about that one time, Mr. Kagan."

"When Judge Nichols was assigned to the Garkov case, Senator Kheel asked me to brief her on what it meant for her potential nomination. I met with the judge at her home. At that time, I told her that the White House was viewing her assignment to the Garkov case as a positive development."

"Did you say anything more specific?"

"Like what?"

It's the first sign that Kagan is there reluctantly. It's one thing for Senator Kheel to serve up his aide, but that doesn't mean Kagan has to go along with it without a struggle.

Donnelly's in no-man's-land for a direct examination. Because Kagan is a prosecution witness, she's limited to open-ended questions and cannot, as they say, lead the witness. But a noncompliant witness on direct is like a dog off a leash, and there's often no way to get them to go where you need them to be.

"What I'm asking, Mr. Kagan, is did you ever discuss with Judge Nichols whether she would be considered for the Supreme Court if Mr. Garkov was acquitted?"

Kagan hesitates, as if he's trying to find a loophole in the question. He must not see one, however, because after a sigh he says, "Yes."

"What did you say to her and what did she say back to you on that point?"

"I don't recall exactly, but I said to her that if Mr. Garkov was convicted, the White House would likely consider her nomination more favorably, and if he were acquitted, there might be opposition to her nomination."

Even though it's far from unequivocal, it's enough. There is now evidence before the jury that if she hadn't been murdered, Faith Nichols was going to convict Nicolai Garkov.

Aaron slumps slightly, but Rosenthal tugs at his elbow, like a father telling his son to sit up straight at the dinner table. It's another important trial rule—never give the impression that things aren't going exactly as planned.

"In other words, you conveyed the idea that she gets the nomination if he's convicted, but not if he's acquitted," Donnelly says. "Isn't that correct?"

Rosenthal is on his feet. "Objection! Your Honor, the witness just testified to what he told Judge Nichols. There's no reason for Ms. Donnelly to ask him if her paraphrasing is correct when the firsthand statement has already been sworn to."

"I'll withdraw that question, Your Honor. I think Mr. Rosenthal is right. We all know what Mr. Kagan said and what he actually meant. I have no more questions."

Rosenthal's cross lasts all of five minutes.

"Mr. Kagan," he says, "you just testified that you made it clear to Judge Nichols that if Mr. Garkov were convicted, the White House would view her potential nomination to the Supreme Court more favorably. Did I hear that correctly?"

"I told her something along those lines, yes."

"I see," Rosenthal says with a nod. "Mr. Kagan, I'm assuming that you know that if you were interfering with a criminal prosecution . . . for example, offering an inducement to a federal judge, such as a nomination to the United States Supreme Court . . . in exchange for her ruling in a certain way . . . for example, convicting Nicolai Garkov . . . well, you would be committing a very serious crime, called obstruction of justice. And so, can I assume that you are confident that you did not make such an inducement to Judge Nichols?"

Even without the benefit of being able to meet with Kagan beforehand, Rosenthal knows Kagan will recognize a softball when it's served up to him. Sure enough, Kagan smiles and then proceeds to hit it out of the park.

"That's right. I did not offer Judge Nichols any quid pro quo, nor did I imply any."

"And is it the case that after your meeting with Judge Nichols, you had no earthly idea how she was ultimately going to rule with regard to the Garkov case?"

"I can only assume that even she did not know," Kagan says with some confidence. "After all, the trial had not even begun yet and it would have been unethical for her to have conducted herself in any other fashion."

"Of course," Rosenthal says. "No further questions, Your Honor."

Like they say about doctors making the worst patients, lawyers are, more often than not, terrible witnesses. A witness's job is to recount the facts, without analysis or context. Lawyers never do that.

Which makes it all the more surprising when Garkov's original trial counsel, Roy Sabato, proves to be a pretty good witness. His answers are short, usually limited only to what he saw and said, and not what he was thinking.

When Donnelly asks, "Please tell us, Mr. Sabato, what you said to Mr. Littman and what he said to you when you discussed the representation of Nicolai Garkov," Sabato's testimony comes out exactly the way Aaron remembers it. Sabato's telling Aaron that Garkov wanted to retain him as counsel, Aaron's initial declination, Sabato's offer of the one-hundred-thousand-dollar fee for a first meeting, and when that didn't do the trick, his claim that Garkov had incriminating evidence he'd make public if Aaron didn't meet with Garkov immediately, which resulted in Aaron's capitulation.

Even though Roy Sabato has told the entire story in his narrative, Donnelly goes back over it, breaking each fact down, one question at a time.

"When you first asked Mr. Littman to meet with Mr. Garkov, what did he say?"

"He said no."

"Did he give a reason?"

"He said that it would cost his law firm more than Mr. Garkov would pay him."

"Is that when you offered him one hundred thousand dollars if he met with Mr. Garkov?"

"I did make that offer on behalf of Mr. Garkov, yes."

"And what did Mr. Littman say to that?"

"He said he was still not interested."

"And then what did you do?"

Sabato looks past Donnelly to Aaron. He gives the subtlest shake of his head, perhaps to suggest that he's not enjoying this.

"That's when I told Mr. Littman that Mr. Garkov had incriminating information about him that he would reveal to the public if Mr. Littman did not agree to meet with him."

"Did you tell Mr. Littman that Judge Nichols was now the judge presiding over Mr. Garkov's case?"

Sabato hesitates. Aaron knows the answer is yes, for he recalls clearly it was that disclosure that put the fear of God in him. Either because Roy Sabato truly does not recall, or because he's trying to curry some favor with Aaron, he says, "I just don't remember. I may have. I just can't be sure."

Donnelly's nostrils flare, a pretty good indication that Sabato was previously more definitive with her on this point. She can't turn on her own witness, however, and so Sabato's testimony will have to stand as the last word on the discussion.

"After you told Mr. Littman of Mr. Garkov's threat to reveal this incriminating information, did Mr. Littman change his mind and agree to meet with Mr. Garkov?"

"Yes."

"Your witness," Donnelly says, smiling at Rosenthal.

With Roy Sabato, Rosenthal finally has a compliant witness, but only so far. Sabato readily concedes that Garkov may have been lying about actually having incriminating evidence about Aaron, but he will not budge on his recollection that he was clear in relaying the message to Aaron, or Aaron's capitulation after the threat was made.

The prosecution has now established that Aaron was being blackmailed. In other words, they have proven motive.

53

Roy Sabato is the last government witness. When he steps down, Donnelly announces in a triumphant voice that the government rests.

"Let's adjourn for the evening then," Judge Siskind says. "Tomorrow morning we'll deal with the defense's motions."

For Aaron, the trial now has the feel of halftime in a football game that's a blowout. There's still a lot of time left to mount a comeback, but it seems that all is already lost.

Aaron thinks back to Donnelly's opening: the promises she made to the jury, the ones that Rosenthal said she could not keep.

Proof of the affair. Check.

Proof of communications between him and Faith on the night of the murder. Check.

Proof of blackmail by Garkov. Check.

Prove that Faith was going to convict Garkov. Check.

Some points might be weaker than others, but in its totality, it's more than enough to convict. There's no escaping the fact that he's in serious trouble.

That is, unless Nicolai Garkov can save him.

Tomorrow will be the decisive moment of the trial. If Judge Siskind rules the defense can get Nicolai Garkov's assertion of the Fifth Amendment before the jury, Aaron's chances of acquittal become real.

But if she goes the other way, Aaron's equally certain that he's going to be convicted.

The next morning the courtroom has an air of excitement. Word has leaked out that today's session will include an appearance by Nicolai Garkov, which has brought the press to a lather.

"On the record," Judge Siskind says, looking down at the court stenographer. "I have excused the jury for the day so that we may take up two items outside their presence. First, the defense has indicated it would like to make a motion for a directed verdict. After that, I will hear from the parties regarding Mr. Nicolai Garkov."

By her phrasing, unintentional or not, Judge Siskind has alerted both sides that the motion for the directed verdict—which, if granted, would end the case with an acquittal—has no chance of success.

Even though he now must realize this is a fool's errand, Rosenthal stands as if there's still hope.

"Your Honor," he says, "at this time, the defense requests that the court enter a judgment of not guilty. Even applying the very liberal standard of permitting the prosecution every reasonable inference, there is simply not enough evidence to support a guilty verdict, and therefore the case shouldn't go to the jury."

Judge Siskind puts up her hand, directing Rosenthal to stop. Aaron knows that Rosenthal has more to say. He was planning on going through a point-by-point rebuttal of every government witness and every document submitted into evidence.

"I'm not sure I need to spend any more time on this, Mr. Rosenthal. I've considered the evidence, and without prejudging the ultimate issue of guilt beyond a reasonable doubt, it's certainly within the jury's domain to conclude the government has met its burden of proof. The evidence presented supports that the defendant and the victim were intimate, and the 9:48 p.m. phone call placed by Judge Nichols to Mr. Littman's office permits the inference that the defendant saw Judge Nichols on the night she was murdered, within the time window that this crime was committed. Mr. Sabato's testimony certainly leaves room for the jury to draw the conclusion that Mr. Garkov knew of the affair and was threatening to make it public if he was convicted, and Mr. Kagan's testimony suggests the odds of that happening were extremely high. Put together, it adds up to motive, means, and opportunity sufficient for a jury to conclude beyond a reasonable doubt that Mr. Littman committed this crime."

"Your Honor—" Rosenthal manages to get out before he sees Judge Siskind's hand again.

"I know what you're going to say, Mr. Rosenthal, and I'd be the first to concede that it's also possible that the jury might reject what I just said. But my point is that a reasonable juror *could* reach a guilty verdict based on the evidence presented. And that's the legal standard. So, on that basis, I am denying the defense's motion for a directed verdict."

Rosenthal sits down. The case will not be dismissed.

Siskind's not finished, though. "I am intrigued, however, Mr. Rosenthal, about the defense's motion with regard to Mr. Garkov. If I understand your position, you would like to call Mr. Garkov to the stand even though he has already notified both you and the prosecution that he will invoke the Fifth Amendment. Do I have that right?"

Rosenthal stands to address the court. "That's correct, Your Honor. The defense believes that Mr. Garkov killed Judge Nichols. Therefore we seek to ask him one question, and one question only: did you murder Judge Nichols?"

"But he's not going to answer," Judge Siskind says. "Isn't that precisely why this should occur outside of the jury's presence?"

"Respectfully, no, Your Honor. Could there be more probative evidence of Mr. Littman's innocence than that Mr. Garkov believes that if he answers the question of whether *he* is guilty of this crime, his answer will incriminate him? It would be a gross miscarriage of justice if the jury decided Mr. Littman's innocence or guilt without knowing that Mr. Garkov virtually confessed to the crime."

Judge Siskind smiles, but it's a gesture that could just as easily suggest that she's enjoying the give-and-take and not that she's inclined to agree. "Well, Mr. Rosenthal . . . I suspect that Ms. Donnelly is going to tell me it will be a gross miscarriage of justice if I rule in your favor. Is that the government's position, Ms. Donnelly?"

"Yes. Yes, it most certainly is, Your Honor," Donnelly says, coming to her feet. "Contrary to Mr. Rosenthal's claim, a Fifth Amendment assertion is *not* a confession. All it means is that Mr. Garkov, perhaps mistakenly, believes that if he answers the question it might lead—*might lead*—to admissible evidence indicating that he is guilty of *some* crime. Not necessarily the crime at issue in this case—the murder of Judge Nichols—but it could well be some *other* crime for which he fears incriminating himself. In Mr. Garkov's case, it's not difficult to see why he would assert that privilege. He's currently under indictment for numerous felonies, and he's a suspect in other murders. On top of which, it is the government's theory in this case that he committed various acts of blackmail. It is far more likely that Mr. Garkov fears incriminating himself in the crimes he's actually committed, rather than the one crime for which someone else has been charged and now stands trial—namely the murder of Judge Nichols. The defense's motion is little more than a request for permission to confuse the jury on what Mr. Garkov's invocation of his Fifth Amendment rights actually means. The jury will equate it with a confession, but Mr. Garkov's assertion may well have nothing to do with this crime at all."

Judge Siskind stares at Donnelly for a beat, then turns on Rosenthal. "I have to say, she's right, Mr. Rosenthal."

Rosenthal appears unfazed by Judge Siskind's rejection of his argument. In a calm voice he says, "Your Honor, there's a very simple solution to this problem. The government should immunize Mr. Garkov on this one subject."

The suggestion causes Aaron to sit up straighter. Sam didn't mention making this proposal, and if he had, Aaron goddamned well would have objected. The last thing the defense wants is for Garkov to testify truthfully. He'll admit to the blackmail and deny the murder.

Siskind, like most judges, jumps at the opportunity for a possible compromise. "Okay, then. Ms. Donnelly, what's the harm if you grant Mr. Garkov immunity with respect to the Nichols murder? Especially because the government believes that Mr. Littman committed the crime, and therefore Mr. Garkov will presumably deny guilt."

"The problem, Your Honor, is that once Mr. Garkov has immunity, he can say anything he wants without fear of prosecution. Obviously, Mr. Garkov is no fan of the United States government. He might admit to the crime just to allow Mr. Littman to go free. Or he might admit to other crimes and then argue that the immunity grant covered them. But it's a moot point. We're just not going to do it."

Some judges draw a line in the sand at being told by counsel that they can't do something and might come back with *Maybe I can't make you immunize him, but I* can *allow him to take the Fifth in front of the jury. Your choice.*

Aaron hopes with all his might that Siskind might be that kind of judge. But with a slight shrug, she indicates that she's not.

"Okay, I've heard enough," she says. "It is exclusively within the province of the executive branch to bestow immunity, and so my hands are tied, Mr. Rosenthal. I'm going to take the witness's invocation of the Fifth Amendment outside the presence of the jury."

Rosenthal is on his feet for one last try. "Your Honor, we respect the court's ruling but request that we be permitted to tell the jury that the reason Mr. Garkov was not called as a witness was because of his assertion of the Fifth. Otherwise, the defense is greatly prejudiced because the jury will not know that we wanted to call him as a witness."

"I'm going to deny that request as well, Mr. Rosenthal. Telling the jury Mr. Garkov took the Fifth is no different than letting him take the Fifth in their presence."

And there it is. Rosenthal's big gamble and Aaron's best shot at a defense goes up in smoke.

After a short recess, and with the jury still out of the courtroom, Sam Rosenthal calls Nicolai Garkov to the stand. The gallery is standing room only for the occasion, and additional court security is conspicuously stationed at the doors.

The tall Russian walks in dressed to the nines in a silk suit, alligator shoes, and a watch sparkling with diamonds. When he passes Aaron, the son of a bitch actually winks. Then he settles into the witness chair as if it were a throne. It might as well be.

Clint Broden is present in the courtroom, and Judge Siskind grants his request to stand next to his client. With Garkov seated and Broden standing, they're roughly the same height.

Judge Siskind nods, telling Rosenthal to proceed. He doesn't even rise, a passive-aggressive show of his dissatisfaction with this turn of events.

"Mr. Garkov, was Faith Nichols murdered on your orders?" he asks.

Garkov shows no emotion at the accusation. Not even a flicker. Broden hands him a three-by-five index card, and Garkov begins to read.

"On the advice of counsel, I assert my rights under the Fifth Amendment of the United States Constitution and all similarly applicable rights available to me by law."

54

The weekend is a welcome respite. The trial is not going well, and Aaron's unsure what type of defense they can mount to change that.

He and Cynthia are still on their first cup of coffee Saturday morning when she says, "I've been thinking of a defense strategy." She stops for dramatic effect and then says, "You lie."

There's silence for a few moments, until Aaron breaks it with a laugh. "Well, it is the oldest defense there is," he says.

Cynthia's expression leaves no doubt that she does not consider this to be a laughing matter. "I'm dead serious, Aaron. You should take the stand and deny everything. The affair. The Garkov blackmail. Seeing her that night. Everything."

Aaron looks at Cynthia with surprise. His wife has always been the moral compass in the household, and yet now she's thrown away any sense of playing by the rules.

"Cyn, it's not that I'm above it, believe me. I just don't see it working. Jails are full of people who took the stand and denied everything. Even assuming that I'm a good enough liar to pull it off—which I'm far from certain about—there's proof of the affair and the jury won't disregard it based on my self-serving denials. I'll just end up burying myself."

"What if it won't be just your self-serving denials?" she says.

"What . . . oh wait, you mean *you*?"

Cynthia smiles and nods.

"But you can't alibi me. Too many people saw you in the hospital. And even if you could, your testimony is hardly worth more than mine. The jury will assume that you'd lie to save the father of your children from jail."

"That's where Rachel comes in."

It's a short list of people for whom you'd do whatever it takes to protect them. For Aaron, that list includes Lindsay, Samantha, and Cynthia, perhaps Sam Rosenthal too.

He's now about to find out if Rachel is willing to make that kind of sacrifice for him. He'd be lying if he said he didn't know how Rachel felt about him, and certainly she made it crystal clear that night at the Pierre. Yet he also knows that he's making an unreasonable request—asking her to put everything she has at risk for him—and he's offering her nothing in return.

Rachel arrives at the Littman apartment less than an hour after Cynthia laid out her plan for a defense based on a conspiracy to commit perjury. Cynthia has gone out, reasoning that Aaron will have more success persuading Rachel if they're alone.

At first Rachel seems happy to once again be in Aaron's company. When Aaron lays out the reason for their meeting, however, she looks far less pleased.

"You want me to testify that we were together the night of the murder?" Rachel says.

"Yes, but only if it's possible you could do that without being contradicted. Can you?"

"I guess."

"No, you have to be sure."

"Well . . . that was the night after Judge Nichols denied the order to show cause, right? I was drafting our brief to the Second Circuit to appeal the ruling. I met with the associates at six-ish, and then not again until about eleven. But I can't swear that one of them didn't stop by to ask a question or call me in the office." She pauses, as if warming to the idea of what she's about to commit to doing. "But even if one of them did pay me a visit, it wouldn't have been for more than a few minutes. I could always say that you went to the bathroom or the kitchen for more coffee or something. The firm's car records will show the exact time I left, but I think it was around midnight." Then with a full-on smile that suggests that Aaron's asked her to go steady and not to commit a crime that carries a five-year prison term per lie, she says, "Yeah. I could definitely say you left after me, which puts you at Cromwell Altman, *not* Central Park, when Judge Nichols was killed."

For a split second, Aaron considers telling her no, that it's just too much for him to ask. But instead he says, "Thank you. I . . . I really don't know what else I can say. But that hardly captures my gratitude. You may truly be saving my life."

She looks at him with laserlike focus, as if she can hold him there just with the power of her gaze, and then says with deadly seriousness, "You should know by now, Aaron, that I'd do anything for you."

Even though he is not being asked to lie under oath, the criminal risk for Sam Rosenthal is every bit as great as it is for Rachel or Cynthia. As the lawyer procuring what he knows to be false testimony, he'll be guilty of suborning perjury. Were he to be convicted of that crime, Rosenthal could very well spend the rest of his life in prison.

Aaron is in Sam's office when he proposes the plan. Rosenthal's first reaction is to question its wisdom, not its ethical propriety.

"I'm not the biggest Victoria Donnelly fan out there," Rosenthal says, "but she's a damn good lawyer. Do you really think that the three of you can hold up under sustained cross-examination?"

Aaron has been thinking of nothing else since Cynthia first raised the idea. Every witness thinks that he can outsmart the questioner, and it's a very rare individual who can. It takes a combination of high intelligence and complete conviction in what you're saying. It's almost like what they say about beating a polygraph—if you believe it's true, it's not a lie.

"I'm not sure," Aaron says. "But it's the best shot I have. More accurately, it's the only shot."

"I wish I could disagree with you," Rosenthal says, "because this is pretty much a Hail Mary pass. But after Siskind screwed us on Garkov, we're left with recalling Stuart Christensen, which I don't advocate, or a character-witness defense and a closing argument based on reasonable doubt, which I think we both agree is a losing proposition."

"Like I said, Sam, this is my only shot."

Rosenthal exhales deeply. "I guess that means we better get everyone down here so we can start to prepare."

They spend the weekend practicing their lies.

On Monday, the curtain goes up on the performance. Cynthia will go first, followed by Rachel, and then Aaron will bring it home.

Sunday night, after the girls have gone to sleep, and Aaron and Cynthia are in bed, Aaron says thank you. He doesn't link his gratitude to the perjury his wife will commit on his behalf the following day, and so it takes on a much deeper significance. Thank you for staying with me, he's saying.

Cynthia acknowledges it with a kiss but not further discussion. After a few moments of silence she says, "I was thinking, you know the way I'm always getting those requests from the University of Virginia med school to come teach for a year or two? Maybe it's time I accepted. With the girls both going off to college, this would be a great time for a change. Charlottesville is really beautiful, and it's only two hours from DC, so it's not totally cut off from civilization."

"Oh. I think that's a great idea," Aaron says.

She must hear the reservation in his voice. "I'm not doing this without you."

Aaron stops himself from reminding her that he may have no choice in the matter. Cynthia is well aware of that possibility. Instead, he decides to indulge her. "So, tell me, what is our new life in Charlottesville going to look like?"

Her eyes light up, even as they well with tears. "I'd like to get a little house," she says, "nothing too fancy. It would be nice if it had a view of the mountains. There would be a guest room for the girls to stay, but it would be more like a cottage. With a small garden. My teaching hours will be limited. Ten to fifteen hours a week, at most. That'll give us a lot of time to do the things we want to do. I'm sure that they'll give you a guest-lecturer spot at the law school if you want it. In fact, I could make it a condition of my deal."

Aaron lets the fantasy swirl beside him, wary of trying it on for size. It's simply too greedy for him to wish for anything other than freedom, however.

"And I'd like us to have a dog, maybe," Cynthia continues. "Not too big, but not a little dog. We'll go to a shelter and pick out one that would otherwise have a sad end, and we'll give him a new life."

"Are you still talking about the dog?"

Aaron has tried to say this with self-deprecating charm, but Cynthia's expression reflects that this is not a joking matter for her. "I don't care if it's here or in Charlottesville or on the moon, I just want us to be together. These last two months with you home have made that crystal clear to me. And if we can be happy under these circumstances, imagine how great it'll be when all of this craziness is behind us."

Aaron nods. The same thought has occurred to him a thousand times, always juxtaposed with the guilt that comes with knowing that he brought this all on himself.

Cynthia's look suddenly hardens. "But it only works if you want to be with me too. And not just because it's better than going to jail. That's not the choice you get to make. There's nothing either of us can do if that happens, but if it doesn't . . . then *you* get to decide how you want to live the rest of your life. The only thing that I ask is that you not spend it with me out of some sense of guilt or gratitude. That's just putting yourself in a different kind of prison."

"I want a second chance too, Cyn," he says. "More than anything."

This is apparently what Cynthia wanted to hear. She presses her body against his, and he immediately feels himself harden. He knows she can feel him too, as she settles herself into him. Aaron's hands drop to cup Cynthia's breasts, and she lets out a low gasp. After they're free of their clothing, Aaron lies on top of her, losing himself in the warmth of her skin. The feeling is so complete that he feels no urgency to enter her, not wanting this sensation to end.

Cynthia, however, is on a different schedule. She immediately guides him inside her, shuddering rhythmically with his slow immersion. When he's fully submerged, just as he's about to pull back slightly, she presses down on his back and wraps her legs firmly around his, locking him inside her, never wanting to let go.

55

Cynthia Littman looks completely composed on the witness stand. She's wearing a cream-colored suit and a single strand of modest pearls. Her hair is down and loose. The idea is for her to present herself as attractively as she can, so the jury believes that Aaron would never have had cause to stray.

Sam Rosenthal's preliminary questions allow Cynthia to establish that she's a woman of substance, not one of those ladies who lunch while their master-of-the-universe husbands oppress the other 99 percent. She tells the jury about her Ivy League education, the fellowships she's received, and finally about her medical practice, leaning heavily on the fact that she specializes in high-risk births.

When Rosenthal asks how she met Aaron, Cynthia answers quickly, so as to head off a relevance objection. It's word-for-word as scripted.

"I was in my last year of med school, and Aaron just came up to me one day in the library and said, 'My name is Aaron Littman. I'm sorry to bother you, but I was hoping you'd let me take you out on a date sometime.' "

Cynthia laughs to herself, as if she's momentarily forgotten she's a witness in her husband's murder trial. "That's Aaron in a nutshell, right there," she says. "The confidence to walk up to a girl he didn't know and ask her out, but also a little bit of insecurity, that maybe he was bothering me. The thing that struck me most, though, was how serious he was. Truth be told, he still is. Nobody said *take you out on a date.* It was always *hang out*, or *buy you coffee*, or something like that. Casual. But that wasn't Aaron. He was always very serious."

Aaron smiles, as if he's remembering that day too. He's not, however. The truth is that they met in a bar, had too much to drink, and had sex that first night. The story that Cynthia weaves, however, is much more romantic.

Rosenthal next turns to the night of the murder. "Mrs. Littman, please tell the jury where you were the night Judge Nichols was killed."

"I was at work, at Lenox Hill Hospital, in and out of the delivery room. My patient was going through a very difficult labor. Several times, the fetal heart rate dropped to dangerously low levels. I stayed with her to get her through a natural delivery, which is always preferable to a C-section. It was one of the hardest labors I had ever seen, and then at the end, the mother developed preeclampsia, which is a spike in blood pressure, and for a moment, I thought I was going to lose her and the baby." Cynthia breaks contact with Rosenthal and looks at the jury. "I'm happy to say that it all ended very well. It was a natural birth and mother and baby are doing just fine now."

Rosenthal concluded patient confidentiality would prevent the prosecution from getting the medical records to refute whatever Cynthia said occurred in the hospital that night. As a result, Cynthia was given carte blanche to make the delivery sound as perilous as possible, even though it was actually quite routine. At worst, the prosecution would track down the patient and her husband, but Cynthia could simply say that it's her job to make it seem that everything is going according to plan, even when it's truly dire.

"When you returned home, what time was it?" Rosenthal asks.

"A little before 1:00 a.m."

"And was your husband at home?"

"He was."

"How would you describe his demeanor when you saw him?"

"Asleep."

There are some chuckles in the gallery. Aaron catches a sideways glimpse of the jury. Cynthia has their rapt attention, and the men are smiling.

"Did you notice anything out of the ordinary when you came home? For example, was your husband acting oddly, or was there any disarray in the apartment? Was there any blood in the apartment or on his clothing?"

"Oh, no. Aaron was so sweet to me when I woke him up. He always likes me to wake him when I come home, and because the delivery was so difficult, I wanted to talk about it a little bit. We stayed up for another hour or so talking." Cynthia says this looking at the women on the jury, who no doubt complain that their own husbands never listen to them.

Again, every word is a lie. Aaron had been drinking when Cynthia arrived home at 1:00 a.m., and she knew instantly that something was wrong. Still, from the nods coming out of the jury box, the only people who matter seem to be eating up this version of the night's events.

Rosenthal takes a deep breath, as if contemplating whether to cross the next Rubicon. Aaron assumes that this must mean he's about to address the affair.

This is the greatest area of danger for the defense. It's always difficult when a witness contradicts a written record, and the Ritz-Carlton documents prove Aaron checked into the hotel about once a week for close to four months, and always paid in cash. To convince the jury Aaron was not having an affair with Faith Nichols, they have to explain away that evidence.

"Did you know Faith Nichols?" Rosenthal asks.

"Not personally, no," Cynthia says. "But I knew that Aaron tried a case before her, and that she was the judge on the Garkov case as well."

"Do you have any reason to believe that your husband had an affair with Judge Nichols?"

Donnelly rises. "Your Honor, it's not my place to invoke the marital privilege, if both Mr. Littman and his wife intend to waive it. But I will object later and ask that this testimony be stricken if the Littmans attempt to use the privilege as both a sword and a shield, testifying to the marital communications between them that they want the jury to hear, and then invoking the privilege to block other communications."

"The defense has nothing to hide," Rosenthal says, looking at the jury. "We will not be invoking marital privilege."

Judge Siskind's expression subtly betrays surprise at the tactic, but it's not her place to say so. "Then continue on, Mr. Rosenthal."

Rosenthal repeats his question and Cynthia emphatically declares her husband has never been unfaithful. Rosenthal walks back to counsel table and Aaron hands him the Ritz-Carlton documents that prove otherwise.

After obtaining the court's permission, Rosenthal approaches the witness stand. He hands the Ritz-Carlton bills to Cynthia.

"Mrs. Littman, before you is an exhibit previously introduced by the prosecution. As you can see, it's a series of photocopies of your husband's driver's license on the letterhead of the Ritz-Carlton hotel, each bearing a date. Also among the documents I handed to you are various Ritz-Carlton invoices indicating that your husband paid for these hotel rooms in cash. My question to you is simple: did you know that your husband was at the hotel on those dates?"

"I did," Cynthia says confidently.

"And why was your husband there?"

"To see me." There's nervous laughter in the gallery. "This is embarrassing . . . but, Aaron and I have been married awhile and, well . . . to put some spark back in our marriage, we would meet at the Ritz once a week or so."

The defense knew that the moment Cynthia laid out this story, the prosecution would scour the hospital charts to see if there was any date that she could not have possibly been at the Ritz-Carlton. But Cynthia said that there was nothing to worry about. She could have arrived at the hotel at any time, and given that the desk clerk couldn't recall Aaron's presence, that also necessarily meant that she couldn't convincingly say her failure to remember Cynthia was proof that she wasn't there.

There's one more thing Rosenthal needs Cynthia to explain away. He asks, "Mrs. Littman, if this was part of a *fantasy*—as you claim—why did your husband pay in cash? It required him to go to the ATM, when he could have easily paid the room charge with a credit card."

Cynthia looks surprised and says, "I honestly didn't know he paid in cash until it became an issue in this case. I was never with him when he checked in, which was also part of the role-play. But that's the thing about Aaron. He's like a Method actor in that way. The part he was playing was to be secretly meeting a woman at a hotel, and so he stayed in character all the way, which included paying in cash."

Out of his peripheral vision, Aaron sees Donnelly's incredulity. But when Aaron turns to the jury, they look far less skeptical.

It's a testament to how well Cynthia's done that when it's Donnelly's turn, she has the look of a boxer storming out for the fifteenth round in need of a knockout.

"You would agree with me, would you not, Mrs. Littman, that the whole point of an extramarital affair is to keep it secret from your spouse?"

"I wouldn't know the whole point of it, Ms. Donnelly. I've never had an affair."

It's a warning shot by Cynthia, telling Donnelly she shouldn't take her on. Donnelly pauses, as if she's rethinking some of the questions she decided to ask.

She must conclude that Cynthia poses more risk than reward, because she then retreats, falling back to the hackneyed questions prosecutors always ask of a testifying spouse. It's smart tactics. Donnelly's not going to get Cynthia to contradict herself and she can better make her points through her cross-examination of Aaron, who will have much less built-in goodwill with the jury.

As a result, the next half hour is composed of the types of questions to which the answers are preordained. *You love your husband, don't you? You'd worry about your children if their father went to jail? You'd do anything to help him?*

For her last question Donnelly asks, "You'd even lie for your husband under oath, wouldn't you, Mrs. Littman?"

"Yes," Cynthia says without hesitation. After a slight pause, she adds, "I'm thankful I don't have to."

The first part of the answer was just about the only truthful testimony Cynthia provided.

56

As soon as Sam Rosenthal says Rachel London's name, Donnelly shouts out her objection and asks to be heard in chambers.

A few minutes later, everyone is reassembled in the judge's office. The judge sits behind her desk with the lawyers standing in a semicircle in front of her.

"What's the story on this witness?" Judge Siskind asks.

Donnelly says, "On Saturday, we received notice of the defense's intent to call Ms. London as an alibi witness. Obviously, Rule Twelve notice should have been made weeks ago."

The defense knew this would be a problem. If they had an alibi witness, the rules of criminal procedure required that they provide notice to the prosecution within fourteen days of its request—one the government made more than a month ago. Rosenthal came up with the only solution that could possibly work, and now it's time to see if Judge Siskind will go for it.

"Your Honor, the failure to file the Rule Twelve notice was entirely mine, and I apologize profusely to the court and to the prosecution. I thought I made the disclosure two weeks ago, shortly after I received the government's discovery, which Your Honor might recall was provided to the defense only the day before the last pretrial conference. Just this past weekend, as I was preparing our defense, I realized the Rule Twelve notice had never gone out, and so I immediately sent it. Certainly, in a case where the stakes are this great, Mr. Littman should not be denied an alibi witness because of a mistake made by his counsel. Just as important, there is no harm done by the late disclosure because, as Ms. Donnelly said, the government has already interviewed Ms. London. On top of which, as the court knows, the defense was denied a witness list in this case, and so the government can hardly complain about prejudice because they only had a few days' notice about this witness when the defense in turn had absolutely no notice of any prosecution witness."

"Your Honor, this is an eleventh-hour desperation move," Donnelly says, sounding a bit desperate herself. "The hard truth is that we believe Ms. London is going to perjure herself to help Mr. Littman. We interviewed Ms. London during our investigation and she never suggested that she could alibi Mr. Littman. It doesn't take a genius to figure out that the defense sees the trial going badly, and so they either lean on a junior partner to commit perjury, or maybe they're bribing her to do so with the promise of, say, a bigger bonus next year, or she's doing it on her own volition out of some misguided sense of loyalty. Whatever her motive, this court cannot let perjured testimony come into evidence."

Judge Siskind furrows her brow. Based solely on her body language—arms crossed, eyes narrowed—Aaron has a moment of panic that Judge Siskind might actually preclude Rachel's testimony.

"Whether or not this witness is telling the truth is an issue for the jury," she finally says.

Donnelly looks apoplectic. "Your Honor—"

"I've ruled, Ms. Donnelly. If you think that Ms. London is committing perjury, you can file criminal charges. Now let's go hear what she has to say."

Rachel is the anti-Cynthia on the witness stand. She's done everything she can to tone down her looks. Her hair is pulled back into a single ponytail, she wears little makeup, and her suit is the most masculine in her closet—she hasn't worn it in years for just that reason. Even so, she looks like the supposedly ugly girl in one of those teen comedies, where the audience knows that once she removes her glasses, she'll be a knockout.

Rachel tells the jury that she is a partner at Cromwell Altman and has known Aaron for more than a decade. She describes her relationship with him as "like a mentor and a mentee."

Rosenthal doesn't ask if she and Aaron are lovers. Better for Donnelly to cross that line and then have Rachel become outraged by the suggestion.

"Were you working with Mr. Littman on the Garkov case?" Rosenthal asks.

"I was."

Rosenthal clears his throat and then limps over to counsel table and pours himself a glass of water. It's an old lawyer trick. He wants to make sure that the jurors are listening for this part.

After he resumes his position behind the podium, Rosenthal says, "Ms. London, I only have a few more questions, but they're very important. First, please tell the jury where you were on the evening that Faith Nichols was murdered."

"I was in the Garkov war room. That's the conference room near my office where we kept most of the Garkov files."

"Are you sure about that?"

"Absolutely positive. After Judge Nichols denied our request that she reconsider Garkov's bail revocation, we had a lot of work to do regarding a possible appeal. So, there's no other place I'd be."

Rosenthal hands Rachel the car voucher she used that evening. It corroborates that she left Cromwell Altman at 12:08 a.m. Ready to gild this particular lily, he then passes it around the jurors, waiting for each one to review it before getting to what he hopes will be the knockout blow.

"Did you see Aaron Littman at the firm that evening?"

"I couldn't help but see him. He was sitting right next to me the whole night."

"Was there a time when Mr. Littman was out of your sight

between . . . let's say 9:00 p.m. and midnight that evening, such that he could have gone to Central Park and committed this murder?"

"No," she says emphatically. "That's not possible. Aside from one of us going to the bathroom, or maybe going to get a soda from the kitchen, we were together the entire evening. In fact, he was still in the office when I left."

Rachel has done as well as Aaron could have imagined on direct questioning. But, of course, cross-examination still awaits her.

Victoria Donnelly surely knows that her sole objective in cross-examination is to convince the jury that Rachel London is a flat-out liar. She wastes no time, immediately zeroing in on Rachel's claim that Aaron was with her at the time of the murder.

"Ms. London, you testified that on the evening that Judge Nichols was murdered, Mr. Littman was with you from about nine o'clock until about midnight. But when you met with me before Mr. Littman was arrested, you didn't tell us that, now, did you?"

"I don't recall everything I said during the interview, but I do know that I told you the truth."

Donnelly stares hard at Rachel. Sizing her up, undoubtedly wondering if she's capable of breaking her.

"Perhaps this will refresh your recollection, Ms. London." Donnelly opens a black loose-leaf binder, which Rachel assumes contains the notes one of the FBI agents took during her interview. With her head in the notebook, Donnelly says, "During that interview, I asked if you had any reason to think that Mr. Littman did not kill Judge Nichols. Do you remember me asking that question?"

"I do."

"But in response, you didn't say that you were with Mr. Littman at the time of the murder, now, did you—yes or no?"

Rachel smiles. The *Answer me, yes or no!* tactic might be a staple on TV dramas, but it never works in real life.

"I recall that I answered that there were a million reasons why

Mr. Littman didn't kill her. Included among those million reasons was the fact that he was with me at the time of the murder."

"But you never said that, did you?"

"You didn't ask me what the reasons were."

Rosenthal shouts, "Objection!" but Donnelly is yelling over him: "In fact, I did, and you refused to answer!"

"Objection!" Rosenthal shouts again.

"Counsel!" Judge Siskind exclaims over both of them. "Approach right now!"

At the bench, Rosenthal hisses, "Your Honor, I am appalled. As Ms. Donnelly well knows, Ms. London did not answer the question on the advice of her lawyer during a voluntary interview. Ms. London had the absolute right *not* to answer. Given that the prosecution previously urged the court to rule that Mr. Garkov's invocation of the Fifth Amendment was too prejudicial for the jury to hear, it's unconscionable for them to suggest to the jury now that there was anything incriminating about Ms. London not answering a question."

"Ms. Donnelly, is this true?" Judge Siskind asks. "Because if it is, I am very unhappy. At least the defense raised the issue of Mr. Garkov's taking the Fifth before just throwing it out there in front of the jury."

Donnelly must know that she's on the wrong end of this one, but she doesn't shame easily. "Your Honor, there is no doubt in my mind that this witness is lying to protect Mr. Littman. Why else wouldn't she tell us during her interview that she could alibi him?"

"Not interested in your mind, Ms. Donnelly. I only care about the evidence you're submitting to the jury, and that's not going to include innuendo or half-truths. Now, here's what I'm going to do. I'm going to instruct the jury that the last few questions and answers should not be considered by them in their deliberations because Ms. London's prior interview by the government is of no importance here. All that matters is her testimony today."

"Your Honor," Donnelly says in a pleading voice, "we have the right to impeach her testimony with prior inconsistent statements."

"That you do, Ms. Donnelly, if you *had* any prior inconsistent statements. Tell me one and I'll consider allowing you to use it. But her refusal to answer a question is not a prior inconsistent statement."

Donnelly returns to the podium to resume her cross-examination. The smart move is for her to regroup and carefully dissect Rachel's testimony. But her expression makes clear that she's not going to pursue a surgical attack. She's out for blood.

"Ms. London . . . on direct questioning, you said that your relationship with Mr. Littman was professional. Mentor-slash-mentee is the phrasing I believe you used. But the truth is that you're in love with him, aren't you?"

Rachel flashes on all of her lying clients over the years. She's already lied about Aaron's presence with her in the war room, but somehow disavowing her love seems harder to do. It takes her only a moment—a pregnant pause, at best—but it's there.

She then says, "Aaron Littman and I work together. Nothing more. What you're implying is an insult to every woman in the workplace, Ms. Donnelly. How would you feel if someone said that you only got to prosecute this case because you were in love with the U.S. attorney?"

Bull's-eye. Donnelly asks a few more questions, largely so she can end on something other than Rachel's rebuke, but when Rachel's testimony ends, that's likely all the jurors will remember.

That, and the fact that she said Aaron couldn't have killed Faith Nichols because he was beside Rachel London at the time of the murder.

57

Aaron spends that evening in a Cromwell Altman conference room, essentially running lines. "A murder trial is no time for improv," Rosenthal says when Aaron deviates from the script.

Only cross-examination will be unrehearsed, and even that has been practiced at length. Rachel has been tasked with playing Donnelly's part, sneer and all. If anything, Aaron's even better at deflecting Rachel's accusations than he was at providing the self-serving responses Rosenthal's questions elicited.

At ten o'clock, Rosenthal announces, "If it all comes in that well tomorrow, I think we'll be way ahead of the game. Go home and get some sleep, Aaron."

Rachel shares the elevator with Aaron.

"You were great today," Aaron says.

"Thanks. But tomorrow's what really counts. No pressure, though."

A sad smile comes to her lips. It's Rachel's way of saying that Aaron's not out of the woods yet.

Cynthia is sitting up in bed reading when Aaron enters the bedroom. She looks sincerely happy that he's finally home, and Aaron lets the feeling of being welcome wash over him.

"So, are you ready?" Cynthia asks.

"We'll know tomorrow, I guess. But if it doesn't go well, it's not going to be for lack of preparation."

"It's not that hard," Cynthia says. Then, with a sly smile, she adds, "It's kind of ironic, don't you think? Now I've testified, and I've even been cross-examined by Victoria Donnelly, but this is new to you. It's a first. I'm giving you legal advice."

"So . . . what's your advice?"

"Be yourself. The jury will like you."

"I doubt that. The thing about criminal trials is that the jury *wants* to convict. That's the only happy ending. If they acquit, it just means that no one pays for the crime."

"That's why we're giving them a different happy ending to want. We're giving them a love story. They'll see that if you're acquitted, we can be together."

If only what she said were true, he thinks. Unfortunately, he knows otherwise.

The jury will not be so interested in Aaron's having a happy ending. They're only going to care about justice for Faith Nichols.

58

It is nearly gospel among defense attorneys that when you put your client on the stand, nothing else matters. The forensic evidence, the other witnesses, expert testimony, all of it goes away. If the jury believes they're listening to a truth-teller, they acquit. If they think the defendant is trying to pull something over on them—and it doesn't even matter about what—they convict.

Simple as that.

It's the reason so few defendants take the stand in their own defense. Only the most gifted liars can pull it off.

Now it's time for Aaron to see if he falls into this dubious category.

The strategy is for Sam Rosenthal to address the most damaging evidence first. This will allow the questioning to end on a high note.

And so, after establishing Aaron's background, Rosenthal gets right to the stuff that matters. "Did you engage in a sexual relationship with Judge Faith Nichols?"

"Absolutely not. Outside of a few times we talked at business functions, I never spoke to her except in court."

"Yesterday your wife testified that you and she met at the Ritz-Carlton hotel. Do you recall that testimony?"

"Yes. Quite honestly, it's something we never dreamed we'd have to share with the entire world, no less our teenage daughters. She saw it on an episode of *Modern Family*. The characters pretend to be other people and meet at a hotel bar. She wanted to try that and then it became part of a 'date night' routine for us."

"Did there come a time when this date-night ritual stopped?"

"Yes. For one reason or another, our schedules didn't sync for a few weeks, and then . . . well, I was charged with this crime and that pretty much meant the end of date night for me."

There are some chuckles in the gallery. A moment of levity that hopefully humanizes Aaron in the jury's eyes.

"Did you ever see Judge Nichols at the hotel?"

"No, never . . . I'm sorry, I take that back. I recall talking to her briefly at a dinner to honor George Vanderlyn, who was her former boss and also someone I know professionally. She was seated at the table with my law firm, an assignment made at random by the organizers of the dinner. I excused myself that evening at maybe nine o'clock, because it was the first of those special date nights with my wife. We decided it would be fun because I was already at the hotel for the business dinner and so it fueled the fantasy a little."

Rosenthal pauses. So far, so good.

"Mr. Littman, I'm going to direct my questioning to something else now. Roy Sabato testified that he told you Nicolai Garkov had damaging information about you. Do you recall that?"

"I recall him testifying to that, yes."

"Is your recollection of that meeting consistent with Mr. Sabato's testimony?"

"The way I remember it, he asked me to take on the matter, and I initially told him that I was very busy. Then Roy offered me the hundred thousand dollars for the initial meeting, and told me that he was concerned that if I didn't agree to it, Mr. Garkov would reveal something about me. I didn't take the threat seriously, of course. Desperate defendants have been known to say whatever it takes. But the practice of law *is* a business, and I did take the offer of one hundred thousand dollars seriously. So I ultimately agreed to meet with Mr. Garkov."

Admitting that Sabato relayed Garkov's threat was risky, but in the end, it was the only play. For Aaron to deny it made little sense. What possible reason would there be for Sabato to lie about that?

Rosenthal asks, "At that time, did you even know that Faith Nichols had been assigned as the judge on the Garkov case?"

"No. The judicial assignment occurred very late at night the day before, and only people who were involved in the case got official notice, which, of course, didn't include me. When Mr. Sabato asked me to meet with Mr. Garkov, I believed Judge Mendelsohn was still presiding over the case."

This, too, wasn't true, of course. But Sabato testified he couldn't remember mentioning that Faith had been assigned to the case, and that opened the door for Aaron to lie without fear of contradiction.

"Did you meet with Mr. Garkov after you met with Mr. Sabato?"

"Yes, I did."

"And what did you two discuss?"

Aaron turns away from Rosenthal so he's looking at the jury. "I need to be careful here because my discussions with Mr. Garkov are protected by the attorney-client privilege, and I have been told by Mr. Garkov's current counsel that he does not waive that privilege. As a result, I can't legally reveal what he said to me or what I said to him. But I can testify about what Mr. Garkov did *not* say, and he most definitely did not threaten me, nor did he ask me to blackmail Judge Nichols in any way, shape, or form."

Rosenthal walks back to the counsel table, leaning heavily on his cane as he does. Once there, he picks up the stack of phone records.

"Did you ever speak to Judge Nichols by phone?"

"We had frequent telephonic conferences during the Eric Matthews case. But whenever that occurred, all counsel were on the phone. So, if your question is whether I ever spoke to Judge Nichols one-on-one, the answer is no. I would never do that because it's improper to have ex parte contact with any judge that you're appearing before."

"Please explain to the jury what *ex parte* means."

"I don't know the literal translation from Latin, but in practice it means that whenever a lawyer speaks to a judge, the lawyer for the other side must also be present. That's true for phone calls and in court appearances. It's even the case when we send letters. The other side gets a copy. That's just standard operating procedure."

Rosenthal asks for permission to approach the witness, and after Judge Siskind grants the request, Rosenthal again uses his cane, clanking it against the floor with each step, as he makes the fifteen-foot trip from the lectern to the witness box. Once there, he hands Aaron the stack of phone bills and then takes even longer to make it back to the podium to resume his examination.

"Mr. Littman, I've handed you the evidence previously submitted by the prosecution," Rosenthal says, "that lists all of the phone calls to and from Judge Nichols's cell phone. Let me ask you point-blank. Did you make or receive any of those calls?"

"No, I did not."

"Have you ever purchased a prepaid phone?"

"No," Aaron says with a head-shake. "I use the cell phone that my law firm provides me."

It's time for Rosenthal to head for home. The night of the murder.

"Mr. Littman . . . did you see Judge Nichols on the night she was murdered?"

"No."

"Where were you that evening?"

"I was at the office all night. Other than a few minutes here and there, I was in a conference room with Rachel London. She called it the war room."

"Ms. London testified that she left before you that night, though. Is that true?"

"That is my recollection, although I did leave shortly thereafter."

There's one problem with this story. There is no evidence of how Aaron got home that night.

His usual practice, like all the Cromwell Altman partners, was to use the firm car service and charge a client for the ride. But that created a paper trail, like the voucher Rachel relied upon to show she had been in the office until a little after midnight. On a few occasions, Aaron walked home, so at least it was not the case that every night was accounted for with a voucher, but he could not plausibly claim that he walked home on a cold evening after midnight.

Rosenthal decided that it was better to bring the point out on direct than to leave Aaron floundering to explain during Donnelly's cross-examination. That way, when she did go after him about it, it would seem like old news. At least that was the hope.

"Mr. Littman, how did you get home that evening?"

"Frankly, at first I didn't remember. It was just another late night at the office, and that's pretty much my regular practice. Even when I heard the next day that Judge Nichols had been killed, I didn't think I'd have to account for my whereabouts. Of course, when the charges were filed, we went back to the vouchers but didn't see one for that night. That could mean the voucher was lost, or that I grabbed a taxi that night."

"Why would you take a taxi rather than the firm's car service?"

"Any number of reasons. There might not have been a car available and a taxi pulled right up. The yellow cabs hover around the area all the time, trying to steal business from the car service. It's also possible I needed to get something from the Duane Reade, which is a block or two from the office, and it's open twenty-four hours. Sometimes after leaving the office, I'll walk a few blocks just to unwind a bit and then hail a cab. Honestly, I just don't remember what I did on that particular night. I wish I did, but I don't."

It's the best he can do with what they have. Rosenthal looked into creating a false voucher, but the risks outweighed the benefits. The car service would likely have complied, given that Cromwell Altman is their biggest client. And a driver might have been paid off too, swearing that he took Aaron from work that night. But it was Aaron who ultimately thought they were going too far out on a limb for a minor point. Putting his trust in Cynthia or Rachel was one thing, but putting it in a limo driver was quite another. Plus those yellow cabs really were like sharks anyway, which made plausible each of the scenarios he had laid out.

And so, after establishing Aaron's alibi as best as lying can do, Rosenthal ends the examination with a closing flurry.

"Mr. Littman, did you kill Judge Nichols?"

"No."

"Just no?"

"What else can I say beyond *no*?"

I didn't do it. You have to believe me.

59

Federal prosecutors don't cross-examine many witnesses. Partly this is because trials in federal court are rare as a general matter, with well over 90 percent of defendants pleading out. And, at least in New York City, the defendants who do go to trial are usually drug dealers and organized-crime figures, and they don't call many witnesses on their own behalf because their associates tend to be criminals as well.

As she prepares to ask her first question, however, Victoria Donnelly doesn't seem the least bit apprehensive. On the contrary, she looks like a predator eyeing prey.

"Mr. Littman," she says as if his name is an epithet, "let me get straight here what you're asking this jury to believe. First, you claim that you never had an affair with Judge Nichols, even though her husband provided sworn testimony that he saw the two of you holding hands as you left the Ritz-Carlton hotel. Do I have that right?"

"I never had an affair with Judge Nichols and I was never with her at the Ritz-Carlton—other than the one time I spoke about, during a banquet that was attended by hundreds of others. Needless to say, that also means that I never held hands with her at any time."

"So, Mr. Christensen, Judge Nichols's widower . . . he's a liar. That's your testimony?"

Aaron knows this is the most precarious part: to maintain his innocence and yet not appear as someone asking the jury to disbelieve everyone but him.

"I don't know why Mr. Christensen testified as he did. Perhaps he's mistaken. Perhaps he lied to you so that he wouldn't be considered a suspect. I don't know. What I do know is that I did not have an affair with Judge Nichols."

I didn't do it. You have to believe me.

"But you did frequent the hotel, didn't you? You're not claiming that the Ritz-Carlton's records are also lying, are you?"

Donnelly's clearly trying to get a rise out of Aaron, to show the jury that he's a man prone to outbursts. His job, therefore, is to remain cool, no matter what she hurls at him.

"As my wife and I both previously testified, we went to the hotel about once a week. It was part of our date nights."

"So just a coincidence, is that your testimony? A clerk at the Ritz-Carlton says that Judge Nichols was often there. Her widower says he saw you hand in hand with his wife at the hotel, and you admit that you were there but claim that you were there with your wife. Do I have all of that right? It's all just one big coincidence?"

"My experience in criminal practice is that the prosecution often takes a fact—for example, my presence at the Ritz-Carlton from time to time—and pressures witnesses to conform their recollection to such facts. So, a clerk at the Ritz-Carlton might be pressured to say that she remembered Faith being there on multiple occasions when the truth could be that she saw her once for a business meeting . . . and like I said, Judge Nichols was at the hotel for the George Vanderlyn banquet. As for Mr. Christensen, all I can say is that a spouse is often a suspect when the wife is murdered, and therefore he might say just about anything to save his own skin."

"Well, finally, something we can agree on, Mr. Littman," Donnelly says. "Some people would say anything to save their own skin. Is Roy Sabato also lying to save his own skin when he says that he told you that Nicolai Garkov would make public some very incriminating information about you if you did not agree to meet with him?"

Aaron's already conceded this, so he's got no choice but to take it on the chin.

"Yes, that is what Roy said."

"And the information he was talking about—the information he claimed Mr. Garkov would make public if you didn't meet with him—that was your affair with Judge Nichols, wasn't it?"

"No. That's not the case. As I testified, I did not have an affair with Judge Nichols."

"But you admit that Mr. Sabato said that Mr. Garkov had information that would be extremely damaging to you?"

"As I've said repeatedly now, Mr. Garkov didn't have any information. He was bluffing when he told Mr. Sabato to say that."

"Yes, yes. That's your story and you're sticking to it."

Aaron doesn't answer, and Donnelly appears content to have the silence permeate the courtroom. When she's played out the theatrics to their fullest extent, she fires off another question.

"Mr. Littman, on the night Judge Nichols was killed, she received two phone calls from the same phone number, and she made a phone call to that number. Is it your testimony that you didn't make those calls or receive a call from her?"

"Yes, it is."

Donnelly pulls a piece of paper from the pile of exhibits that have already been introduced. Then she reads: "*Faith, please call me at this number as soon as you can. Very important.* Are you also telling this jury that you did not send that message?"

"That is correct. I did not send that message."

"If Mr. Garkov was blackmailing you by, let's just say . . . by threatening to reveal your affair with Judge Nichols unless Judge Nichols helped him in his case, that is the kind of text you would have sent, correct?"

Aaron looks across the courtroom at Rosenthal. The question is way out of bounds, but Rosenthal doesn't object. Instead he offers Aaron a slow nod, his way of conveying that Aaron's got to sink or swim on his own, lest the jury believe Rosenthal is trying to obstruct them from hearing the truth.

"The question is based on a false premise," Aaron says calmly. "I can't answer it because I wasn't having an affair with Judge Nichols, and Mr. Garkov was not blackmailing me, and because I didn't send that text."

"And according to you, Mr. Littman, you were in the office the night of the murder with Rachel London?"

"I was in the Garkov war room with Ms. London, yes."

"You and Ms. London are very close, aren't you, Mr. Littman?"

"I'm close to a great many of my partners at Cromwell Altman. I don't know what you mean by *very close*, though."

He knows as soon as he's said it that he should have let Donnelly have that one. But cross-examination is a bit like drowning in that way—when you start to go under, none of your senses work and your actions are often counterproductive.

"Yes, Mr. Littman, I should have known that you *love* all two hundred of your partners equally and completely," Donnelly says. "C'mon, let's be honest with the jury, shall we? There's only one partner that you asked to assist you on the Eric Matthews case. Who was that?"

"Rachel London."

"And there was only one that you asked to assist you on the Garkov case. Who was that?"

"Again, Ms. London."

"Right. And, in fact, Ms. London owes her partnership to you, doesn't she?"

Aaron pauses, contemplating whether he can credibly push back on the assertion. Donnelly takes advantage of the silence to deny him that path.

"Mr. Littman, if I called to the stand any number of your partners, wouldn't they tell me that your blessing alone is enough to elevate an associate to that brass ring, and the millions of dollars in compensation that come with it?"

Aaron feels like he can no longer struggle against the current. "As the chairman of the firm . . . my vote has considerable weight, yes."

"Thank you, Mr. Littman. It wasn't so hard to tell the truth, now, was it?"

Judge Siskind looks over to defense counsel table, apparently expecting Rosenthal to object. But when he says nothing, she takes it upon herself.

"Dial it down a notch, Ms. Donnelly," she says.

Donnelly, however, continues the onslaught. "And you claim that you just don't remember how you got home the night Judge Nichols was murdered. Is that your story?"

"It's not a story, Ms. Donnelly. That's my sworn testimony."

Donnelly smiles at him with contempt. "And it's also your *sworn testimony* that you might have—after midnight on a cold winter night—decided to take a little stroll in midtown Manhattan and then look for a cab, rather than just get inside one of the limousines your law firm has parked right in front of its building to shuttle the partners to and from work. Do I have that part of your *sworn testimony* right?"

"As I testified before, I sometimes do walk for a block or two. Just to clear my head. It's quite easy to find a taxi in midtown Manhattan at that time of night."

"But you didn't submit for the expense, did you, Mr. Littman? So, you have a free ride with the car service, but you're claiming that you decided to pay for the ride yourself."

"That's also not uncommon. A taxi from the office to my apartment is probably six or seven dollars. I don't mean to be cavalier about it, and when I remember to ask for a receipt, I will sometimes seek reimbursement, but given that I'm charging the client fifteen hundred dollars an hour for my time, I don't feel like I have to get reimbursed every time I spend a couple of dollars out of my own pocket."

Donnelly comes to a full stop. Like an athlete psyching herself up, she appears to be preparing for a final onslaught.

Aaron knows that means she's going to question him about the 9:48 phone call to his office. Her smoking gun.

"Mr. Littman, you claim you never spoke to Judge Nichols on the night she was murdered, but you admit, do you not, that there was a call made from Judge Nichols's phone to your office at 9:48 p.m. on the evening she was killed."

"I have seen the records that indicate that, yes."

Aaron can hear in his voice the defensiveness that juries hate. Of greater concern is the fact that he knows it's about to get worse.

"Mr. Littman, you are not suggesting, are you, that the phone company is also lying?"

"No."

"So, Judge Faith Nichols—a judge before whom you were defense counsel—called you from her personal cell phone at nearly ten o'clock at night."

As damaging as the statement is, it's not a question, and so Aaron stays mute.

"Mr. Littman, correct me if I'm wrong, but didn't you testify that you were in the office that night? Your story is that you and Ms. London were side by side all night. But you also admit that maybe . . . just maybe . . . you left her side for . . . I don't know . . . three minutes and three seconds here and there. Enough time for you to be in your office to be on that phone call."

Having put forth this lie, Aaron has no choice but to perpetuate it. "I was in the office at that time, yes."

"And yet you still deny that you spoke to Judge Nichols at 9:48 p.m.?"

"I didn't speak to her," he says.

He might as well have said, *You have to believe me.*

After Aaron's excused from the witness box, the defense rests. Judge Siskind tells the jury that she wants to complete closing arguments that evening and that they can begin their deliberations the following morning. She declares a ten-minute recess so the lawyers can gather their thoughts, and everyone stands as the jury makes their way out of the courtroom.

Rosenthal is upbeat, telling Aaron that he did well. Aaron, however, could feel it all slipping away when he couldn't explain that last phone call.

60

Donnelly's closing argument seems overly strident to Aaron, but it's not uncommon for defendants to feel that way. Hearing someone accuse you of committing an unthinkable act often sounds desperate to you but compelling to a jury.

Even Aaron has to admit, however, that the evidence against him is compelling. The affair is proven by the Ritz-Carlton records and the eyewitnesses. The blackmail by Nicolai Garkov. And the 9:48 call puts Aaron in contact with Judge Nichols right before she was killed.

"And what does the defense say in rebuttal?" Donnelly asks rhetorically. "That none of it is true. No affair. No blackmail. And that the call was made by someone else, someone trying to frame Mr. Littman, perhaps." At this Donnelly pauses, as if she's just thought of something, despite the fact that lawyers practice their closings for hours and almost never ad-lib. "But if there was no affair, as Mr. Littman and his wife claim, how would anyone know to call Mr. Littman to frame him?" Then she just shakes her head. "The defense makes no sense. None. The only reasonable conclusion consistent with the evidence is that Aaron Littman murdered his lover, Faith Nichols, so that Nicolai Garkov would not reveal that Mr. Littman and Judge Nichols were having an affair—news that would have destroyed the defendant's marriage and his career."

Rosenthal's closing pokes holes in what the prosecution presented. As Aaron listens to Rosenthal do the best with what he has, he knows that the defense has not provided an alternative murderer for the jury to consider, which means that he's asking them to reach a verdict in which no one will be held accountable for Faith Nichols's murder.

At six o'clock, Judge Siskind completes her jury instructions. The jurors assemble out of the courtroom without making eye contact with Aaron, but he tells himself not to read anything into that and takes comfort in the fact that the trial is finally over.

All except the verdict, that is.

Aaron enters his home that evening with only one thought in mind: this might be the last night he ever spends here. The sad realization hits him that this will be the case every time he comes home until there's a verdict.

Aaron and Cynthia make love for the third night in a row. Like coming home, he wonders if this, too, will be the last time.

When Eric Matthews was sentenced, Faith read her decision from the bench, going on for ten minutes about the seriousness of the crime and how a message had to be sent to both Wall Street and Main Street that financial fraud was every bit as destructive to the fabric of society as violent crime. When she finally uttered the payoff line—"I sentence you to fourteen years in prison"—Matthews didn't show the slightest emotion. He didn't even turn around when his wife let out a bloodcurdling shriek.

After Faith struck the gavel, while the guards were grabbing Matthews's arms to handcuff him, he turned to Aaron and said, "What happened?"

"She sentenced you to fourteen years," Aaron replied. "We have strong arguments on appeal—"

"No. What did she say about *me*?"

Eric Matthews wasn't even the worst Aaron had ever experienced. Robert Fox, who was at one time considered the most feared man on Wall Street, literally pissed himself when he was sentenced to eight years. And back in the day, when the sentencing guidelines were mandatory, Aaron had two clients commit suicide before sentencing.

Now it's his turn. Above all else, Aaron's determined to preserve some modicum of dignity if the worst is to occur.

Cynthia and the girls are present in the courtroom to wait for the verdict. Aaron wanted to spare them, but Cynthia prevailed upon him that it was important for them to share the experience. Besides, she said, nothing was going to keep her out of the courtroom, and Lindsay and Samantha would be anxiously waiting wherever they were, and she preferred them all to be together.

Midmorning on the second day of deliberations, the jury delivers a note that they've reached a verdict. That most likely means that someone switched sides overnight, as juries usually vote before adjourning for the evening.

"It's a good sign," Rosenthal says.

Aaron knows this is just something lawyers tell their clients to keep them from jumping out of their skin as they wait. He's said it to many a client himself, even as he knew that there is no way of knowing if the switch was from guilty to not guilty or the other way around. Or even if there was a switch at all. It's also quite possible the jury reached a verdict last night and decided to sleep on it, just to make sure no one wanted to change their vote.

Aaron purposefully doesn't make eye contact with any of the twelve jurors as they enter the courtroom. There's no reason to be lulled into thinking that a smile is a vote for acquittal.

It'll be over soon. Less than two minutes.

He imagines he could hold his breath for that long, and a part of him feels like he's doing just that. When everyone is in their place, Judge Siskind strikes her gavel to quiet the gallery.

The silence only adds to the grimness Aaron feels. He turns around to see Cynthia and the twins huddled together, as if they're freezing and sharing bodily warmth.

"Will the defendant please rise?" Judge Siskind says.

Aaron and Rosenthal stand as one. Rosenthal takes Aaron's hand in his and gives it a squeeze. Aaron suspects he means to convey that they're in this together, and yet Aaron has never felt more alone.

"Madame Foreperson, please read the jury's unanimous verdict," Judge Siskind says.

A gray-haired African-American woman stands. She has reading glasses perched on her nose and is holding a piece of paper at arm's length, as if she hasn't memorized the verdict she's about to deliver.

Aaron finally looks at the faces of the twelve jurors. None of them look in his direction. Not one.

He shuts his eyes, trying to tune out all sensory experiences. His complete and total focus is on whether he's going to hear the word *not*.

The foreperson reads in a monotone: "We, the members of the jury, for our unanimous verdict, hereby declare, on the sole count of the indictment, murder in the second degree, that we find the defendant, Aaron L. Littman, to be . . ." And then she looks up for the briefest second and says, "Guilty."

Aaron's knees buckle, and he consciously has to plant his feet to keep himself upright. When his mind flashes on how Cynthia and the girls are reacting, he suddenly becomes faint and tumbles back into his chair.

The court officers converge on him, forming a wedge that makes it difficult for him to move more than a foot from the table. A single word has instantly transformed Aaron into a convicted murderer.

"Poll the jury," Rosenthal says.

Aaron is thankful that someone has done something, even though he knows this will only make it worse. It was bad enough when the foreperson spoke for them, but now each one will declare Aaron guilty.

"Very well," Judge Siskind says. "The defense has requested that each member of the jury state for the record how he or she voted. So, let's go through the jury members, one at a time. Madame Foreperson, you may begin."

The African-American woman stands again. "Guilty," she says, and then she sits down. She's followed by a middle-aged man with a mustache who does the same thing. A younger woman with curly hair, and then a younger man who has shaved his head, and then an older man who is balding all repeat the act. It has the look of a very feeble wave at a sporting event, the orderly rising and sitting, except instead of throwing their hands in the air, each one says, "Guilty."

Midway through, Aaron summons the courage to swing around, and it's even worse than he could have imagined. Cynthia is curled into herself, with Lindsay and Samantha draped over her on either side. Aaron can't see any of their faces, but their bodies are convulsing in a way that indicates suffering.

"There you have it, Mr. Rosenthal," Judge Siskind says when the last juror has spoken. "The jury's verdict is unanimous. I'm going to—"

"Your Honor," Rosenthal interrupts, "at this time, the defense moves for a judgment notwithstanding the verdict and requests to be heard in chambers immediately."

This is the after-verdict equivalent of requesting a directed verdict, and it's even more rarely granted. If judges are loath to take the decision out of the hands of a jury at the trial's midpoint, they are twice as unlikely to overrule it after a verdict is rendered.

Judge Siskind uses her gavel to quiet the gallery. "Mr. Rosenthal, your motion is not unexpected, but I'm going to put this matter down for thirty days from today. In the next month, I expect both sides to review the transcript and prepare motion papers. When we reconvene, I will hear arguments concerning sentencing, in the event that I do not grant the defense's Rule Thirty-Three motion to nullify the jury's verdict."

Rosenthal exhales loudly. It's as if he's expelling the shock of the guilty verdict.

"I know that what Your Honor just proposed is the standard procedure after a guilty verdict," he says, "but there is something . . . something that the defense needs to bring to the court's and the prosecution's attention immediately. Accordingly, I renew my request that the court hear from the defense in chambers at this time."

Judge Siskind looks lost. She likely carefully scripted the trial's conclusion, perhaps even preparing both a guilty and a not-guilty speech, and now Sam Rosenthal is asking her to ad-lib.

"Okay," she finally says. "Let's do this now."

Aaron can finally feel his brain function again. He looks for Rosenthal to provide some type of explanation.

"I would never let you go to jail, Aaron," Rosenthal says.

61

Aaron is escorted out of the courtroom by the guards, who do not extend him the courtesy of unlocking his handcuffs. With each step, he experiences the same sickening sense of anxiety that he did before the verdict. He tries to calm himself by saying that the worst has already happened, but that's hardly a soothing thought.

In the outer office of her chambers, Judge Siskind says, "Do we need to sit down for this, Mr. Rosenthal, or can we do this here?"

"Here is fine," Rosenthal says without emotion.

The stenographer sets up her machine but tells Judge Siskind she needs a chair before she can begin. Judge Siskind's law clerk, a twentysomething woman with long, black hair, says, "Here, use mine," and pushes it in her direction.

Finally, with the court reporter seated but everyone else standing, Judge Siskind says, "Mr. Rosenthal, I assume I speak for everyone when I say we're on pins and needles. What is it that you had to discuss so urgently in chambers?"

"I killed Judge Faith Nichols."

Aaron looks at Rosenthal, but Rosenthal doesn't accept his gaze. He stares straight ahead, looking only at the judge.

No one says anything for a good twenty seconds. The silence is broken by Victoria Donnelly.

"I . . . I don't know what Mr. Rosenthal is trying to get away with here, Your Honor," she says, "but what I do know is that the jury has spoken. They found Mr. Littman guilty. This is nothing more than a stunt to somehow persuade the court that the verdict should be set aside. Or maybe it's a ploy for leniency for when you sentence Mr. Littman. Either way, it's wholly improper."

Judge Siskind doesn't respond at first, but when Rosenthal doesn't rebut Donnelly's charge she prompts him. "Mr. Rosenthal?"

"It's hardly a stunt, Your Honor," he says. "I'm willing to plead guilty and to be sent to prison for my crime."

"Your Honor," Donnelly says, now in an almost pleading voice, "you may not be aware of this, but Mr. Rosenthal and Mr. Littman are very close. Father-son like, is what I've been told. Certainly, many a father would willingly switch places with his son to spare him from prison. Mr. Rosenthal has no family of his own, and while he may think he's doing something noble, he is not. Justice demands that the guilty be punished, and as we have all seen in the trial, and as the jury has found, Mr. Littman murdered Judge Nichols."

After what feels to Aaron like an eternity but is really only a few seconds, Judge Siskind says, "The jury has indeed spoken, and therefore I am ordering Mr. Littman to be remanded to the custody of the Department of Corrections, forthwith."

"Thank you, Your Honor," Donnelly says, relief across her face.

"Don't thank me just yet, Ms. Donnelly," Judge Siskind says. "Mr. Rosenthal . . . I really don't know what to do with you at this point. I don't have any authority to confine you, and so . . . notwithstanding your confession, you are free to go after this hearing, unless Ms. Donnelly's office has the FBI place you under arrest. But, if you truly want to be held accountable for this crime, I will hear from you tomorrow at 10:00 a.m., at which time I would expect you to put forward whatever evidence you have that you, and not Mr. Littman, killed Judge Nichols."

Not every judge permits a convicted murderer time with his family. Aaron intends to make the most of it.

He's standing in the hallway, his hands still cuffed behind his back, when he sees his family from a distance, making their way down the long corridor.

Cynthia is flanked on either side by Lindsay and Samantha, as if they're holding her upright. As they approach, Cynthia rubs her eyes, apparently deciding that she's going to try to hold it together for this farewell. His daughters, by contrast, make no effort to stem their tears.

The girls envelop him, and Aaron takes in the sensation of being sandwiched between them. As much as he wants to lose himself completely in this feeling, he can't quell the fear that he'll never again experience his children's touch.

"It's going to be okay," he says, trying to maintain his composure.

"Girls," Cynthia says, "we'll see your father very soon, but you need to say good-bye to him for now. I'd like to have a few moments alone with him, please."

There is a final squeeze by both of them, and Samantha says, "I love you, Daddy." True to form, Lindsay says only, "ILY," which Aaron has learned stands for *I love you*.

The girls walk away, and as Aaron watches them leave, Cynthia says, "What happened in chambers?"

Aaron hesitates for a moment, not wanting to raise Cynthia's hopes unnecessarily. But there's no way he can keep this from his wife.

"You're not going to believe this, but Sam just confessed to killing her."

"What?"

"I know. He said he killed her."

"Then why aren't you free?"

Aaron smiles. If only it were that easy, he thinks.

"It doesn't work like that," he says. "Donnelly doesn't believe him. She said he was just giving himself up to spare me. Surrogate-father stuff. The judge didn't know what the hell to do. So she said that I'm to stay in custody and she'll hold a hearing tomorrow morning. She told Sam to bring whatever evidence he has to convince her that he's the one that should be going to jail and not me."

"Do you think it's true? Could Sam have done such a thing?"

Before Aaron can answer, two guards are upon him.

"Time's up," one of them says.

They are not gentle. One spins Aaron as if he's a piece of furniture and then the other pushes him square in the back so that he'll start to walk. He turns around for a brief moment to capture a last look at his wife, and he sees that she is sobbing.

Aaron spends the night alone in a cell in the MCC. He doesn't sleep at all, which gives him plenty of hours to think through the last few months.

When Sam Rosenthal first announced he was Faith's killer, Aaron thought it was exactly what Donnelly said—a stunt, by which the old man was trying to spare Aaron. But alone, thinking it through, it makes much more sense.

Aaron has one great advantage over everyone else—the FBI, Victoria Donnelly, Rachel, and even Cynthia—because he knows that he did not kill Faith.

And if not him, then who?

Garkov or Stuart Christensen. One of them makes the most sense. They both had motive, and because they both knew about the affair, it made perfect sense for either one of them to use Faith's cell phone to throw suspicion onto Aaron.

But it also makes perfect sense that when he left Faith in Central Park, with her nomination in peril, she reached out to Sam Rosenthal to fix things. She must have misdialed, calling Aaron's office number out of habit, as she had so many times during the Matthews trial. His number differed from Rosenthal's only by the last digit being a two instead of a one. If Faith had gotten Aaron's voice mail, hung up, and redialed Rosenthal . . . everything would have played out differently. But instead she must have hit zero and asked the firm's receptionist to redirect her call to its intended recipient.

For the balance of three minutes and three seconds, Faith Nichols must have explained her dilemma to Rosenthal, seeking his help, either to control his partner or to smooth things with Senator Kheel.

The wrong number was apparently not Faith's only mistake, however. She made a much graver error in failing to realize that Rosenthal would conclude that it was easier to fix his problems by killing her than to try to salvage her nomination.

62

Aaron's wearing the orange jumpsuit that brands him a convict and is shackled by the hands and feet as he's led back to the courtroom the following morning. The first thing he notices when the side door opens is that none other than Fitz is sitting at counsel table, with Victoria Donnelly in the seat next to him. Sam Rosenthal sits at the defense table, a vacant chair separating him and Rachel London.

The gallery is empty. Judge Siskind must have closed the courtroom, because Aaron can't imagine that anything short of a judicial order could keep Cynthia away. Not to mention the press.

At the MCC, Aaron had been cut off from all news, and he was brought into the courthouse through an internal passageway, thereby avoiding the media. Nevertheless, he's sure that there must be an all-out frenzy in front of the building. It's not every day that one well-respected lawyer confesses to the murder of a federal judge for which another well-respected lawyer has just been found guilty.

As Aaron takes his place between Rosenthal and Rachel, Sam offers him the saddest-looking smile Aaron's ever seen. He places his hand on Aaron's shoulder, but before either of them can say anything, they are interrupted by three loud knocks on the door frame leading to the judge's chambers.

"All rise," the court officer announces.

Judge Siskind approaches the bench with a sense of purpose. A step behind her are two younger women. The black-haired woman who gave the stenographer her chair the previous day sits below the bench, in the same position she occupied during the trial. The other must be Judge Siskind's second law clerk, who to Aaron's recollection never set foot in the courtroom during the trial. She takes a seat in the unoccupied jury box, no doubt anxious to see the show that's about to begin.

"Please be seated," Judge Siskind says after she sits down. "I've closed the courtroom today because I thought it was best to avoid any unwanted commotion. However, there is a stenographer present, and it is not my intention to seal today's transcript. That means this hearing will be a matter of public record." She looks up. "Counsel, please state your appearances."

The prosecution team stands. "Good morning, Your Honor. Thomas J. Fitzpatrick, United States attorney for the Southern District of New York, for the United States." Fitz apparently sees no need to mention Donnelly because after introducing himself, he sits down.

Rosenthal stands and says, "Samuel Rosenthal of the law firm Cromwell Altman Rosenthal and White. Because I'm obviously conflicted, my partner Rachel London is with me. With the court's permission, she will represent Mr. Littman in these proceedings."

"Is it your intention to represent yourself, Mr. Rosenthal?" Judge Siskind asks.

"It is," he says calmly, and then sits down.

"Thank you," Judge Siskind says. "What I'm going to do today is hear from Mr. Rosenthal. At this point, Mr. Rosenthal, all I want you to do is set forth whatever evidence you have to support your claim that you, and not Mr. Littman, murdered Judge Faith Nichols. After you've laid that out, we can talk about how to present the evidence so that the prosecution has an opportunity to cross-examine. I realize that's a bit unorthodox but . . . well, let's be frank, this is an unusual situation."

Rosenthal bends over to the leather duffel bag beside him on the floor. Aaron didn't see it when he entered the courtroom, but he watches intently as Rosenthal pulls out a white plastic trash bag with red string ties. Then Rosenthal methodically opens the bag and withdraws its contents, holding it carefully on the ends to avoid contaminating it.

It's his cane. A different one from the cane that rests beside him now, but Aaron realizes at once that this is the weapon that Rosenthal used to kill Faith.

Rosenthal stands and holds the cane in front of him, as if it's a trophy he's just won.

"This is the murder weapon, Your Honor," he says in an expressionless voice. "It still has blood and other evidence that will prove it was used to kill Judge Nichols. And while I fully appreciate the fact that my fingerprints on it will not be persuasive, any number of people can confirm that it is my cane, and that I used it on a regular basis prior to the murder."

He gently lays the cane on defense counsel table. Apparently he sees no reason to say anything further, because he then sits.

As if a baton has been passed, Rachel rises. "Your Honor . . . at this time, the defense requests that you grant judgment notwithstanding the verdict, pursuant to Rule Thirty-Three of the Federal Rules of Criminal Procedure, and release Mr. Littman from custody."

Aaron has tried to keep his expectations in check, but now his spirits are buoyed. This seems to be more than enough to convince Judge Siskind, and even Fitz, that he did not kill Faith. Of course, until his ankles and wrists are no longer chained together, he will not feel free.

"Mr. Fitzpatrick," Judge Siskind says, "while I know you're going to want to have the cane examined by experts, and someone will need to confirm that the wounds suffered by Judge Nichols could have been caused by a beating with a cane, and that this type of assault could have been committed by someone of Mr. Rosenthal's age, size, and strength . . . let's for the moment assume that all of that is proven to be correct. Would you like the opportunity to cross-examine Mr. Rosenthal now or do you want to wait until after the tests have been completed?"

Fitz looks shaken, and Aaron can't help but enjoy the moment.

Just how the hell is Fitz going to explain *this* to the moneymen backing his campaign for mayor?

"Your Honor," the U.S. attorney says as he slowly comes to his feet, "I have known Mr. Rosenthal for more than thirty years. And I've known Mr. Littman for nearly as long. Let me say, before responding to the court's question, that this is a very sad day. It was a sad day for me personally when we made the decision to arrest Mr. Littman. But I believed that my office acted in the best interests of justice in bringing this case and in securing Mr. Littman's conviction."

Fitz breaks eye contact with Judge Siskind and looks across the courtroom at the defense counsel's table. "I suppose, like everyone else in this room, I want to know why, Sam? Why did you do it? Why did you even let Aaron stand trial? Why are you coming forward *now* when you had every opportunity in the world to do it sooner?"

"Do you want me to put Mr. Rosenthal under oath?" Judge Siskind asks.

"No, we can do that later," Fitz says. "I just want the answers now."

"Mr. Rosenthal?" Judge Siskind says.

Rosenthal smiles at Aaron, his way of saying that it's over. He must believe that Fitz is willing to admit they tried and convicted the wrong man, and accept Rosenthal as Faith's murderer.

Samuel Rosenthal comes to his feet. "Your Honor . . . Fitz . . . Aaron Littman is the closest thing I have to a child . . . or any family, for that matter," he says. "Yes, I should have confessed the moment Aaron was arrested. It was . . . nothing but hubris on my part to believe that I could obtain his acquittal and not have to face the consequences of what I'd done."

Aaron hangs his head. Despite never lifting a finger, he has never before felt so responsible for Faith's murder.

63

Fitz holds a press conference on the courthouse steps immediately after the court appearance, in which he uses the word *justice* at least seven times. He tries his best to spin the recent turn of events as a triumph for his office, emphasizing that now the public will have no doubt that Judge Nichols's killer is securely behind bars. He further points out that it was at his request that Aaron Littman was released on his own recognizance, and that Samuel Rosenthal has been taken into custody, charged with second-degree murder.

It is a performance Aaron has no interest in seeing. He and Cynthia leave the courtroom out the other exit. Although reporters shout at him as he enters the street, he pushes by them without saying a word.

Freedom. Aaron's prayers over the last two months have been answered. For the rest of his life, he will be able to come and go as he pleases.

Rachel has accompanied them out of the courthouse, but when Aaron and Cynthia climb into the back of the Lincoln Town Car that Rachel arranged to meet them at the court, she stops short.

"You two should go on ahead," she says. "Take some time together alone to celebrate."

Aaron steps back out of the car, so he can talk to Rachel without being overheard by the press, which has by now converged on them. He leans over and whispers in her ear, "I can never thank you enough, Rachel."

"You can thank me by being happy," she says.

"Only if you do the same."

They hold each other's gaze for a moment. He knows that Rachel wanted more from him but hopes that she realizes that they will both be happier following different paths.

She smiles, and in doing so answers Aaron's concerns. He doesn't have to worry about her, she's telling him, she's going to be just fine.

"Deal," she says, and then kisses him on the cheek.

Lindsay and Samantha are weeping when Aaron and Cynthia arrive home. It reminds Aaron of the final scene in *It's a Wonderful Life*. He's surrounded by the people he loves, and they love him.

It's an ingrained part of criminal practice, to see how such small things can bring down the high and mighty to depths where even the least fortunate wouldn't change places with them. Were it not for Sam Rosenthal's surrender, Aaron would now be behind bars, a disgrace to his family and friends. And instead he's free, basking in his family's love.

Aaron knows full well that he does not deserve this good fortune. Nonetheless, he will accept it in the hope that someday he might be worthy.

The forensic tests come back a few days later and confirm everything Rosenthal said they would. The blood on the cane matches Faith's, her wounds are consistent with a beating from the cane, and the experts have concluded that Rosenthal is easily strong enough to have done the deed. There are no fingerprints other than Rosenthal's, and the blood spatter is so pervasive that it's not possible that any evidence was wiped away after the crime.

The same day the test results come back, Judge Siskind issues an eight-page written opinion granting the defense's motion. Ever the stickler, she explains that Rule 33 can be invoked only when the evidence presented at trial was insufficient to support the jury's verdict, and that was not true with regard to the evidence considered by the jury in this case. However, she finds that under Rule 29, Aaron is entitled to a new trial, based on the recently discovered evidence. She gives the prosecution ten days to file for a new trial or dismiss the charges.

Two hours later, the U.S. Attorney's Office issues a press release stating that Aaron Littman will not be retried.

It's finally over.

64

Moments after the government announces that Aaron Littman is no longer a murderer, people who shunned him while he was under indictment begin texting, calling, and e-mailing their exhortations that they never believed the charges were true.

Among the first of those calls is one from Clint Broden.

"Nicolai wanted to call himself," Broden says without any hint of recognition of the ridiculousness of the entire gesture, "but given his circumstances, I couldn't allow it, of course. I told him that you, of all people, would certainly understand. He wanted to congratulate you and asked that I tell you that it seems you are less of a categorical imperative guy after all."

Not surprising given that he's a terrorist, a murderer, and a blackmailer, Garkov is also a first-rate prick right up until the end. Aaron is tempted to say just that to Broden but decides that there's no point. Aaron's confident Nicolai Garkov will see prison soon enough, either for the crimes of which he stands accused or something else he hasn't done yet.

"Thanks for the call, Clint," Aaron replies, careful not to wish Broden any luck in his upcoming defense of Nicolai Garkov.

Like Nicolai Garkov, others, especially some members of the press, have recognized that Rosenthal's confession demonstrates that Aaron's entire defense consisted of perjured testimony. There is simply no way to ascribe motive to Rosenthal's crime without concluding that he was protecting Aaron from disclosure of his affair with Judge Nichols.

Aaron's well aware of the collateral consequences of the conduct he's engaged in, and yet he believes that this time there will not be any negative fallout for Cynthia or Rachel for their perjury. Fitz has too good a political ear for that. Any further prosecution only keeps in the public eye that he indicted and tried the wrong man for the underlying crime.

The prison's orange jumpsuit hangs off Sam Rosenthal's slight frame when he enters the MCC visitors' room. Even in the short time he's been here, Rosenthal appears to have lost weight and looks frail, reminding Aaron of the days after Sam's accident a decade ago.

Rosenthal makes his way to Aaron, relying on a metal cane with a four-pronged base, like they issue in hospitals. He isn't shackled at all, perhaps because he's already so unsteady.

More out of habit than irony, Aaron has taken a seat at the same table where Rosenthal was sitting when Aaron entered this room the day after his own arrest. As then, the room is empty, but for the guards who stand at its perimeter.

"I was hoping it was you," Rosenthal says. "The guards don't say who's visiting, just that you have a visitor."

Aaron nods. Of course he knows this.

"You want to hear something funny?"

Aaron is hard-pressed to imagine what Rosenthal could say that would amount to humor at a moment like this.

"Sure," Aaron says.

"I can't get out of my mind this image of Gordon White laughing his ass off. All he ever wanted in life was to have his name before mine."

Gordon White has been dead for more than twenty years, and he exists primarily as the final name on the Cromwell Altman masthead. Rosenthal may be correct that White will move up to third position, but it's more likely both their names will be jettisoned, and the firm will simply rebrand itself as Cromwell Altman. Aaron wonders if this is the saddest stroke of all for Rosenthal, even worse than dying in prison. To have his name taken off his life's work.

"I'm going to resign from the firm," Aaron says. "In fact, right after I leave here I'm going to make it official before the COC."

Aaron expects to be asked about who will take over the firm, but instead Rosenthal says, "And do what?"

"Cynthia was offered a teaching position at the University of Virginia. They say that I can have one too if I want. Guest lecturer or something."

"Don't worry," Rosenthal says with a smile. "I'm not going to try to talk you out of teaching again."

Aaron smiles too, remembering that day in Justice Rellington's chambers all those years ago. "I don't know. I think I might want some time to do nothing. Just think about everything that's happened."

Rosenthal's smile runs away, replaced by an expression of profound sadness. For a moment, Aaron is tempted to provide some comfort, but then he stops short, recognizing that it's wholly appropriate for Sam Rosenthal to suffer for what he's done.

"When she called me that night," Rosenthal begins, even though Aaron hasn't asked him to explain, "she said she'd just seen you. She told me about the affair, and I pretended as if I didn't already know. I told her that I could still save her nomination, but only if she stepped aside on Garkov. She kept saying that she was sure it was all going to come out and how she wanted to do it in her own way. She was going to reveal everything the next day in court. She said she was calling me so that I could tell Senator Kheel, so he didn't feel blindsided, but I think the real reason she was calling me was so I could tell you. In fact, the last thing she said on the phone was 'Tell Aaron not to hate me.'"

That among Faith's final words were those seeking his forgiveness is too cruel an irony for Aaron to fathom. Aaron cannot stop himself from tearing up, even as Rosenthal continues to tell his story without emotion, as if he's recounting a military mission that happened to experience casualties.

"There was no doubt in my mind that if she went public, your career was over, so I asked to meet with her. I knew it was risky. You could be a suspect if she'd told anyone that you'd met her that night, and I could be a suspect if people saw the phone call to my office. I swear, I didn't know she had called your office number by mistake and been rerouted to me. But I had to act then or it would have been too late. So I did what I had to do. There was no other option."

"Of course there were other options, Sam. All that was at stake was a law firm. That didn't justify taking a woman's life."

"A *law firm*?" Rosenthal says with incredulity. "That law firm was *my life*. And I thought it was yours too. And just as I'm sure you would take a life to protect your children's lives, that's what I was doing too."

Aaron has no doubt that this is true. Sam Rosenthal could have gotten away with murder, and yet he didn't.

Rosenthal stands to say good-bye, seemingly to release Aaron from any further obligations. "I don't want you keeping the COC waiting on my account," he says.

For a brief moment Aaron considers telling Rosenthal that he is not forgiven, that some conduct is too horrible to forgive. But Aaron is all that Sam Rosenthal has in this world, and some responsibilities are simply too great to abandon, and so he pulls his mentor into him, hugging him. This is too much for Sam Rosenthal to endure and he begins to sob.

The COC gives Aaron a standing ovation when he enters the conference room. His place at the head of the conference room table is vacant, as is the chair across from it, where Samuel Rosenthal was a fixture for longer than any one of them has served.

"Thank you," Aaron says to quiet the applause of the COC. "I cannot tell you all how much I appreciate all of your support. I would like to tell you that the last few months have reconfirmed how important this law firm is to me, and that I'm rededicated to its leadership and our continued success . . . but the opposite is true. All that I've experienced has made it abundantly clear to me that what matters in life is what goes on not in this office, but in my home, with my family."

Aaron's departure from Cromwell Altman Rosenthal and White has been a matter of negotiation. In exchange for stepping aside and allowing Donald Pierce to finally achieve his life's ambition, Aaron has secured a place on the COC for Rachel London, as well as Abby Sloane's appointment to the newly created position of deputy chairman.

Pierce says, "I speak not only for this committee but for the whole of Cromwell Altman when I say that we are deeply indebted to you and your leadership over these past ten years. We all wish you and your family the very best."

With that, Aaron leaves the COC to continue its business. As he enters his corner office, he thinks he hears the rustle of Donald Pierce changing seats.

Alone in his office, Aaron can't help but stare out the window one last time. He imagines that he'll never again see the world from such a high perch and smiles at the irony that he so rarely appreciated the view. Although his walls are covered with framed clippings of his legal triumphs and photographs of him with various A-listers, when he scans the space for personal mementos that he wants to take with him, he reaches only for a single picture of Cynthia, Lindsay, and Samantha.

Then he leaves Cromwell Altman Rosenthal and White for the last time. The rest of his life now awaits him.

ACKNOWLEDGMENTS

Thank you for reading *Losing Faith*, hopefully enjoying it, and now reading the acknowledgments. Please send me an e-mail at adam@adammitzner.com and tell me what you thought of it. Or find me on my Facebook fan page, www.facebook.com/pages/Adam-Mitzner, and post there. Also, reviews help spread the word, so please post a review to your favorite site.

I am truly fortunate to have had some great people assist me in bringing *Losing Faith* to you. My agent, Scott Miller at Trident Media, deserves special thanks that go beyond just this book, for taking a chance on me way back when. Scott's assistant, Stephanie Hoover, has always been there for me whenever I've had a question or a concern. At Gallery Books, I'm lucky beyond words to work with Ed Schlesinger, who makes everything I write better. Once the book is finished, Stephanie DeLuca helps get the word out, which is just as important as (if not more so than) the work that goes into writing it. I've also been privileged to work with the very talented people at FSB, who tell the blogosphere about me, especially Fauzia Burke and Leyane Jerejian.

My partners and colleagues at Pavia & Harcourt, the law firm where I do my day job as the head of their litigation department, have been incredibly supportive of my nighttime writing activities. Those who know me will appreciate that more than being a lawyer or even a writer, I've always wanted to be a superhero. There are many reasons that dream will not come true, but at least this way I get to have an alter ego.

I once heard someone describe the writing process as being in an empty room and then, slowly, inviting people in. I've been very fortunate that I have some amazing and talented people willing to come into that room and help me: Clint Broden, Matthew Brooks, Gregg Goldman, Jane Goldman, Sofia Logue, Rebecca Nelson, Debbie Peikes, Benjamin Plevin, Ellice Schwab, Jessica Shacter, Kevin Shacter, Lisa Sheffield, Jodi Siskind, Marilyn Steinthal, and Joellen Valentine.

If some of those names sound familiar, it's because after my friends do me the great kindness of reading my unfinished book and providing helpful advice, I reward them by using their names for characters that do not in any way actually resemble them. In *Losing Faith*, I have stolen the identity of Clint Broden (who would like the world to know that he's more academically accomplished than his fictional counterpart but every bit as much a Pepsi man), Harrison Geller, Jane Cleary, Gregg Goldman, Dana Luria, Sara Meyers, Diane Pimentel, Kenneth Sadinoff, Alyssa Sanders, David Sanyour, Ellice Schwab, and Jodi Siskind.

Losing Faith is dedicated to my fifteen-year-old stepsons, Michael and Benjamin Plevin. Benjamin read *Losing Faith* twice in draft and offered insightful comments, and although Michael decided to skip the reading process, that did not in any way impede him from offering his own insightful commentary.

My daughters, Rebecca and Emily, are always at the forefront of my mind when I write—even though neither of them has read any of my work. In Rebecca's case, I think it's because the last thing a teenage girl wants is to know that much about her father's deepest thoughts, and in the case of Emily, who is eleven, it's because the themes are still too adult for her. But I suspect that someday they'll both read *Losing Faith* and I hope that when they do, they not only like it but also remember how happy I was when I wrote it.

Last, and certainly most, my love and utmost thanks to my wife, Susan. She's not only the first person I let into the writing room, but I sometimes make her stay there long after she'd rather have left.

Although she now has me on a strict "I'm only going to read it three times" diet, her assistance to the finished product cannot be measured merely by her critiques. Her presence by my side is what allows me to venture into the writing room in the first place, because I know that what really matters is outside of that room, with her, our family, and our friends.